ALSO BY LOUISE SHAFFER

The Three Miss Margarets

The
Ladies of
Garrison
Gardens

DOUBLEDAY LARGE PRINT HOME LIBRARY EDITION

Ballantine Books  New York

The Ladies of Garrison Gardens

A NOVEL

LOUISE SHAFFER

Copyright © 2005 by Louise Shaffer

All rights reserved.

Published in the United States by Ballantine Books, an
imprint of The Random House Publishing Group, a
division of Random House, Inc., New York.

BALLANTINE and colophon are registered trademarks
of Random House, Inc.

ISBN 0-7394-5660-1

Printed in the United States of America

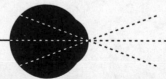

This Large Print Book carries the
Seal of Approval of N.A.V.H.

For Mama,
who taught me to have dreams,
and Roger,
who sees to it that they become a reality

ACKNOWLEDGMENTS

This part of the gig is a joy that keeps on growing because the list of fabulous people in my life grows too. I'm not sure how I got so lucky, but I'm so grateful.

So thank you to and for Eric Simonoff who continues to be the kind of spectacular agent most of us only dream of finding, as well as a good and caring friend whose company I enjoy so much, and thank you to the amazing Lee Boudreaux who works her editorial miracles—I'll always be in her debt for what she's done for this book—while still being fun and funny and the world's best cheerleader.

Thank you to Gina Centrello and all the old and new friends at Random House and

Ballantine: Laura Ford, Kate Blum, Libby McGuire, Robbin Schiff, Thomas Perry, Carol Schneider, Eileen Baker, Toni Hetzel, Dan Rembert, Dennis Ambrose, Johanna Bowman, Janet Baker, Steven Wallace, Rachel Bernstein, and Liz Willner.

Special thank you to Allison Dickens and Mary Siemsen for taking such good care of the Ladies.

Thank you to those who walked me through areas of expertise I lacked and made bygone eras and places come alive for me: the staff at East Fishkill Community Library, especially Carol Reader, Carol Roughgarden, Kristie Simco, and the wonderful Catherine Swierat. Thank you to Tom Tierney, Bernie and Celeste Rudberg, Jerry Foster, Ron Woodward, Sandra Okamoto, Marilyn Piccolo, Phyllis Piccolo, Steven Hudspeth, and to Betsy Gilbert who acted as a special consultant for the more colorful moments.

Thank you to Gerry who could have made a fortune for his dual gig as shrink and researcher, but he did it all because he's just that kind of person. Thank you to Cynthia who acted as a one-woman band, researched, listened by the hour, encouraged, shoved—oh so gently—and in her spare moments fired up her mighty computer to whip out the promotional stuff. I'm not sure I could have done it without you, Cynthia— I know I couldn't have done it on time.

Thank you to Cecile Barendsma who gives my characters the chance to be multilingual.

Thank you to those whose kindness and generosity continues to overwhelm me: Rhonda Johannesson, Marty Reiswig, Ellie Quester, Margaret and Barbara Long, Jody Fasanella, Emma Jayne Kretlow, Jeffery McGraw, Betsy Primm, Keven Haberl, and Wil Purdue.

And thank you to those who just make everything better: Ellen, who is always there with advice, a sounding board, and breakfast, Nimet who has been there for so long I won't count if she won't, Charlie who makes it worthwhile to turn on the computer in the morning, my dear godmother, Aunt Virginia, my sisters Lucy and Marie, and my brother Brad, Bee and Iris, and, of course, Colin, the webmaster past compare, and Christopher.

Like I said, I am one lucky woman.

The

Ladies of

Garrison

Gardens

Chapter One

OLD MISSUS

2004

Something was up. From the hallway outside her bedroom she heard the words *Old Missus* murmured—or possibly they were shouted; her ears were sharp for a ninety-year-old, but even she couldn't hear through thick pine doors the way she used to. For a moment she contemplated protesting. Essie, who had been her housekeeper, cook, and general factotum—for, was it twelve years now?—knew that using the hated *Old Missus* title was a call to arms, even if the sweet young thing Essie had just hired did not. Sharp words were called for. But it would take energy to deliver them. And one had to be careful how one spent that precious commodity at her age. Besides, she wasn't sure she wanted her faithful retainers to know exactly how much of the conversations that swirled around her she managed to pick up. Eavesdropping was one of her main pleasures—there were so few left.

She hoisted herself out of bed as quickly as ninety-year-old joints would allow, so she could begin assembling the various parts— dental bridges, eyeglasses, and medications—that now made up the whole of "Old Missus."

Twenty minutes later, she climbed back into bed. There were additional rustlings and murmurings in the hall, and the sweet young thing entered with a breakfast tray. She had initially balked at hiring the child, whose name was Cherry and whose job description was *companion/helper*. But Essie had put it in terms she couldn't fight. "I can't keep up with this big old barn of a house on my own, and you can't go on living in it all by yourself," she'd said. "I ain't coming in some morning to find you dead in your bed or lying on the bathroom floor with your other hip broken. You let me get someone in here to sleep through the night, or I quit."

So now young Cherry was standing in the doorway, holding the breakfast tray and wearing a fond if slightly patronizing grin. "The *Charles Valley Gazette* is here, Old Missus," she announced.

After delivering that piece of good news, the child could call her Old Missus or Old Mushroom, she didn't give a damn. "Give it here," she said eagerly. The *Charles Valley Gazette* was supposed to be a weekly paper, but it hadn't come for two months, and she had missed it desperately.

The Cherry child carried the tray full of clanking china and cutlery across the room with the concentration of a tightrope walker. Breakfast in bed was an indulgence Old Missus had started allowing herself lately, but she still cringed slightly when it appeared.

The girl finally came to a shaky halt at her bedside. "The paper was in your mailbox down at the post office yesterday," she announced. "They must have sent it out from Charles Valley last week."

"Probably. I'll take it now, Cherry."

"Where is Charles Valley?"

"Lawson County. May I have my newspaper, please?"

But the girl wasn't through cogitating. "I thought it wasn't anyplace around here."

"No." Silently, by reflex, she added, *God forbid!* Although by now it probably wouldn't matter how close she got to Charles Valley. She could march down the main street of the town shouting out her life's story over a bullhorn. No one was still alive who could possibly care. Or would they?

"Why do you get a newspaper from a town that's miles away?" her new helper asked, breaking into her thoughts. Clearly, they were making sweet young things much sharper than they used to. "I mean, it's not like there are any stories in it about the whole state or the country or anything but Charles Valley. You couldn't even buy any of the stuff in the ads over here."

It is never easy to pull yourself up to your full height while fighting bedclothes, but she didn't get to be Old Missus for nothing. "Cherry, dear, I want my breakfast before it congeals on the plate." She was trying for a regal tone, but it came out cranky-old-lady. These days that seemed to happen a lot.

The Cherry child settled the tray over her midsection and helped her adjust her pillows. The *Gazette* was under the bowl of oatmeal that her enthusiastic young doctor said was a real heart saver. What the hell the boy was saving that aged organ for was anyone's guess.

She pulled the paper out from under the bowl and positioned herself under the fancy new natural-light lamp she'd allowed Essie to put on her night table. She'd insisted she didn't need the damn thing, but the truth was it did make the small print easier. And the print used by most newspapers, including the *Charles Valley Gazette*, was infinitesimal. She should start a lawsuit on behalf of elderly Americans across the country being driven mad as they attempted to stay informed.

As usual, the first thing she did was look through the newspaper's table of contents for articles written by Laurel Selene McCready. For the past seven years, Ms. McCready had been listed on the paper's masthead as the assistant to the editor, Hank Barlow, although she also did double duty as a writer. But about three months ago her name had disappeared, after which there was no newspaper for two weeks. When it appeared again, a new assistant was listed on the masthead; soon that name was gone and two others appeared and disappeared in rapid succession. And the arrival of the *Gazette,* which had been a regular feature of Old Missus' Saturdays, suddenly became a random event. Sometimes it showed up on Tuesday, sometimes on Friday—if it showed up at all.

Clearly, the loss of Ms. McCready was a major catastrophe for the paper. And not just because of whatever she had done to make sure it was published each week. Since her disappearance, the damn thing was loaded with typos. But in the humble opinion of Old Missus, it was Laurel Selene's writing that was the biggest loss. The absent Ms. McCready had had a nice way with a phrase and an irreverent slant on life that gave her stories an unexpected and welcome tartness. They were better than the swill turned out by the man she had assisted, that much was sure.

"What's that picture?" asked Cherry peering over her employer's shoulder at the front page of the paper.

"Those are the azaleas at Garrison Gardens."

"I've heard of that—some kind of vacation place, isn't it?"

"It's one of the most important horticultural centers in the country," she responded huffily. "Didn't they teach you anything in school about your own state?" This was an overreaction, but Cherry wouldn't take offense. No one ever did when you were over ninety. No matter what you did, you were cute.

"That garden place is in Charles Valley?"

"Yes."

But mere geographical location didn't begin to explain the relationship of the gardens to Charles Valley, Georgia. The little town owed its livelihood to Garrison Gardens. Students from around the world came to study the work being done by their botanists. Tourists poured into the Garrison Gardens resort to enjoy the lodge, the restaurants, the golf course, the man-made lake, the tennis courts, the RV campground, the hiking and biking trails, the country store, and the phenomenal thirty-thousand-acre Garrison Nature Preserve. Ms. Mc-Cready's boss at the *Charles Valley Gazette* genuflected in print whenever he mentioned the gardens or the resort or the Garrison family that had built them. The family no longer owned the gardens, which were now part of a charitable trust. But the Garrisons—or, more accurately, Peggy Garrison, who had inherited the whole shebang from her late husband, Dalton—had a controlling voice on the board that ran the trust and retained full ownership of the very profitable resort attached to the gardens. The Garrison name—if not the bloodline—remained the eight-hundred-pound gorilla in the area.

"Would you like me to read the paper to you?" Cherry asked brightly. The girl was terminally perky. "You seem to be having a little trouble this morning."

"I'm fine," she answered firmly—not, she hoped, crankily. "I'll call you if I need you, dear."

"Okay," Cherry said, in the indulgent tone that young people used with her now. She vanished and Old Missus reached up to turn on her fancy lamp. She *was* having a little trouble this morning. With her hands, not her eyes, thank you.

Cherry had touched a nerve. It was foolish to keep renewing her subscription to the *Gazette*. Her only connection to the town had been gone for many years. But the little newspaper had become a part of her life. Some names had appeared regularly in it for so many years they were like old acquaintances. She liked to keep tabs on them. At her age, it was hard to make new friends. And it wasn't true that she had no connection to the place—there was still one person whose comings and goings had personal meaning for her. So it was with a gasp that she scanned the front page and read that Peggy Garrison was dead.

Chapter Two

LAUREL

2004

A little alley alongside the one-story brick building that housed the *Charles Valley Gazette* functioned as an unofficial parking lot for the newspaper's staff. Hank parked his car there, and Laurel had too, when she was his assistant. In the past week, a beat-up blue Buick had been in her old spot every time Laurel drove by—which she had done a little too often to be totally healthy. The presence of the new car confirmed the rumor that Hank had hired a new assistant. Again.

But the Buick wasn't in the alley this Saturday morning. Nor was it parked on the street in front of the newspaper office. Hit by a sudden impulse, Laurel pulled into her old space, walked quickly to the big bay windows in the front of the newspaper building, and looked in. No one was inside. When she'd been his assistant, Hank had insisted that she be on duty at the crack of dawn on Saturday. She'd done it because he threatened to fire her if she refused, and because the *Gazette* was the only newspaper in town and it made her feel special to work there. Her other options for employment had all involved food services.

She checked the street quickly. The tourists who would be swarming around in a few hours were still sleeping in their beds in the resort or in the less pricey motels and B and Bs that jammed the area. The locals, who wouldn't be caught dead in tourist territory on the weekend, were nowhere around. She took a set of keys out of her purse—her spare set of the office keys Hank had forgotten to take when he dumped her—and let herself into the *Gazette* building.

Inside, it was dark and still relatively cool. Later in the day, the heat would accumulate under the tin roof and drift downward, de-

feating the efforts of the ancient air conditioner and turning the place into a hot box.
The newspaper took up the entire building,
including a basement that was used as the
morgue. At the back of the ground floor,
where the air rarely circulated, was her
desk—what used to be her desk. In front
was Hank's desk, and in between was the
space with the computers where she and
Hank used to lay out the paper in an all-
night marathon each week.

Hank had paid her a salary that was low
enough to qualify her for food stamps, and
there were undoubtedly laws against the
working conditions she'd put up with, to say
nothing of the hours. She'd had the job from
hell. And she missed it like hell.

She stood in the empty space, breathing
in the quiet. Ironically, what she missed
most of all was the Saturday morning shit
shift. The time alone in the silent office had
been hers for writing and thinking. That was
when she worked on her story for the next
week and checked the issue that had just
come out for mistakes they'd been too busy
to catch. Laurel was murder on punctuation
and spelling, a fixation that would have surprised most people who knew her. She had

a reputation—well earned, she had to admit—for being a wild child. Actually, white trash was more like it.

The newspaper could have been hers. Hank had been toying with the idea of selling it for a couple of years, and Peggy had offered to buy it for her. Peggy Garrison had been her friend, as were the two other members of a trio of older women known in town as the three Miss Margarets. They were Dr. Margaret Long, Margaret Elizabeth Banning, and Mrs. Margaret Garrison, known as Dr. Maggie, Miss Li'l Bit, and Miss Peggy, respectively.

Dr. Maggie was in her late eighties and still ran the clinic where she'd been treating patients since the 1930s. Miss Li'l Bit was in her late seventies and had a pedigree as impressive as the fortune she used to fund charities throughout the state. Miss Peggy was in her mid-sixties, and while her family tree might not have been as illustrious as the Bannings', the fortune she'd inherited when she became the Widow Garrison was even bigger than Miss Li'l Bit's. And she used it just as generously.

Most of Charles Valley addressed the trio

formally with the emphasis on the titles "Doctor" and "Miss." Laurel was one of the privileged few who was close enough to call them simply Maggie, Li'l Bit, and Peggy. She was the only person in town who joined them every afternoon on the porch of Li'l Bit's antebellum home to chat and sip the beverage of her choice as the sun went down.

There could not have been a more unlikely combo than thirty-five-year-old Laurel and the three older women, who were all icons of Charles Valley respectability. Laurel's past was, to put it politely, colorful. Her mother, Sara Jayne, had been a drunk with a high profile at the major and minor honky-tonks along Highway 22. Her daddy, who hadn't lived long enough to see Laurel born or give her his name, was equally well known as a murderer who then went out and got himself killed over the affections of a black woman in a scandal that still lived in the hearts and minds of many of the townspeople, even though it was thirty-six years old. The fact that Laurel Selene, with her family history, was welcome at the sacred afternoon gathering of the three Miss Margarets drove the Charles Valley grapevine nuts.

But two years ago, on a cold autumn evening, the three women had told Laurel a secret—one they'd kept since before she was born. In doing it, they had given her a kind of peace about her past, but they'd put themselves at great risk. If Laurel had chosen to betray them she could have destroyed them and might even have sent them to jail. But Laurel had kept their secret, and the three Miss Margarets considered her a friend for life. Only they weren't the three Miss Margarets anymore, because Peggy was gone.

Laurel swallowed hard, the way she always had to when she thought of Peggy, and looked around the *Gazette* office. She and Peggy had been alone on Li'l Bit's porch the day Peggy had offered to buy the *Gazette* for her. Li'l Bit was inside the house, and Maggie hadn't come over from the clinic yet. Peggy had wrapped up her pitch by saying, "Hank wants to get out of the newspaper business, which does seem to prove there's a God, and I'd love to watch you try your hand at it. What do you say?"

Peggy was sitting in the wicker rocking chair that was her spot on the porch. Her hair was the shade of blond favored by the starlets of her youth; under an expert makeup job, her once-beautiful face showed the wear and tear of her ongoing relationship with Jack Daniel's. She was smiling at Laurel with the kind of affection that felt dangerous if you had spent your whole life not trusting anyone. "I would have loved having a daughter like you, Laurel," she said softly.

For a few days Laurel had been thrilled about the idea of taking over the *Gazette*. She floated around in a happy dream of a revamped newspaper that would never again cover bake sales as if they were hard news, devote its entire editorial page to the ramblings of the elderly minister of the Baptist church, or suck up to the Garrisons. The *Charles Valley Gazette* would be relevant and honest, she told herself.

But then her devil voices kicked in and demanded to know who the hell she thought she was? She'd left college before finishing her first semester. She'd never taken a course in journalism or business. The local merchants who kept the *Charles*

Valley Gazette afloat by advertising in it would never trust her. Hank was one of them; he went to their Rotary and Kiwanis meetings, laughed at their jokes, and sat next to them in church on Sunday. Laurel hadn't been inside a church since her mother's funeral, and her idea of humor did not include hoary dumb-blonde gags, bad puns, or the word *titties*. Add to all of this her family history. And her dicey relationship with Charles Valley's gossip mill.

Laurel walked a fine line with the town of her birth, hating it almost as much as she loved it. She'd never leave Charles Valley; it was her home, but sometimes she wondered how she was going to keep from going crazy living there.

One thing she was sure of, after she thought over Peggy's offer: The *Charles Valley Gazette* was more than eighty years old, and she was not going to be the one who ran it into the ground. So the next time Peggy brought up buying the newspaper, Laurel said no thank you. "It's not that I don't appreciate it, Peggy," she said, stumbling around for the right words. "It's real generous of you, and I'm flattered you think I could do it, and I—"

"I'm sorry I scared you, sugar." Peggy had a way of cutting to the chase that could be unnerving.

"I wouldn't say I'm afraid, exactly—"

"Sure you are. I came at you too fast with the idea. Don't you fuss, we'll talk about it again."

But they never did, because a few weeks later Peggy mentioned she'd been having some pain in her back. So there was a trip to Atlanta for tests, and a couple of desperate weeks of waiting until the doctor at Emory said the words *pancreatic cancer*. Then Laurel got fired, and Peggy had the exploratory surgery that confirmed the doctor's diagnosis. After that there was the roller-coaster ride of radiation that only worked for a while and chemo that didn't work at all. Laurel was on hand for all of it, because she'd said she would be and because she wanted to be. The subject of the newspaper didn't come up again. But by that point, although Laurel didn't know it, Peggy had made other plans.

In the dark office of the *Gazette*, Laurel rubbed her eyes, which had begun to sting. She'd never begrudged the way Peggy's illness took over her own life, but she'd known from watching her mother die that it would have been easier if she'd had something else to keep her busy. So even though she'd been fired, she'd gone back to Hank.

"I don't need a full-time job," she'd said. "I probably wouldn't have the time now, because of helping Peggy. But if you could just let me write a story for you every now and then. Or let me do the copyediting; you know how good I am at that. I need something to take my mind off things, Hank—just a little."

Hank let her beg; then he turned her down with his biggest Rotary Club smile. Even though he had to cancel the paper for the next two weeks because he still hadn't found anyone who could take her place.

Laurel's eyes had stopped stinging. "After everything I did for this place," she said out loud to the *Gazette* office. "After the way I used to stay up all night getting the damn paper out for that dickweed—"

The sound of her own voice rattling around the empty room stopped her. Because she suddenly realized just how much the dickweed would love to find her breaking and entering. Clearly, she should get the hell out while she still could. Instead, she marched to the back of the room where there was a door marked PRIVATE—EMPLOY-EES ONLY.

In a town that prided itself on offering every amenity to friends and strangers, Hank had what was probably the only locked restroom. He was protective of it in a way that suggested an early potty training Laurel didn't want to think about. When she'd first started working for him, he'd tried to make her go next door and use the ladies' room in the Sweet Home Café until she shamed him out of it.

She found the right key on her chain, un-locked the door, went inside, and peed in Hank's sacred commode. Without covering the seat with toilet paper.

After violating Hank's plumbing, she turned on the light and studied herself in the mirror over his sink. The face that stared back at her was a series of circles: round cheeks, round brown eyes, a round mouth, and a rounded nose. It was an old-fashioned country face, free of makeup, because she had no patience for it, and framed by a mass of red hair she usually kept pulled back in an unhip ponytail. She'd never land on the cover of a magazine, but that was fine with her. She'd always had her own way of being memorable. When she was in the mood, she'd let her hair fly free, put on a tank top, jeans with a wide belt, and cowboy boots. It was a tried-and-true outfit that showed off her good boobs, small waist, and the long legs she'd inherited from her ma. With a couple of beers in her she could pretty much get any kind of attention she wanted—and some she regretted after the fact.

Laurel looked at her face in the mirror. "Oh, what the hell," she said. She opened her purse and took out the black and gold makeup case Peggy had given her.

"I hope you don't take this wrong," Peggy had said tentatively, "but you're such a pretty girl. . . ." She'd trailed off. Because that was two years ago and all of the three Miss Margarets were tentative with her then. In some ways, Li'l Bit and Maggie still were. But Peggy had reached out.

"When I was young, I wanted a baby more than anything," she'd said, when she gave Laurel the makeup case. "A little girl. I

was going to name her Amanda. Don't tell
Li'l Bit and Maggie, but I used to talk to her
sometimes. I told her she'd never be afraid
of anything, and if anyone ever tried to call
her Mandy she should spit in their eye." She
let out a wicked little giggle, and for a moment Laurel could see how she'd managed
to capture the heart of Dalton Garrison so
many years ago. Then the giggle died. "I
never did have her, of course," Peggy said.
"But if I had, she'd be about your age."

Laurel dumped the contents of the makeup
case into Hank's sink and found the mascara wand. "This one's for you, Peggy," she
murmured, as she began to unscrew the
top. The mascara was old and dry because
she never used it, although for a while,
when Peggy was bedridden and near the
end, Laurel had tried for her sake.

"Don't you ever let anyone tell you keeping up appearances is shallow, sugar,"
Peggy's tired voice had whispered from the
bed. "You just put on your face and tell
yourself you're doing a public service. No
one ever felt better by looking at a woman
who let herself go."

Two days later Peggy didn't know who

she was talking to. "I fixed everything for you, Amanda," she'd said.

Her voice was so far gone by then that Laurel had to bend over to hear her. But the wasted hand that held Laurel's was amazingly strong. And hot—even now, Laurel could still remember the heat.

"They'll try . . ." Peggy had started to say, but the mists that had been carrying her in and out of consciousness took over, and she had to struggle to pull herself back, "Don't let . . ." she got out before the mists took over. "Don't let them. . . ."

"It's okay, Peggy, I won't let them do it," Laurel whispered, and wished to God she knew what they were talking about.

A dried flake of mascara, the size of a boulder by the feel of it, had lodged itself under Laurel's eyelid. Which could have been an accident. Or a warning from on high about the morning ahead of her.

"Stop stalling," she said to her reflection in the mirror. "You promised you were going over there today." Because this was the day when she had to deal with the way in which Peggy had "fixed" everything for her.

Chapter Three

The speed limit on Highway 22 was fifty-five miles an hour, but according to her speedometer Laurel was doing forty-five. It was because of her streaming eye, she told herself, not because she didn't want to get where she was going. She mashed on the gas, and drove past Garrison Gardens and the resort, plunging into a forest known as the Garrison Nature Preserve that spanned both sides of the highway. A triangular piece of land was wedged in the middle of the highway, splitting it for several miles. On this pie-shaped chunk of prime Charles Valley real estate were the homes of the three

Miss Margarets. Li'l Bit and Maggie shared a swatch of land bordered by a ridge of hills at the wide end of the triangle, owning eighty and thirty acres, respectively. At the top end of the wedge, starting with the tip, were the two hundred and sixty acres that came with the huge log home Peggy had lived in for the forty-five years of her marriage and widowhood. This house was Laurel's destination.

She reached it and turned off the highway. In front of her were two stone pillars and a wooden gate. On the right-hand pillar was a sign proclaiming that you had arrived at GARRISON COTTAGE. The innocuous-looking gate was wired to alert the security system at the Garrison resort if an unauthorized person attempted to enter the grounds. Authorized persons like Laurel had a plastic ID card they swiped through a scanner that was concealed on the back of the left pillar.

Laurel leaned over to check her eye in her rearview mirror—it was red and mascara smeared. She looked like shit. Well, it had been that kind of day. Actually, it had been that kind of a month—no, make that many months. And the worst was ahead of her.

She drew a deep breath and started down the long driveway to Garrison Cottage.

To call Peggy's former home a cottage was to wallow in old-money understatement. "Let's face it," Peggy said once. "It's ten thousand square feet of house, not counting the porches and the patio around the pool. The damn thing's a castle. I don't care if it *is* made out of logs they cut right here in Charles Valley. Dalton wasn't the one who wanted a big house, you know. That was Miss Myrtis. Peggy was referring to Dalton's first wife, her predecessor, Myrtis Garrison. The daughter of a wealthy and powerful Georgia family, Miss Myrtis had cast a long shadow in Charles Valley. Even after Dalton married Peggy, the legend of the first Mrs. Garrison lingered.

"Miss Myrtis designed Garrison Cottage," Peggy continued. "She wanted it to be like Monticello—a place where important people would come to talk and change the world."

It hadn't quite worked out like that.

The driveway wound through what seemed to be a forest that had been left to grow wild. It was only after you'd driven through it several times that you realized that there was no kudzu choking the pines and oaks. The shade-loving azaleas that flourished under the canopy of trees had not gotten where they were by accident, nor had the magnolias or the crape myrtle, scattered artfully throughout. The land on either side of the river-rock drive was as exquisitely manicured as Garrison Gardens itself.

"Just one of the perks," Peggy said, of her home and grounds.

Peggy had had the entire staff of the resort at her command. Maids from housekeeping cleaned her house, the mechanics who serviced the resort vehicles kept her car humming, the restaurants cooked her meals and delivered them to her. If she wanted to throw a party, trays of the cheese wafers and tiny biscuits with country ham for which the resort was famous would appear as if by magic, along with waiters wearing the white gloves that were a hallmark of Garrison service. And gardeners in Garrison overalls showed up every day, starting in the early spring.

"Since they go to all that trouble anyway, I'd just as soon they dug up the damn for-

est primeval and planted a pretty lawn,"
Peggy complained. "When I come home
late at night, all those trees are downright
creepy." But she hadn't changed so much
as the placement of one shrub.

The drive up to the house had never
seemed creepy to Laurel, and by the end of
Peggy's life she was doing it every day.
Peggy had wanted to die at home instead of
in the hospital, but she hadn't wanted Maggie and Li'l Bit taking care of her. "It'd be too
much for them, but they'll try anyway,"
she'd said.

"Not if they know I'm going to be there,"
Laurel had said.

Of course, Maggie and Li'l Bit knew what
Peggy was doing.

"Peggy wants to spare us," Li'l Bit said.

But Maggie, who sometimes saw things
more clearly, said quietly, "She needs Laurel
now."

Laurel's eye had stopped tearing—*Thank
you, Jesus*. She followed the driveway
through the forest until it suddenly gave way
to a meadow of wildflowers. And there, rising out of a sea of pink, red, blue, and white,
was the great log castle. It was built in three

parts. The central section was two stories tall, capped with a gable roof and skylights. Two side wings, each one story high, were attached to the center at a slight angle, giving the house a curved look. In front of it was an oval garden full of daylilies, daffodils, hollyhocks, and hydrangeas, anchored on either end by a massive oak. When she first saw it, the place had seemed beautiful but overwhelming to Laurel; later it had become familiar and sad. Now she wished someone would burn the damn thing down.

She parked under one of the oaks and sat for a moment, hoping she wasn't the first one there. Sure enough, another car was parked on the other side of the oval. But instead of the ancient Volvo she was expecting, it was the brand-new gray van Maggie had recently bought for the clinic. Only one person drove that van, and for the first time that morning Laurel felt herself relax. As if on cue, the front door of the house opened and a man stepped out into the sunlight. He was tall, probably six two or three, and slim, but with enough muscle to make him interesting. High cheekbones, strong features, and straight jet-black hair reinforced the legend that his daddy's great-grandmother had been part Cherokee; his deep-blue eyes and the dimple that appeared at the side of his mouth when he smiled were a gift from his Irish great-granddaddy. He had been named after the television character Perry Mason, because his mama thought the law was an admirable career and she wanted a professional man in the family. She'd gotten her wish, although the profession wasn't the one she'd had in mind. Her son was a doctor. And he was stuck with the name Perry. Laurel was privy to all his family lore because she'd known him all of his life and for most of hers. To the rest of Charles Valley, he was a hero, the local boy who had gone north to Harvard University and medical school and then chosen to come back home. To Laurel he would always be The Wiener, also known as her best friend Denny's annoying baby brother.

"Hey, Wiener," she called out.

He gave her a lazy, dimple-producing grin that would have turned her knees to jelly if she hadn't been old enough to remember him when he was teething.

"That would be Dr. Douglass to you, girl." His voice had the intimate smoky quality of a TV spokesperson for women's hair products. No matter how many times she heard it, it came as a shock to Laurel, who remembered the years when it had been a nasal squeak. She also remembered The Wiener's impressive collection of preadolescent zits, the glasses that always seemed to be sliding off his nose, and the days when the white T-shirt that was now clinging so nicely to pecs, abs, and biceps would have been stretched over a bulging stomach that bounced violently when its youthful owner attempted to run after Laurel and Denny. The summer air would echo with screeches of "Take me with you or I'll tell Mama!" and Laurel and Denny, who were usually embarking on some form of hell-raising, would have to turn around and inflict bodily harm on the pest to teach him not to mess with his elders. There had been a time when The Wiener's punishment for calling her *girl*, as he just had, would have been swift and merciless. But that was before he went away from home and came back tall, gorgeous, and licensed as a physician. His first act after coming back to Charles Valley had been to charm Maggie into admitting that, as she approached her ninetieth birthday, perhaps she could use a little assistance at the clinic. Afer three months, she was admitting that she didn't know what she'd do without him.

He'd also been Peggy's doctor in the months before she died, and Laurel had come to depend on him for help that went way beyond medical expertise. The Wiener could get a smile out of Peggy no matter how sick she felt, he organized the squadron of nurses who took care of her, and he could always get Laurel to talk when everything got bottled up and she was ready to explode. The Wiener was one of those rare souls who really wanted an answer when he asked you how you were doing, and while that kind of Oprah-speak could drive Laurel bat-shit, it was what she needed during those horrible days and weeks. Now he came down the steps to get her.

"Are you ready for this?" he asked gently.

Since she'd rather be walking over hot coals barefoot, she added mind reading to the list of The Wiener's gifts. She remembered her mascara-stained cheek and rubbed it. "Are they here?" she asked.

He nodded. "I brought them over. I figured Li'l Bit didn't need to be driving."

"You're right. I didn't think of that." But he had. Of course.

He held out his hand to her. "Come on," he said. "It won't be as bad as you think it's going to be." She took his hand and followed him inside.

They walked into the single large room that encompassed the foyer, dining area, and living room. The huge space was topped by a soaring cathedral ceiling with four skylights, commissioned by Myrtis Garrison and designed by a local glassblower. Each one featured a tree: a magnolia, a dogwood, a live oak, and a pine. Visitors gasped when they saw those skylights. As Laurel gazed upward, she wondered for the first time what would happen if the suckers leaked.

Halfway between the first floor and the ceiling was a mezzanine. The family bedrooms and the most imposing guest bedrooms were up there. Five smaller guest bedrooms were downstairs in the left wing of the ground floor. Laurel had never been up on the mezzanine. The little room where Peggy had slept and died was in the left wing. Laurel hadn't looked in that direction since she came in.

She turned instead to the outsized sofa Myrtis Garrison had had made specially for the big living room. The two women who had been seated on it stood up. One was six feet tall, with a square body and a mass of unruly gray hair imperfectly secured in a net. Her nose was too large, her chin was too small, she wore thick glasses, and there was no way she'd ever been pretty, not even when she was young. But her blue eyes behind the glasses shone with intelligence, and her stern face had a kindness she couldn't hide no matter how hard she tried. At her side was a little doll, as ethereal as the tall woman was solid, who was barely five feet tall, with a delicate face framed by silky white curls. At eighty-nine she still retained the prettiness that had always masked her tough mind and even tougher will. The large woman was Li'l Bit, the doll was Maggie. Losing Peggy had been a huge blow that had put new pain lines in both faces, and being in her house had to be killing them. In spite of that, they stood side by side with backs so ramrod straight they would have been the envy of any marine commander. Then they broke ranks. Li'l Bit got to Laurel first, hugging her tight.

"Thank you for coming." Laurel managed to get the words out in spite of the golf ball that had lodged itself in her throat. "You shouldn't have, but I'm glad you did."

"Nonsense," Li'l Bit said, in the fluty aristocratic voice Laurel used to think was snotty. "Did you honestly think we wouldn't?"

"You'll be all right, Doodlebug," said Maggie, whose voice was deep and low. "You'll see."

They were trying to encourage her. They'd lost a friend who had been with them for decades, but they were smiling and trying to help her. In another minute she was going to lose it. But from behind her, Perry's voice cut in. "You probably should get started, Laurel," he said.

She turned to him, because facing Maggie and Li'l Bit wasn't possible. "Yeah. The sooner the better, right?"

"Right." His eyes held hers until they were steady. "I have to get back to the clinic. Call me when you're done."

"I'll drive Maggie and Li'l Bit home."

He nodded and started to go, but then he turned back and gave her a quick hug. "You know, they don't give a Tough Girl Prize," he whispered in her ear. Then he left.

She turned back to her two friends. "I suppose we should go upstairs," she said.

"Whatever you want, dear one," Maggie said.

So Laurel led the way up the stairs to the mezzanine of the castle—the castle she, Laurel Selene McCready, now owned. She owned Garrison Cottage, she owned the resort, and she had a seat on the board of Garrison Gardens Charitable Trust. Because, when she died, Peggy Garrison had left the whole mess to her dear friend Laurel Selene McCready.

Chapter Four

OLD MISSUS

2004

She wanted to scream. The *Charles Valley Gazette* was maddeningly uninformative about the death of Peggy Garrison. There was a goopy tribute to her by Hank Barlow, and a brief mention of church services that had already taken place, but that was it. Frustrated, she threw the little newspaper on the floor. As if on cue, Cherry came hurrying in.

"Did you drop your paper? Let me get it for you."

"I don't want it anymore. Take it away."

"Yes, ma'am." Cherry picked up the offending paper and was about to walk out.

"Wait." The girl stopped obediently. "Go to Buddy Dogget's and get me any copies he has of the *Atlanta Constitution*."

"Why don't I just go to Eckerd's? It's right there in the middle of the shopping center. Dogget's is all the way downtown—"

"Buddy doesn't always get around to returning the newspapers he doesn't sell. Tell him it's for me, and I want all the back issues of the *Constitution* he has. And he can throw in the last three months of *Southern Living* while he's at it. I'll pay full price."

"Yes, Old Missus," Cherry muttered rebelliously, under her breath.

"Cherry," she called out, timing it nicely so the kid was almost out of the room, "I believe I've told you and Essie that I prefer to be called Mrs. Rain."

It was sheer cussedness on her part to insist on being called that, and she knew it. The southern way would have been to call herself by her first name with a respectful "Miss" tacked on the front. That was what everyone expected, because she was an old lady and they figured her for Old South. Over the years it had always been a struggle to get the various maids and cooks and gardeners to call her Mrs. Rain.

In the beginning she'd insisted on using the name as a way of hanging on to a scrap of everything she'd had to give up. It had been an act of defiance, silly, sentimental, and maybe even a little dangerous. But it was her way of shaking her fist at the sky. And there had been a time when she needed to do that.

But now she was just torturing poor Cherry because the girl was young and didn't have achy joints and diminishing eyesight. And because the death of Peggy Garrison brought back memories of other deaths. Even though she'd never met Peggy, she'd always wished she could have. She would have asked the woman if she liked being Dalton Garrison's wife, if being a Garrison had made her happy. But now Peggy Garrison was gone. And the last link in the chain was gone with her.

Chapter Five

LAUREL

2004

"The bedroom suites used by the family were at the back of the house," Li'l Bit said, when they got to the top of the staircase.

She and Maggie weren't even breathing hard after their climb to the mezzanine. Laurel was.

"The guest rooms were on both sides and the front," Maggie added. "I remember they were quite opulent. Each one had a bathroom and a dressing alcove."

On each of the guest bedroom doors there was a small brass plaque documenting the fact that someone of note had spent the night there and giving the date on which the historic sleepover had occurred. Laurel read a couple of names she probably should have recognized from her high school history classes but didn't. Finally she found one she knew.

"I thought it was just talk about Franklin Roosevelt staying here," she said.

"Actually, he visited twice," said Li'l Bit.

"The last time was right before the war," said Maggie. "The rumor was that he was meeting with one of Churchill's people, but that never did come off. Although Dalton and Myrtis did have a picnic for President and Mrs. Roosevelt over at the gardens."

Laurel stared at the plaque for a moment. Suddenly, the whole thing seemed wildly funny. "I have a house with little brass things on the doors," she said unsteadily. "I have bedrooms and sitting rooms and dressing rooms and a room for cutting flowers." Laughter she couldn't control was gurgling up inside her. "There were times when Ma was gone on a bender and I didn't have enough to eat. I slept on the couch when I was a kid, because we only had one bedroom. A month ago I was trying to figure out how to pay for a new air conditioner."

The laughter was coming in waves, and

she could hear it sounding a little shrill. She was afraid of what would happen next. But, God love them, Maggie and Li'l Bit started giggling along with her. Then somehow they were all holding on to one another and laughing. Then they weren't laughing anymore, they were just clinging to one another.

"What the hell am I going to do?" Laurel asked.

Maggie said, "You're going to go through your new house, Doodlebug."

And when Laurel couldn't seem to make herself move, Li'l Bit opened the door to the nearest bedroom and gently nudged her inside.

From behind her, Maggie snapped on a wall switch, but it only produced a dim light. Through the gloom Laurel could see creamy wallpaper featuring urns and some kind of pink flower. Thick pale rugs were scattered over the floor. There seemed to be a lot of padded chairs and love seats and round tables with skirts, and the twin beds shared a tufted headboard.

"I'd fight not to spend a night in this room," Laurel said. But Li'l Bit and Maggie were staring at it transfixed, so she added quickly, "But what do I know? It just doesn't seem like Peggy."

"No wonder," Maggie said softly. "Peggy never touched this room. This is the way Myrtis decorated it, two years before she died. She showed it to me."

"That was before I was born," Laurel said. "It was . . . I don't know how many years ago."

"It was nineteen-fifty-six," said Maggie. The date seemed to echo around the room as they all stood quietly, trying to digest what this said about Peggy.

It was Li'l Bit who broke the silence. "That little writing desk over there belonged to Myrtis's grandmother," she said, in a hushed voice. "Her father bought it for her as a wedding present. The initials on that sewing basket—*M. B.*—stand for *Myrtis Benedict*. Her father's people were Benedicts."

"Peggy kept all Myrtis's stuff," Laurel said, needing for some reason to state the obvious.

"Yes," said Li'l Bit.

"Maybe it was only this room," Laurel said hopefully.

*   *   *

But it was the same in all of them. The fan in the glass case on one sitting-room wall was the one Myrtis's mother had carried at her deb party. Myrtis's aunt had painted the music box on the nightstand in another bedroom, and the little china clock. The Benedicts seemed to have had a fondness for monograms; a big fancy *B* with swirling curlicues was painted or carved on almost every available surface. But even worse than the damn *B*s were the family photographs sitting in silver frames on the tables with the fancy skirts. In room after room, Li'l Bit stood immobile, her face going from scarlet to white as Maggie quietly identified sepia-toned pictures of Benedict women in hobble skirts and Benedict men wearing white summer suits and boater hats. The Garrisons were represented too, mostly brandishing sporting equipment; tennis rackets and croquet mallets. There wasn't one picture of Peggy's family. Or of Peggy.

"All those years . . ." Maggie said, when they'd walked out of the last gloomy bedroom and were back in the sunny brightness of the mezzanine. "Peggy lived here for all those years. . . ."

"And she never changed a thing," said Li'l Bit, with a sadness that cut.

"She never asked either one of us to come upstairs." Maggie smiled an achy little smile. "This is the first time we've been up in this part of the house. I guess now we know why."

"She was so afraid," said Li'l Bit. "All her life she was afraid."

Of what? Laurel wanted to scream. *Of the goddam Garrisons?*

Laurel had grown up among folks in Charles Valley who *didn't* revere its leading family. "Sons of bitches who wouldn't let any other industry in here, refused to pay a living wage, and then called themselves Christians" was the way she'd always heard it. The exception was Miss Myrtis. Even the most ardent critics of the Garrisons said Miss Myrtis was a good person. Laurel thought she sounded as bad as her menfolk. The woman stood by while her husband ripped off his workers; then she gave wads of money to the needy—most of whom wouldn't have been needy if it hadn't been for Mr. Dalt. Miss Myrtis had also been a rotten mother, whose son had caused misery for everyone who knew him, including Peggy. Especially Peggy.

Peggy was worth a dozen of Miss Myrtis. A million! Laurel wanted to shout. But she didn't. Because Li'l Bit and Maggie were hurting enough. And when your friends are old and fragile, you don't get to shoot your mouth off. Once, when Peggy was talking about her friendship with Li'l Bit and Maggie, she told Laurel there had been a time when she stopped being the youngster and became responsible for them. "It just seemed to sneak up on me," she'd said. "I always wondered when it happened."

Well, I sure as hell know when it happened for me, Laurel thought. *When you died, Peggy.* And she could almost hate Peggy for it.

They had walked to the back of the mezzanine where the family bedroom suites were, and now they were facing the door to the master bedroom. Li'l Bit took a deep breath, opened it, started into the room, and then stopped. She and Maggie stood in the doorway and stared at the ornately carved canopy bed in the middle of the room.

"Let me guess," Laurel said. "The frigging bed was in Miss Myrtis's family for a million

years, and they carried it here from Savan-
nah on their backs. . . ." She trailed off because Li'l Bit and Maggie were looking up at
the canopy. Laurel looked up too and saw
that the fancy *B* she'd come to hate was
carved over and over on the frame.

Every night of her married life, the last
thing Peggy had seen before she went to
sleep was a reminder of Myrtis Garrison.
She'd been reminded of Myrtis when she
woke up in the morning and when she
made love to her husband.

"Shit," Laurel said.

"Would you like to go in?" Li'l Bit asked.
But Laurel could tell that neither she nor
Maggie wanted to know what was in there.
After Dalton had died, Peggy had moved
out of this room and closed it up. Whatever
sad, mean little details it would reveal about
Peggy's life and marriage, she hadn't meant
to share them with anyone but Laurel. Going into the room with Maggie and Li'l Bit
would expose her when she wasn't around
to put a pretty spin on what they would see.
For Peggy, who would rather chew glass
than go out of the house without her
makeup on, it would be a violation. Laurel
closed the door. Maggie and Li'l Bit stood in

the hallway looking like lost children. She had to make it better for them.

"I'll take us to lunch," she said desperately. "The Magnolia Room at the resort. We'll order champagne and have a party for Peggy. She'd love that."

But Li'l Bit was sagging with weariness, and Maggie was looking every one of her eighty-nine years. Laurel knew they'd rather go back to the big porch that wrapped around Li'l Bit's house.

"I could fix us some sandwiches," Li'l Bit said, and Maggie nodded eagerly. Laurel could picture the scene. Maggie would pull herself up on the old porch swing and Li'l Bit would settle into the big chair that used to be her father's and they'd eat the soggy sandwiches Li'l Bit had made. And they'd be okay with seeing the empty wicker rocker where Peggy used to sit. But Laurel knew she couldn't stand it. Not today.

She delivered them to Li'l Bit's house and took off.

There had been a time when Laurel would have headed for the Sportsman's Grill after a rotten morning. It was a local hangout, not one of the tourist traps. Denny and The

Wiener's father owned it, and she would have gone there because even though it was morning and the place wasn't open yet, Denny would have been inside setting up for the lunch crowd. Denny had been her friend since they were in grammar school. When they were kids they'd discovered Hank Williams and Patsy Cline together, and the music plus their friendship was probably what had gotten them through the bad times when Denny was doing drugs and Laurel wasn't, but she'd get plastered enough to sleep with any boy who asked and some who didn't. And after Denny got clean, on Friday nights when his band played at the Grill, sometimes Laurel still got plastered and sang harmony with the guys.

Over the years, it was Denny who made sure she got home when she'd had one beer too many and who patched her up when she'd fallen for yet another son of a bitch who turned out to be as bad as Denny said he was going to be. Denny was always there for her. Until he met Jennifer, who really wasn't as awful as Laurel tried to tell herself she was.

The next thing Laurel knew, Denny was wearing a tux and standing next to his little brother, who had come home to be his best man, and she was one of Jennifer's ten bridesmaids who traipsed down the aisle of the First Baptist Church. After the ceremony, the happy couple moved to North Carolina and even though Laurel and Denny swore they'd never lose touch, she knew they already had.

And that was why she couldn't go into the Sportsman's Grill anymore, so she'd lost it too. It was coming up now, on her left. She pushed the gas pedal to the floor, with the usual lack of response from her ancient Camaro. She couldn't even speed past the damn place.

"I'm tired of losing!" she yelled as she drove.

But of course, most people would say she hadn't. Most people would say she was one of the luckiest women alive. Because of the way Peggy had "fixed" everything for her.

Chapter Six

MRS. RAIN

2004

The back issues of the *Atlanta Constitution* weren't any more satisfactory than the *Charles Valley Gazette* had been. A quick skimming of six weeks' worth of Sunday papers yielded not one single mention of Peggy Garrison. There was nothing left for Mrs. Rain to do but go through the obituaries, a gloomy prospect and definitely tiring to ninety-year-old eyes. She hit pay dirt in the second newspaper in the stack, but her triumph was short lived. Of the three columns devoted to Peggy, almost all of it was blather about the great man who had been her husband. It would have been funny if it hadn't been so typical. Dalton Garrison was never worthy of either of the women who married him, but there he was, downstage center in Peggy's obituary, hogging the spotlight. The damn thing had probably been written by one of the PR people who worked for the resort and the gardens.

Finally, in the very last paragraph, Peggy was mentioned in her own right. She was a beloved figure in Charles Valley who would be missed, said the *Constitution*, as if delivering hot news. Then it added that the late Mrs. Garrison's place on the board at the Garrison Gardens Charitable Trust would be taken by Laurel Selene McCready, who was also the new owner of the Garrison resort complex. *That* was news—big, strange, exciting news! Maybe the old connection to Charles Valley wasn't broken after all. Or if it was, maybe there was a new connection to be made. Suddenly, creaky joints and failing eyes didn't seem to matter.

Essie had planted a new walkie-talkie thing by the side of her bed next to the natural-light lamp. Mrs. Rain wasted several valuable minutes trying to work it, then gave up and called out in the voice that could once hit the back wall of a 1,500-seat theater, "Cherry, I want you!" She was pulling herself out of bed, as Cherry raced into the room.

"What's wrong?" the girl panted anxiously.

"I'm not dying, dear, I just need to get dressed. And I want you to brush out that bird's nest at the back of my head." She always thought better when her hair was brushed. And now she needed to think. She wanted to find out everything she could about Ms. McCready.

Chapter Seven

LAUREL

2004

Laurel turned onto Highway 22 heading north toward I-85 and Atlanta, for no reason except it was the opposite direction from Charles Valley. She floored the gas pedal, and a Volvo station wagon with a mommy and two kids in it whizzed past her, which had to be a new low for the Camaro. Just once she wanted to fly down the highway at the speed of traffic. Or better yet, she'd like to outrun everything on the damn road. She floored the gas pedal again. But she was going up a hill—not the Camaro's best event—so the speedometer didn't even waver.

* * *

When Peggy's lawyer dropped the bomb-shell and told her she was Peggy's heir, Laurel's first thought was that someone should have warned her. Then she realized that Peggy had, in her own way. A week after Peggy's tests at Emory—when, as far as Laurel knew, she was still waiting for the results—she'd invited Laurel to have supper at the Magnolia Room. This was unusual. Peggy might make use of the Garrison family perks in her own home, but she kept a low profile around the resort. But that night Peggy had seemed so insistent that Laurel was sure she had good news.

Laurel had left the *Gazette*, even though it was a Thursday, the night when she and Hank put the paper to bed, and raced over to the Magnolia Room. She'd sat across the table from Peggy, waiting for her to say they were celebrating because it wasn't cancer, after all. The doctors were wrong, Peggy was going to say, it was a false alarm.

But Peggy wasn't following the script. "What do you think about this place?" she asked, after a moment.

"I understand the food is good," said Laurel cautiously.

"I meant, what do you think of all of it? Garrison Gardens? The resort?"

This was another first. Peggy never talked about anything Garrison, which was a blessing, given Laurel's feelings on the subject. Now Laurel measured her words carefully. "If the gardens and the resort weren't here, a lot of people wouldn't have jobs," she said.

"That's not what I asked."

Candlelight from the table flickered over Peggy's face, outlining hollows and jutting bones that had never been there before. Her eyes were tired.

How did she get so thin? Laurel thought. *How did I miss seeing it?* That was when she knew the news was not going to be good.

She wanted to say whatever would make Peggy happy. "The gardens do a lot of good," she said. "Everyone would miss them if they weren't here."

Peggy nodded and opened her menu. Then she shut it. "I've made a lot of bargains, Laurel. And a lot of mistakes. I've done my best, but I could have done a lot better."

"We all could," Laurel said, knowing

something awful was coming and trying to brace for it.

"I'm not apologizing," Peggy went on. "I wanted money, and I've had it. I'm proud of some of the things I've done with it." She eyed Laurel thoughtfully. "But I don't want to mess up now."

Because she couldn't stand the suspense even more than she didn't want to hear the bad news, Laurel said, "Peggy, please tell me what you're talking about."

That was when Peggy drew a deep breath and said what Laurel already knew, that the preliminary cancer diagnosis was confirmed.

Laurel made all the usual noises about how Peggy could beat it. And Peggy agreed that, yes, of course she could. But her eyes said differently and so did her voice.

Suddenly, as she sat across from Peggy with the candles on the table flickering, Laurel remembered being in her first semester of college at Jackson State, when her mother Sara Jayne called. Laurel could hear the panic in her ma's voice as she said, "I've been feeling like shit for almost a year now, not that you'd ever notice, college girl."

Remembering her mother's phone call,

Laurel wanted to run. She wanted to get away from the Magnolia Room and Peggy and everything she knew was coming in the months ahead.

I can't be there for you, Peggy, she wanted to say. *I've been through it once, and I can't do it again.*

But then Peggy said, "Would you mind if we got the hell out of here? I'm not hungry." So they left.

Peggy insisted that she wanted to go home and swore she didn't mind being alone. Laurel watched her drive off and then she went to the Sportsman's Grill to see Denny before going back to the newspaper. But Denny was off with Jennifer and her mother, planning seating arrangements or some such crap, so she had a beer—which turned into many beers.

Maybe that was the reason she did what she did next. Or maybe she wanted to give Peggy the answer she'd been too chicken to give her at the restaurant. If Denny had been at the bar, he might have seen that something was wrong and stopped her. But she finished her beers, went back to the newspaper, and told Hank she'd finish laying out the paper if he wanted the rest of the night off.

After he was gone, she went out to her car and brought in the six-pack of Bud she'd picked up at Brown's Convenience Store, put Patsy Cline on her portable CD player, and, when she had a nice mix of pissed-off and righteousness going, wrote a slightly meandering but comprehensive editorial about everything that was wrong with Garrison Gardens and had been since it came into being. By the time she finished writing her opus and redoing the layout, it was nearly morning. She drove home, wondering if Hank would bother to read her work before he printed.

She found out later that the guy who made the deliveries was the one who noticed there was a piece by Laurel Selene McCready on the editorial page—something that had never happened before—and alerted Hank. Otherwise the *Gazette* would have broken a decades-long tradition of kissing up to the Garrisons and run the most scathing commentary on the town's cash cow that had ever seen print.

Hank didn't even bother to fire her in person. He left a message on her answering machine.

Three days later, Laurel had presented herself at Peggy's door and said, "Let me help you."

"When I need you, I will," Peggy had said.

"Promise."

"I promise," Peggy had said. Then, as Laurel turned to go, "And you promise me something, Laurel Selene. No matter what happens . . . afterward, I mean . . . remember to have fun. I never had enough fun."

At the time she couldn't figure out what Peggy meant. Now she knew it had been a warning.

There was a stoplight ahead and Laurel realized that while she'd been wandering down memory lane, she'd reached the junction where I-85 cut into Highway 22. The road, which had been uncluttered up to that point, suddenly turned into a stretch of strip malls, fast-food places, car dealerships, discount shopping clubs, motels, and a Wal-Mart the size of a small town. If the state of Georgia ever gave out an Ugly Road Award, this part of Highway 22 would be a contender. It went along with her mood—

which was getting uglier by the minute. And trying to tell herself how grateful she should be just made it worse. Because it was real sweet of Peggy to say have fun. "But how the hell do I do it?" she asked the air—or maybe the absent Peggy.

"Here's what I've got, Peggy," she said, abandoning the pretense that she wasn't talking to a dead person, "I've got lawyers. I've got a bunch of people, including me, who don't think I should have any of what you've given me. And I've got the house that was your personal jail for forty-five years. How do I find the goddamned fun in that? Do I go buy things? When you've been broke all your life, you train yourself not to spend money. I don't even know what to want—"

Then, without warning, she did. Right there in front of her was something she wanted so bad she could taste it. It was a car. But this wasn't just any vehicle, it was wide and low and built to move, what Denny used to call a mean machine. It sat on a platform high above all the other cars at the Dodge dealership across the highway. She must have seen it before, the way you see Hollywood mansions or pricey getaways on television commercials, but they never really register because they are so far out of reach. But now the car was beckoning to Laurel from four lanes over. She crossed the highway and hauled butt into the dealership parking lot.

"It's the new Viper," the salesman said. "We keep it up there for display purposes."

"But it *is* for sale, right?"

"Uh-huh," he said doubtfully, "but that's a lot of car. It isn't what I'd show to a girl—"

"Show it to this one." There was no need to explain that she'd learned to drive by tearing around town in the 1970 'Cuda that Denny had souped up when they were teenagers.

"It's stick shift. Six to the floor."

"Okay. How much?"

"I've never sold one. I don't even know if it comes in any color except red."

"Red is fine. I'm real fond of red."

"You want to buy that one? Right now?" She nodded. If he made her wait she'd lose her nerve. He stole a look at her Camaro parked outside the showroom. "I can't give you any kind of trade-in on that thing."

"I'm not asking for one."

"That Viper is an eighty-five-thousand-dollar car. Plus tax."

"I'll write you a check," she said, trying to sound as if she tossed around eighty-five-thousand bucks plus tax every day of the week. To her ear she pulled it off rather well.

So naturally, when it came time to actually sign the check, her teeth began to chatter. Which was what happened when she was doing something insane and she was still rational enough to know it. She was about to go into full castanets mode, but by then the salesman—who had insisted on checking with her bank to make sure she could cover the check—was smiling at her, and the guys on the lot had brought the Viper down off its platform and it was sitting right outside the showroom window, and it seemed to be grinning at her too. So she clenched her shaking jaw, wrote her name, took the car keys, and, waiting for she didn't know what retribution from God, walked out to claim her property.

On the inside the Viper was a spare two-seater, frills like leg room had been sacrificed for engine space. Any passenger who was over six feet tall was going to ride with his knees under his chin. Laurel had to climb in left foot first, and swing in over the seat, which made her feel like Tom Selleck in *Magnum PI*. Then she turned on the ignition.

She'd forgotten what it felt like to have a beast like this under you. The engine roared to life, straining to take off, and she alone could unleash it. She shifted gears and felt the power surge. The urge to find out what her new sweetheart could do was overwhelming, but Laurel kept the leash on until she reached a deserted back road behind the car lot that the salesman had pointed out to her. Then, finally, she mashed on the gas pedal. In seconds the wind was whipping her hair and burning her eyes as the Viper gobbled road. She pressed harder; the car roared and sped ahead. She could lose control and flip over going so fast, but that was why God made cars like this, for the danger and the rush.

The road had looped around and now she was heading back to the highway. A stop sign was coming up and, good citizen that she was, she pulled back on the gas and drove demurely up to it. But then three teenage guys in a pickup, riding high off the ground on monster wheels, pulled up be-side her. The kid riding shotgun—cute, she noted—looked down on her and grinned a challenge. There was a traffic light at the end of the road where it met the highway. She pointed to the light and held out five fingers. The kid nodded and they peeled out.

The race wasn't even close. The boy be-hind the wheel did his best, but the monster truck wasn't in the same league as her monster. She waited for the boys at the traffic light, holding out her hand for the five bucks her vanquished opponent slapped into it. Then, with a tap on her mighty gas pedal, she sped onto the I-85 ramp headed toward Atlanta.

Chapter Eight

Laurel's destination was a shopping plaza in Buckhead where Peggy had once taken her for what she called *a girls' lunch.* Laurel parked in a landscaped lot and walked through a main door worthy of Disney's Magic Kingdom. There were two floors of classy stores jammed together side by side, one shiny window after another, all full of expensive stuff glittering under bright lights. Music played and fake fountains splashed and women with perfect hair floated around looking rich. None of the shoppers seemed to have kids—at least not the kind that made noise. It was a far cry from the Sam's

Club where Laurel made her annual trip to stock up on blue jeans and T-shirts, and for a moment she thought about splitting. But she had a mission. She was going to buy things and give them away and have fun doing it, like Peggy told her to. She plunged into the nearest store, determined to splurge for the first time in her life.

She started looking for a gift for Maggie, who was an easier nut to crack than Li'l Bit. "I want something warm. A sweater, maybe," she told a saleswoman she'd hunted down. Maggie was cold all the time these days, but she refused to admit it because she didn't want to dress like a little old lady. "But it's got to be pretty too."

The saleswoman, who had been eyeing Laurel's Sam's Club ensemble like it wasn't quite clean, reluctantly produced a sweater in a buttery shade of yellow.

"Luscious, isn't it?" she cooed.

Out of force of habit, Laurel checked the price tag—and thought she was going to need CPR. "Four hundred and twenty bucks for a sweater?" she gasped, and started to give it back. But the saleswoman held out her hand to take it with an air of triumph—like she was glad she'd been right about the low-rent chick who was diminishing the value of her merchandise by standing near it—so Laurel said, "I'll take it."

After that, it got easy. The car had been an emotional purchase, born of impulse, and so outlandish it still didn't seem real. But the sweater was a deliberate choice and once she'd made it she seemed to cross some kind of line. A mindless calm came over her, as she went up and down escalators and in and out of stores. Soon she'd accumulated a fortune's worth of brightly colored sweaters and shawls, wrapped in tissue and tucked in discreetly glossy boxes and shopping bags with logos on them. But she still hadn't found the perfect gift she felt was out there. She continued her quest with a vague sense that she'd know it when she saw it.

And she did. It was on a rack of coats in a store that bore the name of a designer Laurel recognized from seeing his clothes on Nicole Kidman in *People* magazine. Except the word *coat* didn't begin to describe this garment. It was made out of a silky brocade and cut like a kimono. It was tiny—just long enough to come to Maggie's knees. But it was the colors that took Laurel's breath away. The brocade was a deep rosy pink; the glistening lining and cuffs were a pale pink satin. She grabbed it and knew the search for Maggie's gift was over.

Clothes were out of the question for Li'l Bit, who had been wearing the same uniform of shirtwaist dress and Natural Bridge oxfords since the 1940s. But empowered by her success so far in the world of haute couture and consumerism, Laurel took off with purpose.

Li'l Bit had two great passions in life: her gardens and opera. Every day for a week after Peggy's funeral, Li'l Bit had pulled her ancient phonograph out on the porch, hooked it up to an extension cord, hauled out a pile of scratchy old 78s, and played them at full screech—which, thank you, Jesus, wasn't very powerful on the aged equipment.

"This is Richard Wagner's *Twilight of the Gods*," Li'l Bit said. "I boycotted Wagner the day we all heard about Kristallnacht, and I've stuck to it all these years." But the boycott was momentarily suspended for Peggy. Miserably unhappy as Li'l Bit was, Laurel could see how much she loved the opera.

"Anyone who feels that way about music

should have a CD player," Laurel had said to Maggie.

"I've told her and told her," said Maggie. "She says she's used to her phonograph and it's too late for her to change." Maggie gave an impatient little snort. She adored any new gadget that came her way and had kept the service guy from the appliance store a virtual prisoner for most of an afternoon when he came to install her TiVo, making him explain the intricacies of it over and over until she could negotiate it and her satellite dish with an assurance Laurel envied.

"You wouldn't believe what it took to get her to use the TV remote," Maggie said. "That is, after she finally agreed to allow a television in her house. If Bobby Kennedy— God bless his soul—hadn't been shot, I still don't think she'd have one."

But Li'l Bit had adjusted to the loathesome TV and was now devoted to her remote. So Laurel strode into the high-end electronics store at the far end of the plaza and purchased the most user-friendly sound system she could find. Before she bought it, she had the salesclerk turn up the decibels until she satisfied herself that Li'l Bit, whose hearing wasn't what it had been, could get every note—and so could the rest of the country if she had her windows open.

After arranging to have the CD player and speakers delivered to her car, Laurel went on to her final stop. Next to the electronics store was a glitzy emporium dedicated to the sale of CDs and videos. She informed a bemused young man who asked how he could help her that she wanted every opera he had in the place. Then she was done.

Her sense of well-being started fading somewhere on the way back to Charles Valley. The highway was full of traffic, and her new car idled loudly, which didn't seem like a good omen for a future that would be spent driving to the supermarket rather than racing around a track. In her haste to get behind the wheel of the Viper, she'd left her tapes and CDs of vintage country music in the Camaro. The only country stations she could find on the radio played crossover stuff that didn't drown the devil voices that were now yelling in her head.

Throwing money away the second you got it, like rich white trash, the voices mocked as Faith Hill sang some rockabilly crap on the radio. *Couldn't you be a little more original? You think Li'l Bit and Maggie want presents you bought with money you got because Peggy is dead?*

And there it was. Peggy was dead. Laurel turned up the radio until Faith was loud enough to be heard three cars over.

Even with the devil voices, she probably would have made it home okay if she hadn't seen the Camaro. But when she turned off the Charles Valley exit from I-85 there it was, in the Dodge dealership lot. It sat by itself in the back, bathed in the cruel white glare of fluorescent lights, looking dirty and alone. The least she could have done before she deserted it was wash it. It had been her car for eighteen years, bought used in a moment of wild hope during her first and only semester at college when everything seemed possible. It had come back home with her in defeat when her mother got sick, and it had been one of the few constants in her life since. And she'd dumped it unclean and unloved on strangers who had painted a humiliating SELL FOR PARTS sign across its windshield in garish yellow.

The road ahead of her blurred, her eyes

filled with tears, and she had to fight to keep from sobbing. She held on until she reached the Sportsman's Grill and pulled into the parking lot to get off the road. The sobs were coming from a place so deep she didn't know she had it. She cried for Peggy, who was gone forever; and Denny, who might as well be; and the job that had been her only source of pride; and her mother, who hadn't been much but was all Laurel had; and the father she'd never known; and the Sportsman's Grill, where Denny's band had been replaced by a DJ who did Elvis impressions at parties; and her poor, sad Camaro, thrown away without as much as a good-bye. She cried for all the changes she didn't want in her life, and the empty spaces inside her that no amount of presents in spiffy boxes would fill up. She bent over so her head was on the steering wheel of her new car and cried for things she didn't even remember.

Chapter Nine

Having a major meltdown in the middle of a parking lot was embarrassing, especially when it was in front of the hangout you once considered your turf. So when Laurel lifted her head from the steering wheel after about twenty minutes of blubbering, she offered a quick *thank you* to heaven that no one had seen her and began rooting around in her purse for a tissue. It was a useless exercise because she never remembered to carry them, not even when she had a cold. But she searched anyway, which, she told herself, did not have anything to do with stalling or not wanting to go home alone, or wishing that Denny was back at his old station in the Sportsman's Grill.

She was about to dump the contents of her purse on the seat next to her when a familiar voice at her side made her jump.

"Laurel?" Perry was standing next to her car; she remembered he ate supper every night here at his dad's restaurant. Given what Maggie could pay him at the clinic, it was probably the only decent meal he had all day.

She knew he was going to take one look at her swollen red eyes and kick into Kindly Doctor mode. That would lead to one of those chats that had helped in the past when the subject of the chat was Peggy, but tonight it was going to make her want to throw things. The thing to do was cut him off with a breezy, Hey, Wiener, gotta run, and get the hell out of there. Instead, for reasons she couldn't control, she turned her tearstained face up to his and said, "Hi, Perry," in a voice that cracked pathetically.

But instead of offering sympathy and a comforting shoulder to cry on, the fool was staring at her Viper. "Is this yours?" he asked reverently.

Dr. Sensitivity hadn't even seen her tearstained face. The car had brought on an in-dustrial-strength attack of Guy's Toy Lust. Which was pretty much the same lust that had attacked her, so she should have un-derstood it.

"What's the top it can do?" asked the Wiener. In another second he'd be drooling. She wanted to snatch a handful of his T-shirt and yank his head down so she could bang it on her steering wheel. She wanted to turn on the ignition and drive the Viper over his feet. Instead, she grabbed his hand and said, "Wiener, please. You've got to help me get my car back."

The desperation in her voice finally pene-trated. He dragged his gaze away from the Viper.

"Are you okay?" he asked.

"I want my car back!" She choked.

"This isn't yours?" His eyes wandered back longingly to the Viper.

"Yes, it's mine! I want my Camaro back!"

"Why?" His hand stroked the side door in an involuntary motion. She was losing him again.

"Because she's my baby and she's at the Dodge dealership out by I-Eighty-five, and I need to get her home before someone buys her and chops her up for parts. Please, Wiener, I can't let them do that to her. She was my first car!"

The words brought him back from whatever automotive la-la land he'd been inhabiting. He looked down at her with the same understanding she'd seen him give Peggy so many times. "Too many changes going on right now, aren't there?" he said gently.

She wanted to tell him just how bad it really was. But if she did, she'd go to pieces.

"It's not that big a deal—getting the Camaro back," she lied. "I just thought I'd like to have a second car for"—she searched for a second—"for backup. If I have to—you know . . . haul things. This Viper isn't a good hauling car." The Camaro wasn't much in the hauling department either, but she rubbed a couple of late-blooming tears out of her eyes with her fists and gave him a spunky little smile. "So what do you say? It'll only take about an hour, maybe a little longer."

He glanced down at the passenger seat, crammed with packages.

"I'm going to take all that stuff back," she said inanely. "I wanted to give Maggie and

Li'l Bit something—presents—you know? But Maggie is so fussy about what she wears, and Li'l Bit will never figure out how to use the CD player, and I've never been any good at picking out things to give people—"

"If you open your trunk I can put the packages in it," he cut in.

"You're gonna come with me?"

"Are you kidding? I want to see you drive this thing."

She handed him the packages to put in the trunk. But he couldn't fit them in because Li'l Bit's CD player was taking up all the room, so he stowed the overflow in the front seat of his own car. Then she watched as he slid into the passenger seat of the Viper with admirable grace. He eyed the Viper's gearshift.

"You do know what you're doing, right?" he asked. By way of an answer, she turned the ignition key and peeled out of the parking lot.

"Am I scaring you?" she asked sweetly, over the roar of the motor.

"Girl, do your thing!" he shouted. And as she hit the gas, the ever-so-dependable Dr. Douglass threw his head back and let out a rebel yell. Proving that Charles Valley's very own Doogie Howser was still a kid.

Laurel had been the one who'd asked Perry to take care of Peggy. When Peggy first came back from the hospital, she'd dutifully continued going into Atlanta to her oncologist at Emory for her treatments. But as she got weaker and her prognosis worsened, she didn't want to undergo the exhausting trip anymore. Her specialist wasn't about to trust the widow of Dalton Garrison to some local practitioner out in the sticks, and he wanted her to stay in Atlanta, but Laurel thought of Denny's beautiful baby brother who had just moved back home and was working for Maggie.

"Peggy needs to watch the sunsets with Maggie and Li'l Bit," she'd said to him.

And he understood. The city doctor hadn't, but The Wiener was a Charles Valley boy who knew all about the three Miss Margarets sitting on Miss Li'l Bit's porch every afternoon. The next day he'd taken his Harvard-educated self up to Atlanta to meet with Peggy's specialist, and then Peggy was home for good.

After a while, when Peggy was too sick

for sunsets on Li'l Bit's porch and Laurel was spending all her time at Peggy's house, Perry started coming by every day after his work at the clinic. He brought Peggy's favorite foods: pulled pork sandwiches with the sweet sauce (not the hot) from Lenny's Barbecue, fried chicken from the Sportsman's Grill, and, once, a bag of tomatoes from the garden he'd planted in his backyard.

Laurel had opened the bag and was hit with the smell of sun and dirt that always accompanies fresh-picked tomatoes. They were at their absolute peak, bright red, and so full of juice it felt like it was going to burst through the skin when she touched them. She put down the bag and started out the kitchen door. "Don't you do a thing with those," she said over her shoulder to Peggy's night nurse, who was saying something about a nice healthy salad.

Laurel came back twenty minutes later with a jar of Hellmann's mayonnaise, a giant economy-size roll of paper towels, salt, pepper, and the freshest loaf of Wonder Bread she could find in Brown's Convenience Store.

"The bread's got to be soft," she told the

nurse, who hailed from somewhere up north. While Perry and Peggy looked on in happy anticipation, Laurel spooned up mayonnaise in big dollops and spread it on the bread. She cut the tomatoes into slices, laid them on top, and then she added lots of salt and black pepper—not the pepper you had to grind, the kind from a little red-and-white can.

" 'Mater sandwiches," Peggy informed the nurse, a big smile on her too-thin face. "Wait until you taste!"

The sandwiches were the best Laurel had ever made, creamy and juicy and salty and sweet all at once. The bread had just the right degree of squishiness. They taught the nurse to bend over the sink to eat it so the juice wouldn't run down her elbows.

"Oh, that is good." The woman groaned with pleasure and reached for a second one. Even Peggy managed to get down a half a sandwich.

"I've never eaten so much mayonnaise at one time in my life," the nurse said.

So Peggy and Laurel started showing off, listing the specialties based on one of the South's basic foods.

"We even make a cake from it," Laurel bragged.

"Maggie makes the best," Peggy said.

"I love Maggie to death, but you can't beat the one they serve at McGuire's," Laurel protested.

Perry suggested a contest, promising to produce cakes from both Maggie and McGuire's for the nurse to judge. Laurel offered her ten bucks as a bribe, which made Peggy laugh. It was the kind of silliness Peggy needed—or maybe they all needed it. All Laurel knew was that Peggy ate the second half of her tomato sandwich. "Oh, we're having *fun*," she said, over and over, like a kid at Christmas. And for that night, thanks to The Wiener's tomatoes, they were.

Later, after Peggy had been helped into bed and given her meds, Laurel went in to say good night. Peggy took Laurel's hand in hers and kissed it. "I'm so lucky," she whispered. "I'm the luckiest woman in the world."

And the ravaged little face looking up at her was so alive and hungry for happiness that Laurel wanted to punch the wall. But she made herself nod and kiss Peggy's cheek. "I'll see you tomorrow," she said, with a big fake smile. "Now get some sleep." And she kept herself from running until she got out of the room.

Perry caught up with her outside in the driveway.

"She's lucky?" Laurel whispered, although she wanted to scream. "Peggy never had a lucky day in her life. And now it's over. The whole goddam thing is over for her, and she never got what she wanted."

"Maybe she had more than you know," Perry said.

"She wanted a baby, did you know that? She wanted a daughter, and that old bastard Dalton wouldn't let her have one."

"But she got herself one anyway. I think that's what she was trying to tell you."

And just as suddenly as the anger had come, it vanished. Because Perry was right. "We didn't have enough time," she said. "I've only known her for a little while."

"Yeah. It isn't fair to you."

But this time he was wrong. "No. I'm lucky too," she said.

They stood quietly for a moment; then, without her asking, he walked her over to her car.

"Are you okay?" he asked.

"Yes."

There was a breeze stirring the night air and a star-packed summer sky above her. For a brief insane second she almost forgot Perry was Denny's baby brother. But then he opened her car door for her and said, "Drive safe, Laurel Selene," just the way Denny always used to, and she remembered. She drove off, resolving not to forget again.

Which was why she freaked when she saw him the next day in the SuperSave Market. He was leaning over to pick up a package of chicken parts, and she watched him for almost a minute before she realized what she was doing. *You are not checking out The Wiener's butt!* she told herself furiously. *You are not!* She had run out of the store, narrowly missing a display of banana-pudding samples in the produce section.

Now, as the Viper roared through the night, Laurel could feel her cheeks burning all over again when she remembered the moment in the SuperSave. The Wiener was cute, there was no getting away from that, but she was eight years older than he was, and there was something deeply wrong about having the hots—even momentarily—for the infant sibling of the guy who had been your spiritual if not your biological brother for most of your life. No matter how attractive Dr. Douglass was, noticing how well his jeans fit certain parts of his anatomy made Laurel feel like she was tiptoeing close to incest.

Chapter Ten

If the guy at the Chevy dealership thought Laurel was strange for wanting her Camaro back, a check for twice what the parts could ever be worth quickly changed his mind. Mercifully she didn't do anything really embarrassing like kiss the car keys when he gave them to her. She handed them to Perry and drove the Viper home behind him.

Laurel lived in a cabin that had been in her family for generations—it sat, inconveniently for the Garrisons, in the middle of the Garrison Nature Preserve across the highway from Li'l Bit's antebellum home. As Laurel followed Perry up the dirt road that led to her little house, the sound of frantic barking greeted them. Peggy's adoptees were hungry.

Peggy had rescued stray dogs, "my furry babies," she called them, and after she died Laurel had moved the poor things—all ten of them—to her own place because she couldn't face going over to Garrison Cottage to feed them. Now the dogs were crammed into her tiny two-room house, where they exchanged canine hostilities with Patsy Cline, the stray Peggy had once foisted off on Laurel.

Perry had already gotten out of the Camaro and was waiting for her when she drove up. As she opened her front door it occurred to her that this was the first time he'd ever been to her home. And it was the first time she'd been alone with him for any length of time—without talking about medications or nursing schedules—since he'd been old enough to shave. Fortunately, before she could start feeling weird, the dogs descended on them, and for the next half hour he helped her fill food and water bowls, let the dogs in and out of the yard she'd fenced in for Patsy, scratch tummies, and head off a potential fight.

"Your dog doesn't seem to like the others much," he remarked.

"Patsy's strange."

The dog wasn't the only one. Now that the canine contingent was no longer demanding her attention, she was feeling weird again. The Wiener, damn him, seemed perfectly comfortable. Of course it wasn't his turf that was being invaded, or his family history that was on display. She snuck a quick look over at the four shelves she'd put up in the center of her living room wall, defiantly placing them where they could not be missed. On those shelves was a collection of frayed, ancient books. There were paperbacks and hardcovers, old how-to manuals, murder mysteries, *Reader's Digest* Best of the Year anthologies, one-time potboilers like *Valley of the Dolls*, and classics like *The Complete Works of Shakespeare* all jumbled together. These books were the only inheritance she'd ever had from her father. He'd bought them at a garage sale before he was killed a few months before she was born. Not knowing if she was going to be a boy or a girl, he'd printed the name BABY MERRICK in pencil in a large childish scrawl on the first page of each book. Below that, in her own prissy penmanship, Laurel had written *Laurel Selene McCready* when she was seven. From everything she'd heard about her father, the man had never read a book in his life, but he'd wanted her to have these and she would probably insist on being buried with them. To hell with what anyone had to say about her notorious daddy.

There was one more relic of her childhood in this room. On the floor, propped up against the corner, was her ma's guitar. Drunk or sober, Sara Jayne could always make music, and no matter how mad Laurel got at her memory she could no more toss the guitar than she could ditch the books. The damn thing would probably be buried with her too.

"Sara Jayne sure could sing." The Wiener was reading her mind again.

"When did you ever hear her?" The places where her ma did most of her singing would have been off limits for the young impressionable Wiener.

"Once, when you were away at college. She came into Daddy's bar and sang with

Denny and the boys the way you used to. I think she did it because she missed you."

It was funny the way someone could say something that would get you in the gut, and they'd never know it. Or did he? For a brief moment she flashed back to the pudgy nine-year-old Wiener, who always seemed to be watching her. The present-day Wiener moved to her sofa and sat on it, sprawling out his long denim-clad legs like he was at home.

"Do you ever wear anything but jeans?" she asked.

"It's a habit I got into up north. Hanging on to my redneck cred."

"Did you like it up there?"

"I got a good education, good training, it was nice to get away from home. Yeah, I liked it."

"Why the hell did you come back?"

He was about to answer her but something flickered in his eyes and he changed his mind. "Why did you?" he asked. "You went away to college. I remember when you left."

"To Jackson State. I had a scholarship— everything covered," she said, and then could have kicked herself. Mentioning the scholarship was beyond pathetic. "Ma got sick, so I had to come back to take care of her. But it was okay. She said I'd never make it at college, and she was probably right,"

"I'm sorry, Laurel." He really was. She could tell.

"Hey, I wouldn't want to break a fine old family tradition of screwing up." There had been a lot more to it all than that, but she'd never told anyone—not even Denny—about it. Still, if Wiener were to ask her the right questions, right now, this minute, maybe she would. She waited, but he didn't. Which, she told herself, was just as well.

"Your turn," she said. "Why did you come back?"

He paused again, but this time he decided to say it. "Well, there's this girl."

There was a tiny pang of regret somewhere in her stomach and a much bigger pang of relief.

"You came back home for some girl you knew in high school?"

"Earlier than that."

Laurel ran through a list of the girls his age who had stayed in town, looking for one spectacular enough to make him return to

Charles Valley. She came up empty. "She must be a knockout."

He nodded enthusiastically. "She's beautiful, and she's very smart. . . ."

The litany was starting to piss her off. "Does she have a name?"

"Laurel."

"Yes?"

"No. Her name is Laurel Selene Mc-Cready."

He hadn't said that. And if he had said it, it didn't mean what she thought it meant. And if it did mean what she thought it meant, if she ignored it, it would go away. She got up and headed for the kitchen. "Can I get you something to drink?" she asked. "I've only got sweet tea in the fridge, but I can make up some without sugar if you'd like."

He wasn't going to let her dodge it. He was going to say *You have to deal with this*. She knew it. What he said was, "Thanks, but I should probably get back to my car." He was going to let her dodge it. He *was* still a child.

"Right," she heard herself say. "You need to get your rest. You have to get up early tomorrow, and . . ." He nodded and stood up, unfolding long limbs with an athlete's grace; where had he learned to move like that? "I'll get the car keys," she finished lamely.

After a silent drive that felt awkward as hell to Laurel although it didn't seem to bother Perry—the little creep—they finally pulled into the Sportsman's Grill parking lot. Perry took her packages out of his car and put them in her front seat.

"Are you really going to take these back?" he asked.

"Probably."

He started to say something and stopped.

"Thank you for the help," she said.

"Sure."

Before he could get into his own car, she peeled out. She could feel him watching her.

Chapter Eleven

When Laurel got home, she carried the pile of presents into her bedroom, where she closed the door over the protests of the dogs and spread her loot out on her bed. And thought about gifts. And the story she'd almost told Perry.

The night before Laurel was leaving for Jackson State, her ma had come into the living room where she was packing. Sara Jayne lit a cigarette and watched for a while. "Think you're getting out, don't you, college girl?" she said. Her voice had the edge that said tonight's drunk would be a mean one. "You're going to walk out of here and get your hot shot degree, and you'll never be back. But it doesn't work like that with us. You think I didn't want more than the shit life I had? You think I wanted to screw up? But that's what we do, college girl. We always screw up." And then, having delivered those words of maternal wisdom, she took off for the night.

The next morning, Laurel figured she'd get out of the house before Sara Jayne was awake. But as she finished loading up her car, her mother appeared on the porch behind her looking shaky and red-eyed, in the way Laurel knew only too well. Watching Sara Jayne standing there, Laurel had to admit that she would have done anything to get away from Charles Valley and her.

"I know you think I'm a bitch for what I said last night," Sara Jayne said. "I just don't want you to be disappointed." Which was so stunningly close to an apology that in spite of herself Laurel went back up to the cabin to give her a hug. "Take care, Ma," she said.

"You'll be back," Sara Jayne whispered.

For the first time, Laurel heard the fear in her ma's voice and understood that her mother didn't want Laurel to go because she was terrified to be on her own.

Her ma wasn't right about college—not totally. Laurel hadn't screwed up, but it hadn't been the new start she'd been dreaming of either. The students in her classes seemed young, in ways she had never been. She missed Charles Valley, Denny, and the Sportsman's Grill where the bartender slipped her illegal beers when she sang with Denny's band.

Still, she stayed in school, and she called Sara Jayne once a week. It was one of the few expenses she allowed herself. She made the calls every Friday night at seven, and to her surprise Sara Jayne was always there, even though Friday had always been her big night for partying. Not only was Sara Jayne at home, but she sounded pleased to hear Laurel's voice. There were other signs of change too. Sara Jayne had started wait-ressing at one of the restaurants at the Garrison resort, and she seemed to be sticking with the job. In spite of reason, history, and all her instincts for self-preservation, Laurel found herself hoping. She told herself it was just the distance and homesickness, but the part of her brain that had always been labeled *sucker* where her ma was concerned wouldn't listen.

So one Friday night, after Sara Jayne talked about a rich lady who had come into the restaurant wearing a string of pearls exactly like Joan Collins on *Dynasty*, Laurel decided to risk buying a Christmas present. It was something she hadn't done since her ma whipped her with a belt years ago for trying to give her a surprise birthday party.

There was a jewelry store near the college, where she ran up a whopping $178 on her brand-new credit card for a pearl necklace the guy swore was real, although it was cultured. For the first time in her frugal life she was in debt, but the small scrap of hope demanded it.

She wrapped the jewelry box in red-and-gold paper three times before she got the creases right and spent hours looking for a card before she finally settled on one with a cat dressed like Santa Claus on it. She drove home with the pearls on the seat next to her. About twenty miles outside Charles Valley her teeth started chattering. About ten miles out of town she began holding a conversation with Sara Jayne.

"You're going to hate those damn pearls, aren't you?" she berated her absent mother. "Or something else will go wrong, something I shouldn't have done or should have done. Because we can't have a good Christmas, can we? There is no way you could just smile and like what I've given you." But the scrap of hope—and her sucker's brain—kept her driving.

When she got home, Sara Jayne wasn't there. She knew Laurel was coming home because Laurel had repeated the time and date of her arrival every Friday for a month. But Sara Jayne wasn't there. Laurel's teeth stopped chattering. And she felt a sour little smile spread over her mouth. And in spite of how much a part of her wanted to cry, another bigger part of her was saying *I told you so.*

As she went through the empty house she thought of all the scenarios for a disastrous Christmas that she'd been imagining on the drive home. The one thing she hadn't anticipated was a no-show. You really had to hand it to her ma.

Sara Jayne didn't turn up for the next three days. On the morning of the fourth day, December 23, Laurel placed the jewelry box and the card on Sara Jayne's dresser and went back to college to spend the holiday alone in the room she was renting from a third-year biology student.

Later on, Laurel would piece it together and realize that while she was driving home to Charles Valley, Sara Jayne was getting her diagnosis. And while Laurel sat in the empty little house waiting, Sara Jayne was coping with her terror the only way she knew how. But by the time she figured out the sequence of events, Laurel had already left school, and Sara Jayne was in the hospital, and their new lives centered around bedpans, and IV drips, and finding the right kind of wipes to moisten cracked lips, and new phrases like *pain management* and *do not resuscitate.*

Then came the night when the floor nurse called to say Laurel should get herself back to the hospital immediately. Laurel walked into her mother's darkened room and saw something gleaming on Sara Jayne's arm. The pearls had been twisted around her wrist.

"The doctor wouldn't let us put them

around her neck," the nurse said. "But she insisted on wearing them, so we made them into a bracelet." Two hours later, Sara Jayne died.

Chapter Twelve

The next morning Laurel got up early, before Li'l Bit and Maggie were awake, and went to Li'l Bit's house. She left the entire mountain of glossy boxes and bags on Li'l Bit's front porch and slipped away.

For the next few hours she told herself she was not in hiding. She had reading to do. On Tuesday night she was going to have supper with the Garrison lawyer, who was now her lawyer. His name was Stuart Lawrence, Jr., and he had billed the evening that lay ahead of her as a *little chat*. If that wasn't scary enough, his secretary had sent her an auto-graphed copy of the book he'd written and self-published about the resort and the gardens. It sold in the Garrison gift shop for an outrageous sum and it featured a picture of Stuart Junior with his father, Stuart Senior, who had been the Garrison lawyer before him. Clearly, she had to read the book. That was the only reason she was staying home instead of going over to see how Li'l Bit and Maggie were doing, she told herself.

After forty-five minutes of Junior's clunky prose, she gave up and drove across the highway to Li'l Bit's.

She heard the music as soon as she started down the driveway. One of Li'l Bit's Italian operas was blasting away, reaching decibel levels that were way beyond the capacity of her old phonograph. Laurel stopped her car and got out as Li'l Bit, who had been sitting on the porch, came down the steps and made a beeline for her.

"Do you hear how glorious?" she demanded in her high voice. Big loopy melodies swooped through the air. Li'l Bit's face was pink and glowing, and her hair was flying out of its net. "Do you hear how perfect?" Li'l Bit hugged Laurel. "You shouldn't have done it," she shouted happily above the music, "but I'm so glad you did! I'm such an old stick-in-the-mud, I never would have gotten one of those machines for myself, and just listen!" She stood still, letting the sound wash over her like a dog under a sprinkler on a hot day. "I'm truly in your debt, Laurel."

And the only thing Laurel could think to say was, "How did you get it hooked up so fast?"

"Perry did it. He came over early this morning. I thought you'd asked him to," Li'l Bit said.

Before she could find out more, Maggie appeared from inside the house wearing the rose brocade coat. She saw Laurel and blew her a kiss; then she did a little turn, showing off the shimmering pink silk lining like a runway model. She finished with a slightly arthritic curtsy.

The opera was blasting, Maggie and Li'l Bit were both laughing, thrilled with their loot, and she'd made it happen. She realized she was getting a glimpse of what having the Garrison money could mean. And for the first time since she sat in Stuart Junior's office and heard that Peggy had turned her into the Garrison heiress, Laurel felt like everything was going to be okay.

Chapter Thirteen

MRS. RAIN

2004

Finding out about Laurel Selene McCready had become a mission. Unfortunately, Mrs. Rain admitted to herself, it seemed to be a doomed one. Phone calls to her two main contacts in the outside world—her lawyer and her man of business—hadn't turned up any information, nor had Cherry's visits to the library and the historical society. After four frustrating days, Mrs. Rain was ready, reluctantly, to admit defeat.

It seemed that Laurel Selene McCready had no important family behind her, and no social or political connections. Obviously she was a local girl—her writing seemed like that of a young person—from Charles Valley who had somehow caught Peggy Garrison's attention and then earned her loyalty.

And now Ms. McCready was the heir to the Garrison fortune. God help her, or maybe not. It depended on how well she dealt with Stuart Lawrence Junior. And that would depend on whether Stuart Lawrence Junior was anything like his late father. Of course, Stuart Senior had had leverage.

Thinking about it all was tiring. Her infant doctor had warned about avoiding stress, which meant avoiding life, a concept that seemed to elude the boy.

However, his word was law, so she'd been bundled off for a nap. Essie and Cherry had turned down her bedcovers and tucked her in as if she was a geriatric five-year-old! Well, she might be lying down but she was damned if she'd sleep. She fumbled around for her glasses and focused enough to read the clock on her bedroom wall. It was four in the afternoon.

In an hour, Cherry would serve her her supper in front of the television. Then she'd watch the news and stop brooding about things that were none of her business. Especially since there was nothing she could do about any of it, no matter how much she wished she could.

She sighed into the murky half-light of her bedroom. Just one more time in her life she'd like to be relevant. No one ever told you how incredibly boring life could be when your major accomplishments were keeping your bowels regular and remembering to take your blood pressure medication. And if you'd played for the kind of high stakes she'd known in her time . . . well, best not to think about that. After all, Charles Valley and its residents had been off-limits to her even before she became a doddering old relic. Once, she had resented what the place cost her, but she'd given up on that long ago.

So here she was with her breakfast trays, her television, Essie, Cherry, and the child prodigy doctor. Laurel Selene McCready would have to fend for herself. Still, it was a pity that the young woman didn't have the kind of family or background she would probably need to go toe to toe with Stuart Lawrence Junior.

Chapter Fourteen

LAUREL

2004

Stuart Lawrence, Jr. ("Just call me Stuart," he'd begged) had asked Laurel to come to supper so he could explain what he referred to as her holdings. That, it seemed, was the correct word for what she'd been calling "the stuff Peggy gave me in her will." And the Lord knew she needed someone to explain it to her, because Garrison Gardens and the Garrison resort were so tangled up legally and financially she'd never figure it out on her own. So it was very kind of Just Call Me Stuart to invite her, and there was no reason for the little shiver of dread that made its way up her spine every time she thought about it. The shiver came from the same place as the sweaty palms she always had when she did her income taxes, which on her yearly salary were a joke, but anything official and monetary had that effect on her.

Just Call Me Stuart and Mrs. Just Call Me had lived in Charles Valley since he took over his daddy's duties at Garrison Gardens. Before that, they'd had a home in Atlanta, so there were many people in town, including Laurel, who had never seen the couple up close. She'd met Junior for the first time when he summoned her to his office at the gardens and gave her the news about Peggy's will. At that time she'd been in shock, and she hadn't registered much about him. She'd taken away a sense of a generic middle-aged guy in a muted plaid sports jacket. The wife was a complete mystery.

On Tuesday night, before supper at the Big House, instead of putting on her usual jeans and T-shirt as she had sworn to herself she was going to, Laurel grabbed one of her skirt-and-blouse outfits from her days at the *Gazette*.

"But I'm not wearing pantyhose for any-one," she said defiantly to the dogs, who were watching her. However, she did shove her feet into the sandals with the one-inch heels. When she checked the address Stu-art Lawrence had given her, she realized she'd be eating her supper in Fairway Es-tates, Charles Valley's only gated commu-nity. She probably should have painted her toenails.

Fairway Estates backed up to the Garri-son golf course. The enclave, which was ten years old, had been the subject of much controversy in Charles Valley because the land on which it was built had been owned by Garrison Gardens. The board that ran the gardens sold it to a developer, which was unthinkable to the locals. Not so much as an acre of Garrison land had been sold since the Great Depression, when the Garri-son family acquired it by ripping off desper-ate farmers. Most people in town thought the gardens were protected by the Garrison Gardens Charitable Trust. It came as a nasty surprise to discover that the board of the trust could do pretty much whatever the hell it wanted.

Laurel arrived at the entrance gate, was

waved through, and drove down treeless streets to her destination. SUVs were clearly the vehicle of choice in the neighborhood, and the houses were built right up to the property lines, giving the place a claustrophobic feel in spite of the obvious wealth. But for such a densely packed area, it was as quiet as the surreal shopping plaza in Atlanta. Where the hell did rich people stash their kids? she wondered. Or their pets? Then she remembered she was a rich person. A rich person who had come to discuss her holdings.

A maid wearing a Garrison resort uniform opened the door to the Lawrence manse, but the man of the house was right behind her. "Laurel, welcome," he said, with what seemed to be genuine enthusiasm.

Just Call Me Stuart wasn't bad looking. He was in his middle sixties, not quite six feet tall, with a compact body that was probably the result of upscale enthusiasms like swimming, tennis, and, given the game of choice at the resort, golf. He had a full head of snowy hair and a pair of mild brown eyes behind little square glasses. For dinner at home he wore a sports jacket in a plaid that was so muted it was practically nonexistent. He was also wearing a bow tie, a nerdy touch Laurel tried to tell herself was endearing.

"Come into the living room, please," he said, ushering her in. Laurel had an impression of high ceilings, oversize windows looking out on the unreal green of the golf course, and puffy furniture covered with pale silks that made her want to wash her hands before she touched them. Some kind of overhead system provided selective pools of mood lighting around the living room. The effect was probably supposed to be warm and cozy, but it made Laurel uncomfortably aware that her skirt and blouse had cost twenty-two bucks on sale. She focused on the bow tie and reminded herself to keep an open mind.

Stuart's daddy had been known in Charles Valley as Mr. Dalt's man behind the scenes. The gossip in town was that the son was no match for the father in the Great Man Sweepstakes. Still, there was something about Junior that said he thought he was smarter than most of his fellow humans, and that those mild brown eyes could go cold in seconds if he was crossed.

Stop it, Laurel told herself. *You hated the*

three Miss Margarets before you got to know them.

A voice sang out, "You must be Laurel Selene."

"Laurel, my wife," Junior said, as a woman swept into the room and grasped Laurel's hand.

"I'm Lindy Lee Lawrence," she announced. "Isn't that name like every bad joke you've ever heard about the South? It took me two years to decide to marry Stuart because of it." She exploded in a surprising cackle of mirth. It was the sound of someone who laughed alone a lot.

Lindy Lee was probably in her late fifties, and when she was young she'd been a beauty. The remnants of it still clung to her, especially in her blue-green eyes. But she'd chosen not to go the Botox/surgery/hair-dye route, and nature was taking its toll. Her thick mane of hair was as white as Junior's, and her jawline was beginning to sag. She was taller than Laurel, but it was hard to tell what her figure was like because she was wearing a top made of yards of filmy blue-green cloth over a pair of wide black pants. Her jewelry was large and plentiful, featuring blue stones and gold, but her feet were bare. Her toenails, Laurel noted, were not painted.

Throughout supper, it seemed to be the job of the lady of the house to keep the conversation afloat. Laurel learned that her hostess was born in Mississippi, "in the golden buckle of the cotton belt." She had refused to "come out" as her mama had wished her to, and she had marched with Dr. King from Selma to Montgomery, which was presumably something Mama had *not* wished for.

"I wanted to be a writer, like you, Laurel— a newspaper writer. Well, I guess almost everyone did. Gloria Steinem was our heroine. She proved the pen was mightier than the sword."

"Especially when she was wearing that Playboy Bunny outfit," Junior said, with a chuckle.

"She wore that to go undercover and write an article about the exploitation of women," Lindy Lee protested—but very mildly. Her husband didn't seem to notice. Lindy Lee went back to her monologue, flowing seamlessly from Ms. Steinem to the Lawrence daughter, whom she had named Gloria, although Lindy Lee referred to her as

My Child. It was obvious that My Child was the light of her mother's life.

"She's about your age, Laurel. Lives in New York City and works for television. As a producer and a writer, if you please, in the news department of that new women's channel—you know, the one that isn't Oprah's."

"Her show goes on at five-thirty in the morning, and six people watch it," put in Junior. Laurel got the feeling that My Child was not the light of *his* life.

"She's living her mama's dream and giving me an excuse to make regular visits to the big city," said Lindy Lee, exploding into her cackle laugh.

"She'll be lucky if she doesn't get herself raped and killed," said the loving father.

Without missing a beat, Lindy Lee changed the subject again. "Have the charity vultures descended on you yet, Laurel?" she asked.

"No," Laurel said, startled.

"Well, they'll be swooping down on your poor battered head, darlin', just as soon as word of Peggy's will gets out."

"I hadn't . . . thought of that."

"Peggy funded all kinds of charities, you

know. Everyone will be frantic to get to you. I might hit you up myself for a little cash for a friend of mine who's running for the state senate—"

"A run your friend is going to lose," Stuart cut in. "Laurel might as well burn her money." He stood up, indicating that the conversation was over. "Laurel and I should get started. Lindy Lee, will you have the maid bring coffee and dessert to my den?"

His wife hadn't finished eating. When he stood up, she was in the process of chewing a forkful of peas. But she scrambled to her feet. "Of course," she said brightly. "Dessert is peach mousse. I do hope you like it, Laurel. It's Stuart's favorite in the world."

In the den, the maid served a pinkish mess and took herself out. Junior sat behind a heavily polished and carved table that seemed to double as his desk and indicated that Laurel should settle into a puffy silk chair. There was a nasty-looking pile of documents at his elbow. "This money you've inherited is going to change your life, Laurel," he said. "It's my challenge to make sure the changes are for your own good."

His eyes behind the glasses were earnest, and he seemed very sincere. True, he did treat his wife as if she were the household pet, but Laurel had learned long ago not to judge a man by his marriage.

"Inheriting a fortune is not the lark everyone thinks it's going to be," he went on. "If I may be blunt, it helps if you have a few generations of being wealthy under your belt."

"That lets me out."

He gave her a conspiratorial little grin. "You and me both. My daddy was not to the manner born. Lindy Lee's family is from the crowd that says 'my people' when they mean 'my kin.' But my daddy was just a small-town lawyer from Nowhere, Georgia."

I'm not sure that puts you in the same class as the bastard kid of the town lush, Laurel thought, but she nodded politely.

"Miss Myrtis was the one who discovered my father. Did you know that? She brought him to Mr. Dalt's attention. Over the years they both came to rely on Daddy, and I'm proud to tell you he never let them down." Junior sorted through the pile of papers and pulled out a folder that he handed to Laurel. "I put together some material you can look over at your leisure. About one-third of your portfolio is invested in the Garrison resort. You own the entire company. The gardens do not belong to you; they are a part of the Garrison Trust, which is a charitable organization. However, the board of directors makes all decisions concerning the gardens, and you have the deciding vote on that board."

Laurel's head snapped up from the pages she'd been trying to read. "Excuse me?"

"Because the interests of the resort and the gardens are so closely intertwined, when the charitable trust was formed, the Garrison family retained control of the gardens by giving the deciding vote to the owner of the resort. That means you."

"Me?" She swallowed hard. "I'm in charge of the gardens?"

"And the resort—since you are the sole owner."

For the second time that week, she felt laughter bubbling up inside. "Did you ever meet my ma?" she asked.

Junior shot her a relieved look. "Good," he said, with a sigh. "I'm glad you see the . . . incongruity in the situation."

"It's bone-ass crazy."

"Fortunately, there's a way to handle it. If I may, I'd like to give you a little history. When Miss Myrtis married Mr. Dalt she had a substantial fortune of her own, much of which she sank into the resort. That entitled her to a voice on the board of the gardens and shares of stock in the resort. But since she felt, as you feel about yourself, that she wasn't equipped to be a part of the decision-making process, she signed over a limited power of attorney to my daddy."

"Which meant . . . ?"

"My father voted for her at both entities. And after Miss Peggy inherited everything from Mr. Dalt, she followed in Miss Myrtis's footsteps and let my father continue in the role he had filled for so many years. On his passing, Miss Peggy transferred the authority to me." He opened his briefcase and pulled out a form, which he slid across the table. "This is the power of attorney. As you can see, it's renewable every year."

Laurel scanned the paper in front of her. "Miss Myrtis was the one who started doing this?"

"Yes. She felt my daddy could best look

out for her interests. And Mr. Dalt's too. Although he voted for himself."

I bet he did. The old tyrant would make his wives sign over their authority, but Mr. Dalt would vote for himself.

"Of course, in the last years of his life, Dalton let Daddy represent him too." *Which shot that theory.*

"And Peggy always signed? Every year?" But she already knew the answer to that. Poor Peggy hadn't had the courage to change the master bedroom in the house she'd called home for forty-five years. No way would she have insisted on having her say at the gardens and the resort, if the great Miss Myrtis hadn't done it.

"Miss Peggy saw the value of the precedent that had been set." Junior just happened to have a pen handy. He placed it in front of her.

"And now you want me to sign too."

"It's your decision, obviously. But you've made it pretty clear that you don't think you're prepared to take on a responsibility of this nature."

"I'm not." But she didn't pick up the pen.

"Signing in no way affects your ownership

of the assets. I will not be making any decision about your stock portfolio. You'll have people to advise you about that. You will still get the same allowance, the house in Charles Valley is yours, you can use the apartments in Atlanta and New York and the lodge in Colorado, you get services from the gardens and the resort, the Garrison jet is at your disposal, and all the other amenities—none of that changes."

"I see," she said, to say something.

"Is there anything you don't understand that I can explain?"

He wanted her to sign—wanted it bad—but was that unreasonable? Would anyone in their right mind want her making the decisions for the gardens and the resort? It sure as hell wasn't what *she* wanted. But she still didn't pick up the pen.

"Let me tell you about the men who work for . . . well, actually, many of them work for you," Junior said. "At the resort, Peter Terranova, who was a rising star at one of the largest hotel chains in the world, is our CEO. He's put together a senior management staff of eight of the top men in the field, who run the hotel and the facilities connected to it. Sitting on the board of the foundation, we have two CEOs of major corporations, one former senator, a former head of the Canning Arts Foundation, and three lawyers who are all senior partners in highly respected firms, including yours truly. Dr. Michael Whittlesey, who headed up the Grenier Botany Project, oversees the gardens. Most of us have been involved with the gardens or the resort in some capacity for at least five years. I've been there since I took over for my father back in the eighties."

"That's . . . impressive."

"It is indeed. With all due respect, Laurel, do you think you belong in the room with us?"

"No."

"Then is there some other reason why you don't want to sign that power of attorney?"

She didn't have a reason, only a mindless resistance. "I just don't know if I'm ready to give up something I didn't even know I had twenty minutes ago."

He leaned back in his chair. "I realize this is all coming at you very quickly. But we're in a fast-moving industry. Sometimes Pete and Mike and I have to make decisions overnight. Right now we're paralyzed at both the gardens and the resort because I don't have any authority. If I seem to be pushing you, that's why."

She smiled to show that she didn't mind his pushing. But she couldn't give in.

Stuart leaned forward again. "Laurel, I know this is going to sound old-fashioned and corny, but I feel I'm a keeper of the flame. My father helped build the resort and the gardens. Miss Myrtis, Mr. Dalt, and Miss Peggy gave him the privilege of representing them, and that torch was passed to me. Three people—all of whom were highly intelligent—chose my father and me to perform this service for them. Business aside, I have personal and sentimental reasons for hoping you want to let me continue a proud family tradition. Through me, I see a line stretching from Miss Myrtis to Miss Peggy to you."

Maybe that was why she was balking. Stuart Junior and his power of attorney were a legacy from Miss Myrtis, just like Miss Myrtis's log house and her damn Benedict antiques. So maybe Laurel Selene McCready didn't feel like trotting obediently in the great lady's footsteps. Or maybe she was just being bullheaded.

"Can I have a couple of days to think about it?"

He wasn't happy about it, but he knew when to back off. "Take your time."

He ushered her out into the hallway, and Lindy Lee materialized magically at his side to take over with the social chitchat as she and Stuart walked Laurel to the front door. "I've been wanting to tell you how much I admired you for the way you stepped in with Peggy," she said. "All of us who cared about her were so grateful to you. And of course, dear Perry! Aren't we lucky he's come back home? I've been racking my poor old brains trying to find some delicious young thing for him to fall in love with, to keep him here for good."

It would not be ladylike to tell her to mind her own business, Laurel decided.

Lindy Lee's verbal avalanche continued. "Well, now, I guess this is good-bye. You must come back and see us again soon. My, what a pretty car! It's so . . . low. Drive carefully, the deer are all over the place this time of year."

She paused long enough for Stuart and Laurel to murmur "good night" at each other, and then Laurel was free to climb into her car and drive away. The ordeal was over.

Chapter Fifteen

Laurel woke up early the next morning and was on the road by seven. She'd put on another of the skirts Hank had forced her to wear to work. Originally she'd paired it with the matching blouse that had come with it, but on her way out of the bedroom she'd caught sight of herself in the mirror and had quickly ditched the demure top for a scoop-neck T-shirt. It was an improvement, but still not right. She'd been about to change into her jeans when she'd had a burst of inspiration. She grabbed one of her wide belts and hiked the skirt up so it was just above her knees. The result wasn't

trashy, but it didn't look like she had anything to hide either.

Now, as the Viper roared along, the skirt
flared nicely over her thighs. She was
headed for the old part of Charles Valley,
where, sixty-odd years ago, a young Dr.
Maggie had set up her clinic in an aban-
doned sweet potato warehouse next to the
railroad station.

The trains had stopped running to Charles
Valley and the railroad station had long
since been turned into a tourist restaurant
that featured down-home cooking, quaintly
mismatched crockery, and mason jars used
as drinking glasses. But Maggie's clinic
hadn't changed since she'd had air-conditioning put in back in the 1960s. Entering it
was like walking into a time warp. The old
kitchen chairs in the waiting area had worn
a pattern on the bare wooden floor, and the
small icebox in the corner still held cold
lemonade for those who wanted to help
themselves. Hours at the clinic hadn't
changed either; it was open six days a
week, from seven-thirty in the morning until
four-thirty in the afternoon, with half an hour
off at eleven-thirty for lunch. However, now

that she had a partner, Maggie allowed herself the indulgence of sleeping in until eight and didn't arrive at work until nine-thirty. Perry handled the early morning hours by himself until the nurse came in.

Laurel found him drinking a cup of coffee and looking out the window at some squirrels fighting on the rusty old railroad tracks. He was wearing a crisp white doctor's coat over his jeans.

"Hi," she said.

He turned and his eyes lit up appreciatively when he saw the skirt. Which was no reason for her to blush, for God's sake.

"Hi," he said happily.

"I wanted to thank you. For fixing up the CD player for Li'l Bit. She loves it."

"You're the one who gave it to her."

"But you're the one who set it up."

"Well, you said you were afraid she wouldn't be able to."

"I was. But you made it so she could." There had to be a way the conversation could be more lame, but at the moment she couldn't think of it. "I gotta go," she said.

"You do?"

"Yeah. I just wanted to . . . you know . . . say thank you and now—you're busy."

He looked around the empty waiting room. "Not really."

"You will be. And I am. Busy."

"Oh, I thought maybe you'd come over here to say you've seen the way of the truth and the light."

"Excuse me?"

"About what I said last night. I figured it would take about twelve hours to sink in, and here you are—"

"No."

"No, you don't see it my way, or no, it hasn't had a chance to sink in yet?"

"You're Denny's little brother."

"I know."

"I babysat you. I changed your diapers."

"Not lately."

"I used to beat you up."

"I forgive you. I know it's going to take awhile for you to get past the age thing. And the fact that I'm Denny's brother."

"Denny's *baby* brother. Listen, Wiener—"

"Could you not call me that?"

"This is sweet. And I'll admit it's flattering—"

"You're just scared."

"What? You think I'm scared of you?"

"Of what people will say."

"I've never been scared of that in my life!"

"That's my girl."

"I am not your girl!"

"Yet."

"Listen, you little—"

"You really should stop calling me little. I have about five inches on you."

"Will you shut up and let me talk?"

"Okay."

"We're going to pretend we never had this conversation."

"Like we did last night?"

"You're impossible." She started for the door.

"Go out with me, Laurel Selene. I promise you'll be able to handle it. We start slow, maybe grab a little supper."

She walked out the door without answering and heard him open it again as she strode to her car, where she lowered herself into the front seat with dignity and—thanks to the hiked-up skirt—a display of what she knew were the best legs in the county.

"I'll call you about that date," he yelled, as she roared off.

She hadn't gotten her message through to him. He still didn't understand that they couldn't be anything but friends and that that was a good thing.

Men, and getting involved with them, were bad topics for Laurel. Not that The Wiener fell into the category of men in the getting-involved-with sense. That was ridiculous. But given her history with members of the opposite sex, when she fell for a man, it was never a positive experience. As Denny had once put it, "Honey, if you like him, I don't want to meet him alone in a dark alley." That hadn't been altogether fair. None of her pre-vious love interests had been dangerous; her taste ran more to cheaters and users. But since she'd started hanging out on Li'l Bit's porch she'd been avoiding the kind of one-night stands that had made up so much of her social life. It could have been the influence of the three Miss Margarets, or the fact that Peggy's illness had taken over her life. Or it could have had something to do with Josh, her last—or perhaps her first—semi-serious attachment.

Josh was a magazine writer, in his late forties, who had come down from New York to do research on a book he was writing. At first he'd run true to form, pumping Laurel for information about her father because the scandal surrounding John Merrick's death had been part of his story. But that had changed. He was the only man besides Denny who'd ever recognized, or cared, that she had a brain in her head. He even offered to stake her to a new start in New York City. She'd turned him down. While she'd never regretted it, there had been a night after Denny announced his engagement when she'd almost used the private cell phone number Josh had given her in case she changed her mind.

Three days later she'd read in *People* magazine that Josh and the fourth Mrs. Josh—an actress half his age—were on their honeymoon. The bride, who was noted for playing roles in unpleasant independent films, looked intense and a tad anorexic in the pictures. Josh beamed at her with the kind of total appreciation Laurel remembered well. And she finally admitted she missed it. Because even if he did look a little silly next to his young bride, Josh had been the pick of the litter in Laurel's romantic life.

And now there was The Wiener and his childhood crush. Which he would get over.

This time next year he'd have some totally appropriate young woman on his arm, and he'd be wondering what had possessed him to ask Laurel for a date. She shifted gears and let the Viper fly down a deserted stretch of road, wishing she felt more cheerful.

Chapter Sixteen

One thing was clear to Laurel: She had to start dealing with her holdings. It wasn't going to be easy. The fact that Garrison Cottage was stuffed with Miss Myrtis's antiques was enough to make her want to burn the place, and not just for Peggy's sake. The myth of Miss Myrtis as a great lady had always made Laurel want to gag, but now she knew about the power of attorney Miss Myrtis had signed. Unlike Peggy, who had been young and penniless when she married Old Mr. Dalt, the great Miss Myrtis had been an heiress with her own fortune, an education, and some major family clout behind her. But she'd signed over her power of attorney like a good little lapdog instead of stopping her husband and his henchmen as they set up policies that were still keeping wages in Lawson County the lowest in the state. Low wages meant low taxes, which meant lousy schools, which meant uneducated kids who had nowhere to go for jobs except back to the Garrisons. *And Myrtis Garrison could have stopped it all years ago!* Instead, she'd given handouts to people who could have helped themselves if they'd had a level playing field and she'd picked up a reputation for saintliness. Laurel hated the way everyone bought the hype about the old bat who had once been named the First Lady of Garrison Gardens by the society writers of her day.

Now Laurel was the new lady of Garrison Gardens, not to mention Garrison Cottage—which she had to finish looking over. It would be easier to do that than sitting at home and staring at the power of attorney Stuart Junior wanted her to sign. At least she could put off becoming a lapdog for a little longer. She left Maggie's clinic, drove to the big log house, went upstairs, and picked up her tour where she'd stopped it, in the master bedroom.

The room was surprisingly girly, with pink dominating the carpets and draperies. The wallpaper was badly faded, but Laurel could see that the roses in the pattern were pink too. The hateful canopy bed and a chaise with a Tiffany lamp next to it were the only freestanding pieces of furniture in the room. There were no bureaus or dressers, but two of the walls were lined halfway up with built-in drawers and shelves painted a creamy white. There were large closets on both sides of the room. In one corner, a small makeup table had been built in with a mirror and itty-bitty lamps alongside it. There certainly wasn't enough light or counter space for a woman who loved fooling with cosmetics as much as Peggy had. But then, this room hadn't been Peggy's. The inadequate makeup area made a right angle with a padded window seat that ran the entire length of the back wall under the windows. It was covered with pink silk too. Pink had never been Peggy's color.

The bed was still made up, as if waiting for Peggy and Dalton to turn in. Or Dalton

and Myrtis. The pillowcases were monogrammed with the swirly Benedict *B*. Laurel
turned her attention to the drawers instead.

The right side of the room must have
been Dalton's. There were drawers full of
men's socks that had been folded into neat
little bundles and laid out in straight rows.
Other drawers held stacks of men's under-
wear, also neatly folded. In his closet, several pairs of identical brown-and-white ven-
tilated wing tips were impaled on racks that
climbed up one wall, and at least a dozen
identical lightweight summer suits hung on
nice-smelling wooden hangers, along with
pants, jackets, shirts, and sweaters. Old Mr.
Dalt had been a natty but not very adventur-
ous dresser.

Peggy's side of the room was empty. This
made sense, since Peggy had moved herself to the little bedroom downstairs after
Dalt's death. But to Laurel it felt like a sad
summary of Peggy's life in the house. She
wanted to lock the bedroom door and walk
away, leaving it the way it was. But this
house was already too full of memorials to
the dead. She found some black plastic
garbage bags in the kitchen, brought them
back to the bedroom, and began filling

them with the clothes that had belonged to Peggy's husband.

It was late in the afternoon by the time she was done. In spite of the air-conditioning she'd turned on, she was sweaty, tired, and covered with about three decades of undisturbed dust. It was time to quit. Tomorrow she'd call the ever-helpful resort staff and request that someone haul the bags down to the rescue mission. But before she left, she looked around the room one last time, to make sure she'd gotten everything. That was when she noticed that part of the window seat's top was actually a lid, evidently opening to a storage compartment. Curiosity trumped weariness, and she lifted it up. The area was much larger than she expected. Its farthest corners were dark, and the wood was raw and unpainted. At first she thought the entire space was empty, but as she was about to close the top, she saw a glint of something that looked like gold in the corner. Hoping the tetanus shot she'd gotten in grammar school was still active, she reached in, dodging rusty nails, and found the handle of an old-fashioned suitcase. It was good sized, made of leather that had once been beautiful and very expensive, with a handsome brass latch. Laurel brushed off cobwebs and a layer of grit. The leather was cracked and water stained, and it smelled moldy. Obviously it had been in the window seat for some time. But why had Peggy put it there? Laurel turned it over and found the swirling *B* for Benedict on the front. The suitcase hadn't belonged to Peggy. Like everything else in the house, it had been the property of Miss Myrtis. Who, for some reason, had wanted to hide it.

It took Laurel forty minutes and a trip to the gardener's shed for a toolbox before she finally managed to pop the rusty lock on the suitcase. Inside, she found an old-fashioned pinafore and dress. Laurel pulled them out gingerly. The pinafore was a lacy ruffled affair that had once been white but now had yellow fold lines. Threaded through the lace ruffles was a faded pink ribbon, and there was a pink sash with a big squashed pink silk rose on it. The dress, which was also liberally supplied with white lace ruffles, had probably been bright green at one time, with more roses printed on it. Both the dress and the pinafore looked like something out of a picture book of Victorian children. The getup wasn't garish, but the girl who'd worn it would have stood out in a crowd. She must have been over five feet tall and hard on her clothes. The apron had been torn and mended several times, as had the dress. The seams of the dress had been let out, and there were inserts of pink fabric on the sides—obviously, its owner had worn it long past childhood.

Laurel looked back in the suitcase to see if there was anything else. On the bottom of the case was a yellowed paper. She pulled it out carefully and found herself staring at a page of sheet music for a song by Stephen Foster called "Beautiful Dreamer."

Chapter Seventeen

MRS. RAIN

2004

The house was dark and she was supposed to be asleep. But her legs ached. More important, so did her heart. Not the pumping muscle her young doctor was so diligently preserving, but her real heart, that non-organ that was somewhere deep inside. Her heart was where the music had come from, the singing and the laughing, and it was where the memories were kept—memories that were triggered easily because they were so much more real than anything that was going on in her life today. The death of Peggy Garrison had started a flood of them.

Clearly, sleep was out of the question.

She got herself out of bed and went into her closet. It was big—in her time she'd slept in rooms that were smaller—and there were two shelves above the clothes racks, far too high up for her to reach. She fought her way through the robes and nightgowns that seemed to make up too much of her wardrobe these days, until she found a stepladder folded up in a corner. She opened it and carefully climbed up—her boy doctor would have a fit—feeling around on the top shelf through a mess of scarves, gloves, sweaters, bits of string, old newspapers, and other debris she refused to let Essie touch until she found a large gray envelope hidden behind some shoe boxes. Clutching her prize, she climbed back down and settled herself in the large wing chair where she sat to watch television. She turned on the lamp, opened the envelope, and pulled out an ancient sepia-toned photograph of a young girl wearing a long old-fashioned dress with roses printed on it and a white pinafore with ruffles, a wide sash, and a big artificial rose. If the picture had been in color, the roses and the sash would have been pink.

She slid the picture back in the envelope

and made her way downstairs to the living room where the piano was. She'd never actually learned to play the thing, not more than just fooling around and picking out a melody with one finger, but she'd always liked having it in her house.

She put the envelope in the piano bench, sat down to play, and she caught sight of her hands resting on the keyboard. When you were young you never believed that the day would come when your fingers would be twisted and your pretty voice would become a croak, something you couldn't bear to hear. Still, you had to do the best you could. Slowly she began to tap the notes with one finger while, in a soft voice, she sang the lyrics she knew by heart:

*"Beautiful dreamer, wake unto me,
Starlight and dewdrops are waiting for
thee."*

Chapter Eighteen

IVA CLAIRE

1927

"Beautiful dreamer, wake unto me," Iva Claire sang, as she walked slowly across the stage of the New Court Theater. She sang loudly into the empty house, checking for dead spots, those places onstage that seemed to swallow up the sound of your voice so it never reached the audience. A civilian wouldn't know what to look for, but at twelve Iva Claire was a seasoned professional who could tell when her voice had stopped carrying. Whenever she and Mama played a town for the first time, she always went to the theater before rehearsal to run through their numbers so she could warn

Mama about any problems. Mama never thought of things like that.

Iva Claire and her mother were vaudevillians. Their last name was Rain—Mama's full name was Lily Rain—so their act was called Rain and Rain: The Sunshine Sisters. Mama called it their *nom de théâtre*. Being in show business was Mama's dream. Getting out of show business was Iva Claire's dream.

"Starlight and dewdrops are waiting for thee," Iva Claire sang, as she finished working her way across the stage. There were no dead spots in the New Court; it had been well built seventy years ago. Now it was old and dirty, and it had the peculiar smell Iva Claire had come to associate with the South. She was used to the normal backstage odor of dust and sweat; she'd been breathing that since she'd started working at five. But theaters in the South—the New Court was in Beltraine, Georgia—also smelled from dampness that never completely dried because of the hot, humid air.

Actually, Iva Claire didn't mind the heat or the dampness or even the smell. She'd been wanting to play a southern circuit ever since she found out she and Mama had family below the Mason-Dixon line. But no matter how broke they were, Mama would never take a booking in the South. Iva Claire was pretty sure the reason had to do with Mama's family, but Mama refused to talk about it, and if Iva Claire pushed her she would get one of her headaches. There were lots of things that Mama wouldn't talk about. Like the fact that she was scared to be in Georgia. She said she wasn't, and she had screamed at Iva Claire for suggesting it, but Iva Claire knew that ever since they'd gotten to Beltraine, which was their first stop in the state, Mama had been having trouble breathing—a sure sign she was upset. And it was all Iva Claire's fault.

Don't think about that, she told herself firmly.

She walked to the middle of the stage where the movie screen was to see how shallow their playing space would be. The New Court was a vaud-and-pic house, which meant they showed motion pictures and offered a live vaudeville show in between. It wasn't a great booking, but it was a miracle that the Sunshine Sisters had gotten it. They wouldn't have if another act on the tour hadn't dropped out in North Carolina. Mama and Iva Claire had joined the troop there two months ago. They were what was known as a disappointment act.

If she was honest about it, Iva Claire knew the Sunshine Sisters were a disappointment in more ways than one. Their act was terrible—what performers called a *fish* because it stank. Part of the problem was their material. Vaudeville audiences liked funny patter, snappy songs, and pretty girls who showed a little leg. The Sunshine Sisters wore old-fashioned costumes with long skirts, they sang droopy songs by Stephen Foster, and they didn't have any patter at all. Then there was Mama's performance. Mama had a pretty voice but she tried too hard, which made her movements stiff and her singing shrill. When the audience didn't like her, she tried harder—and got stiffer and more shrill. Iva Claire sighed. The Stephen Foster act was new; Mama had put it together and she loved it with all her heart. She'd never see how bad it was—and Iva Claire would never tell her.

"The sight lines in this old dump are as good as the sound," a light high voice called out from the darkened house. "I've been watching you while you were singing, and there's no place where the audience can't see you." Iva Claire whirled around to see Tassie walking up the center aisle of the theater. Tassie was about a year older than Iva Claire, and she traveled with a couple known as Benny Ritz and Irene DeLoura. Ritz and DeLoura were the headliners of the troupe. Their comedy routine was the best thing in the show.

Iva Claire and Tassie hadn't said more than a couple of words to each other since the Sunshine Sisters joined the troop, but Iva Claire had been curious about the older girl and her connection to DeLoura and Ritz. Tassie was way too young to be their daughter.

"I brought you your sheet music," Tassie announced. As she came closer, Iva Claire could see through the gloom that she was carrying a pile of papers. "And I got us a couple of gum erasers," she added.

Iva Claire felt herself stiffen. "How did you know . . . ?" she stammered, too embarrassed to finish the sentence.

"It's okay," the other girl soothed. "I know what you do before the show each time we play a new house. I've seen you erase what those jerks write."

The jerks were house musicians. Each vaudeville theater had its own orchestra, and sometimes if an act was really bad, like the Sunshine Sisters, the men in the pit would amuse themselves by writing notes in the margins of the music. *This act is a bomb*, the clarinetist in one town would scrawl on the clarinet part. *A real Thanksgiving dinner,* his counterpart in the next town would add. Each guy would try to be wittier and meaner than the last one. It would have hurt Mama to read what they wrote, so as soon as they hit a new town, Iva Claire would sneak into the orchestra pit to clean up their sheet music.

"Don't feel bad. I'd do it, too, if I was you," Tassie said.

Iva Claire tried to smile, but she was too embarrassed. She might not want to be in show business, but since she was, she hated being the worst act on the bill. Going out in front of an audience five times a day and dying was bad enough. Getting caught erasing comments from her sheet music was downright humiliating.

But Tassie was trying to make friends, that was clear. Iva Claire had never had a friend her own age. There had been people in the boardinghouse back in New York that she'd loved. But that was before she and Mama had had to run from New York and the boardinghouse, because of what Iva Claire had done. Now she'd never see any of her old friends again.

Don't think about that. "Thanks," she said to Tassie.

Tassie climbed up on the stage and they divided up the music. Each of them took an eraser and went to work.

"How long have you and your ma been doing a sister act?" Tassie asked, as she flipped through the pages.

"About a year. When I got taller than Mama, we switched from mother and daughter."

"Benny says you're the glue that keeps your act together."

"Really?" It sounded like a compliment, but Iva Claire knew she was no performer.

Tassie nodded eagerly. "Benny and Irene like to keep an eye on the show, so they watch all the acts. Benny says you and your ma get away with playing sisters because you're such a good mimic."

That was another secret of hers. Iva Claire had learned if she could copy

Mama's gestures and poses, the audiences seemed willing to believe their age difference was closer to ten years than twenty. Makeup and distance from the stage helped, of course, but it was the imitating that did it. It wasn't just that she could copy Mama's movements either; she could also get inside Mama's head and think like her. For some reason that made it work. Iva Claire wasn't much of an entertainer, but she had trained herself to be good at getting inside other people's heads.

"What gets me is, you and your ma don't even look alike," Tassie went on.

It was true. At twelve, Iva Claire was already two inches taller than her mother, and her dark hair was stick-straight. Mama's hair was dark too, but it was so curly it wouldn't lie flat even after she'd just had it bobbed. Iva Claire's eyes were blue, her perfectly proportioned nose was straight, and her face was square with a jaw that Mama said made her look determined. Although she wasn't heavy, she looked solid. Mama was tiny and looked like you could blow her away just by breathing hard. Her eyes were dark brown, her delicate little face was heart shaped, and her button nose turned up at the end. The only feature mother and daughter shared was a full curvy mouth. Yet they passed as sisters. It was proof—if Iva Claire had ever needed it—that you could make people see what you wanted them to.

Tassie echoed her thoughts. "People will believe anything if you do it right. We toured with a two-headed boy once. He turned out to be twins who worked behind an illusion curtain. The one who played the second head told me the whole trick was in the way he held his neck—in the angle. Can you believe that?"

Iva Claire did believe it. Completely.

"How did you start traveling with Benny and Irene?" Iva Claire asked.

"Benny and Irene knew my mother because she was in the business. When she died, they took me in. They got it all written up legal that they were my guardians. That was Benny's idea. It took us a couple of months to find a lawyer who would do it, since I was so young and we were trooping, but Benny wouldn't quit until he had those papers." She said it calmly, as if being taken in by strangers was the most natural thing in the world.

Tassie wasn't really pretty—her round blue eyes were too big for her face, and her front teeth stuck out a little—but even though she was small, she already had the kind of curves Iva Claire was learning were to be envied. At first Iva Claire thought she was tough. Tassie smoked cigarettes and played craps with the stagehands, but she was actually very sweet. The big dream of her life was to be in show business, and her idols were Gracie Allen and Irene DeLoura. She stood backstage in the wings at every performance, watching all the acts, laughing at jokes she'd heard dozens of times, sometimes clapping louder than the audience.

Now she looked over at Iva Claire. "So why are you doing this tour? Your ma hates playing this part of the country. She says so all the time."

For a brief crazy moment, Iva Claire played with the idea of telling her the truth. But she could never tell anyone what she'd done back in New York.

"You've seen our act." She shrugged. "We have to take whatever we can get."

"You're not that bad."

"Then why are we sitting here cleaning up my sheet music?"

"Are you going to let a bunch of hillbillies calling themselves musicians get you down? The hick playing base in Wynward was the town barber, for Christ's sake. It's not like we're playing houses with real orchestras."

"Our act is a bomb," she said flatly.

That stopped Tassie. Iva Claire put down her eraser. "Your songs are real pretty," she said carefully. "I still like listening to them, and I've heard them every night for two months. Hell, I can sing along with you by now."

"But the act is a bomb."

"Well, it could be a little more . . . loose. The way your ma has every hand gesture worked out. . . ." She smiled apologetically.

"I know." Iva Claire picked up her eraser and started working again, but she could feel Tassie watching her. Finally, she looked up. "Thanks for helping me," she said, with a smile. "It would hurt Mama if she saw this."

Tassie smiled back. "I like your ma. I like the way she loves the business, you know?"

"Oh, yes," Iva Claire said. Her voice had

slipped into what Mama called her *snide tone.* "One thing you can say about my mama, she loves the business."

Tassie was fidgeting with the piece of paper in front of her; there was something on her mind. "Benny and Irene, they're quitting," she finally said. "This is their last tour. Irene says they're too old. They bought a little piece of land in New Jersey, and they want to try to grow vegetables. If you can believe that."

"It'll be nice for all of you, living out in the country."

"The hell it will!" The big blue eyes were filling up with tears. "I don't know how I'm gonna stand it, Iva Claire, living out in the middle of nowhere. And they're so happy, I don't know how to tell them—" The tears were starting to overflow; she blinked them back. "I was thinking maybe you and your ma . . . well, maybe you might need someone to go around with you. She has trouble helping you carry the trunks sometimes, and I'm very strong. And I could keep up the costumes, I can sew."

It was the first time in Iva Claire's life that she'd had something to give someone. She was always on the other end, begging for a job or a paycheck. But now Tassie was doing the begging. The new role of Lady Bountiful was too heady to resist. "I'll talk to Mama," she said recklessly.

The response was instantaneous and gratifying. Tassie threw her arms around Iva Claire, then started dancing around the stage. "Thank you, thank you, thank you!" she said.

"I can't promise anything."

"Your ma will do it, if you ask," Tassie said confidently. Which only went to show how little she knew about Mama. Tassie sat back down and started piling up the sheet music. Mercifully for Iva Claire's pride, they'd both finished erasing. Suddenly Tassie looked up. Two shrewd blue eyes were studying Iva Claire. "Now that we're going to be traveling together, you want to tell me why you and your ma really took this gig?"

Once again, for a moment, Iva Claire was tempted. It would be so easy to just spill it all. And it might feel better if someone else knew. But what if Tassie didn't understand?

"Like I said, we take what we can get."

She could see from the look on Tassie's face that Tassie didn't believe her, and she held her breath. If Tassie pushed her, Iva

Claire would have to cut off what her instincts told her could be the best friend she ever had. Suddenly she realized she'd hate that. Tassie seemed to realize the same thing, because she backed off. She got to her feet and picked up the sheet music. "I'll put this down in the pit. You better get up to the rehearsal room. Your ma will be waiting for you." She started for the wings, but she turned. "Maybe someday you'll tell me," she said, before she left.

Iva Claire sat alone on the stage. She closed her eyes and tried to make her mind a blank. But the memories of New York and the awful thing she'd done came flooding back. It had all started when she and Mama were rehearsing the Stephen Foster act.

Chapter Nineteen

"Beautiful dreamer, queen of my song," Mama sang a cappella, her light soprano filling the small room she and Iva Claire rented in Big Hannah O'Brien's boarding-house. They were going through the block-ing—the moves and gestures—of their new act. Mama held her left hand up in the air near her head as if she was listening. With-out knowing she was doing it, she tilted her head slightly to the left too. Iva Claire watched the little gesture and filed it away to be used when they did the performance.

"Iva Claire, sing!" Mama said. "We're opening in a week."

Iva Claire felt something twist in her stomach. She didn't want to open in a week. The new act was going to be awful. Of course, that was nothing new.

There had been a time when she'd hoped that Mama would realize they didn't have what it took to make it and let them quit. They'd stop going on the road, stop renting rooms, get out of Hell's Kitchen, and settle down in a little town somewhere. Iva Claire would go to school full time, not just for a few months whenever they were laid off. She knew she'd be good at school, much better than she was at performing, because—and this was something she could never tell Mama—she was too smart to be an actor.

She was already surprisingly well educated. After spending so much dead time on trains and backstage, she'd already read more than most adults, and geography was a natural for her. Languages came easily too. Since many of the vaudeville performers they knew came from other countries, she'd already picked up a smattering of Italian and Yiddish and an Irish brogue that Big Hannah said sounded like she'd been born in the Old Country.

"Beautiful dreamer, out on the sea, Mermaids are chaunting the wild Lorelei;" Mama sang, her eyes glowing happily. Iva Claire felt her stomach twist again. Somehow Mama had wangled a booking out in Brooklyn. It was the closest the Sunshine Sisters had ever gotten to playing Manhattan, where audiences prided themselves on being tough. She and Mama were going to be killed. And Mama had no idea.

"All the booking agents for the Big Time circuits go out to Brooklyn to see the talent at the Chevalier," Mama had said when she announced the news. Ziegfeld sends his scouts there to find new acts for the Follies. "The manager of the Chevalier—his name is Lenny—swore to me."

Iva Claire knew important booking agents went to demonstration theaters like the Jefferson in Manhattan, where they could catch up-and-comers like Bob Hope, but she wasn't sure they schlepped all the way out to Brooklyn. However, Mama had been giving this Lenny an awful lot of what she called "special attention"—which probably explained how they got the gig—and Mama was no fool when it came to men.

"Beautiful dreamer awake unto me!"

Mama finished the song, and her face was radiant. When Iva Claire was little she used to try to win that look for herself. Now that she was older, she knew only Mama's dream could bring it on.

"Oh, Lordy!" Mama said, holding her hand to her chest and plopping down on the sofa. "That's enough rehearsing for now. Let me catch my breath!" Mama always had to catch her breath when she got excited. Iva Claire waited until she'd calmed down. There was something she and Mama had to talk about, and Mama wasn't going to like it.

Finally, her mother looked at her. "Such a serious face! What's wrong with my little Claire de Lune?"

Iva Claire braced herself. "Mama, I saw the roses for the costumes when they came yesterday," she began.

For a second, Mama looked nervous, but then she spotted the window across the room. "Did you close that?" she demanded.

"Those roses were made of *silk*."

"What are you trying to do, Iva Claire, asphyxiate us?" Mama leaped to the window, opened it, and said, "That's better!" She turned and smiled, but the nervousness was still there.

"I guess it was a mistake—the roses be-ing silk—because we can't afford them."

Her mother didn't answer.

"If you want me to, I'll take them back to the shop."

"Silk really isn't that much more expen-sive."

"Mama, those roses cost *three times* what you said you were going to pay."

"You have to spend money to make it."

"You promised you'd be careful!"

"This one time I want everything to be perfect. Just this once we're going to have the best. We deserve it, Claire de Lune."

She said it defiantly, but she couldn't meet her daughter's eye and Iva Claire felt herself shiver. She knew money had been going out—when you were doing a new act you had to have new pictures, costumes, and musical arrangements—but every time she asked Mama what it was costing, Mama swore she was sticking to their budget. "Trust me, Claire de Lune," she'd said. And because Mama was so happy and Iva Claire hated to fight, she had trusted her. But now her mother couldn't meet her eye.

Before she could force Mama to say how

much she had spent, there was a knock at the door. Glad for the interruption, Mama said, "I'll get it." Big Hannah was standing outside.

"There's someone calling for you on the telephone," the landlady said. There was one telephone in the boardinghouse, in the downstairs hall. Iva Claire and Mama lived on the top floor. "It's probably important," Big Hannah added needlessly. In their world, a phone call always was. Mama left quickly. Iva Claire could hear her running down the stairs. She noticed the landlady hadn't moved.

Iva Claire admired Big Hannah almost more than anyone she knew. Unlike most show folk, Big Hannah hadn't blown the money she'd made. When she retired from her dancing act, she'd bought this boardinghouse, where she gave tenants like Iva Claire and her mother a clean place to live for the lowest rent in the city. It was known throughout the neighborhood that Big Hannah could always lend you a few bucks if you needed it, and any performer who was down on his luck could get a hot meal from her and a place to sleep on her parlor sofa.

The big woman was giving Iva Claire a

worried look as she squinted through the smoke from the cigarette tucked in the side of her mouth. Iva Claire had practiced that squint—and the way Big Hannah talked around her cigarettes—until her imitation was perfect. Mimicking people was fun as long as you didn't have to do it onstage.

"You and your ma been rehearsing?" Big Hannah asked. Her worried look was probably because everyone in the boarding-house had heard about the new act, and they all knew it was going to be a stinker.

Iva Claire nodded.

"How's it going?"

Iva Claire smiled brightly. "Good," she said. The performers' code said you didn't show doubt—not even to someone as nice as Big Hannah. Big Hannah smiled back just as brightly because she knew the rules too. But Iva Claire could tell there was something on her mind.

"Iva Claire, is your ma planning to move after you open the act?"

At first, Iva Claire thought she was joking. Except there was nothing funny about the possibility of losing their rooms at the boardinghouse.

"We wouldn't go anywhere. We love it here, Big Hannah. Why?"

The big woman looked uncomfortable. "You know I'll carry my people for as long as I can, but—" She stopped short. "Never mind. It's got nothing to do with you, child." She started for the door, but Iva Claire stopped her.

"How long has it been since Mama paid the rent, Big Hannah?" she asked quietly.

Big Hannah hesitated. Then she said, "Don't you worry your head about it. I'll talk to your ma," and let herself out.

Iva Claire and Mama had two rooms, a bedroom for Mama, and the sitting room where Iva Claire slept on the sofa. Mama kept their money in a wooden box in the top drawer of her dresser under her clothes. Normally Iva Claire wouldn't have dreamed of going into Mama's dresser, but now she ran into Mama's bedroom, got the box, and started counting. They had eleven dollars and forty-six cents. She counted again, thinking she'd made a mistake. She hadn't. Frantic, she went through the rest of the drawer, feeling in the corners for bills or change. Nothing. She pulled the other drawers open, searching through Mama's clothes. There were stockings, blouses, sweaters, and under-wear all jumbled together, but no money. Mama had done the unthinkable—she'd spent all their money on the new act. And they weren't due to get another check for four months.

Chapter Twenty

The checks were what Mama and Iva Claire
lived on. Mama liked to think they supported themselves, but the Sunshine Sisters didn't work enough. The checks came
in the mail every spring and fall in long white
envelopes; their arrival was one of the few
dependable things in Iva Claire's life. If she
and Mama were on the road, a check would
be waiting for them at General Delivery in
whatever town they were playing. If they
were laid off and staying in New York, it
would show up at Big Hannah's.

The checks were one of the many taboo
subjects Mama refused to talk about. Iva

Claire knew the envelopes always bore the same return address in Georgia but she didn't know who sent the allowance or how much it was. What she did know was, the money was the only safety net they had, and even Mama, who spent their pay as soon as she got it, was careful with the check money. Until now.

A floorboard behind her creaked, and she turned fast. Her mother was staring at her. "What are you doing in my room?" she demanded.

"Mama, I didn't hear you." Her mother's eyes were wild and black. Something was wrong, something more serious than finding Iva Claire in her bedroom. "Who called you?" Iva Claire asked. "Is everything all right?"

"You were spying on me."

"Big Hannah said we haven't paid the rent. . . ."

Mama moved to the dresser so fast Iva Claire didn't know it had happened. "You want to know how much I spent?" she screamed. She yanked open the top drawer. Her clothes spilled out as she grabbed the box and threw it against the wall. Bills and coins scattered on the floor.

"Are you happy now? There's your precious money! That's all we have left! Get down on your knees and pick it up, since you love it so much."

"Mama, don't—"

"I wanted this to be a good time for us, but you take the joy out of everything!"

"Mama, please don't cry—"

But Mama had already started. "You've ruined my life from the day you were born! I had a career. I was on my way. But I couldn't work with a baby. For five long years I couldn't work because of you. Do you know what that does to an actress?"

Iva Claire knew. She'd heard it before. She wished it didn't still hurt.

"I could have given you up. That's what I was told to do. But I kept you!"

"Mama, I didn't mean to upset you. . . ."

Mama was sobbing now. The tears were pouring down her face. Soon she'd start having trouble breathing. "I was young and pretty, and there were plenty of men too. But no man wants a girl with a baby. Do you know how boring it is to be locked up with a three-year-old child night after night? Do you know how it feels to watch everyone get ahead of you? Girls who don't have half your talent are working, and you're trapped?"

"Mama, please. . . ."

"And now you're blaming me? After you took everything?"

"I never said—"

"Well, damn you, I won't let you break me. Do you hear me? You will not do it!" She ran through the apartment to the front door; then she turned. "I could have gotten rid of you, you know," she gasped. "There are ways to do it."

That was something she'd never said before. Mama left, slamming the door behind her.

Over the years, Iva Claire had learned that there was no point in crying. But there were times when it was hard to keep from doing it. The best way was to stay very still with your eyes closed tight so no tears got out. And it was important to make your mind a blank. So she stood in the middle of the room without moving, squeezed her eyes shut, made her hands into fists, and tried to make her mind behave.

Don't think about it, she told herself.

I could have gotten rid of you, Mama's voice said in her brain.

Don't think.

There are ways, said the voice.

Don't think, don't think, don't think!

Chapter Twenty-one

Iva Claire waited until she was sure she wasn't going to cry. Then she opened her eyes, went into Mama's bedroom, and started putting the clothes back in the drawer. She was folding a blouse when she heard a knock on the door. Mama hadn't taken her key when she ran out.

She thought about not opening it, but sometimes after her mother had been really mad, she got dizzy and had to lie down. Iva Claire walked slowly to the door.

Mama wasn't there. No one was. Thinking she'd been imagining things, Iva Claire was about to close the door when a little growl at her feet made her look down. A small white dog stood on her hind legs in the doorway. She was dressed in a red velvet hat and a matching red jacket, both trimmed with gold braid, like a bellhop in a fancy hotel. In her mouth she was holding, by a string, a box from Pozo's bakery down on Ninth Avenue. After a second, she dropped to all fours and let the box go. Then she sat back up, showing off the most dazzling part of her costume, the collar around her neck. It was a band, about two inches wide, that Iva Claire happened to know was made of eighteen-carat gold and had come from Tiffany's jewelry store. It was because of her collar that the dog had been billed as FRITZIE, THE THOUSAND-DOLLAR DOG during her performing days.

"Hey, doll, Fritzie and me just got some fresh cannolis and we thought you'd like one." A little man appeared from behind the door where he'd been hiding so Fritzie's entrance would have its full effect. Pete Massoni lived in a single room next door to Mama and Iva Claire. For years he'd had an animal act with his wife, Sally, but after she died, he and their last dog, Fritzie, had retired. Now he was another of Big Hannah's tenants, an old man living off his small savings supplemented by her low rents and kindness.

Iva Claire knew Pete had heard Mama yelling—the wall between Mama's bedroom and Pete's single was thin—and he'd dressed his little dog in her costume and put on her special show collar just to cheer up Iva Claire. Pete believed nothing in the world was so bad that watching Fritzie wouldn't help. But he was wrong this time. Iva Claire was trying to think of a nice way to get rid of him when he got down on his knees next to the dog.

"She wants to do her whammo finish for you," he said. He held the little dog's face close to his. The two of them were looking at Iva Claire, Pete with his anxious smile and Fritzie with her sweet tired old eyes. Iva Claire gave up and got down on the floor next to them.

"Let me see you do the finish, Fritzie," she said.

Frtizie was fourteen, and Pete had to stay close to her when she did her tricks these days to make sure she didn't fall. But she was still a trouper. She got up on her hind legs, put her two front paws out in front of her in a way that was part begging and part saying *I love you* to an imaginary crowd, and turned slowly to the left and then to the right. Then she turned around once, sat back on her haunches, lowered her head as far as it could go, and bowed. Iva Claire clapped loudly.

"You shoulda seen her do that on the stage," Pete said, as he scooped up the little dog and gave her a kiss. "Every night she found the light so it bounced off her collar." He got to his feet, picked up the cannoli box, and held it out to Iva Claire. "My wife Sally always used to say she liked something sweet when she was feeling blue," he said.

She couldn't take the box because she'd start crying. But she couldn't say no to Pete either. She stood there staring at him.

"Your ma didn't mean it, doll," he said gently. "She just wants"—he searched for the right words—"someone to see her. That's all."

"I see her," Iva Claire said. "I see Mama all the time."

"She needs an audience. I ain't saying it's right, it's just what we all want," Pete looked down at Fritzie in his arms. "Maybe it's because we don't want to be who we are. Look at me, doll. Not smart, nothing to look at, no matter what my Sally used to say. But when I was on that stage, I was Rudolph Valentino! If it hadn't been for show business, I'da been just another schlub, working at the clock factory like my old man and my brothers."

"You're not a schlub—" Iva Claire started to say, but Pete cut her off.

"All I'm saying, you don't know what your ma doesn't want to be."

"Big Hannah's happy being who she is."

Pete nodded. "But not everyone is a tough cookie like Big Hannah. Or you, you're one of the strong ones too, kiddo. Just remember that. Now, how about that cannoli?"

She took the box. "Thank you," she said.

He nodded happily and went back inside his room.

Iva Claire dropped the cannolis on the sofa and returned to the hallway. She hurried down the narrow passage to the black metal door at the end. In spite of a sign that said DO NOT ENTER, she opened the door and began climbing a steep staircase to a second metal door, which she also opened and stepped out onto the roof of the boarding-house. Behind her, the door slammed shut with a clang.

The roof was flat with a rim around it that was about a foot high, like a low wall. Mama was nestled against the rim with her face buried in her hands. She must have heard the door slam shut but she didn't look up. Iva Claire moved to her.

"It's getting dark, Mama. You need to come inside."

In the beginning darkness, Iva Claire could see she was still crying. Iva Claire sat down next to her and put her arms around her mother's little body, knowing it was the only way to stop the shaking that would come next.

"It's all right, Mama," she crooned. "It's all right."

"You're all I have, Claire de Lune. There's no one without you."

"I know." Iva Claire stroked the curly black hair. And then, even though it wasn't fair, she said, "I'm sorry I made you mad, Mama." After all, she was the strong one. "Now, get up," she added cheerfully. "We have to go downstairs and finish rehearsing. We open in a week!"

Mama cried harder.

"Mama, you're going to make yourself sick. I'm sorry I looked in the money box." She meant it now; she really was sorry. "Mama, you're scaring me."

Mama gulped back sobs until she was finally quiet. Then she stood up so she was facing her daughter.

"You should be scared," she said. "Things are worse than you thought."

They'd been canceled. That was what the phone call had been about. They were going to lose the fifty bucks they would have been paid, and they weren't going to be seen by any booking agents. Whatever small chance they'd had of getting a longer run in Manhattan was gone. Mama's gamble hadn't paid off and the dream act was finished.

What had done them in was the Gerry Society. That was what show-biz people called the New York Society for the Prevention of Cruelty to Children, after its founder, Elbridge Gerry. In New York, children could appear onstage as long as they were out of the theater by 9:05 P.M., but they couldn't sing or dance unless they had a special permit from the Gerry Society. When Lenny realized that the younger of the two Sunshine Sisters was only twelve, it didn't matter what kind of promises he'd made to Mama, he wouldn't let them go on. He'd had run-ins with the Gerry Society before.

"And the worst part is, there's an inspector at the Gerry Society who will look the other way for fifteen dollars a day," Mama said.

Thirty bucks—that meant they'd have twenty left over. It wasn't much, but if they put it together with what they had, and if Big Hannah would carry them awhile longer, they might be able to hang on until they could scrape something else together. There was always the chance that their lousy act would get a booking.

"Tell the inspector we'll give him the money as soon as we get paid," Iva Claire said.

"He wants it before we go on."

"I'll lie about my age. I get away with it in the act—"

"Lenny already knows you're too young, and he won't take the chance unless we bribe the inspector." Mama took in a deep shuddery breath. "I'm sorry, Iva Claire."

It was the scariest thing she could have done. Mama never apologized. "I spent every dime we have." Mama's mouth made a funny, twisted little smile. "My father always said I couldn't do anything right." This was even worse than apologizing. Mama never mentioned her family. It was like she'd suddenly become someone Iva Claire didn't know. "Daddy used to say I was stupid," Mama went on. "Looks like he was right. He always was."

Iva Claire couldn't stand it anymore. "We're going to do the act," she said. "We will, Mama." Anything to get rid of this calm sad stranger who sounded so beaten and bring back her mother.

"You don't even like the act."

"Yes, I do! It's beautiful. There's nothing else like it. We'll knock 'em dead."

Mama shook her head, but she was starting to smile. Iva Claire rushed on, grabbing at words, not knowing where they came from.

"We can't quit show business, Mama. What would we do? We're not civilians."

And if there was a small voice inside her

saying this was her chance for a real home and a real life, a much bigger voice commanded, *Don't think about it*.

"I want to do the act." She was lying as hard as she could.

And finally, Mama showed signs of life. "You do?" she said eagerly. "Really, Claire de Lune?"

"More than anything."

Mama started pacing. "We need money." she said. "We have to find some money."

That was when they heard Fritzie barking in Pete's room below them.

Chapter Twenty-two

The world is full of *ifs* and *maybes*. If Fritzie hadn't barked at that very moment, maybe Mama never would have thought of her terrible plan. And if Charles Lindbergh hadn't flown across the Atlantic Ocean and had a ticker-tape parade, maybe Mama wouldn't have come up with a way to make her plan work. But Fritzie had barked, Lucky Lindy had landed safely in Paris, his parade was scheduled for the following Monday, and Mama had her plan. When Iva Claire heard it, her heart sank.

"You want to steal Fritzie's collar and pawn it?"

"I won't steal it, Claire de Lune, I'll *borrow* it. We'll give it back."

They were back downstairs in their sitting room now. Mama had closed the window in case their voices carried out to the street, and they were whispering so no one could hear them through the walls. The whole idea was so unreal, it was funny, but Mama wasn't laughing.

"We'll pawn the collar and get enough money to pay the inspector. Then when we're paid, we'll redeem the collar and put it back where we found it."

"Mama, you can't."

"The old man will never know it's gone. He doesn't put it on the dog every day."

"But what if Pete looks for it?"

"It'll be gone for three days, that's all. Your precious Pete will never know."

"Maybe we could borrow the money, Mama." But the only people they knew well enough to ask were Pete and Big Hannah. Pete didn't have it to spare, and they already owed Big Hannah for the rent. Then she thought of something. "Mama, what about the checks? Maybe whoever sends them could give us some more—"

"No." Her mother's voice cracked like a whip.

Years later, when she looked back on the moment, Iva Claire thought maybe if she'd been a little older she would have resisted Mama. Or if she'd had a life of her own with school and friends her own age maybe she could have put up more of a fight. But she was only twelve. And trying to make Mama happy was what her life was about.

"All right, Mama, we'll do it," she said softly.

Mama's eyes filled with tears, and she hugged Iva Claire hard.

"It'll be easy, Claire de Lune, you'll see. Everyone in the boardinghouse is going to Lindbergh's parade. I'll take the collar then."

Iva Claire looked at her mother and thought about how quickly Mama got angry and how easily she cried. She thought about how Mama got carried away and spent all their money even when she didn't mean to. And she made a decision.

"Let me do it, Mama," she said.

And for a long time after that, she would remember that her mother only hesitated for a second before she said yes.

Chapter Twenty-three

The morning of the parade, it seemed like the whole city of New York was having a holiday that was as good as Christmas, your birthday, and the Fourth of July all rolled into one. As she walked to Fifth Avenue surrounded by laughing, excited people who were going out to celebrate, Iva Claire wished with everything she had that she could be one of them.

Don't think about it, she told herself.

She'd been telling herself that all morning. It had kept her from crying when she looked at Pete across the breakfast table, and when Big Hannah handed her a box camera, and said, "Here, child, this is for you. You'll show your grandchildren the snapshots you took today."

Don't think about it.

The parade was starting at the Battery and coming up Fifth Avenue. The group from the boardinghouse was going to watch from the front of the New York City Public Library. They left right after breakfast, but by the time they reached the library steps a big crowd had already formed. This was what Iva Claire and Mama had been counting on. Iva Claire asked Mama if she could go off on her own and try to get closer to Fifth Avenue. Mama said yes, but if Iva Claire got lost, they would all meet after the parade near one of the lions in front of the library. Then Mama told her to have fun, gave her a quick kiss, and sent her off.

Iva Claire was careful to turn back a couple of times and wave at her mother as if she was trying to keep her in sight. Then she ducked in and around the clumps of people as fast as she could until she was out of the crowd. At the outer fringe she stopped, took a deep breath, and started walking fast back to Hell's Kitchen.

*   *   *

As she was taking out her key to unlock the boardinghouse front door, it occurred to her that someone might see her there on the stoop. She and Mama had assumed everyone would go to the parade, but what if one of the neighbors hadn't? What if one of them was home right now looking out the front window?

Don't think about it.

She went in.

The parlor was dark, but she knew what she was looking for. There was a rolltop desk where Big Hannah kept a spare key for every room in the house. It took less than a minute to find the one with Pete's name on it, and a couple of minutes more to climb the stairs and unlock his door. She stopped on the threshold with her heart beating hard. Pete had never asked her to come into his room.

The box camera was in the way—she hadn't known what to do with it—so she put it on the floor outside the door and went in. Pete's single room was the same size as the one Mama used as a bedroom, but Mama's room always looked like she was about to move out of it. Pete's was crammed full of things. There were shelves full of scrapbooks and the kind of knickknacks people pick up in hotels and train stations. Framed publicity stills of a young Pete with Sally and their dogs were on the walls. This was Pete's home.

Don't think about it.

Iva Claire scanned the room for Fritzie's costume trunk, where Pete had once told her he kept the collar. The trunk was in a corner near the bed. She started for it. A sound from behind made her jump. She whirled around to see Fritzie sighing in sleep on the bed.

Iva Claire made her mind a blank and waited, watching the bed. Fritzie shifted position but she didn't wake up. Iva Claire moved quickly to the trunk. It was the same size as the one she'd had when she started touring with Mama, back when she was five. But this one was painted gold, with FRITZIE spelled out in hundreds of rhinestones across the front.

The trunk was latched but not locked. Being careful not to scrape it on the floor or move it out of position, she pulled it open. Fritzie's costumes were folded neatly in the little drawers—tiny brightly colored outfits trimmed with gold braid.

The collar was in the bottom drawer, hidden under Fritzie's red jacket. Iva Claire took it out slowly, being careful to put the jacket back exactly the way she found it. The gold collar gleamed in her hand. Suddenly there was an explosion of barking from the bed. For the second time she jumped and whirled around while ice water poured down her spine.

An ecstatic Fritzie was wide awake, making a racket and wagging her tail. She'd seen the collar and thought she was going to do her act.

"No, Fritzie," she heard herself say. "Please."

Fritzie didn't jump well anymore, but she managed a stiff-legged leap off the bed.

"Please."

The little dog pulled herself up on her hind legs and began her bow with her front paws outstretched, turning to the left and the right. But there was no Pete to help her. As Iva Claire watched, she lost her balance and fell.

"Fritzie, I'm so sorry," she whispered.

She started for the door. The little dog

scrambled to her feet and ran around in front of her. Iva Claire closed her eyes to keep the tears from spilling out. Soft fur brushed her legs, little paws scratched at her shins; if she opened her eyes or looked down, she'd be lost. Blindly she grabbed the doorknob behind her, opened it, and ran out. From the other side of the door she heard Fritzie's mournful little yelps. The sound followed her as she remembered to pick up the camera, hid the collar under the mattress in Mama's bedroom, returned Pete's key, and raced out of the boarding-house.

Don't think about it, don't think about it, don't think about it.

She ran back to Fifth Avenue, where she stopped in dismay. The crowd had gotten bigger. There was no way she could ever get close enough to the curb to see the parade. But she'd have to be able to talk about it. In a few days, Big Hannah would ask to see the pictures she'd taken. What was she going to say?

Later, all she would remember was how easily all the lies had come to her and how calm she'd felt. First, she opened the camera and exposed the film to the light. When the ruined negatives came back from the pharmacy, she told herself, she'd have to try to cry in front of Big Hannah.

Next, she got herself as close as she could to Fifth Avenue and waited. She thought she saw something that looked like ticker tape coming from the windows in the buildings across the street, but she really wasn't sure. It would be best not to mention that, she decided. Through the crowd, she heard a band playing, and then there was some clapping and cheering, but only in spots, and it seemed far away. Then the applause became a roar that surrounded her and went on and on. Obviously, Lucky Lindy was going by. She kept on waiting.

Finally the crowd began to break up. Groups of people were walking away from the avenue, laughing and calling out to one another. She watched them pass, until she spotted two kids, younger than she was, walking behind a man and a woman who were obviously their parents. She cut in next to them and began walking.

"Which part did you think was the best?" she asked the boy. Before he could open his mouth, his sister was offering her opinion.

By the time they reached Broadway, Iva Claire knew Lucky Lindy hadn't walked in the parade, he'd been in a car. She knew approximately how long the parade had been, and that the little girl's favorite float had models of the Statue of Liberty and the Eiffel Tower with the Spirit of St. Louis flying between them. The family turned to go south on Broadway and Iva Claire hurried back to the lions in front of the New York Public Library. She was in place just minutes before Big Hannah, Mama, and Pete came to find her.

The walk home wasn't difficult. She talked about the Statue of Liberty float and all the pictures she'd taken of Lucky Lindy in his car. Big Hannah and Pete both laughed, enjoying her childish pleasure in the great day.

And a voice inside her head said, *I'm good at this. I lie to people who are my friends and take things that aren't mine and I'm good at it.* And suddenly she felt very cold. But then another, more familiar voice came to the rescue.

Don't think about it.

*　　*　　*

Where is it?" Mama whispered, when they were back in their rooms. Iva Claire went into the bedroom and got the collar from under the mattress.

Mama sighed with relief. "I knew you could do it."

She wanted to throw the collar out the window. She wanted to confess what she'd done to Big Hannah and Pete and apologize with all her heart. She wanted to promise God or someone she'd never ever do anything terrible again. And a week ago, maybe even yesterday, she would have believed she could make that promise. But now she knew better. Because now she knew too much about herself.

She handed the collar to her mother. "Yes," she said. "I did it."

Chapter Twenty-four

When they finally did perform the Beautiful Dreamer act at the Chevalier, Iva Claire didn't really care whether it was good or bad. Mama had taken the collar to a pawnshop, gotten the money, and the Gerry Society inspector had taken the bribe. But none of it mattered.

Their first show was at eleven thirty in the morning. She and Mama sat side by side in their cramped dressing room, sharing the makeup mirror and the communal makeup table. Out of the corner of her eye, she saw Mama's hands shake from stage fright as she lined her eyes with clown white, but her own hands were steady. Mama was chattering in a high, scared voice about agents and scouts and their wonderful future. All Iva Claire wanted to do was get through the next two days so they could get paid and buy back Fritzie's collar.

Finally, the last bead of mascara had been applied to the false eyelashes, and the final coating of powder was dusted over the greasepaint. Mama had tweaked and puffed their costumes, and the silk roses that cost so much had been pinned in their hair. Downstairs the movie was halfway finished, and below the stage, the musicians were making their way into the darkened orchestra pit where the sheet music for "Beautiful Dreamer" had already been placed on stands. Mama kissed the rabbit's foot she always carried with her, and they hurried down the metal stairs.

Backstage, as they waited in the wings to go on, Mama grabbed a passing stagehand by his sleeve. "Who's out there? What agency?" she whispered. The man shrugged and walked away. But then the movie screen went up, the show curtain came whooshing down, and they were on.

Mama's voice was shaky at first but it got

better as they warmed up. She still sounded tight and careful, but that was the way Mama always was in front of an audience. Iva Claire blended their tricky harmonies to her mother's melody by rote. They left the stage to scattered applause and a few cat-calls.

"The house is empty," Mama gasped, as she stood backstage catching her breath. "Where the hell's the audience?"

Iva Claire didn't even try to come up with something comforting to say. She just stared at the place on her mother's face where the sweat had streaked her rouge.

Mama gulped some air and managed a smile. "That was just the first show. The agents will come later in the day. Don't worry, Claire de Lune. They'll be here."

There was no point in saying that she wasn't worried about anything except getting paid. They had nine more shows to go, and the collar would be back in the drawer in the little gold-painted trunk, and Pete would never know it had been gone.

We just have to last through tomorrow, she thought, as she and Mama trudged back up to their dressing room.

*   *   *

Mama kept on believing until the last show on the second day. Then, as they stood in the wings waiting to go out for the last time, Iva Claire watched reality hit her. She finally understood that there weren't going to be any big agents in the audience and no one was going to book them on the Big Time or give them a spot in Ziegfeld's *Follies*.

"I'll kill Lenny," Mama said. As she went out onstage with her mouth stretched into her big performance smile, there were tears glittering in her eyes. And something interesting happened. For that one performance, Mama started to sing the way she did in rehearsal. They had never sounded better in their lives. When they took their bows, the applause was almost enthusiastic.

After the show, they packed up in grim silence. They were headed for the assistant manager's office to pick up their pay— Lenny had made himself scarce—when the stage doorman called them over. He was holding out a slip of paper.

"Somebody sent this back," he said.

Mama couldn't talk; she grabbed the note and started to read. For a moment Iva Claire believed in miracles. But then Mama's face went white and she looked sick, like she was going to faint.

"Mama?" Iva Claire started to her, but Mama pushed her away. She crumpled up the note and threw it against the wall. Iva Claire picked it up.

It was from a small-time agent named Teddy Fitz, and he had a job for them. He had a tour that had started a month earlier and one of the comedy teams had left it. He needed an act to fill in. The problem was, Teddy Fitz booked the South. His note mentioned Virginia, North Carolina, Tennessee, Alabama, Louisiana, and Georgia.

Iva Claire turned to her mother. "Mama, we need the money. Couldn't we? Just this once?"

"No," Mama said. Iva Claire was pretty sure it was having to work Georgia that cinched it.

Iva Claire crumpled up the note again. It would have been nice to have a job that could carry them until the next check came, but it really didn't matter all that much. What mattered was putting Fritzie's collar back where it belonged.

"I'll go get our pay, Mama," she said.

* * *

The next morning Mama cashed the paycheck, and they had the money. Before she went off to the pawnshop, Mama hesitated as Iva Claire had known she would and said, "If we get that collar back now, we won't have anything. Maybe we could wait until—" She looked at Iva Claire's face and didn't finish the thought.

Two hours later, Mama had locked the door to her bedroom and was lying down with a headache. Iva Claire was sitting on the sofa in their living room holding Fritzie's collar. She and Mama were broke. Eventually, Big Hannah would have to ask them to leave because even she couldn't keep two deadbeats around forever. Iva Claire didn't know where they'd go or how they'd live. But for the first time in three days she felt light and free.

She'd taken Pete's key from the rolltop desk earlier that morning while Big Hannah was out doing her daily food shopping. Now all she had to do was wait for Pete to leave his room. Every noon he went out to have lunch with a couple of song pluggers who'd retired about the same time he had. The threesome always went to a little place on Forty-eighth Street near the Friars' Club.

*   *   *

It only took her five minutes to put the collar back. And even though Fritzie woke up and started barking just as she was closing the trunk, she didn't panic. The little dog barked a lot and everyone in the building was used to it. No one would come upstairs to check Pete's room. Iva Claire took a quick look around to make sure everything looked the way it had when she came in. Then she left.

In the hallway she closed the door and leaned against it with her eyes closed. It was over! She'd gotten away with it! She turned around to lock the door. But as she was about to take the key out of her pocket, a sound behind her made her turn. Big Hannah was halfway up the stairs, staring at her.

Chapter Twenty-five

"What were you doing in Pete's room, child?" Big Hannah asked quietly.

Don't run, she told herself.

"The door was open—" she started to say, but Big Hannah stopped her. "Pete's key isn't in the desk. What were you doing, Iva Claire?"

She couldn't answer. Big Hannah came up the rest of the stairs. "I still know people in the business," she said. "Word is, you and your ma had to pay off that jerk from the Gerry Society. I asked myself how you could do that when you didn't have enough money for the rent." She paused and looked at Pete's door.

Suddenly Iva Claire was tired—of lying and thinking and trying not to think. She slid down so she was sitting on the floor, and she told Big Hannah about the collar. "Please don't tell Pete," she whispered. Big Hannah stared down at her for a long time; there was a hard look in her eyes. Then the hard look softened. She tucked her skirt around her knees and lowered her large body to the floor to sit next to Iva Claire.

"No, honey," she said. "I won't tell Pete." One big arm pulled Iva Claire in to her ample chest. It felt so good to have someone older and bigger hold her, Iva Claire thought she would never move. But then Big Hannah said, "I don't know what's to be done. Your mother should be reported."

When she said that, Iva Claire had to pull away. She couldn't let Big Hannah hurt Mama. But she knew something important now. Big Hannah had a soft spot for her, and she could use it.

"Big Hannah, we got a job last night," she said in an eager little-girl voice. "A tour. If you don't tell anyone about Fritzie's collar, we'll leave tomorrow and you won't have to worry about what to do."

She could see Big Hannah waver.

This is how Mama gets people to do what she wants, she said to herself. Then *Don't think about that!*

"But it isn't right," Big Hannah fretted. "You're just a child, and she used you. You can't go on like this."

"I know what I—what *we* did was bad. But Mama's sorry, and so am I. We brought the collar back as fast as we could. And now we have a chance to make a fresh start." She made her voice quiver. *Someday when I'm old enough, I'll do good things, I'll help people and I'll make up for this.*

"You'd be going on the road?" Big Hannah asked. "I had an idea you wanted to stay put."

"I want to do the act. We worked so hard on it, Big Hannah."

Big Hannah was troubled. She wanted to do the right thing, but she wasn't sure what it was. She was such a good person.

Don't think about that.

Finally the woman hoisted herself to her feet. "Give me Pete's key," she said. Iva Claire stood up and handed it over. "Tell your mother I want her out of my house and on the road, saving her money and taking care of you. And if she ever does anything like this again and I hear about it, she won't be able to send you to do her dirty work. I'll take care of her myself."

And that was why, in spite of everything Mama had said before, they ran over to Teddy Fitz's office that afternoon and took the job. Rain and Rain, the Sunshine Sisters, were heading south.

Chapter Twenty-six

"Iva Claire!" Tassie's urgent voice called out from the back of the house, breaking into her daydream. "Come quick! Out here to the lobby! There's something you've got to see!"

Iva Claire climbed down from the stage and ran through the theater to the dark lobby where there was a curved double staircase leading to the second floor. The theater balconies and boxes were on the second floor, as was the rehearsal room.

"Over here!" Tassie said. She was standing near the right wall of the lobby. There was a glass case on the wall where the management put up the pictures of everyone who would be performing on the bill that afternoon. "Look," Tassie said.

Iva Claire's picture wasn't on the wall. When your publicity still was taken off the lobby wall that meant you'd been canned. For a horrible moment Iva Claire thought somehow the theater manager had heard how bad the Sunshine Sisters were. But Mama's picture was right there in its frame, although there was no sign under it announcing the name of their act. Obviously someone had made a mistake, and with Mama already hating the entire state of Georgia—

"Your ma is gonna be mad," Tassie said.

With Tassie at her heels, Iva Claire ran up the stairs to the rehearsal room. Mama was already there, pacing and breathing hard.

"I've been looking everywhere for you," she said. She hadn't seen Tassie. "I need to tell you something."

"If it's about them not putting my picture up, I bet they just forgot. I'll go find the manager right now, and—"

"No, you won't."

"I'm sure they didn't mean to insult us. If I go talk to him—"

"I didn't give them your picture. You're not doing the act until we're out of Georgia."

Iva Claire's first thought was that she was free. For three whole weeks she wouldn't have to go onstage. Then she pictured Mama going out all by herself in front of an audience.

"It's a two-person act, Mama."

"For now, it's a solo."

"Mama you need me—"

"That's enough!" Mama snapped. Her eyes were wild; she was scared to death to do the act alone, but for some crazy reason she was going to. Iva Claire looked up at the clock on the rehearsal room wall. There was no time to argue. The rehearsal pianist would be there any minute. She had to do something. She couldn't let Mama die onstage. She looked around the room for something, anything . . . and saw Tassie standing off to the side staring at her feet.

"Tassie," Iva Claire said.

Tassie looked up at her, and Iva Claire knew they were both thinking the same thing. "You said you know all our songs, didn't you?" Iva Claire asked.

Tassie had gotten very pale, but she said, "I've been watching your act every day."

"Do you know the music well enough to sing it onstage?"

"I couldn't learn all the fancy harmonies you do," Tassie managed to get out. "Not in time for the show today. But I have a good ear, and I've always sung parts."

It wasn't a perfect solution, but it was better than Mama trying to fill twenty minutes as a solo. Iva Claire nodded at Mama. Finally realizing she was about to be rescued, Mama turned to Tassie. "Could you do it?" she demanded eagerly. "Could you do the act?"

"Rehearse with her and see, Mama," said Iva Claire. But she already knew what Mama was going to decide. For a second, it felt like something sharp had gotten inside her chest. Not because Tassie was going onstage in her place; Tassie was welcome to that torture. But Iva Claire's biggest pride, the one thing that made her different from every other kid she met was the fact that her mama needed her. And now, it seemed, Mama might not.

Don't think about that.

The pianist came in. Mama and Tassie

began to sing. And somewhere in the whole mess of everything that was going on, the question of why Mama refused to let Iva Claire perform in Georgia got lost.

Chapter Twenty-seven

Iva Claire's costume was six inches too long for Tassie. And since the first show was at two-thirty, there was no time to shorten it. Nor was there time for her to learn all the gestures and moves Iva Claire did; watching an act from the wings was very different from performing it. On a more positive note, Tassie hadn't been lying when she said she had a good ear, and she'd actually picked up quite a lot of their harmonies as well as all the lyrics just by listening. What she didn't know she faked, so the music rehearsal had gone pretty well. All three of them agreed she could carry off the singing.

As for the stage movements, she'd just have to try to do what Mama did.

It was time to get ready for the first show. Mama and Tassie raced to the dressing room to slap on some greasepaint. Iva Claire followed them, trying not to think about all the things that could go wrong.

Half an hour later, she stood with them backstage as they waited to go on. Tassie seemed all right, but Mama was panicking. The music started, and Mama went onstage like someone in a trance.

Then without warning, Tassie froze. "I can't," she whispered.

"You've got to."

Tassie didn't move. Mama was already in position. Iva Claire gave Tassie a little shove—just enough to get her moving. Tassie made it out of the wings and on to the stage, but she'd forgotten to pull up her long skirt, so she stepped on it. Then she walked up it until she couldn't go any farther. Her big eyes now even bigger with fright, she smiled a fake smile at the audience and began tugging at her skirt—which didn't move because she was standing on it. There was a snicker from the house.

Meanwhile, in the middle of the stage,

Mama struck their opening pose with both hands clasped over her heart.

Tassie's struggle had loosened the silk rose Iva Claire had pinned to her hair, and it started to slip down on her forehead. She blew frantically at it to keep it from falling, tugged at her skirt, and smiled idiotically at the audience. Then she blew at the rose again. And tugged at her skirt. And smiled. Now she had a routine going; blow, tug, smile, blow, tug, smile. Downstage center, Mama stood like a statue. The snicker from the house turned into giggles.

Finally Tassie yanked her skirt free, hiked it up around her hips, scurried to her place at Mama's side, and clasped her hands over her heart. More giggles from the audience, and someone clapped. That was what did it. Iva Claire saw something flash in Tassie's eyes and knew she was going to play it for laughs. Her rose fell into her face again, and she blew at it explosively, but this time she looked straight out, so she was giving the audience the raspberry. She got a small hand. And she was on her way.

When she and Mama started to sing, Tassie did all the gestures a beat after Mama did them. At one point, she stopped singing and walked around so she could see what Mama was doing and copy her. She kept up the battle with her rose and her skirt. What made all her bits even funnier was Mama, who went on singing and gesturing as if the mayhem at her side didn't exist. When they finished, the Sunshine Sisters got real applause, the kind where the audience is saying "Thank you!"

Backstage, Iva Claire braced herself for an explosion. Mama was going to be furious. Tassie had turned her beautiful act into a joke for a bunch of hicks to laugh at, and Iva Claire knew it was going to be her fault. She waited for the onslaught.

Mama came offstage first. She threw her arms around Iva Claire, her eyes glowing under the heavy makeup.

"Listen, Claire de Lune," she said, as the audience clapped. "Did you ever hear anything like that?"

Tassie, whose eyes were glowing the same way, came off and hugged her too, whispering in her ear, "I hope you're not mad."

She wasn't, not really. She could never have done what Tassie had just done, and she never would have wanted to. But she did wish she had been the one who had put that light in her mama's eyes.

For the next four shows, Tassie didn't get a single laugh. She repeated all the business she'd done before, but it fell flat. She tried harder and harder, tripping over her skirt so wildly that she almost fell into the orchestra pit, but she didn't get a peep from the house. The Sunshine Sisters were back to stinking again. Instead of the act being overrehearsed, it now looked like Amateur Night in Dixie—literally. After the last performance, Mama left the theater without saying a word. Iva Claire stayed with Tassie, who cried all the way back to the hotel.

The next morning, just as Iva Claire and her mother finished getting dressed, there was a knock on the door. Benny and Irene came in with Tassie, wearing her costume with her rose pinned in her hair.

"We gotta get this act in shape," Benny said briskly, as Irene handed Mama a cup of coffee. "We can't have our girl laying an egg out there. Now, Miz Rain, you sing that opening number, and we're gonna work the shtick where Tassie trips on her skirt."

Iva Claire thought she knew what it meant to rehearse, but she'd never seen anything like the kind of drilling Benny did with Tassie that morning. Every accident that had been so funny the day before was now analyzed and broken down into minute movements, which were then repeated over and over. And throughout it all, Benny kept saying, "Remember how scared you was when this happened the first time? That's what made it funny. Don't never try to repeat that feeling—you can't. Once you get the moves locked in, you gotta find a fresh way to keep the feelings real for yourself. And they've gotta be real every night. That's what John Q Public wants: fresh and real."

When he was finally convinced that Tassie was ready, he gave them all one last bit of advice. "In comedy you gotta have a part of your head checking the audience. Not your whole head; think of it like you've gotta split your brain in two."

Mama and Tassie looked at him blankly.

"Listen," he said. "Serious actors, the ones who do all the high-hat plays, they gotta keep their mind on what's happening onstage. They gotta ignore the audience. But a comic's gotta be aware of the house so he can time his laughs and pace himself. You gotta do two things at once." He paused. "Before I met Irene I had a mind-reading act—called myself the Great Otto. Talk about doing two things at once—you're saying your patter for the audience and all the time you're watching the mark like crazy, so you know when you're hitting home. Same thing you do when you're getting laughs. Being a mind reader is the best training for a comic I know of."

Tassie listened breathlessly. Iva Claire couldn't imagine putting that much time and thought into making people laugh.

When it was time to go to the theater, Benny gave Tassie a kiss on the cheek and said, "You're as ready as you'll ever be. Break a leg, sweetheart."

By the end of the day Tassie has gotten back most of her laughs. By the end of the week she and Benny had worked in several more. The Sunshine Sisters were almost as good as DeLoura and Ritz. And for the first time since she was five, Iva Claire was unemployed.

Chapter Twenty-eight

MRS. RAIN

2004

"Mrs. Rain? Mrs. Rain? I've been looking everywhere for you. What are you doing in the living room?" Cherry's voice, shrill with anxiety, sliced through her dreams and woke her.

She opened her eyes and looked around. The child's question was an excellent one. She was indeed in her living room, in one of the most uncomfortable chairs she owned, and had obviously dozed off. What the hell she was doing there was a mystery. She forced her brain to address the issue.

"What time is it?" she asked.

"Seven."

That wasn't much help. "Day or night?"

"It's morning, Mrs. Rain."

She continued prodding her unwilling brain until it produced the memory of yet another sleepless night in which she had come downstairs to the living room. She leaned back, the mystery solved. Then she frowned and straightened up again. Her brain, now panting to be helpful, had just provided another memory. She had taken her picture out of the piano bench where she'd stashed it a couple of nights before, and she'd been looking at it when she'd drifted off. But now it wasn't in her hands, which meant—

"What's this?" Cherry asked. The girl leaned down to pick up the picture, which had fallen with its envelope on the floor.

"That's mine." She held out her hand.

The girl was staring at the publicity still. "Who is that?" she asked.

"Just a picture."

"Is it you? The eyes are the same."

She could have lied. But she'd never been any good at that. "It was me. A long time ago."

"What's that weird thing you're wearing? Did people dress like that back then?"

"That, my dear, was a costume."

"For Halloween?"

Before Peggy Garrison died she might have let it go at that. But now there wasn't much point. Besides, she hadn't talked about the old days in so long. "It was a theater costume. I was in an act called the Sunshine Sisters."

"You had a sister? I've never heard you say anything about your family."

She looked down at the picture. "Yes," she said. "I had the best sister anyone could ever ask for."

Chapter Twenty-nine

IVA CLAIRE

1927

At first, Iva Claire went to the theater, because she didn't know what else to do. She sat in the dressing room while her mother and Tassie put on their makeup and waited to see if Mama needed her. Mama often had headaches and had to have her back rubbed. When the Sunshine Sisters were onstage performing, Iva Claire stood where Mama could see her and know she was there. But Mama's headaches seemed to have vanished and she never looked to the wings for reassurance anymore. Finally, on the third day, Iva Claire stayed away from the theater as an experiment. Mama didn't seem to notice. The sharp object in Iva Claire's chest twisted a little, but the heady prospect of freedom balanced the twinge. Mama wasn't her responsibility anymore; Tassie was making her happy now. Long empty days with nothing to do—no performances, rehearsals, or making the rounds of the booking agents—suddenly stretched out ahead of Iva Claire.

She read every book, magazine, and newspaper she could get her hands on. When she could find a radio, she listened to the news. She walked around the little town of Beltraine and looked at the civilians' houses with their gardens and trees and front yards. She began to dream again, about living in one place and going to school. There were so many new professions opening up for college girls in these modern times. Iva Claire already knew she wanted to be a social worker. Back in Hell's Kitchen there was a neighborhood settlement house run by a social worker named Miss Forsythe, and Iva Claire had admired her even more than Big Hannah. But you had to have a real education to be a social worker, and Iva Claire knew she'd never get one if she was always on the road.

Meanwhile, as she was dreaming about her future, Mama and Tassie were knocking 'em dead at the New Court Theater five times a day. Mama was happier than Iva Claire had ever seen her, and Tassie was walking on air. But when the company left Georgia and moved on to Alabama, Iva Claire was supposed to go back into the act.

After a whole week of freedom, Iva Claire didn't want to be a Sunshine Sister ever again. She knew Tassie was dreading having to leave the act as much she was dreading having to go back into it, but she'd thought of a way that they could both get what they wanted. There were schools— they were called boarding schools—where a kid who didn't have a regular home could live. She knew about them because she and Mama had once played the same circuit as Ethel Barrymore. When most vaudevillians went on tour, they just stuck the whole family into the act, whether they were talented or not. But Miss Barrymore was a classy legit actress, and her daughter went to boarding school. Iva Claire was going to try to convince Mama to let her go to one too. But she had to do it fast. They only had two more weeks in Georgia, and Mama wanted her to start rehearsing to take over from Tassie.

"Benny can teach you what Tassie's been doing," Mama said.

"I'll never be able to do what Tassie does."

"Of course you can. All she does is stumble around and fall down."

"Mama, Tassie's wonderful. She changed the whole act."

"That was an accident." After all the hours of rehearsing with Benny, Mama still didn't see how hard it was to do Tassie's shtick. "Besides," Mama added, "the audience laughs because I'm standing in front of her singing. We'll be just as funny when you're doing Tassie's part."

Mama was taking credit for the laughs Tassie was getting. *Well, of course she was,* Iva Claire thought. *I should have known.*

"I'm not a comic like Tassie. You know that."

"You can do it, Claire de Lune!" Mama smiled happily. "I know you can. Start working with Benny tomorrow morning, and by the time we get to Alabama you'll be perfect."

"Mama, you're a hit now. Why do you want to change things?"

"This is *our* act!" Mama was pleading now. "We're the Sunshine Sisters, Claire de Lune, you and me."

"But I'll ruin everything."

"You have to come back! It's supposed to be you and me together! That's the dream, Claire de Lune. You and me!"

And that was why Mama couldn't see that Tassie was the real star of the act, because it didn't fit her dream. She'd never see that her Claire de Lune didn't want to be in show business, because that didn't fit her dream either. So they'd drop poor little Tassie and break her heart, and Iva Claire and Mama would be back where they'd always been, broke, with a stinker act and no bookings, waiting for the checks that came twice a year.

It was such a waste. All three of them could have had exactly what they wanted, but Mama was going to throw it all away. Suddenly Iva Claire knew she couldn't go along with it. Somehow she was going to go to school. She'd make the plans behind Mama's back and tell her about it after it was all settled. Mama could cry and yell, but there wouldn't be any way she could stop Iva Claire once the school was paid for. And if the act was a really big success, eventually Mama would get over feeling bad. She hoped.

Obviously there were big hurdles to be overcome, the first and most important being money. Going to a boarding school had to be expensive. But Iva Claire thought she knew where she could get help. She was going to get in touch with the mysterious benefactor who sent their checks.

She knew the person's address; she'd seen it dozens of times on the back flaps of the long white envelopes: a street, a street number, a town, and the state of Georgia. The sender's name was never included, but Iva Claire had always assumed that it must be a member of Mama's family. Over the years she'd pictured a grandmother who looked like Miss Barrymore and a grandfather who was a taller version of Pete Massoni. Or maybe it was an aunt or uncle who had been supporting her all these years. Whoever it was, if she could contact them, she thought maybe she could persuade them to help her. They had been generous in the past. And there was the possibility that they might even like her. She decided it would be best if she could meet her unknown relative—or relatives—face-to-face.

At the railroad station she learned that Beltraine was an hour south of Atlanta and the address from the checks was an hour north of the city. She could go and come back in the same day. The fact that she would have to steal money from Mama's purse for the ticket made her feel guilty, but it was for a good cause.

She didn't want to show up unannounced on her family's doorstep, they might not like that. So, even though it would take time she didn't have, she wrote a letter. Finding the right words when she wasn't sure who she was writing to was hard. She couldn't figure out how to begin. *Dear Person Who Has Been Sending Checks to Mama and Me* clearly wasn't right. Finally she wrote a brief note in which she told them who she was, said that she was in Georgia, and offered to come to their house to meet them if they would tell her how to get there. She told them she was staying in Beltraine and asked them to contact her at General Delivery. She thought about giving them the name of her hotel but decided it was too risky; the desk clerk might give her mail to Mama.

Two days after she sent the letter, she went to the General Delivery office to see if there was an answer, even though she knew it would take at least a week. She and Mama had never been churchgoers, but she was praying for a reply before they left for Alabama.

Meanwhile, because Mama insisted, she began sitting in the wings and marking Tassie's moves in the act—and trying not to see the pained look on Tassie's face. She wanted to tell Tassie how she was going to save them all, but she was afraid Tassie might say something to Mama by mistake.

It took four days. The answer wasn't a letter, it was a cablegram that the telegrapher at the railroad station took across the street to the General Delivery office. The message didn't start out, "Dear Iva Claire," and there was nothing in it about being glad to hear from her. There were just instructions. She was to go to Atlanta to the Georgian Palace Hotel. She was to look for Room 1021.

At first she was disappointed. The tone of the cablegram was so cold, and a hotel room wasn't exactly what she'd pictured. But then she read the final sentence and saw the way the sender had signed off. And she didn't think anymore about how bad it was to steal money from Mama. She'd do anything to go to Atlanta now. Her whole life could change after this.

Chapter Thirty

The streetcar was moving up Peachtree Street. Iva Claire got up from her seat and made her way to the conductor at the front.

"Are you sure the Georgian Palace Hotel is on this street?" she asked, for the second time in three minutes.

"Yes, miss. It's just up a ways."

She sat down behind him so she could ask again if she had to. She couldn't miss the hotel. She just couldn't.

This might be the most important day of my life.

She still wished the meeting wasn't taking place in a hotel. It felt a little too much like going to a bank or a booking agent, neither of which had been pleasant experiences for her and Mama. But she had to take what she could get. The important thing was to make a good impression today. Her hands were sweating. Just in time she remembered not to wipe them on the skirt of her dress.

If things went really well, maybe she wouldn't have to go away to school after all. Maybe she'd have a real house to live in, full time, and she could go to school in her own neighborhood with kids who were her friends. The possibilities were endless, if she played this right. She hugged the suitcase she was carrying to her chest.

Bringing the suitcase had been a last-minute idea. She knew how dirty you could get on a train, even for a short trip. If the person sitting next to you was dumb enough to open a window, you'd get a face full of smoke and cinders, and the seats were never clean. So she'd packed her best dress in her suitcase with a hairbrush and some soap. At the station she'd washed up and changed into the clean dress.

I need to be pretty and charming and as smart as I can be.

But how could you stay pretty when the air was so hot and sticky that your hair which you'd set in rags the night before had gone stick straight? She could feel herself start to panic, and she knew right away what was wrong.

I'm having stage fright, she thought with a start. She'd never had it before. She'd watched Tassie and Mama standing in the wings, hands shaking as they waited to go on. She'd seen performers throw up from stage fright. But the fear had never touched her because she'd never cared if a bunch of strangers liked the Sunshine Sisters. Today she wouldn't be able to stand it if her audience didn't like her.

The streetcar stopped. Across the street was a big white building.

"That's the Georgian Palace Hotel, miss," said the conductor.

She grabbed her suitcase and got off. The hotel rose in front of her, ten stories high with a wide terrace across the front. It was the kind of place where only rich people went. The Sunshine Sisters could never afford to stay at a fancy joint like the Georgian Palace. But she was going in. She had to. And she was going to go in as if she belonged there. No matter what happened. Heart pounding, she crossed the street.

She made her way across the hotel lobby, not looking left or right, holding her head high the way Mama did when she went out onstage. Some part of her brain registered a green and white pattern on the floor beneath her feet, lots of polished marble, and many doormen, bellhops, and other hotel personnel in uniforms. A man in a particularly elaborate costume asked if he could help her, but she smiled regally and said no thank you, and he melted into the air. She reached the elevator and got in. She was committed now.

She found Room 1021 quickly—too quickly. Now that she was here, she wanted to run. Ever since she'd set up this meeting, she'd been trying to believe it would be wonderful; now she would find out if she'd been right. She watched her hand reach out and knock on the door. It opened right away. She couldn't look up.

Please let him like me. Please.

She raised her eyes and looked into her father's face.

Chapter Thirty-one

She'd thought she was ready, but she hadn't expected to see a masculine version of her own features staring at her. He had her eyes, her nose, and the chin Mama had always called *determined*. His hair was lighter than hers, and he'd lost some of it, but it was stick straight. He was tall and big, but not even a little fat. Even as her mind was whirling, she was pleased that he was good looking.

"My God," he said, in a hushed voice. He hadn't been expecting the resemblance either.

"Hello." She wanted to say something

memorable to mark the moment, but that was all she could get out.

"Come in," he said. He took her arm and pulled her into the room. She wasn't ready for him to touch her, and he didn't seem to be either. As soon as she was inside, he dropped her arm and backed away. He was still staring at her.

"Well, we certainly do look alike," she said, which she knew was stupid, but she had to say something. She tried to smile at him. He didn't smile back.

He crossed his arms over his chest and looked down at her. She felt very small. "All right, what does your mother want?" he asked.

"Mama?" she asked, surprised. "She doesn't even know I'm—"

"If she sent you for more money, go back and tell her she's not getting another cent out of me. And if she ever does anything like this again, she can whistle for her allowance."

"Mama doesn't even know I'm in Atlanta!" Then she realized the danger of what she'd done. If seeing her made him angry, he might stop sending the cheeks. And it would be all her fault. "You've to got believe me! Mama would be so mad if she knew I was here. I left before she was awake; I had to sneak out. This wasn't her idea. She never even wanted to come south. She hates being in Georgia!"

There were anger lines on the sides of his mouth. They started to soften slightly.

"You're telling me she didn't know about that letter you sent? You wrote that by yourself?"

"Yes! I wrote it and I mailed it. You always put your return address on the envelope when you send us our checks, so I knew where to send it."

"How did you get here?"

"On the train."

"You just bought a ticket, got on a train, and came to Atlanta? All by yourself?"

There was no need to tell him about the money she'd taken from Mama's purse. "It wasn't that hard. I travel on trains a lot."

"How old are you now?"

"Twelve."

"My God."

Please don't let him be mad, she prayed. *Please let him smile now*.

But he didn't. He crossed his arms over his chest again and kept on looking down at her. It would be easy to copy the way he did that, but she would never, ever mimic him.

"Well, if your mother didn't send you, then you must be the one who wants something from me," he said. "What is it?"

After what he'd said about Mama, she didn't want to ask him for money for school. Not yet.

"Could I sit down for a minute?" They were standing in the foyer of his suite. Behind him she could see a sitting room with big comfortable-looking chairs and green draperies drawn across large windows to keep out the sun. "And I sure am thirsty, if you could spare a glass of water." She put down her suitcase to make it seem more like she was staying. He had other ideas.

"Look, I got this all wrong. It sounded like you were threatening to come to the house. I thought your mother was trying to . . . well, that doesn't matter now. But if you're really here because you wanted to see me—"

"Yes, that's it," she reassured him eagerly. "And I was so happy when I heard from you! I used to ask Mama about you all the time when I was little, but she never would tell me anything."

He didn't offer to let her come into his sitting room. Instead, he moved closer to the door. "I think you'd better go."

She was stunned into silence.

"I never should have done this."

"Don't say that, please!" She finally managed to get out. "I just got here. And I came so far. Couldn't we talk for a while? I have so many questions I want to—"

"This was a mistake. I thought you were going to ask me for money. I wasn't expecting this." His hand was on the doorknob. He was going to open it.

"I did come for money!" she blurted out.

He looked relieved. It was as if he'd rather fight about money than talk to her.

"But it's not what you think—" she started to say. He cut her off.

"The answer is no. Your mother and I have an agreement. I give her a very generous allowance. I'm sure she squanders every penny of it, but there's nothing I can do about that."

"I need the money for school. Boarding school."

"Your mother gets enough money from me to support you very nicely. I'm keeping my end of the bargain. I won't do any more. Now I'm going to have to ask you to leave."

She couldn't go, not like this. Not while he still disliked her.

"All right," she said quickly, "I take it back, I don't want anything. Just let me stay for—"

"It won't accomplish anything." His polite way of dismissing her was worse than Mama's screaming.

"But . . . don't you want to get to know me . . . just a little?"

"There's no point."

Don't cry! the voice inside her head warned. But it was already too late. The tears were starting to spill down her cheeks.

Her father made an exasperated sound. "This is just what I was afraid of."

"I'm sorry," she whispered. "I'll stop."

But she couldn't. Blindly, she picked up her suitcase and tried to open the door. She knew she'd failed. He hadn't liked her before she started crying, and now he hated her. She had to get out.

But she couldn't get the door open. She pulled at the doorknob with the suitcase still in her hand. The suitcase was old, and with all the yanking and pulling, she banged it against the door several times. The rusted lock broke, the lid opened up, and everything inside flew out: the soap she'd brought, her hairbrush, and the dress she'd worn on the train. Crying harder now, she got on her knees to pick up her belongings.

Behind her, the man who had given her his chin and his eyes looked at the items on the floor and said, "Oh, Lord, were you expecting to stay here?"

Don't say anything, warned the voice inside her head. But now she was way past the point of heeding it. She stood up so she could face him. "I brought a clean dress because I wanted to look nice for you. I wanted to be pretty, so you'd like me! But I was stupid. I didn't know there was *no point*!" She mimicked his cold polite voice.

She got back down on the floor to pick up her things, but she was crying so hard she couldn't see. He got down on the floor beside her and gathered up everything. Then he piled the whole mess on a table, helped her to her feet, and led her into his sitting room. Her crying made him uncomfortable, she could tell, but he made her sit on his sofa and waited until she finally stopped. Then he went into the bathroom and came back with a glass of water. When she'd finished drinking it, he sat in the chair opposite her and sighed.

"What did you want to ask me?"

I won! she thought, *He's letting me stay. But he's not happy about it.*

Don't think about that.

"I'd like to know about you and Mama," she said.

He sighed again. "I guess I owe you that much."

Chapter Thirty-two

"I met Lilianne right here in Georgia."

"Lilianne? Mama's name is Lily."

"Maybe now it is. When I knew her she was Lilianne. She's a Venable," he said. "Did you know that?"

She shook her head. "What's a Venable?"

We're talking! Her heart sang. *I'm talking to my father!*

"Not what, who. The Venables are show folk; they have been for generations. I think they're the only family like that in the South. They own an old theater, the Venable Opera House. It's been in the family since . . . I think it was built around eighteen-eighty. At least that's the story Lilianne told me."

"But Mama's last name is Rain."

"Her mother was the Venable. Her father was an actor who worked for his in-laws. A real son of a bitch from what I could make out." He stopped himself. "Excuse my language."

"I've heard worse," she said quickly.

"I'm sure you have," he said grimly, "given the life you've had."

There was a part of her that wanted to tell him about her life. Maybe he'd change his mind and help her after all. But that would mean telling on Mama, and she couldn't do that. "It wasn't so bad," she said. "Not all the time. We've had some good bookings, and Mama . . ."

The anger lines at the sides of his mouth were getting deeper. She wasn't explaining this properly. She tried to find a better way.

"You see, being an actress was Mama's dream and no one ever believed in her. . . ."

"So you had to," he said softly.

"Yes. But I'm not very talented, except I do have perfect pitch, and I—"

"How old were you?" he broke in.

"I don't . . . understand. . . ."

"How old were you when Lilianne put you onstage for the first time?"

"Five."

"Damn!"

"It was all right. I got to travel all over the country and see all kinds of things. . . ." He was upset; she had to make him feel better. "I like being in the business. Even if we're going through a dry spell, it's better than being a civilian." She was parroting every performer she'd ever met. Then she smiled to show him how happy she was. It didn't work.

"What the hell was going through her crazy head?" he asked no one. "Dragging a baby around the country—"

"I love the Sunshine Sisters," she insisted frantically.

"The what?"

"The Sunshine Sisters. That's our act. Rain and Rain, the Sunshine Sisters." She was just making it worse. She had to change the subject. "But you were going to tell me about you and Mama. I want to know how you met her, and were you with her for a long time, or was it just . . ." She trailed off, thoughts of Lenny coming to mind. She moved on quickly. "I don't know anything about my past, you see."

He was still upset; for a moment she was afraid he was going to tell her to leave again. But then he leaned forward in his chair, his hands clasped around his knees, so he was looking at the floor instead of her.

"Lilianne was in a play. Some kind of operetta, I don't even remember the name now. She was in the chorus. I went backstage with a couple of friends to ask the girls to have supper with us. Lilianne came along. We got to talking. . . ." He leaned back in the chair and gazed at the wall. "Lilianne wasn't like anyone I'd ever met. She knew about theater—in those days she wanted to be an actress, not a singer—and she could talk about Shakespeare for hours. She wanted to have a career; she didn't want to get married and have a passel of—" He stopped as he remembered who he was talking to. "She was so different from everyone I knew. I was fascinated. I guess you'd like to hear that I was in love with her. But I wasn't. Neither was she. We just . . . suited each other for the moment. Besides, I was married.

"In those days, I wanted something. Lord

knows what I thought it was. From the time I was a boy, everyone knew I was going to take over the family business. I was the oldest son." He sighed. "I didn't want that for myself back then. I wanted to travel, see things. But I'd gotten married, and my wife was ill, and the business was sitting there waiting for me. So I gave in. I went to work for my father and tied myself down." He paused. "Anyway, Lilianne came along at the right time."

Iva Claire nodded. She wanted him to keep talking, although the things he was saying were hard to hear.

"She was touring through a lot of little towns all over Georgia and Alabama. I saw her whenever I could get away. I guess we were together on and off for about five months. We both knew she was planning to go to New York." He shifted his gaze to another wall, still avoiding looking at Iva Claire. "When Lilianne told me about the baby, I didn't . . . ." He was searching for words, and the polite tone in his voice was gone. Iva Claire held her breath and waited to hear what he would say about her.

"I wanted—" he began. "I told Lilianne I'd help her find a home for it."

Iva Claire told herself not to get hurt about being called *it*.

"Lilianne wouldn't listen. For a while, I thought she was trying to get back at the Venables. They were real proud, always trying to prove that even though they were theater people they were just as good as anyone else. It would have embarrassed them to have a bast—an illegitimate child in the family. Especially her father; he was the one she hated the most. He told her she wasn't a good enough actress to work in the family theater, and she never forgave him. One thing about Lilianne, she could really carry a grudge. . . ." He trailed off, taken by some memory.

Get back to the part about me!

As if he'd heard her thought, he said, "When she told me she was going to keep the baby, I said she was on her own. I had to. I can't tell you what kind of pluperfect hell there would have been if anyone knew I'd gotten some actress in the family way.

"Lilianne was fine with me not being in her life. She didn't want any interference from me, just money. She said she'd go to my father if I didn't pay up. But I wanted to do it. I didn't want the baby to starve.

"I knew she'd be a bad mother, but I couldn't stop her. I did make a deal with her. She had to stop acting and stay in one place until the baby was five years old. I hoped that she'd call it quits after that." He shrugged. Clearly Mama's dream was much stronger than he'd imagined.

"After five years she was free to go wherever she wanted in the North or the West. I didn't want her coming south—especially not to Georgia. I told her if she came down here, the checks would stop." For the first time he looked at Iva Claire. "You want to know how I felt when I left you with her? Guilty. I'd never felt so guilty about anything."

It wasn't as good as if he'd said, *I wanted you, and I hated not being able to keep you with me*, or, even better, *I loved you and I made the mistake of my life when I gave you up*. But it was something. The rest would come after he got to know her.

"You seem like a nice girl," he said. "Very intelligent. Can I give you some advice?"

She nodded eagerly.

"Don't let Lilianne use you."

"Mama wouldn't."

"You know better than that."

"Mama may not be like other mothers, but she loves me."

"Just be careful," he said gently.

He got up and went into one of the closets. A few seconds later he came back with a suitcase. It was made of caramel-brown leather with hinges and a lock that shone like gold. There was a fancy gold monogram on one side. It probably cost several months' worth of food and rent money for her and Mama.

"That's beautiful," she breathed. He started packing her belongings in it. "You're giving it to me? I can't take that!"

"Yours is broken," he said. He finished packing and handed the suitcase to her.

"You want me to leave? Now?" she asked.

He nodded. He couldn't look at her.

"But you haven't gotten to know me yet. I can guarantee you'll like me when you do. I'm very—"

"Iva Claire, stop!" It was the first time he'd used her name.

"But we haven't had enough time—"

"This isn't going to lead to anything. You're not a part of my life. We've seen each other. You've asked some questions, and

I've done my best to answer them. But this is as far as it goes."

It was like getting hit really hard. Then she went numb.

"I know you think that's cruel of me," she heard him say, "but it's the kindest thing I can do for you."

Actually, he was right. The numbness killed all feeling. She knew if she could have felt the pain, it would have drowned her. But she was able to take the expensive, beautiful suitcase he was holding out to her and stumble toward the door. He got there first and opened it for her.

"Good luck," he said. She didn't tell him that you never say *good luck* to someone in show business.

She left the hotel and started to walk down Peachtree Street. She didn't get back on the streetcar, because she couldn't sit still. She had to keep moving. The beautiful suitcase bounced at her side, her father's gift bruising her leg.

"You're not a part of my life," he'd said.

Don't think, don't think, don't think.

It started to rain the way it did in the South, a sudden downpour that happened so fast the sun was still out. Her dress got soaked and stuck to her body, flapping heavily around her legs. The water squished out of her shoes. The beautiful suitcase was getting ruined. She cradled it in her arms, trying to protect it with her body, but the rain kept coming down, spattering and staining the smooth rich leather.

She walked the entire mile from the Georgian Palace Hotel to Terminal Station. She'd always thought of herself as a person who was very realistic—Mama had had enough dreams for both of them—but now she knew that in her own way she'd been dreaming too. She'd dreamed that she'd find a way to make a new life for herself. Now she knew better. She didn't have money for school and she never would. She couldn't leave Mama because Mama was all she had. She was trapped. She bought her ticket and boarded the train that would take her back to Mama and Tassie and the New Court Theater. And the Sunshine Sisters.

Chapter Thirty-three

The train was late getting in to Beltraine, so she walked into the hotel room just as Mama was coming home from the theater after the last show. The first thing Mama saw was the suitcase. And, of course, she recognized the gold monogram on the side.

"Oh, my God, Iva Claire. What have you done?" she demanded. "You went to see him, didn't you?"

It would have been silly to pretend she didn't know who Mama was talking about. Besides, she was too exhausted to try. Iva Claire nodded and braced herself for screaming and crying and things being thrown around the room. But Mama didn't move.

"So now you know what he's like," she said quietly.

Iva Claire nodded again.

"You were hoping he'd take you in, weren't you? Do want to get away from me that much?"

If there ever was a time to try to explain how she felt about show business and school and having a real home, this was it. But Mama's big dark eyes were begging not to be hurt; she was holding herself stiffly as if she was waiting for a blow.

"Am I that bad, Claire de Lune?"

She was so small. So very, very small.

"Mama, I don't want to leave you." She'd never felt so tired. But she walked across the room and put her arms around the rigid little body. "I'll never leave you, Mama."

Mama pulled away to face her. "Then why did you go?"

"I was . . . curious. You never talk about him. You wouldn't tell me where I'm from. I wanted to know . . . that's all. Now I do. And I'm sorry I went." That last part was honest, at least.

"Are you sure?" Mama's eyes were still

begging. "I know sometimes I can be . . . hard on you."

"You're the best mama there ever was."

Mama's smile was bright enough to light up Broadway. "I'm so glad!" She hugged Iva Claire. "Now you'll come back into the act and everything will be wonderful. We're going to be so happy, Claire de Lune, I promise."

It was Benny who solved the problem of keeping Tassie in the act.

"We'll make it a trio," he told Iva Claire. "You know that stuck-up way you act when you're onstage? Like you're too good for everyone around you? We can use that. And we'll find some places where you can mimic Tassie too. That's a real gift you got."

So Iva Claire became the third Sunshine Sister. She wore Mama's costume even though it was too small and they had to adjust it. Tassie kept on wearing Iva Claire's, which was too big for her, because that was crucial to the shtick. They made a new dress for Mama out of a shiny pink fabric. Benny rehearsed them in a new routine; Tassie was still the sister who couldn't do anything right, and Iva Claire became the snooty one who tried to keep her in line, while Mama was oblivious to it all. Tassie did all her bits, walking up her own skirt, battling with her rose, but now Iva Claire gave her dirty looks that eventually led to shoving and a carefully choreographed fight. By the end of the act, Tassie and Iva Claire were rolling around on the floor, while Mama sang her heart out about starlight and dewdrops.

"We got ourselves a female knockabout comedy team!" Benny said proudly. Then he added, "We gotta drop the Rain part of the name though; it's too hokey. Just call your- selves the Sunshine Sisters, plain and sim- ple. Has a nice ring to it."

Tassie was overjoyed to have Iva Claire back in the act. "I'll never forget what you did, giving me your part," she said. "But it's much better this way."

Iva Claire could never explain that she hadn't done it for Tassie. She had simply tried to escape.

The new act worked. In the old days, Rain and Rain had always played the deuce, which meant they were the second team to go on. It was the spot reserved for the worst act on the bill. But when they opened in Alabama, the manager of the Melody took them out of the deuce and put them just ahead of DeLoura and Ritz for the closing. For the first time in their history, the Sunshine Sisters didn't have to worry about getting canned.

When the tour ended in Louisiana, there was a new decision to be made. The Sunshine Sisters were going back to New York, and Tassie was supposed to be going with Benny and Irene to the farm they'd bought in New Jersey for their retirement. Everyone knew what Tassie wanted to do, and it didn't include growing vegetables.

"She's got the business in her blood," said Benny.

"When I was her age, if someone told me I had to live on a farm I'da run like hell," said Irene.

But Benny had one stipulation. "Tassie's underage. We gotta get a lawyer and make this a legal arrangement," he said. "We'll go to the same one in Georgia who wrote up the papers when we adopted Tassie."

Mama tried to get him to go to a lawyer in

Louisiana, but no amount of arguing would change Benny's mind. "You don't know what a hard time we had finding a lawyer who would do this the last time," he said. "All them other legal beagles said we had to wait for a court hearing, even though we was on the road and couldn't stay in one place. Couple of them wanted to put our girl in an orphanage, said the stage was no place to grow up. This guy did everything nice and simple and quick in his office. I had to pay an arm and a leg, but he done fine by Tassie."

So after the last night in New Orleans, Mama, Iva Claire, Tassie, Benny, and Irene took a train to Georgia. Benny's lawyer drew up papers saying Mama was Tassie's new guardian, and he changed her name from Tassie Ritz to Tassie Rain. Or at least, that was what he said he'd done. Iva Claire had her doubts about him. In fact, she didn't like him at all. His name was Stuart Lawrence.

Chapter Thirty-four

MRS. RAIN

2004

The Cherry child was a good listener. Or maybe it was just that after so many years it was a pleasure to remember the old days and talk about them. It was carefully edited talk, to be sure, with the names changed to protect the not-so-innocent, but it still felt good.

She never would have told Cherry any of it if the girl hadn't seen the picture of her in her Sunshine Sister costume. "You were an actress?" the girl had asked.

She could have nodded and left it at that. But Cherry was looking at her the way no one had in seventy years. Once again she had an audience. It was a feeling you never ever forgot. Or stopped missing.

"I was a vaudevillian, dear. There was a difference."

And that was how she started digging up the past for the entertainment of her young companion.

"You tell such good stories, Mrs. Rain," the girl said. "You make me laugh."

Well, of course she did. She'd been a performer, for heaven's sake. That was something you didn't lose just because you weren't as young as you used to be. Look at George Burns. Of course there were some stories she couldn't tell, some that weren't funny, that could make you cry—or worse. Those were not for young Cherry's ears.

But shouldn't they be told to someone? At first the thought was too frightening, and she refused to let herself dwell on it. But her mind insisted on playing with it anyway, the way a person standing on the roof of a high building might play with thoughts of jumping. She could feel the idea taking hold of her.

She wondered about her motives. Was she trying to assuage her Maker at the eleventh hour? After all, she couldn't live forever, and confession might clean the slate, celestially speaking. But the God she'd come to believe in was too hard-nosed to be taken in by contrition under duress. And confession for its own sake had a mawkish quality. She'd let her record stand and take her judgment when the time came. But it hadn't yet. And while she was still present on earth—however margin-ally—she couldn't shake the feeling that knowing the truth might be useful some-where, somehow, to someone. Or perhaps it was just that, good or bad, her story was all she had, and she wanted someone to know and remember it after she was gone. The idea that kept her awake at night, re-peating itself over and over in her brain, was that Laurel Selene McCready was the per-son who should become the keeper of her particular flame. After all, Ms. McCready had already inherited the loot—and Stuart Lawrence, Jr.

Chapter Thirty-five

LAUREL

2004

The old water-stained suitcase sat on Laurel's bed. The dress and pinafore were inside, folded the way she'd found them, but she'd kept the sheet music out. The name of the song, "Beautiful Dreamer," was familiar. But she wasn't sure she'd ever heard it.

She'd taken the suitcase home because it fascinated her so much she couldn't leave it in Garrison Cottage. What the hell did it—and its weird contents—have to do with the great Miss Myrtis? A nasty little part of her was hoping the artifacts were connected to something so heinous in the saintly lady's life that it would trash her rep for good. But there was probably some simple—and saintly—explanation.

Laurel looked down at the yellowed page in front of her. Someone had written something in the margin, in pencil, but the note had either been erased or it had faded too much to be read. She put the sheet music back into the suitcase, closed it, and put it on the floor of her closet. She'd have to ponder it later. Right now she had something more urgent to deal with. She went into her kitchen.

The power-of-attorney form Stuart Junior had given her was on her kitchen table. It had been five days since he'd asked her to sign it.

"Junior's daddy helped build the damn gardens," she said to Patsy Cline, who had refused to go out with Peggy's mutts and was sitting at Laurel's feet in a way that was meant to let the intruders know once and for all who was the alpha dog. "He knows a hell of a lot more about them than I ever will."

Silence from the fearless watchdog guarding her feet.

"But something about it doesn't sit right. Myrtis Garrison passes Senior on to Peggy, and then Senior passes Peggy on to Junior, and then Peggy passes Junior on to me."

It was a system that had worked since before she was born. And if Myrtis and Peggy had been okay with it, what was her problem?

"That's the difference between a lady and me. They say *please* and *thank you* and they pass the tea. They do what's expected of them. Tell *me* what to do and I say, *Kiss my ass*. Dumb."

There was a grunt from Patsy Cline.

"You weren't supposed to agree with me."

Patsy yawned and closed her eyes.

"I can't put it off anymore. I'll go to his house right now and sign the damn thing in front of him. That should make his Sunday."

She found the phone number he'd given her and dialed, but before anyone could answer, she hung up. She refolded the power-of-attorney form, marched into her bedroom, and shoved it into the drawer where she kept her underwear. "I'll take care of it tomorrow," she said. "Today, I have a date with a peach cobbler."

She dragged the protesting Patsy Cline outside to play with the other dogs, got the keys to the Camaro because there was no way she could picture Maggie climbing into the Viper, and took off.

Every Sunday, directly after mass, Maggie went out to the nursing home to visit her old friend Lottie. Lottie's parents, Charlie Mae and Ralph, had worked for Maggie's family and lived in a cabin on their land. Maggie and Lottie had been best friends when they were children and, in spite of race, time, sickness, and tragedy, the friendship had endured.

Six years ago, Lottie had had a stroke and had to move to the nursing home, and the Sunday visits began. For years Maggie had driven herself, with a freshly baked treat carefully cradled in a white linen towel on the passenger seat next to her. Peggy had put a stop to these trips after Maggie had a fender bender with a family of tourists who hadn't known that when Dr. Maggie's ancient Volvo was on the road you had to watch out for her tricky left side. After that, Maggie still drove herself for short runs around the town of Charles Valley, but for longer hauls, like the fifteen-mile trip to the nursing home, Peggy had taken over. Now, as with so much else that had been Peggy's, Laurel had inherited the weekly nursing-home trek.

Not that she minded it. The drive was pretty, and Maggie's baking was not to be missed. She rotated Lottie's favorite cakes—red velvet, lemon, pound, and whiskey pecan with caramel icing—with a variety of seasonal cobblers and pies.

Maggie was waiting for Laurel on her back porch. She came down the steps wearing a snazzy ensemble: cream-colored slacks, a matching blouse, and one of her new cardigans tied schoolgirl style over her shoulders. She looked relieved when she saw the Camaro.

"I'm sure that new car of yours is perfectly lovely, Doodlebug," she said, as soon as she and the cobbler were settled in the passenger seat, "but I think I'd feel like Dale Earnhardt Junior hopping into it." Laurel shot her a startled look and tried to make her brain grasp the idea of Dr. Maggie, NASCAR fan.

As usual, most of the staff and several of the residents turned up for the cobbler, and

Maggie's eyes shone the way they always did when she was with Lottie. Lottie was confined to a wheelchair and her speech was limited, but Maggie managed to communicate with her just fine, holding Lottie's big stroke-gnarled hands in her small, beautifully manicured ones. There was something so connected about them, Laurel thought.

It wasn't until the visit with Lottie was over and they were heading out of the nursing home that the shit hit the fan. That was when Maggie caught sight of a young aide in the hallway.

"Grace," she called out, "why didn't your mama go for those X-rays I ordered? When I didn't get the report, I called radiology at St. Francis, and they said she'd never come in. She needs to have—"

"She will, Dr. Maggie," Grace said. She was in her early thirties, tall and slim, with golden-brown skin and hazel eyes. Those eyes were filled with a fear that Laurel recognized only too well. "My sister and me, we just found out about it," Grace said nervously. "Mama didn't want to tell us because she didn't have the money, and she knew we'd try to pay—"

"Pay for X-rays? Why would she have to pay for them? Your mother's still working at the resort, isn't she?"

"Yes, ma'am."

"All the Garrison employees have health insurance. That'll cover it."

"No, it won't. Mama canceled hers."

"*Canceled* it?"

"The resort has been making people pay more for their premiums—"

"I heard," Maggie said grimly. "But I told your mother to pay whatever she had to."

"She did. But a month ago they told everyone in housekeeping that they were going to be raising the co-pay again. It's over two hundred dollars a month, and Mama said she couldn't afford it."

Maggie's pretty little face was red with anger. "How could you let her, Grace? With her history?"

"She didn't tell us until after she'd done it. They laid her off last winter during the slow season, right when she had to get the new propane tank for her house and she's still trying to pay that off." There were tears in Grace's eyes now. Laurel remembered the day she first heard Sara Jayne's diagnosis, followed by the news that temporary employees at the Garrison resort—which meant her mother—didn't qualify for benefits at all.

"Reetha and I will pay for the X-rays," Grace was saying. "It'll take us a couple of weeks—"

"No!" Maggie shouted. Then she stopped and took a deep breath. "Your mama can't wait. I'll call St. Francis on Monday and make an appointment for her. I'll talk to them, get them to hold off on the bill, or—something. Just get your mama there!"

"I will, Dr. Maggie. I'm sorry I—"

But Maggie had already started down the hall, moving so fast that Laurel had to run to keep up. Their dash ended in the parking lot outside the nursing home. Then a little ball of fury exploded next to Laurel.

"May Stuart Lawrence rot in hell!" Maggie yelled. "May he be damned and rot in hell!"

"They always do stuff like that, Maggie. Those sons of bitches at the resort and the gardens have always—" Laurel stopped. She'd just remembered who owned the resort and had a controlling vote in the gardens.

Maggie was looking at her. Clearly she'd remembered who owned the whole mess too. "Oh, Doodlebug," she said softly, as if something tragic was unfolding in front of her.

And in that moment, Laurel made a decision. "Wait right here," she said. And she dashed back inside the nursing home.

Grace was still standing in the hall where Maggie had left her, trying to get herself together. Laurel rushed up. "Don't worry about the X-rays," she said.

Grace pulled back. "My sister and I will be fine," she said politely.

"I'll take care of it. Tell them to send the bill to me. I'm Laurel McCready. I own the resort."

"Oh, my land! You're the one Miss Peggy—"

"Yeah, I am. What's your name?"

"Grace Marshall."

"Well, Grace, you get those X-rays and any other tests your mama has to have. And then, if it turns out she has a problem, you let me know what you need—Emory, anything. You hear?"

"But I can't—"

"I've been where you are, okay? I'm for real. You can ask Dr. Maggie. Here, let me write down my name and my phone number."

Grace began to cry now—not just tears, big wrenching sobs. "I don't know what to say."

"Don't worry about that. Just do what you've got to do for your mama."

"Thank you! Oh, thank you! I've been so scared. If Mama needed . . . it can cost so much. I didn't know what we'd do."

Feeling like Wonder Woman and Oprah and Stuart Lawrence's worst nightmare all rolled into one, Laurel hugged her. "It never should have happened. And it won't anymore. The resort is my responsibility now, and this bullshit is going to stop." And before Grace could start thanking her again, she ran out to Maggie in the parking lot.

"Are you all right?" Maggie asked, when they were driving back from the nursing home.

"Couldn't be better."

"Wasn't that a stop sign you just ran?"

"Sorry." She slowed down a little. But she needed to get home. She had a phone call to make.

Chapter Thirty-six

Stuart Lawrence was not happy about meeting with the redneck chick on his day off. Sunday was church and golf day for Garrison execs and he was teeing off, or whatever the hell golfers did, at two. On the other hand, he needed her to sign his power-of-attorney form, so he sighed, to let her know how pushy she was being, and allowed as how they could probably meet in his office over at the resort for just a few minutes. She agreed without apologizing, which was clearly what he expected her to do, and hung up.

*   *   *

The executive offices for the resort and the gardens were housed in three white stone buildings at the back of the resort, connected by red brick pathways that were bordered with low boxwood hedges. Stuart's office was in the middle. Laurel strode up to the front door, banged on it, then let herself in and yelled into the empty entryway that she was there. Stuart appeared and conducted her to his office.

After the splendor of his home, Stuart's office was a surprise. The room was small, furnished with commercial carpet, an old wooden desk, a couple of padded chairs, and a lamp. On the walls were pictures of the Lawrence men—Junior and Senior, separately and together—shaking hands and posing with other men, all of whom looked rich and pleased with themselves. On the desk was a picture of Stuart's father standing with Mr. Dalt on a dock near a large body of water. One of them had caught a huge fish, but it wasn't clear which of the men had actually bagged the thing, since they were holding it between them. Possibly they had double-teamed it.

Stuart's office—specifically the rattyness of it—was interesting. Obviously someone at the resort had decided he didn't rate more than cast-off furniture and cheap floor covering. That could give a person one hell of an inferiority complex, never a good thing in a man.

At the moment he was sitting behind his desk, looking patient and slightly martyred in his golfing clothes. Which, for some reason, made Laurel even madder. "Do you have health insurance?" she demanded.

"I don't understand."

"I'll take a simple yes or no."

"Of course I have health insurance."

"Well, I just met a woman whose mother doesn't. Her mother is a maid at the resort, and she dropped her insurance because you—*we*—made it too expensive for her. Now she's sick—"

"Laurel, I can see why you find this upsetting."

"Upset? I'm pissed. I told this woman—her name is Grace Marshall—that I was going to pick up her bills, whatever they are—"

"Do you have any idea what that could cost you?"

"Probably better than you do. I went through it all before when my ma was dying and the resort wouldn't lift a finger to help. I know damn well I can't pay for everyone."

"I'm glad you realize that."

"That's why we're going to make sure people have insurance."

"Laurel—"

"You've been rich all your life. You don't know what it's like when they tell you your mother has something real bad and you're scared it's going to kill her. But you're even more scared that there might be something they could do for her that you'll never even hear about, because you don't have the money to pay for the best treatment." He sat back in his chair. He'd given up trying to interrupt. "You don't know what it's like when you come home from the hospital and the mailbox is so full of bills you don't even bother to open it, because if you do you'll throw up. Or when you're sitting next to your mother's hospital bed, and all you can think about is how much it's costing her to die. You don't know any of that, but I do. And I'm not letting anyone else go through it. Premiums for employees at the resort have got to go down."

He waited for a moment. Then he said, "Are you through?"

"I am." She sat back.

"Do you have any idea how much it costs to provide benefits for our employees?" he asked. Every inch of him said how much he resented having to explain his policies to the likes of her. In spite of herself, she felt guilty for bothering him. She fought the feeling.

"No, I don't," she said.

"We employ over three thousand workers at the gardens and the resort. Insuring all of them—with a minimal plan, mind you—runs over ten million a year."

She couldn't keep from being shocked. He saw it.

"Exactly," he said. He finally looked at her. He had the coldest eyes she'd ever seen. They were looking at her like she was beyond stupid. "It's an astronomical sum. Even after raising the co-payments, we're still looking at a figure in excess of seven million. I don't have the precise numbers on hand."

"But if someone gets sick?" A tone of pleading was creeping into her voice and she hated herself for it.

"Laurel, with all due respect, you don't begin to understand what's involved here!"

Stuart's coldness was rapidly giving way to anger. "A few years ago, we were facing the prospect of *bankruptcy* at the resort. And we were considering closing down the gardens."

That was a stunner. There were always rumors that the gardens and the resort were doing badly, but this was coming from a source who knew what he was talking about. "You guys were going out of business? Seriously?" she asked. It would mean hundreds of people losing their jobs in a one-industry town.

"It was a very real possibility. Of course we kept it quiet; it wouldn't have helped our image with potential visitors if it had been known. I'm sure you can see that."

Laurel nodded, trying to make herself absorb the idea of the gardens and the resort not existing.

"We've managed to stay open, but our revenues are still down—not through any fault of ours, I might add. In fact, we've done remarkably well considering the challenges we've faced. Times have been difficult, and families have cut back. A vacation is one of the first items on the budget to go.

"Furthermore, we're going to have to upgrade our facilities if we want to remain competitive. And we should be expanding. We've been exploring the idea of building adult-living residences near the golf course. Our architects are projecting an initial cost of between fifty-eight and sixty million dollars. I promise you no one will invest with us if our financial picture looks the way it did."

Stuart's anger had subsided. Now he sounded reasonable and responsible again. She tried to remember the panic in Grace's eyes.

"Meanwhile," the reasonable and responsible voice went on, "our health insurance costs are rising at an annual rate of twenty percent. We simply can't afford that."

Grace's face was fading away.

"There's got to be some other way," Laurel said, knowing she was losing ground.

He let out a deep sigh. "Laurel, the decision to increase the premiums was not taken lightly. We held off as long as we could. But sometimes you have to make the tough calls. I'm sure if you were to ask any of our employees if they'd rather have cheap health insurance or know that the resort and the gardens will still be here next year, they'd opt for their jobs."

He was right. People might bitch about the gardens, but no one in their right mind would want the Garrison cash cow to tank.

"I'm sure what we've done seems harsh to you. But it had to happen. And that's why I advised you to sign your power of attorney over to me. You hear a story like the one this maid told you—and I admit it's heartbreaking—and you react emotionally. All you want to do is make it better for her. That does you great credit. But I'm responsible for the livelihoods of three thousand people. I have to look at the bigger picture. These are complicated, difficult questions. Only an informed, experienced person can wrestle with them and still hope to sleep at night."

She should have known he'd get around to the power of attorney.

"I hope I've answered your concerns," he said.

She hated him, but she nodded.

He got up to let her out of the office, and she had to keep herself from running out the door.

Chapter Thirty-seven

By the time Laurel got home she hated herself as much as she hated Stuart. She wasn't fit company for the dogs. Naturally, the phone rang.

"So, I'd like to take you out for that date. How about supper?" a familiar husky voice said in her ear.

"Wiener."

"It's got to be the Sportsman's Grill, because you own all the nice restaurants in town."

"Don't say that."

"I know you don't spend every night

meeting and greeting at the Magnolia Room, but you do own—"

"I told you not to say that, goddammit!"

"Laurel? What's wrong?"

"I don't want to hear about the gardens or the restaurants or any of the shit I own!" And she slammed down the phone.

Two seconds later, as she was trying to find his number, her phone rang again.

"I'm sorry," she said.

"Okay."

"It's not about you."

"Okay."

And then before she could stop herself, she was spilling the whole story: about Grace and Maggie and her power of attorney and the loathesome Stuart Junior. "I didn't fight," she said. "I hate that son of a bitch and everything he stands for, but as soon as he started talking I started thinking, *What do I know?* Those bastards are going to screw hundreds of people, and I couldn't think of a single way to fight it."

"Laurel, it's all right."

"I've never been to college. I've never run a business."

"And he knows that."

"I've messed up everything I've ever tried to do in my whole life."

"No, you haven't."

"I can't do this. I can't be the person who owns the whole goddam town. Peggy was either out of her mind when she made that will or she was drunk."

"I'm coming over."

"I sat in that man's office like a fool."

"It'll just take me a couple of minutes."

"Don't come. I'm going out to get something to eat."

"Stay where you are."

"It's better if I'm alone—"

But he'd already hung up. She found her keys and ran for her car, figuring if she drove fast she'd be all the way into town before he reached her dirt road. She got as far as turning on the ignition, but then she turned it off again. When Perry drove up fifteen minutes later, she was sitting on her porch, waiting for him.

"For the record, you're not a fool," he said. "The guy's a bully, Laurel. Stuart Junior threw a lot of numbers at you because that's how he intimidates the peasants when they get out of hand."

"I should have said something."

"He shut you down, honey. He's been running things here for a long time, and he doesn't want interference."

"I wasn't trying to—okay, I *was* trying to interfere. But somebody should!"

"And that somebody is you. But you've got to know what you're doing. You've got to be totally clear, totally prepared. With facts and figures—"

"I can't do that."

"What do you mean, you can't? You have to, if you want to take him on."

"I don't want to take on Stuart Lawrence. I don't want to know about the facts and figures. I just want people to have health insurance."

"Damn it, Laurel, you can't waltz into the man's office trying to be a hero with nothing but the steam coming out of your ears!"

Which, of course, was exactly what she'd done.

"Is this supposed to make me feel better?"

"Okay, that was the wrong way to say it." He regrouped. "Lawrence is a shit heel. But he's a disciplined shit heel; he knows his stuff. If you want to deal with him—if you want to do anything more than just sign that power of attorney and turn everything over to him—you have to do your homework. Make him give you the books." She could feel her face go blank. "The financial statements. Learn the operation. See for yourself where the money's going. Know what you're talking about."

She could imagine the look on Stuart's face when she informed him that she wanted to inspect his finances. As usual, Perry did his mind-reading thing. "You'll be okay," he said. "Why does this matter so much to you?"

"This is my town too. You're not the only one who hates the way the gardens and the resort Bigfoot everyone." Then he smiled, a big spectacular dimple-producing smile. "Besides, I want to watch Laurel Selene McCready kick some good ol' boy ass."

The best—and the worst—of it was, his smile said he really thought she could do it. No one had had that kind of faith in her since Peggy died.

"Let's get something to eat," she said.

They didn't go to the Sportsman's Grill because it was too late. After ten the grill morphed from a place for family dining to a place for serious drinking. Laurel and Perry drove to McGuire's, a little all-purpose store with the best home-cooked takeout in the state. They picked up two fried chicken suppers, with an order of special fried okra and a can of bug spray, and took the feast back to eat on Laurel's porch. Perry sat across from her, not next to her, and didn't try to touch her once. And if she'd been afraid he was going to start up with his foolishness again, she needn't have worried. He kept up a stream of the kind of chitchat he'd have had with an elderly female relative, talking about his work with Maggie and how his mama was going back to school after all these years so she could be a teacher. By the time they finished eating, Laurel could almost tell herself she'd imagined his declaration of passion and the follow-up scene in the clinic the next morning.

As she walked with him to his car, she was congratulating herself on how well she'd handled the situation when he stopped and said, "Now, I'd say we're making progress, wouldn't you?"

"Huh?"

"You haven't called me Wiener in at least

three hours. I told you you'd start adjusting your thinking."

"I haven't adjusted a damn thing!"

"Well, you always were bullheaded. You'll come around." Before she could put him in his place, he added, "But about Stuart Lawrence. It wouldn't hurt to do some research on him."

"I should research Junior?"

"Trust me, he's done plenty of research on you." He gave her a quick peck on the cheek, said, "You'd better go inside. It's past midnight and we've been sitting here so long we're going to be out of bug spray," and on that romantic note he left.

Chapter Thirty-eight

Perry had said she needed to go over the financial reports for the gardens and the resort. A grown-up would have called Stuart at his office and asked him to give her the account books. But the idea of making that phone call after her last encounter with the man made her teeth chatter. So early the next morning, she drove to Lenny's Barbecue, which was the place in Charles Valley where the entire sheriff's department went for breakfast.

Laurel's quarry was a blonde in a cop's uniform who still favored the big hair so beloved by women in the 1980s. Her name was Sheralynn, and during the years when Laurel was having an affair with the very much married sheriff, Ed Hood, Sheralynn had been the token female on the force. Ed, not exactly a liberated thinker, had assigned Sheralynn to a desk in the station house and turned her into a glorified secretary-receptionist, frustrating her lifelong ambition of becoming a highway patrol officer. Since Laurel was locked into her lousy relationship and hanging around the station a lot, she and Sheralynn had bonded over their mutual resentment of the man who was, in very different ways, doing them both dirt.

Since that time, mercifully, both of them had moved on. Laurel had found Josh, who was a massive, though brief, step up on the dating food chain, and Sheralynn, having outlasted Ed's defeat in the last county election, was now following her bliss in a shiny new patrol car.

When Laurel found her, Sheralynn was eating Lenny's breakfast specialty, two cinnamon-raisin biscuits liberally covered with gooey white icing. Laurel pulled up a stool and quickly got down to business.

"Do you have any family working for the accounting department at the resort?" she asked. Sheralynn came from a huge clan, and it was a sure bet that she'd have a cousin or a nephew working in every branch of the place.

"Let's see, Ruthie's at the information desk and Tommy's in the sales department. . . . Probably Mary Lou's young'un, Jessie, would be the best. That child is a whiz at numbers. She's just two night courses away from her CPA, and I know she's got an office job over there. Why?"

Laurel told her what she needed. Sheralynn shot her a suspicious look. "You want Jessie to sneak you copies of the account books? Don't you own the resort and the gardens?"

"Just the resort. Technically—" Laurel was about to launch into an explanation, but to her horror she felt her eyes begin to pond up.

Sheralynn said hastily, "Hey, it's not a problem. As far as I can see, it's not illegal for you to borrow something you own. I'll call Jessie as soon as she gets to work." She studied Laurel thoughtfully. "You know, since we heard—about Miss Peggy—doing what she did and all, a lot of folks have been real jealous of you.

"Don't be."

"Yeah, I'm beginning to think maybe that jackpot isn't all it's cracked up to be."

Sheralynn promised to be in touch as soon as she'd spoken to Jessie and took off in her patrol car with an ostentatious squealing of tires. Laurel picked at the remains of the cinnamon biscuit she'd left unfinished and tried to plot out her next move according to the precepts laid out by Perry. "Do research on Stuart Lawrence," he'd said. Presumably that meant doing more than reading the author's biography that appeared on the back cover of the book he'd written on the Garrisons. She got up and made a phone call.

Chapter Thirty-nine

"I asked Maggie to come over too," Li'l Bit said. "She'll be here as soon as she can get away from the clinic. Perry overslept this morning and they're backed up. It seems he was out quite late last night."

"Really?" Laurel said. She told herself she didn't feel responsible—or uncomfortable. Li'l Bit produced two cups of the undrinkable instant coffee she made with hot water from the tap and settled into the big rocking chair that had been her father's. Laurel sat in her usual spot on the front steps.

"Now, what can I tell you about Stuart Lawrence that you don't already know?" Li'l

Bit mused. "I have to admit I always thought he was an unpleasant youngster. I used to have swimming lessons in my pond for all the children in town. Stuart came one summer when he was nine. He was large for his age, and it was just evil the way he delighted in dunking the little ones."

Perry had called it right. Junior was a bully, and he always had been.

"The man had poor Peggy completely bamboozled." Li'l Bit sighed. "Isn't it odd how you can know someone for so many years and never realize the most basic thing about them?"

Used to the loopy routes Li'l Bit's mind could take, Laurel didn't make the mistake of thinking they were still talking about Stuart. "You mean Peggy?"

Li'l Bit nodded. "Maggie and I were closer to her than anyone. But we never knew how frightened she was."

"You think Stuart frightened her?"

"There had to be some reason why she put up with him."

"Maybe she trusted him."

"I can't imagine why. He's totally lacking in gravitas. His father was truly awful, but he was tough." She paused. "I always thought there was a story there."

"Stuart Lawrence Senior and Peggy?"

Li'l Bit shook her head. "Myrtis."

Laurel realized the route was going to be loopier than usual. But she perked up at the mention of Myrtis Garrison. Since finding the mystery suitcase she was hungry for any new insights on the woman. "The way I heard it, Miss Myrtis was the one who brought Stuart Senior to work for the Garrisons," she prompted.

"That's right. I always thought that was odd. He wasn't her kind of person at all. . . ." Li'l Bit drifted off, lost in thought. "You never knew her, of course."

"I've heard about her. Everyone talks about Miss Myrtis like she was the mother of Jesus."

"The first time I met her, I thought she was the kindest person I'd ever known. It was at a dinner party. I was young and rather awkward, I'm afraid, and Mama was being unpleasant. Myrtis defended me. No one else ever tried to curtail Mama when she was on a tear, and Myrtis didn't even know me." It would not be helpful to ask for details about that meeting, Laurel decided; Li'l Bit was wandering down some elusive memory lane and it was always better not to interrupt the trip. "There was always something a little reserved about Myrtis," Li'l Bit went on, "even in the beginning. Most people put that down to her having been educated in England. In those days, people around here were very suspicious of anything foreign."

"I never heard about Miss Myrtis going to school in England," Laurel said.

"Myrtis never talked about it. It was considered strange that her father sent her abroad. Northerners did that with their daughters all the time—well, look at dear Mrs. Roosevelt—but here in the South we didn't as much. Myrtis's father was a restless soul, and her mother died quite young. They lived in England on and off for several years when Myrtis was a child. Her father sent her back to England to attend Gracewood Academy when she was fifteen, because he didn't want to hand her over to his mother-in-law, whom he didn't like. That was the story we all heard. I always thought he did it because he was a terrible womanizer, and having an adolescent daughter around would have been—Good Lord, she's going to hit that tree!" This last in reference not to the adolescent Myrtis but to Maggie, who was careening up the driveway in her Volvo.

Maggie swerved out of danger, got out of her car, and came up on the porch while Li'l Bit made dire predictions of death and destruction if she didn't stop driving. Maggie dismissed them serenely. "I'm sorry I couldn't get here sooner," she said. "Perry was late this morning. I can't imagine what—"

"Li'l Bit and I have been talking about Myrtis Garrison," Laurel said hastily.

"I was telling Laurel about Myrtis's years at Gracewood Academy," said Li'l Bit.

"It was supposed to be a progressive school for the time," Maggie said, as she hiked herself up on her porch swing. "Personally, I always thought her father, the old goat, sent her there so she wouldn't cramp his style. But I thought Laurel wanted to hear about Stuart Lawrence."

"Yes," Laurel said. She told them about the power of attorney. Li'l Bit and Maggie exchanged glances.

"So that's how he did it," Li'l Bit said softly.

"But why did she go along with it?" asked Maggie.

"Who?" Laurel asked, feeling the conversation was slipping away from her.

"It does explain some things," Maggie said.

Li'l Bit nodded. "The clinic."

"Exactly."

"What clinic?" Laurel asked, in a desperate bid to keep up.

"When Myrtis was first married, she was going to help me set up my clinic," Maggie said.

"Back in those days, no one wanted a female physician," Li'l Bit added.

"The only patients I had were the ones who were so poor they couldn't afford to go to Dr. Brewster."

"Which was precisely the point." Li'l Bit beamed at Maggie before turning back to Laurel. "Maggie was living in Atlanta, and she came back home because this was where she was needed. It was very brave of her."

"But since none of my patients could pay me, I couldn't support myself. Myrtis was very enthusiastic about setting up a clinic on the grounds of the resort and running it as a service to the community. Then, suddenly, she dropped the whole idea. I never understood why, but now I realize she backed off right after Stuart Lawrence came to work at the gardens."

"If she was letting him make the decisions for her . . ." Li'l Bit said.

"That would account for it." Maggie finished the thought. "But why did she let him do that?"

"Exactly. I hate to admit it, but I can see Peggy signing over her voting rights, if she was put under enough pressure," Li'l Bit said. "She wasn't strong."

"But Myrtis was," Maggie said.

Li'l Bit nodded. "In the beginning, she was full of ideas. She was a big admirer of Mrs. Roosevelt—which was a rarity in these parts."

"Most people of Myrtis's background thought Eleanor Roosevelt was a traitor to her class—and race," Maggie said.

"Myrtis used to argue with old Mr. Grady—"

"He was Dalton's father," Maggie clarified.

"Laurel knows that," Li'l Bit said, irritated. "As I was saying, Myrtis used to argue with her father-in-law all the time about labor unions. She believed in them strongly. She wanted to integrate the staff at the resort and the garden thirty years before anyone heard the term *civil rights*."

"Then Stuart Lawrence came," Maggie said. "And suddenly Myrtis didn't have a word to say about the resort *or* the gardens. Dalton, on the other hand, had always been a bit of a nonentity, but he came into his own after Stuart showed up,"

"Not in a good way," Li'l Bit added.

Maggie nodded. "Stuart and Dalton were two of a kind—put them together and they had the compassion of a rock."

"And the vision of an avocado," Li'l Bit chimed in.

"But you say Myrtis signed that power of attorney," Maggie said, shaking her head in disbelief.

"And now Stuart Lawrence's son wants *you* to sign," said Li'l Bit.

Laurel nodded.

Maggie inspected her fingernails and Li'l Bit looked off into space. Like the late Myrtis Garrison, Maggie and Li'l Bit held political and social beliefs rooted in the glory days of FDR. Maggie kept true to her ideals by working in her clinic and charging only twenty dollars a visit. Li'l Bit supported her long list of charities, worked tirelessly as a volunteer, and had been known to pay the electric bill or a month's rent for a hardworking family that got behind. They weren't the only people in Charles Valley who disapproved of the way the gardens and the resort were run, but they were probably the most active in trying to combat the results. And for thirty years, Peggy had had the power to change everything they disliked, but she hadn't. Laurel wondered what it must have cost Li'l Bit and Maggie to keep their mouths shut for three decades. They had, because they loved Peggy, and because the three Miss Margarets didn't meddle. If Peggy hadn't wanted their advice—and clearly she hadn't—they hadn't offered it.

Now, it seemed, the old rules held for Laurel. The question of her signing the power of attorney hung in the air. Li'l Bit and Maggie had to be bursting with opinions and suggestions, but Laurel hadn't specifically asked to hear them—although she might have been glad if they'd been offered—so her two friends changed the subject and began a lively debate about the exact date in the 1930s when the Fair Labor Standards Act was passed. The argument lasted until the bad coffee was finished and the little party broke up. Laurel left for home, Maggie went back to her clinic, and Li'l Bit bustled off to work in her garden. No advice was given.

Back at her house, Laurel went to her bedroom and took the old suitcase out of her closet. The damn thing was starting to haunt her. So was the ghost of Myrtis, as she'd just been described by Maggie and Li'l Bit. Laurel opened the suitcase and took out the child's dress and the sheet music. She laid them on her bed, smoothing out the yellowing paper and running her fingers over the darned places on the dress. She still resented the great lady whose legend had terrified her beloved Peggy, and she would always hate the fact that Peggy had lived in a shrine to Myrtis's ancestors. But Li'l Bit and Maggie had given her a picture of young Myrtis that was very different from the Myrtis Garrison of the legend, who gave money to charities but would have had to go lie down if she'd actually met a poor person face-to-face. That didn't sound like the eager young woman who wanted to start a clinic and got into arguments over labor unions. Laurel imagined her coming to Charles Valley, full of ideas from her progressive school in England, wanting to make a difference. She'd been strong enough to stand up to her father-in-law—a tough old coot, by all accounts—but she'd somehow let herself be bulldozed by the elder Stuart Lawrence. Pretty much the same way Laurel was being bulldozed by Junior. So when you stopped to think about it, the town tramp and the great lady had something in common. Wasn't that a kick in the pants?

Laurel looked down at the strange old-fashioned dress she'd spread out on her bed. Why had Myrtis caved? And if classy, rich, educated Myrtis Garrison couldn't fight the first Stuart Lawrence, how the hell could redneck, uneducated, perpetually down-and-out Laurel Selene McCready fight Stuart Junior? But wouldn't it be another kick in the pants if she could?

Why does it seem like everywhere I look

these days I keep coming back to Myrtis Garrison? she wondered. And what the hell did the contents of this faded old suitcase have to do with Charles Valley's great lady?

Chapter Forty

MRS. RAIN

2004

She'd had an incident. That was what the infant doctor called it—a *minor incident*—which was a tidy if inadequate way to describe the terror of waking up at dawn to discover that your left side has stopped working during the night. Fortunately, her vocal cords were functioning and she had called for help, which brought Cherry running. Thank God for the child's sharp young ears and quick young mind.

Cherry had made the necessary phone calls, which resulted in an ambulance and a hospital room and the early morning appearance of the boy physician with a colleague versed in such problems as clots, embolisms, and strokes. This was followed by several frightening days of being *under observation* before the specialist declared that she could go home.

While she'd been gone, a sickroom had been set up for her in the sunroom on the first floor. It was her least favorite place in the house. She wanted to be in her own bedroom, where she'd lived with her ghosts for so many years. But her bed, her dresser, and her old wingback chair were now in the hated sunroom. She wanted the freedom to roam her own house at night, but Cherry now slept across the hall and those sharp young ears meant the girl would be up like a shot at the first creak of a floorboard.

The infant doctor had assured his dear Mrs. Rain that her new sleeping quarters were not permanent and her life would get back to normal as soon as he was sure the new medications were working. The pills were to be taken on a precise schedule; otherwise she could *stroke out*. That was not supposed to scare her. To ensure that she got the dosage right, she'd been given a string of seven little boxes, which were to be filled with the proper number of pills for each day of the week, thereby doing an end run around her suddenly dicey short-term memory. It was all very efficient and, the boy explained kindly, designed to help her maintain her independence. But the idea of counting up the piles of pills and dropping them into the tiny boxes with her arthritic fingers was too much. She turned the whole mess over to Cherry, who handed her the right medications twice a day. To hell with independence; she was too tired to fight for it.

Instead, she let herself drift into a new daydream that had rapidly became as comforting as her memories. In her fantasy, she was in Charles Valley, where she had contacted Laurel Selene McCready. Sometimes she pictured Ms. McCready as a small Irish brunette, like Gracie Allen; sometimes she was built more along the lines of Myrna Loy. They met in the field of wildflowers in front of Garrison Cottage—which Mrs. Rain could visualize because a picture of it had appeared in the *Charles Valley Gazette* some thirty years before.

Laurel Selene was standing in the sunlight with a smile of welcome. But as she came forward to shake hands, there was a little frown of curiosity creasing the spot between her eyebrows. So before Laurel Selene could ask a single question, Mrs. Rain said, "I have a story you need to hear."

Then, in her beautiful daydream, they sat on the ground in front of the big log house, and as Mrs. Rain started to talk she could feel the tightness in her chest that had been there long before her incident loosening at last.

"Did you ever have a time in your life when it felt like things happened in a chain?" she asked Laurel Selene. "And when you look back on it, you realize that everything that happened—every single link—led to the next thing. And if you could have stopped it anywhere along the way, your whole life would have been different? I had a time like that. It started back in the summer of 1933."

Chapter Forty-one

IVA CLAIRE

1933

Indiana could get hot in the middle of summer, and Iva Claire's hands were sweaty. The handle of the costume trunk was slipping out of her grasp.

"You okay?" Tassie panted.

"I need to change sides."

They stopped to lower the big trunk down onto the sidewalk; they were both out of breath. "How much farther?" Tassie gasped.

"The clerk at the hotel said five blocks."

"It feels like we've come five miles."

"There's just two more to go. You ready? I want to get the costumes unpacked tonight."

They changed sides, heaved up the trunk, and continued their trip down the Main Street of Washtabula, Indiana. Normally, they'd have hired a taxicab to carry the costume trunk to the theater. But the Sunshine Sisters were making half their normal pay for their three-week booking at the Egyptian Theater in Washtabula, so they had to save their pennies. Iva Claire wished they could have turned the gig down, but these days beggars couldn't be choosers, and like most vaudevillians they were beggars.

A lot had happened in the six years since Tassie had joined the act. For one thing, Tassie and Iva Claire had grown up. Tassie was nineteen now, and while she still wasn't classically pretty, she had fulfilled her early promise as a cute little trick with her big eyes and her small hourglass figure. At eighteen, Iva Claire had grown into her strong features; her tall body had slimmed down, her blue eyes had darkened, her complexion was creamy, and when she piled her stick-straight hair on top of her head, she was usually described as handsome.

A lot had happened to the Sunshine Sisters too. At first, they had worked steadily. Not on the Big Time—they were never headed for the Palace—but for most of 1927, 1928, and 1929 they had toured the country with an act that could be fairly described as a modest hit. They played decent theaters and earned enough to support themselves. For the first time that Iva Claire could remember, the checks from Georgia were used strictly for luxuries. And if she felt trapped in her life as a Sunshine Sister, Mama and Tassie were blissfully happy. Two out of three wasn't so bad.

But while the Sunshine Sisters were touring and growing up and getting their laughs, the world around them was changing. In 1927, Al Jolson sang in a moving picture called *The Jazz Singer*, and the talkies were born. At about the same time, RCA brought out a new line of Radiolas that ran on the electricity people had in their houses instead of big old-fashioned batteries. The new radios, as they were called, were compact and simple to use, and people were buying them as fast as RCA could make them. Now families could stay in their own homes and be entertained for free or go to movies for a lot less than it cost to see a live show. Vaudeville was hit hard. But what really did it in was a certain Thursday in October 1929. WALL STREET LAYS AN EGG was the way *Variety* described the day the stock market crashed.

Initially, most of the entertainers Iva Claire knew shrugged off Black Thursday. "It's not like I ever had any money to invest," she heard, in dressing rooms and greenrooms. No one understood that life had changed for good.

They caught on when theaters started closing around the country. Shows in New York went dark by the dozens, road shows were canceled, permanent stock companies went under, and work dried up. The Sunshine Sisters got occasional gigs, mostly on weekends, always for increasingly smaller paychecks. Every once in a while they were booked as the entertainment at marathon dances, going on to perform during the fifteen-minute rest periods when the exhausted contestants were off the floor. But even that humiliating work became less and less frequent until, once again, the money from Iva Claire's father was the only thing keeping them going. Then, without warning, he had skipped their last check. Mama refused to write to remind him. She insisted that they should wait and see if he sent it on his own. After five months, the check still hadn't come and their finances went from surviving to desperate. By the time the booking at Indiana's fly-by-night Egyptian Theater came up, there was no way they could turn it down.

Iva Claire adjusted her grip on the trunk handle. She already had a nice set of blisters on one hand.

"I think it's that building at end of the block," she gasped, indicating a white stone and brick monstrosity with a marquee jutting out over the sidewalk. Tassie nodded, too winded to speak.

There were several reasons why Iva Claire would have liked to turn down the booking in Washtabula. The Sunshine Sisters had been booked as a solo, which meant the theater was a cheap operation that was only offering the audience one act; plus, the theater management had changed hands twice in the last six months, which did not bode well.

But the main reason Iva Claire wished they could have stayed home was Mama. After a lifetime of touring, traveling seemed to exhaust Mama now. Everything did. When they were back in New York, she still read *Variety* from cover to cover, but there were days when she couldn't get out of bed until it was too late to make the rounds. And right now, instead of running over to the theater to look it over, she was lying down in their hotel room, so tired she couldn't catch her breath. In spite of the heat, Iva Claire shivered. If something really was wrong with Mama . . .

Don't think about that, said the voice she'd been trusting since childhood.

The marquee was a few feet ahead of them. They lugged the trunk up to an impressive front door with glass panes and wrought-iron curlicues. There was a large padlock and chain threaded through the wrought iron. The big marquee was blank. Tassie and Iva Claire dropped the trunk and stood on either side of it, staring at the theater in disbelief.

"It's closed," Tassie said.

I knew it, Iva Claire thought. *I had a feeling about this job.*

"I'm going around to the stage door," Tassie said. "There's got to be an explanation."

"There is. The Egyptian is out of business."

"They can't do that. We came all this way. We have a contract."

Tassie wouldn't believe what had happened until she went into the pharmacy next door, and the boy behind the soda fountain confirmed their worst fears.

"The management was leasing it," she reported back to Iva Claire. "They went belly up about a week ago."

Which meant that the Sunshine Sisters wouldn't be reimbursed for their train tickets back to New York. How were they going to get home? Silently, they picked up the trunk and began the long walk back to their hotel.

The Normandy Hotel was not the kind of place where the Sunshine Sisters usually stayed. Mama said it was one step up from a flophouse, which was an exaggeration although not a big one. But it was cheap. And now they couldn't even afford to stay there. There was no way out; Iva Claire was going to have to write to her father. It would be humiliating, but she'd remind him that they hadn't received their last check. If he knew they were stranded, he'd send the money; she was sure of that.

Then, when they were back in New York, she and Mama would have a talk. They couldn't go on like this. Vaudeville was dead and it was time to quit. Mama would scream and yell, but in the end she'd have to accept reality. Somehow, in spite of the Depression, Iva Claire would have to find a civilian job. It would be boring and awful and she'd have to keep herself from thinking about how much better she could have done if she'd had a high school or—dream of dreams—a college diploma, but that was reality too. Tassie could stay with them for as long as she wanted. Of course, if they didn't have an act anymore, she might move on. The leather handle slipped a little in Iva Claire's hand. She looked over at Tassie, her dress streaked with sweat and street dirt as she struggled to hang on to her side of the trunk. *What will Mama and I do without her? She's the only friend I've ever had.*

Don't think about that.

"You need a rest?" Tassie asked.

"No. Do you?"

Tassie shook her head. They continued on to the Normandy to break the news to Mama that the Sunshine Sisters were all washed up in Washtabula.

The desk clerk at the hotel saw them coming and hurried over. For a moment, Iva Claire hoped he was going to help them carry their trunk upstairs; he'd been very taken with Tassie when they checked in. But the clerk wasn't smiling and he ignored the heavy trunk.

"Your ma had a bad turn while you were out," he said breathlessly. "I called the doctor for her. They come and took her to the hospital."

They spent money they didn't have on a taxicab and Tassie prayed with tears running down her cheeks. Iva Claire was numb. All she could think of was the time six years ago when she'd gone to meet her father. She'd wanted to leave Mama then. Now she bargained with God. *I'll never complain about her again. Just let her be all right, and I'll take care of her for the rest of my life.*

When they got to the hospital, Mama had already been admitted. She'd had a heart attack.

Chapter Forty-two

Iva Claire didn't like her mother's doctor. He was old, with a voice that sounded like two pieces of something very dry being rubbed together. Without her wanting to, her mimic's brain recorded the sound and stored it away.

"There is no way to predict when or if another heart attack will come," Dr. Wilbur croaked. "I've given her some medicine to decrease the fluid around the heart, but above all we must keep her calm."

Mama's never calm.

"Rest, both physical and mental, is the most important element of treatment. These early days are critical. A sudden heart failure like the one she just suffered is often followed by other attacks. We do see the rare patient who recovers and is able to go back to a normal life, but I must stress that that is not the rule."

Mama will be one of them. She'll be fine. Once I get her back to New York.

She and Tassie wanted to stay with Mama, but Dr. Wilbur said her mother needed to sleep. Iva Claire let herself be led out of the hospital. She had to get back to the hotel so she could write her father.

There had been a time, after her disastrous visit with him, when she hated the sight of the envelopes he sent. When the act was making money, she wished she could tear up the checks and send them back to him in little pieces. But the extra money meant better hotels and sleeper cars on trains when they had long jumps—little treats that Mama loved—so the checks were always cashed. To hell with dignity.

Now she didn't try to be dignified. She told her father the facts and asked him to send the money quickly because Mama was sick and she shouldn't be under a strain and they needed to get her home.

She printed the address of the Normandy Hotel very clearly for him. She sent the letter. And she began to wait.

When Mama was released from the hospital they brought her back to the Normandy. The doctor told Iva Claire to watch for signs of another attack. If Mama had trouble breathing or felt chest pain, there were some pills she had to take immediately. But Mama brushed it off. "I'm fine, Claire de Lune. I've had trouble catching my breath all my life."

Dr. Wilbur told Iva Claire, "Keep exertion to a minimum. This hotel doesn't have an elevator and you're living on the fourth floor. Perhaps you should try to move to the first."

But until they had enough money to settle the tab they'd already run up, they couldn't afford to move.

"Limit her salt intake. She needs light, nutritious foods," said the doctor.

But light, nutritious food cost money.

"Above all, don't let your mother get overexcited," said Dr. Wilbur.

But Mama was already overexcited, or, to be more accurate, she was terrified. There was only one thing that would make her feel safe. "When can we get out of this godforsaken town and go home?" she wept, the way Iva Claire had known she would.

"I would have preferred to wait before she undertook the trip back to New York," said Dr. Wilbur, "but she is so unhappy that I think it is better to risk it. Her heart cannot stand the strain of all this emotion."

But the check hadn't come.

The bills were piling up. There were medicines to be paid for, the hospital had cost ten dollars a day, and even though Dr. Wilbur hadn't charged them yet, he wasn't coming to the hotel every afternoon for free. Iva Claire raced down to the lobby every three or four hours to ask the clerk if any mail had come for her. The answer was always the same—there was nothing.

Tassie was spending time in the lobby too, but with much better results. She was flirting with the desk clerk, who expressed his appreciation by "forgetting" to send up their weekly account. But that couldn't go on forever.

"I got a job," Tassie announced one day, when things were looking so bleak Iva Claire hadn't even ventured out of their room. With the help of the smitten desk clerk, Tassie had landed a gig for three

nights singing in a roadhouse on the out-
skirts of town.

"The crowd can get kind of rowdy, but I'll
make sure no one gives her any trouble,"
said the desk clerk. But they couldn't live
very long on Tassie's tiny paycheck.

Iva Claire wrote to her father again, pleading this time.

> Mama has to go home. Staying here
> is making her upset and her heart is too
> weak to take it. The doctor says it's a
> matter of life and death. . . .

"There must be something wrong," said a
voice behind her.

Iva Claire jerked around in her chair to see
her mother. She covered the letter quickly
with her hands. "Mama!"

"He wouldn't cut me off unless something
was wrong."

"He hasn't cut us off, Mama."

"You've already written him once, haven't
you?"

"Yes."

"And he didn't answer."

"Not yet."

Mama sat down on the bed. She looked

off into space. "He was so handsome when he was young," she said. "I think if I had really cared about him, I probably could have had him, even though he was married. Not that that matters now."

"Mama, he'll send the money."

"There's something wrong, Claire de Lune."

She couldn't say she was thinking the same thing, because Mama had to stay calm. "Maybe the letter got lost, or he was away from home. So many things could have happened," she said brightly. But her mother shook her head. She looked tired— and old. When did Mama get old? "I don't want you to worry—" she started to say, but her mother cut in wearily.

"Finish your letter," she said. "We need the money."

They waited three more weeks, but there was nothing. No check, no answering letter.

"He did it," Mama said softly. "He finally cut us off."

Mama went to bed early that night and got up the next morning before either of the girls were awake. By the time Iva Claire went into her room to see how she was, she was gone. She hadn't left a note, and her best dress and hat weren't in the closet. Fighting panic, Iva Claire woke Tassie, who yanked on some clothes and raced downstairs with her. The barber who ran the shave parlor in the hotel lobby said he'd seen Mama walk out about an hour earlier.

"We all heard how sick she was, so I was glad to see she was better," the barber said. "Ain't it a miracle what doctors can do these days?"

But no one in the lobby, or the newsstand, or the hotel restaurant had seen which way Mama was going.

I should have slept in her room last night, Iva Claire thought wildly. *I knew she was upset. I shouldn't have left her alone.*

"It'll be better if we split up and look for her," Tassie said.

They went in opposite directions, Tassie headed for the railroad on the edge of Washtabula. Iva Claire raced to the center of town and the Egyptian Theater.

Mama wasn't at the theater, but the boy behind the soda fountain at the pharmacy had served a small woman wearing a hat with a big pink rose on it. She'd bought a newspaper and taken an order of ham and eggs with her in a paper bag. But she'd left awhile ago.

Iva Claire ran back to the hotel. The lobby was empty now. The barber who had been so helpful hadn't seen Mama come back in, but then he'd been busy with customers. The desk clerk hadn't seen her either, but he took one look at Iva Claire's face and went into the restaurant to get one of the waitresses.

"Millie, keep an eye on my desk, will you?" he asked. He locked up the cash register and turned to Iva Claire. "I'll go up to your room with you," he said. They climbed the stairs together.

Please let her be in the room, Iva Claire prayed. *Please let her be mad at me for making such a fuss.* But she knew better.

Mama had made it up all four flights and into the hallway before she collapsed. Her face was white and twisted with pain; her breath was coming hard. She was holding her purse against her chest. Next to her on the stairs were a newspaper and the ham and eggs that had spilled out of the bag when she fell. Iva Claire grabbed the purse and began searching through it.

"Forgot my medicine," Mama rasped. "Sorry, Claire de Lune. . . .

Iva Claire found her mother's room key and threw it to the clerk. "Her pills are on the table next to her bed," she said, in a voice she didn't recognize. She was aware of the man rushing to the apartment door, opening it, and going inside. It seemed to take hours.

"Wanted to . . . have . . . something that tasted good," Mama said. "You give me slop. . . ."

"Mama, don't talk."

"Read in the newspaper . . . Bob Hope has a new show. . . ." The pain had to be bad, but Mama was trying to smile. Her eyes were big with fear. Where the hell was the desk clerk?

"Mama, if I help you, can you walk to your bed? It's only a few feet."

"I have the pills." The clerk was back and shoving the bottle into her hand.

The pills worked their magic. Some of the color came back into Mama's face, and the grimace of pain relaxed.

Thank you, God. Thank you, thank you.

Between them, Iva Claire and the clerk

half carried Mama into the room. While he went to get the doctor, Iva Claire settled Mama into her bed.

"Lie back, Mama."

But Mama wanted to talk. "Bob Hope has a new show . . . on Broadway. A vaudevillian on Broadway. He went legit."

"Please lie back, Mama."

"We worked with him. Remember?"

They'd played the same theater in Cincinnati, but he'd been there the week before them.

"Yes, Mama, I remember."

Her mother lay back in her bed and closed her eyes. Iva Claire took her mother's hand and kissed it. "I love you, Mama," she said. "I don't know what I'd do without you."

Mama didn't open her eyes, and for a moment Iva Claire thought she'd fallen asleep. But then she murmured, "Bob Hope and the Sunshine Sisters. We're good . . . aren't we, Claire de Lune?"

"Yes, Mama. We're the best." She held her mother's hand hard. Mama was breathing easily now, more lightly than she had since Iva Claire found her.

I'll have to go clean up that mess in the

hall, Iva Claire thought. Then the little hand in hers went limp. In the tiniest fraction of a second, the breathing stopped. And the whole world froze.

Chapter Forty-three

She wanted to put an in-memoriam ad in *Variety* for Mama, but they couldn't afford it. She wanted to take Mama home to New York so she could be buried in the place she loved, but they couldn't afford that either. There was no money for pink roses for Mama's funeral, no friends to sing "Beautiful Dreamer" for her.

I could have done it right if he'd sent the check. Damn him!

The town of Washtabula was generous to strangers, particularly to two young girls who were all alone. The funeral home buried

Mama for free, but her grave was in the pauper's field. Iva Claire knew she would never go back there.

After the brief service, Dr. Wilbur handed Iva Claire two train tickets to New York.

"I'm on the township board and we authorized this last night," he said.

She wanted to say they didn't need charity; she wanted with all her heart to give the tickets back.

"Don't be an idiot," Dr. Wilbur said softly. "Keep them."

"Thank you," she managed to say, through the pain and humiliation. She thought of her father. *Damn him*.

Tassie and Iva Claire didn't own much in the way of personal belongings, and now they wouldn't be needing the Sunshine Sisters' music, costumes, and publicity stills; everything they had left fit into two suitcases. They finished packing for themselves, then they turned to Mama's room. Iva Claire went in first, and collected all of Mama's street clothes out of the closet. She would have liked to have given them away to someone whose face she could see, like one of the hotel maids, but Tassie had found a junk dealer who bought secondhand clothing and they needed the money. Iva Claire piled the garments on top of the theatrical trunk, which was going to be sold too. They'd already emptied it, and sheet music, costumes, and pictures were heaped on the bed. Tassie pulled out a picture of herself and laid it aside. Iva Claire picked up the first page of the sheet music for "Beautiful Dreamer" and did the same. Then they threw out the rest of the pictures and music, and Tassie added the costumes to the pile for the junk dealer. At the last second, Iva Claire grabbed her costume and crammed it with the sheet music into her suitcase with the swirling *B* monogram on the side.

Mama's room was empty now.

"Don't look," Tassie said. "Just keep going."

Iva Claire nodded, and they each picked up a bundle of clothes. When they were coming back from the junk dealer, the desk clerk called out, "Miss Rain, this came for you." He was holding an oversized envelope with the familiar return address on it. Tassie was the one who finally reached out to take it. Iva Claire didn't touch it until they

were upstairs in their rooms. She sat on
Mama's bed to read it.

Her father had received both of her letters. He had opened them, read them, and
torn them up, and sent back the scraps so
she would know. There was no check. And
he hadn't written one word to say why he'd
done it.

"I'm going to see him," Iva Claire said.

"Honey, let it go," Tassie said.

"I'm going to find him."

"Why?"

She didn't know. "I'm going to his house,
in the town where he lives. The son of a
bitch wouldn't let me go there the last time,
but he can't stop me now."

"It won't do any good, Iva Claire. It's too
late," Tassie pleaded. "We have other things
to think about."

"It won't take me long. You can go back
to New York, and—"

"I'm going with you," Tassie cut in.

It took Iva Claire a moment. "No, Tassie."

"If you're serious about this, I'm not letting you go alone."

"You can't."

"You and Lily gave me my chance to be in

the business. You took care of me, even when we weren't making a dime. You're my family. If you want to do this, I'm going with you."

They cashed in their tickets for New York. Instead of going home, Iva Claire and Tassie boarded a train and headed for Beneville, Georgia.

Chapter Forty-four

MRS. RAIN

2004

Thoughts about heart attacks and memories of the summer of 1933 were coming back to haunt her all the time. She couldn't shake them. Cherry knew something was bothering her and tried to help.

"Why don't you tell me some more of your stories, Mrs. Rain," she suggested. "You know that always makes you happy. And I like hearing them."

But the story that was haunting her was the one she wanted to tell Laurel McCready. She was starting to think she should write it all down now, while her mind was still intact. She could send it to Laurel as a letter. The idea appealed to her. A missive that would tell all her secrets. A dangerous missive. Or would it be? That was the question she kept coming back to: How risky would it be after all this time? And would it really help Ms. McCready to know the secrets? She'd been going back and forth over that in her mind for days. It was one thing to daydream about pouring out her soul; it was quite another to actually find out where Laurel lived and write her a letter laying out the terrible truth. She wasn't sure she could do it. She hated not being sure. Sometimes she thought she'd never been sure of one damn thing in her life—she looked around the hated sunporch—except how much she wanted to get out of this room.

"Cherry, when am I going to start using my own bedroom again?" she demanded.

The girl looked uncomfortable. "Mrs. Rain, you know what the doctor said."

Cherry meant the genius specialist, not the infant physician, and what the genius had said was, "I'm afraid we can't be running up and down stairs just yet. Not until we get this pesky little hitch in our git-along under control." It seemed he was famous for his bedside manner with the elderly.

"The doctor is a jackass."

"Yes, ma'am," said Cherry, "but he's the doctor. And until he says you can move—"

"All right, all right," she snapped.

It was unfair to take out all her frustrations on poor Cherry when she was really angry at herself for being so indecisive. From what she'd been able to piece together, Laurel McCready was young and inexperienced, with no family to support her. The girl must be trying to cope with the overwhelming legacy Peggy Garrison had left her. Picture her reaction if she got a letter telling her the truth about that legacy. Would it help her? Did she need help? Mrs. Rain sighed; she had to have something more to go on than the nagging voice in her head that said things were going badly for Laurel Mc-Cready.

"Cherry, run over to the post office and see if the *Charles Valley Gazette* has come this week," she said. But instead of leaving the room, Cherry was staring at her as if she'd lost her mind. "What is it?" she demanded impatiently. "Why are you looking like that?"

"Don't you remember?" Cherry said gently. "The last issue said they were going out of business. We won't be getting the *Gazette* anymore."

It had slipped her mind, that was all. There was no need for young Cherry to look at her like she was in the early stages of gaga-dom. She simply hadn't wanted to remember that the *Gazette* was gone. She'd hoped to keep track of Laurel Selene through the little newspaper. At some point they'd write an article about the new Garrison heir. And by reading between the lines, she'd know if Laurel Selene was all right. And then she'd know what to do.

"Of course I remember," she said firmly to Cherry. But her voice just sounded tired and querulous. "Go away, Cherry dear. I want to rest," she said.

"That's a good idea," said the youngster, obviously relieved. "Shall I pull down the blinds for you?"

She nodded, but it didn't matter. Because she was going to close her eyes. And as soon as she did that, she'd be in her daydream again. She'd be sitting in front of Myrtis's big log house in Charles Valley, and she'd be telling Laurel Selene the story—all of it—about the young girl who had hidden away her past in a water-stained suitcase with a swirling *B* on the side.

Chapter Forty-five

LAUREL

2004

Laurel tossed the old leather suitcase on the passenger seat of her car and took off for Li'l Bit's, where she knew she'd find Maggie and Li'l Bit together on the porch. It was Saturday afternoon, and she'd made a decision. It was time to let the Myrtis Garrison experts have a crack at the mystery. It was strange how her attitude about the great Miss Myrtis had shifted. At first she hadn't wanted to talk about the woman. Now she had a spooky feeling that there was a story attached to the suitcase and its contents that she needed to hear.

Part of the feeling came from the fact that

she was still crammed into her tiny cabin with eleven dogs because she couldn't make herself move into the log palace she had inherited. The power-of-attorney form still sat in her drawer under her underpants because Sheralynn's cousin hadn't yet produced the resort's financial records. Meanwhile, for the last three days Stuart Junior had been leaving increasingly hostile messages on the answering machine she'd installed so she could dodge his phone calls.

She drove up Li'l Bit's driveway faster than usual, hoping she wasn't spraying gravel on Li'l Bit's carefully tended front yard. She was eager to get on with her proposed show-and-tell. She pulled up next to the brick path leading to the front porch, but before she could take the suitcase out, Maggie and Li'l Bit waved and Li'l Bit called out, "Laurel, there's someone I want you to meet."

Then she noticed the vehicle parked directly ahead of her. It had a squashed-in back, a snub-nosed front, and it looked like a car Daffy Duck would drive in the old-time cartoons. It was one of the virtuous new hybrids, which operated on a combination of gas and electricity. She turned to the porch and saw who had to be the owner of the cartoon car, a young woman her age, sitting in Peggy's chair. An attack of kindergarten-level jealousy hit. Li'l Bit's place was her turf, and the sacred afternoon hours on this porch were her special domain. Who was this intruder? She shoved the suitcase down on the floor of her car, got out, and slunk across the front lawn, trying not to pout too visibly.

Li'l Bit handed her a beer. "This is Gloria," she said, as the young woman pulled herself out of the wicker chair.

Gloria was almost as tall as Li'l Bit, but a lot skinnier. She wore neat dark shorts, a dark shirt, and a pair of clunky sandals that Laurel assumed were as comfortable as they were ugly. There was something vaguely familiar about her face.

"I'm Gloria Lawrence." The young woman amended Li'l Bit's introduction, sticking out her hand. Then she exploded in her mother's unmistakable cackle. "I'm afraid you already know my daddy."

Laurel realized she was shaking the hand of My Child.

"Gloria has decided to leave her job in New York—" Li'l Bit began.

"I got fired," Gloria interrupted. "I suggested doing a story on the downside of Botox, and the former model now hosting my show objected on the grounds that it was 'so totally a bummer.' Plus she couldn't say all the big words in the script."

"So now Gloria is here in Charles Valley," Li'l Bit went on, obviously uncomfortable about something.

Maggie was examining her nails, which meant she was uncomfortable too. "Gloria has come to interview us," she murmured.

"She's going to do a story about Peggy," Li'l Bit fluted nervously.

"For the *Charles Valley Gazette*," Maggie added. "I'm sure you know Hank isn't going to be continuing with the newspaper."

Everyone in town knew it.

But what the hell did that have to do with the smiling Gloria? And why were Li'l Bit and Maggie shooting her such worried looks?

"Gloria bought the *Gazette*, Laurel, dear," said Maggie, ending the mystery.

My Child had bought the newspaper? Laurel's *Charles Valley Gazette*? Gloria was sitting again. She sipped something from a can. She'd not only co-opted Peggy's chair and Laurel's newspaper, she was drinking one of Laurel's beers!

"We wanted you to hear the news from us," Li'l Bit put in.

"Gloria just told us," Maggie added.

"There wasn't time to call you—" Li'l Bit said.

"Not that there was any need," Maggie cut in quickly.

They were making a mess of this and they both knew it, but they were too concerned about her to be graceful, which was so sweet it almost took away the sting. Laurel had to bail them out. "Congratulations," she said to Gloria. "The *Gazette*'s been around for eighty years, and people will be real grateful to you for keeping it from going under."

"Actually, it's my mother they should be thanking. She put up the money. I'm going to be the editor, but she owns it."

So it was a family effort. Daddy would probably vet all the stories about Garrison Gardens and the resort.

As if reading her mind, Gloria said, "My

mother has her own money. My father had nothing to do with this." Laurel smiled as if she believed that horseshit. Gloria turned to Li'l Bit. "I'll come back and do the interview later," she said.

"Please, don't let me stop you," Laurel said, telling herself she should offer to go but knowing there was no way she was leaving. After the briefest of pauses, Gloria whipped out a tape recorder and began asking Li'l Bit and Maggie questions.

The interview seemed to go on forever, but maybe that was because Laurel was working on her not-pouting-and-being-a-good-sport technique, and it was going down hard. Finally, Gloria turned off the recorder.

"It's such a pleasure to talk about Peggy," Maggie said. "What a lovely idea—writing an article about her in the newspaper, Gloria."

"You ask excellent questions," Li'l Bit added.

"The dogs will be starving. I've got to run," said Laurel. "Nice meeting you, Gloria."

"I should go too," said Gloria.

Which was how Laurel found herself walking down to their cars together.

"So just how emotionally invested were you in the *Gazette*?" Gloria asked.

"Emotionally invested in working for Hank?"

Gloria did one of her mother's cackling laughs. "I meant, how much do you miss the newspaper?"

"I like writing, but I've been thinking lately that it wasn't really what I wanted to do or I'd have done it—" She broke off. Why was she spilling this to the woman who had just drunk two of her beers? "My job at the *Gazette* kept me from being a waitress," she said briskly. "Working there was a bitch."

"According to what I heard, Miss Peggy offered to buy it for you."

So Gloria really did do her homework. Laurel shrugged. "Running things isn't a big strength of mine."

"Isn't that going to be a little rough? Given your new . . . situation?"

"Not according to your daddy. I don't have to bother my purty little head about any of it."

"My father gives new meaning to the

word *retro*. So you're cool with me being editor of the *Gazette*?"

The woman didn't let up. "Of course."

"Good. Then can I interview you too?"

"Why?"

"You're the new Garrison. A story on you will be a nice companion piece for the profile on Miss Peggy."

"I'm—" Laurel stopped. "Look, I still haven't wrapped my brain around all of this."

"I understand. It'd be freaking me out, too, if I were in your place." Laurel decided Gloria must be one of those people who regularly put themselves in other people's places. "If you decide to do it," Gloria continued, "there's an article I found in the archives that you wrote. I'd like to use some of it. It's very good."

"Thanks. Can we talk about it later?"

"I'll call you in a couple of days. I want to get my first edition out next week. From what I can see, delivery of the paper's been erratic lately, and I don't want to lose the six or seven readers I still have."

Obviously, Stuart Junior's daughter wasn't going to have any trouble running things.

"Nice car," Laurel said, as they approached the Daffy Duck-mobile.

Gloria looked at it vaguely. "Is it? I'm not into cars. The dealer said it was earth-friendly."

Chapter Forty-six

"She said it out loud!" Laurel told Perry that evening. One of his patients from the clinic had made fresh strawberry ice cream for him, and he'd brought it over in a cooler to share since it was too much for him to eat alone. That was his excuse for getting together. "Gloria Lawrence actually said her car was *earth-friendly*," Laurel said. "Without laughing."

"So you don't like her because she doesn't have your automotive flair, or because she's running the *Gazette*?"

"Who says I don't like her?"

"Come on."

"I worked at that paper for eight years! I watered the plants, and took Hank's mama to the dentist, and covered every single one of the damn library Christmas craft shows. And now Gloria Lawrence waltzes in from nowhere and her mother writes a check and she's the new editor!"

"And Peggy could have written a check and you would have been the editor, but you turned her down."

"That's beside the point. Doesn't it bother people that this woman has a conflict of interest?"

"How?"

"Three-quarters of the articles in the *Gazette* are about the Garrisons—the family or the business."

"And in the past those articles were written by that model of journalistic integrity, Hank Barlow."

"At least he wasn't directly connected to the empire. Is the entire town going to pretend they don't know what Gloria's daddy does for a living?"

"The way I've heard it, her daddy isn't so happy about his baby girl's new profession. She won't be sucking up to the Garrison shrine."

"Who told you that?"

"Gloria."

"You know her?"

"We've met."

"How?"

"I get around."

He did. It was unnerving how many people seemed to consider him a close personal friend. Not that she was keeping track. "Gloria wears ugly shoes," Laurel said. "And while she's wearing them, she talks about emotional investments."

"And she doesn't eat meat. Fortunately, Chrissie doesn't seem to mind."

"Who is Chrissie?"

"Her partner."

"Gloria told you all of this already? I didn't even know she'd come to town."

"I'm friendly. I like people."

"Unlike me?"

"Change of subject." He paused to scoop a second helping of ice cream into his bowl. "So, how's it going with you and Gloria's father?" he asked.

"It's in the works," she said vaguely. She'd been hoping she'd have more to report to him by now.

"What about the books? Do you need

someone to go over them with you? You probably should hire an accountant to help you."

She took a deep breath. "I haven't seen the books," she admitted.

"They haven't given them to you yet?" he said indignantly. "Honey, if Lawrence is stonewalling you—"

"I didn't ask him." She told him about Sheralynn's cousin.

"You're stealing your own financial records?" he asked sharply. It had occurred to her that he might disapprove of the Hail Mary pass she was trying to do around Stuart, but she wasn't prepared for his tone of voice.

"I'm going to catch him off guard," she said crisply, to end the discussion. "Can I have more ice cream?"

She should have known crispness wasn't going to do it. "You were afraid to ask Lawrence for the records, weren't you?"

"This seemed easier."

"Bull. You were afraid you were going to piss him off."

"All right! I'm scared. I've never pretended I wasn't."

"Well, get over it."

"It's not that easy for me."

"It's not that easy for anyone!" The dogs, hearing the edge in his voice, were trying to find cover behind or under the furniture. "Of course you're scared. You're a smart person, being scared is a fact of your life. But you don't give in to it."

She couldn't believe he was going at her like this. "I am not giving in, damn it!"

"Stuart Lawrence isn't going to respect you until you force him to. You *own* those financial statements. You have a right to see them."

He was right, and somewhere in the back of her brain she knew it. "Maybe I don't want to see them. Maybe I don't want any of this crap!"

"Laurel—"

"Maybe I don't want to be respected. Maybe I shouldn't be! Hell, I wouldn't respect me if I were Stuart Junior!"

He was watching her and shaking his head. She wasn't his fantasy woman now, that was for sure. "When are you going to stop buying what they're selling?" he asked softly.

"Buying what?"

"All your life, the *nice* people said you were trash and you believed them."

"That's not what—"

"It's exactly what this is about. The sad thing is, you've always been worth ten times more than the *nice* people. You had the mother from hell, but you got yourself to school every day. A perfect attendance record, and straight A's right up to your senior year. You read Faulkner for fun, for Christ's sake; you turned me on to *The Great Gatsby*—"

He was bringing up things she didn't need to think about. "And it's been downhill for me ever since. Maybe the apple doesn't fall that far from the tree. Ever think of that?"

"You're not Sara Jayne!"

"Go ask them about that at your daddy's bar. Or better yet, I'll give you a list of names to call." That would get him. He'd walk out now. Except he didn't.

"You want to match lists, honey? I'll give you mine. Anyone your age—or mine—who doesn't have one doesn't have a pulse."

"Says the perfect son. The doctor from frigging Harvard."

"Get something straight. I'm not afraid of your big bad past. I don't feel sorry for you because you had a bad time. And I'm not going to be your goddam babysitter like Denny. If you want to fight Lawrence, I've got your back. If you want to take the money and run, that's fine too. But I will not watch you fuck up so you can keep on feeling rotten about yourself."

"You won't watch me do anything. Because you're going to get the hell out of my house, and you're going to butt out of my life!"

That was when he left.

After he was gone, her house seemed way too quiet. The red light on her answering machine was blinking. She pushed the button and Stuart Junior's voice—surprise, surprise—came at her.

"Laurel, I don't want to pressure you," he lied. "You've had several days to get that power of attorney to me. We're facing many challenges at the resort and the gardens, and we need to be able to make decisions." There was a pause. "I wouldn't say this if I didn't feel I must make you understand the gravity of the situation, but"—pause for dramatic effect—"there's never been a will that couldn't be overturned. Laurel, I'm speaking now as a lawyer and—" Laurel erased the rest and headed for her bedroom. For the first time in months she knew exactly what she wanted to do.

It was ten-thirty on Saturday night. The drinking crowd at the Sportsman's Grill would just be getting started. It took her five minutes to pull on her tightest tank top, ram her feet into her red cowboy boots, and wriggle into her snuggest jeans. "The girl is back!" she told the dogs. "Don't wait up!"

The Viper roared happily down the deserted highway while Patsy Cline sang "Crazy" from the CD player. Laurel Selene Mc-Cready was gonna party. She was gonna dance and sing and get shit-faced. Because she was celebrating. Stuart Junior had given her a way out.

"I'm quitting," she sang, putting her words to Patsy's music. "I'm dumping the whole mess and splitting."

She was going to tell Just Call Me Stuart to overturn the damn will. Let him take the log palazzo, the money, the financial statements, and even her beloved car if she could just stop being worried all the time. She'd never owned stuff before and she wasn't going to miss it now. And she really wasn't going to miss being responsible for the livelihood and well-being of three thousand people.

"And Perry can go to hell," she sang.

Whatever crowd now hung out in the Sportsman's Grill was there in force. The parking lot was jammed, mostly with pickups, souped-up racetrack wannabes, and motorcycles. The Viper slid into a spot right down front, the best auto in the place, doing her proud.

She got out of the car and gave herself the little tug that always made her tank top settle just a bit lower in her cleavage and turned to lock the car. Then she saw the suitcase. It was on the floor of the car in front of the passenger's seat, right where she'd left it.

And she knew she wasn't going to be dumping a goddam thing—not the house or the resort or the decision about signing the power of attorney. It was too late for that. Because at some point while she'd been hanging out with the three Miss Margarets and helping Peggy and talking to Perry, she'd changed. It wouldn't solve a thing for her to walk away now, because she knew people were going to be hurt. And it was her responsibility to make it better if she could. And if she didn't try, she'd be no better than the people she'd hated all her life.

"Fuck," she said. And she got into the Viper and went home.

Chapter Forty-seven

Monday morning, Laurel got up early and drove to the imposing gate that protected the residents of Fairway Estates from the rest of the world. She figured catching Stuart at home would be less intimidating than seeing him in his bare little office at the resort. Besides, she wanted him to know she was up early and ready to take care of business. Unfortunately, she'd forgotten there were guards at the gate.

"My name is Laurel Selene McCready," she said, trying to be impressive. "Mr. Lawrence will want to see me."

It was Lindy Lee who actually okayed her to the guard.

"Stuart's gone to work," she said, as she led Laurel into the dining room. She was dressed, made up, jeweled, and coiffed, although still barefoot. Laurel wondered if it was a fashion statement or if her feet hurt.

"Have some coffee with me," Lindy Lee said.

"I should go. I need to talk to Stuart—"

"And he needs to talk to you. You're driving the poor darling tee-totally mad, you know."

"I'm sorry."

"I'm not." She looked at Laurel and laughed. "Bless you, don't look so bewildered. And if you won't drink my coffee, at least sit down and talk to me. I believe you'll find it interesting."

Laurel sat.

"Before I start, are you planning to do that interview for the *Gazette*?"

"That's right. You're the owner now."

"And a more silent partner you'll never meet. But I know Gloria wants to ask you about some things that are going on at the gardens, or maybe it's the resort, or both. I make it a point not to know about that kind of thing myself."

It was probably how she managed to stay married.

"Has Gloria asked her father about what's going on?"

There was a sad little cackle. "He wouldn't tell her if she did. My Child and my husband do not have a copacetic relationship. He's never approved of her politics or her—uh, friends. Stuart can be . . ." She trailed off, then started again. "Stuart is a good man—well, he could be. But he's spent his whole life covering up for the old bastard." She smiled. "That would be my late unlamented father-in-law."

"Mr. Lawrence Senior?" Laurel tried not to sound surprised. Had anyone besides his son liked the man?

"He was a rotten lawyer, as well as being a world-class bully," said Lindy Lee. "I never knew old Mr. Dalt, but do you really think he meant for poor little Peggy to have control of his beloved resort and gardens after he died? You know as well as I do how people like the Garrisons work. Ask yourself: Would *you* have been his pick to carry on the glorious family legacy?"

"It doesn't matter what he would have wanted. I'm here."

"My point exactly. Stuart's illustrious daddy drew up a will so full of loopholes it looked like bad crochet work. And when my poor husband tells you he can overturn Peggy's will, he's whistling in the dark. Thanks to his father, only a blood relative of Peggy's could challenge that thing. And Peggy didn't have any family." She sipped her coffee. "I overheard my husband leaving his message on your answering machine last night."

"And you're letting me in on this be- cause . . . ?"

"I'm tired of watching Stuart turn into his daddy. To know the old man was to despise him."

"He must have done something right. Peggy trusted him."

"Peggy hated his guts. And from some- thing she told me once, I gather Miss Myrtis loathed him too."

"But Myrtis brought him here."

"She did, but she must have had second thoughts. But by then it was too late. He had no gift for the law, but he was a great manipulator, and I gather old Mr. Dalt was putty in his evil hands." She shook her head, "With that man for a role model, it's no wonder my Stuart is so awful. Try not to hold it against him, will you?"

She actually seemed to want a response. "Uh, sure," Laurel managed. Then, before the conversation got any weirder, she stood up. "Thanks for the talk, but I probably should be going."

Lindy Lee got to her feet and saw her to the door. "Just remember, Laurel, you hold all the cards," she said. "Now go see my husband."

When she was back in her car, Laurel took out the cell phone she'd gotten when Peggy was sick but never bothered to turn on. She dialed the number she used to know as well as her own and waited for an automated voice to tell her to leave a message after the beep. Instead, a living person answered.

"This is the *Charles Valley Gazette*, Gloria Lawrence speaking."

One thing you had to say for the Lawrences, they believed in getting an early start on the day.

"Gloria, I've decided I'd like to do the interview," Laurel said.

"Great," Gloria said flatly. Obviously her mother was the exuberant one in the family. "When can you do it?"

"Could you give me a couple of days? I'm clueless about the way things work at the gardens and the resort, and I'd like to have some idea of what I'm talking about."

"Excuse me, but are you expecting my father to educate you?"

"Not exactly. But I *am* going to take a look at the books."

"He's turning them over to you?"

"I'm going to ask him for them today."

"I'd love to hear that. So, I'll call you—when?"

"Let's say Wednesday?"

"Perfect. Gives me just time to write the story before I put the paper to bed. Can I use that article you wrote?"

"Sure."

"And Laurel? After you pry those books out of my father's cold dead hands, if you want help breaking down the math into something the human mind can grasp, my partner Chrissie is an accountant. She can translate most of the legalspeak for you too. I'll ask her to give you a hand, if you'd like."

Turning her down because she was a

beer thief with a bad taste in footwear would be childish. "Thanks. I was going to ask around. I figured no one local would want to go up against the resort and the gardens."

There was a pause. Then Gloria said, "You *are* the resort and the gardens. You do realize that, right?"

"I'm working on it."

Chapter Forty-eight

She'd been right about Stuart Junior. When she showed up in his office asking for the books, there had been a little vein throbbing in his left temple that said how badly he wanted to throw her out on her unworthy redneck ass. But she'd walked in like she owned the place—which come to think of it, she did—and he hadn't given her a fight. He even said he was sorry for the crack about overturning the will, which was definitely the first time in her life someone who sounded and looked like Stuart Junior had apologized to her. An added bonus was the feeling of pride when she called Sheralynn to say Jessie didn't have to sneak the books to her after all. Then Chrissie had given her a crash course in corporate bullshit that was so infuriating she couldn't sit still when she reported it all to Li'l Bit and Maggie on the porch the following afternoon.

"The CEO, Peter Terranova, the vice presidents of This and the directors of That—there's about a hundred of them," she ranted, as she paced back and forth on Li'l Bit's porch, "you better believe *they* aren't worrying about paying for a hospital visit! The damn suits protect their own. Know how they do it?"

"No, Doodlebug," said Maggie, "but maybe if you sat down—"

"They can't cancel the coverage for everybody, because the Feds would come down on them. They get a tax advantage if they offer everyone health insurance." Two days ago she wouldn't have known how to use the term *tax advantage* in a sentence. In spite of her anger she was impressed with herself. "But they can ask the workers to pay an enormous percentage of their premiums. As long as everyone is paying the same percent, it's legal. Of course, they jack up their own salaries to cover the cost of their own premiums. Everyone else takes the full hit. People like Grace Marshall's mama drop their health insurance because it's gotten too expensive. Which is what Stuart and his friends wanted all along! Plus at the gardens, they're planning to lay off a thousand full-time employees—"

"My God!" said Li'l Bit.

"They can't run the gardens without a staff." Maggie said.

"They replace full-time employees with part-time employees. If you work less than forty hours a week, you're not entitled to any benefits *at all*."

There was a long silence on the porch as her two old friends took this in.

"Human beings never change," Maggie said at last.

"Remember the old days. It's better than it was," said Li'l Bit. But she sounded weary.

"It's more subtle. But more insidious." Maggie grumbled.

"I haven't told you the worst stuff," Laurel said. "The big boys all get bonuses—and we're talking in the millions—but the freebies are worse."

"Freebies?" Maggie asked.

Laurel nodded grimly. "Chrissie calls

them 'executive perks'." She ticked them off as she continued to pace. "Three times last year, Pete Terranova's wife hopped on the Garrison jet to go to Los Angeles. It costs six thousand bucks a trip. All the top execs have their kids in private schools, and a Garrison scholarship fund picks up the bill. The execs get special rates on their home mortgages, financed by guess who? Their SUVs are company vehicles, so they don't so much as pay for the goddam gas. Everything at the resort is free for them—the golf courses, the spa, the swimming club, the tennis courts, the restaurants—and they get huge discounts at all the shops. And if they need to get away from the stress of robbing everyone blind, they can go hang out in an apartment in Atlanta, which costs twenty thousand dollars a year, or a 'bunga-low' the size of a supermarket next door to the movie stars in Aspen."

And that was just the big stuff. The vice president in charge of food and beverages had charged hot-rock massages for his secretary, who—if the employee brochure was anything to go by—was considerably younger and blonder than his wife. The di-rector of marketing had been reimbursed for the mouthwash he used, on the grounds that it was a professional expense.

"When Chrissie showed me all of it, I was . . . it was just amazing," Laurel wound up. Which didn't begin to express how shocked she'd been. Like all Charles Valley locals, she'd always assumed the boys who ran the resort and the gardens were helping themselves to extras on the side, and as long as they kept the place functioning and providing jobs, no one thought about calling them on their petty larceny. But what she'd seen was grand theft.

"This Terranova guy came to Charles Valley five years ago from Los Angeles. He was working for some big hotel chain. He brought in a whole bunch of people from outside to run the gardens and the resort. And Stuart Lawrence has been giving them a free ride."

"What are you going to do, Laurel?" Li'l Bit cut to the chase.

"Have another talk with Stuart. I may not have a diploma from a big-deal business school, but even I know you can't steal everything that isn't nailed down and then say you're bankrupt."

"Yes," Li'l Bit said carefully. "Obviously, you have to talk to Stuart."

"I've got all the facts this time. I made Chrissie walk me through the numbers until I could recite them in my sleep. And we worked out a budget that'll keep the premium costs where they are for right now. Long-term we'll have to make other plans, but this will be a start." Maggie and Li'l Bit exchanged one of their looks. "What do you think? I really want to know." She sat down on the porch between them.

"I assume your budget doesn't include bonuses and executive perks?" said Li'l Bit.

"Everyone will have to make some sacrifices."

Li'l Bit leaned over to hand her her untouched beer. "I'd be very strong when I talked to Stuart," she said.

Maggie brushed a wisp of hair out of Laurel's eyes. "But I wouldn't use the word *freebie*, Doodlebug," she said.

When she got home, Laurel called Stuart Junior and asked politely if she could come to his office in the morning. She thanked him when he said yes. Then she went into her bedroom and got the power-of-attorney form out of her drawer and, in front of the admiring dogs, lit a match and burned the damned thing.

That evening after supper, she drove to the small house Perry was renting. He'd heard the Viper roaring up his driveway and was in the front yard waiting for her.

"Sometimes I can be an asshole," she said.

"Yes."

"I forget who my friends are."

"Yes. Want to come inside?"

"I can't. I have a big day tomorrow."

"You came over here just to say you're an asshole?"

"That's it." She turned to get into her car, but he came down off the steps and stopped her. Which pleased her a lot more than it should have.

"I'd have your back even if you did fuck up," he said.

"That might not be the smartest thing you've ever said."

"I'll take my chances."

It took her a moment. "I was going to go to the Sportsman's Grill Saturday night. I figured I'd get into as much trouble as I could and forget the whole mess. I didn't."

"I know."

"How?"

"I followed you. Just in case." And before she could say anything more he put an arm around her and started walking her to her car. "Now go home and get some sleep. You have a big day tomorrow." He helped her into the Viper and stood in the driveway smiling as she drove off.

Chapter Forty-nine

Junior's secretary hadn't been on the scene the first time Laurel had gone to see him, but this morning she was waiting.

"Stuart would like you to meet him in the conference room at the end of the hall," she said, with a friendly smile. "That's three doors down on your right."

Later, Laurel would realize that the words *conference room* should have put her on guard, but she felt so confident it never dawned on her. She found the right door and breezed in.

At first it seemed like there were fifty men sitting around the long table staring at her.

Then she realized there were only eight of them. Stuart, who was seated at the head of the table, got up to do the honors.

"Laurel," he said, "I'd like you to meet our team." He began rattling off names and labels like Director of Special Events and Vice President of Sales. In her shattered state, only "Peter Terranova, CEO of Garrison Gardens" actually stuck. Stuart finished his laundry list of Garrison big guns, gave her a moment to let it sink in, and then said with a chilly little chuckle, "That's the entire cast of characters, and don't worry, there won't be a quiz." There was a collective—and equally chilly—chuckle from the boys at the table.

Junior, the son of a bitch, had ambushed her.

The faces staring at her were well groomed and doubt free, because the men who owned them knew they were entitled to run the world. Faces like these had been scaring the hell out of her all her life. She'd been prepared to deal with one of them, but eight was another matter. She gulped. "Stuart, I thought we'd be talking alone."

"I felt this would be more efficient. If you

have questions for any of our executives, you can ask them directly."

So now she could ask the food and beverage director about the hot-rock massages to his face.

"Whenever you're ready, Laurel," Stuart prompted with a smirk. The smirk was a mistake. He thought he'd backed her off with his posse. Well, that kind of bullshit might work with Peggy and Miss Myrtis, but Laurel Selene McCready came from people who never backed down from a fight—not even when the entire damn bar was lined up against them.

Her hands were shaking, and her teeth were starting to do their castanet imitation, but she clenched her jaw and said loudly, "I do have some questions. Like how come we're making health insurance so expensive for some people and not for others."

"Every employee at Garrison is offered the same package of benefits," someone began.

"Yeah, but everybody here at this meeting gets a boost in their salary to cover the premiums when they go up." If she'd been expecting guilty, or even shifty, looks, it wasn't happening. They all seemed bored. "You get bonuses too, and a whole lot of free-bies," she added, and then remembered she'd promised Maggie she wouldn't use the word. She wanted to kick herself.

"Laurel, there are a variety of circum-stances—" Stuart began, but a voice cut him off.

"I'd like to hear more about these free-bies," Peter Terranova said. He stood up and strolled to the opposite corner of the table. To address him, she had to speak over the heads of seven hostile execs. Ter-ranova wasn't big—at the most he was five feet eight inches tall—but he gave off a street fighter vibe that was impressive. His neck was thick, and his shoulders were massive. If Laurel had had to guess she would have said he'd been a wrestler at some point in his youth. Or maybe he just overdid it with his trainer at the resort spa. At the moment every fiber of him was bris-tling.

She took a deep breath, reminded herself that facts were facts, and started in.

"There are certain . . . extras," she said, getting the terminology right this time. "There was a trip to the West Coast for your wives at the resort's expense. And a scholarship fund that only gets used for kids whose fathers are already making six figures."

Terranova leaned against the wall behind him. "Go on," he said.

So she did. Heart pounding, she listed every one of the "perks" the boys were heaping on themselves and added up the expense to the resort and the gardens. Terranova was still leaning back; he seemed to be listening. The rest of the room seemed to be listening too, although it was hard to tell with those bland faces. At least they were being quiet. Her mouth was dry and swallowing was hard, but she kept on, launching into the suggestions she and Chrissie had put together for the next fiscal year.

"First, there're the bonuses. They're only supposed to be handed out when business is going well. But you all know it's not. If we get rid of that expense, cut all the free—extras, and I don't take any profits for the rest of the year, we won't have to raise the percentage the employees are paying for health insurance right now. I know that's not going to fix things forever, but it gives us a little time to try to find another way to take care of this mess."

She looked at the silent men sitting around the table. They didn't like what she'd said, but no one was arguing with her. How could they?

Then Pete Terranova straightened up. "When I told my wife I wanted to leave LA and drag her and the kids to Bumfuck, Georgia, she started looking for a divorce lawyer," he said. The line got him loud snickers around the table. He wasn't the only one who had had a rough time selling the family on Charles Valley.

"She was right. I was on my way up the ladder at Benchmark Hospitality; everyone who knew me said I was out of my mind to leave. But I liked the idea of trying to save this old place." He turned to Laurel. "Trust me, coming to this little mom-and-pop operation was not a career move for anyone in this room. God knows, we didn't do it for the money. You can't even offer stock options. That bonus you say I didn't earn? It isn't a tip toward what I could be making."

"I didn't mean—" Laurel began, but he talked right over her.

"The only thing you have to offer me, besides the work I happen to love, is a lifestyle. So, damn straight, I expect the resort to make sure my kids don't go to the shitty public schools, and Lindsey's horse gets boarded at the Garrison stables, and if my wife is getting cabin fever and she wants to fly out to Beverly Hills to see her friends, yes, she goes on the company jet. Because none of that is a freebie. I've earned it." His eyes were hot with anger. "I've worked my balls off for this place. When I came here, it was gurgling down the tubes. You're so fond of checking the books, check out how close this place was to Chapter Eleven."

"I know about—" Laurel started to say.

"It took me three years to put together the team that's sitting at this table. And it took us another two years of beating our brains out to get the resort turned around. We're not totally there yet, but we haven't gone belly up. With a recession, and a war on terror and nobody wanting to leave the house, and gas prices going up and down like a goddam yo-yo, we've kept this place going. We've even managed to grow a little. I worked a minor miracle here, and everyone in the industry knows it. I can exercise my out clause, walk out the door today, and I'll be up to my ass in job offers. So will my entire team."

Stuart tried to break in. "Now, Pete—"

"What I won't do is put up with any more of this crap. If I ever, *ever* have to sit through a meeting like this again, I'm gone. Is that understood? You can run this place yourself, Ms. McCready, since you think it's such a cakewalk."

"I don't," Laurel said. But no one could hear her because Pete Terranova was slamming the door on his way out.

There was silence in the room for a minute, and then one by one the men sitting at the table got up and followed their leader out of the room. Only Stuart Junior stayed behind with her.

"He meant every word he said, and I don't blame him," Stuart said.

If she had to look at him she was going to do something childish like spit in his eye. She walked to the window and looked out at the pretty little garden in front of the building.

"It would be nice if every person were equally valuable, Laurel, but they're not. Not from a business point of view," Stuart said gently. "We give Pete Terranova what he wants because he's worth it. That maid you told me about is replaceable. I'm sorry if that sounds elitist or unfair. My father always used to say, *I never got a job from a poor man.*"

That would be your father the rotten lawyer.

"It took us a year to talk Pete into coming here," Stuart went on. "He's right; he has worked a miracle. Part of our appeal for him is that he's been his own boss. He's not going to take interference, from you or anyone else." He started for the door. "Neither am I. I'm through fighting with you. If you don't want to sign that power of attorney, you'll have to replace me too." At the door he turned. "By the way, next summer, a new theme park will be breaking ground forty-five minutes away from here. They should be ready to compete with you by 2006."

Then he walked out of the office.

Chapter Fifty

When Laurel got home, the spreadsheets and papers she and Chrissie had gone through were still stacked up on her kitchen table. She dumped them in the trash and called Gloria to say she was canceling her interview.

"But the paper goes to press tomorrow night," Gloria said.

"I'm sorry."

"Laurel, today all the employees at the gardens and the resort got notice that their premiums will be going up. It's not a secret anymore. I'm doing an editorial on that story, and as of this moment I'm saying that approximately three thousand workers are going to be shafted. Is that accurate? Are you going to let that happen?"

"I can't stop it. I don't know anything about business. There are people who know what they're doing, and they say this is the way it has to be."

"That's it? You don't even have an opinion about what's going on?"

"My opinion doesn't make any difference."

There was a pause on the other end of the phone. "You're signing my father's damn power-of-attorney form, aren't you? What the hell did they do to you?"

"Gloria, you want to fight with your daddy, do it on your own time, okay? I'm doing what I have to do."

"You really believe that?"

"Yes." And Laurel hung up.

She took the trash out. She fed the dogs. She made herself a lunch she didn't eat.

She sat on her porch swing and told herself she was being responsible. She was going to give in to Pete Terranova and Stuart Junior and their team. Because if they walked out, she'd be up shit creek without a paddle. More important, so would all the

Garrison employees. If the resort and the gardens went *gurgling down the tubes*, they'd take everything with them.

So Pete Terranova's spoiled wife would fly to California to see her friends on a private jet, and people making minimum wage like Grace's mama would get sick without having health insurance. Laurel Selene McCready was going to roll over and play dead. Because she had to. Every now and again, over the years, she had run across the word *heartsick* in a book. Now she knew what it meant.

When she saw Maggie and Li'l Bit, she was determined not to cry.

"Are you sure that's what you want to do?" Li'l Bit asked.

"Why not give yourself some time to think it over, Doodlebug?" said Maggie. "It won't hurt Stuart to wait a little longer for his power of attorney."

"If I'm going to do it, I want to get it over with," she told them. So, of course, they let it drop, even though Maggie looked worried for the rest of the afternoon and Li'l Bit looked thoughtful.

*   *   *

She was going to need a new form to re-place the one she'd burned. Asking Stuart for it was going to be the ultimate defeat. He'd probably have a good idea of what had happened to the first one. But it had to be done, she told herself. First thing in the morning.

But the next morning she slept late and it was almost noon by the time she got herself dressed and ready to go. She told herself she'd wait until after lunch. After lunch, she decided she should call first to see if he was in his office. Then, finally, she faced the fact that she wasn't going to make herself do it at all. Not that day. As Maggie had said, it wouldn't hurt Stuart to wait a little longer. And she'd still have the rest of her life to feel like shit.

She got undressed, put on her bathrobe, and turned on the television. On one chan-nel a chef with a French accent was mold-ing the Brooklyn Bridge out of chocolate. On another, a woman was making lamp shades. She opted for a rerun of a cop show she'd watched when she was a kid.

She stayed in front of the television as the afternoon sun set and it got dark outside. She didn't go over to Li'l Bit's porch. She went to bed telling herself that tomorrow she was going to suck it up and do what had to be done.

But on Friday the first copy of the *Charles Valley Gazette*, now under new management, was delivered to its faithful customers.

Chapter Fifty-one

MRS. RAIN

2004

Cherry came in and paused dramatically, hands behind her back. "Mrs. Rain, guess what?" she demanded.

She couldn't have guessed what if she'd wanted to. She'd fallen asleep sitting up in her wingback chair, and now she was totally disoriented. For a second she couldn't even remember what she was doing in the sunroom.

"Mmmnnn," she murmured, vamping for time. Was it Friday or Saturday?

"The *Charles Valley Gazette* came today. They sent it by overnight mail."

"Give it to me!" she commanded, no

longer caring what day it was. The *Gazette* was back in her life—and so was Laurel Mc-Cready. She took the paper from Cherry and began peering at the tiny print.

"Here," Cherry said eagerly. "Let me read it to you."

She was about to say she'd be damned if she would. But then she looked up and saw affection in the child's face. Somehow, young Cherry had become her champion. She handed over the paper and leaned back into the depths of her chair. "See if Mr. Barlow explains why he changed his mind about shutting down," she said.

"He didn't." Cherry skimmed the front page. "It says here the paper is under new management. The publisher is Mrs. Lindy Lee Lawrence, and the new editor in chief is Gloria Lawrence."

She was upright again. "Lawrence? Their last name is Lawrence?"

"That's what it says."

It could have been a coincidence, of course. Lawrence was a fairly common name. But still, to have it turn up in the same small town? Did the old man's son ever have a child? She should have found some way over the years to know these things.

"Is there anything else about Gloria Lawrence?" she asked.

"Uh-huh. She wrote an article in a part of the paper that says IN OUR OPINION."

"That's the editorial page. Read it."

"Yes, ma'am." Cherry took a breath and began reading Gloria Lawrence's editorial aloud. " 'When I took over the *Gazette*, I found the following column in the archives. It had never been printed. It was written by Laurel Selene McCready, a seven-year employee of this newspaper. This is a quote from Ms. McCready's article:

" '*The time has come to be honest about Garrison Gardens and the Garrison resort. Because they are the main employers in Charles Valley, they have been getting away with abusive treatment of their workers for far too long. We all know about layoffs that hit without warning and employees who have worked overtime without being compensated for it. We know about wages that are the lowest in the state and unsafe working conditions that result in serious injuries. We know about these things, but we don't say anything. We give the gardens and the resort a free pass because they have power. They've become the elephant in our living room. We need to stop ignoring it.' "*

Cherry looked up from the newspaper. "That's the end of the stuff Laurel McCready wrote," she announced.

"Go on with Gloria Lawrence's editorial."

Cherry nodded and began reading again. " 'According to my records, the day after she wrote this column Ms. McCready was fired from this paper. Ironically, the vehement Ms. McCready is now the owner of the resort, and she has the deciding vote on the board of trustees that makes policy for the gardens. And, according to yesterday's announcement, the gardens and the resort are now planning to raise the cost of health insurance premiums for those workers for whom Ms. McCready expressed such concern. When asked to comment, Ms. McCready replied, "I don't know anything about business. There are people who know what they're doing, and they say this is the way it has to be. My opinion doesn't matter." In our opinion, it does matter what Ms. McCready thinks, and she got it right the first time.' " Cherry looked up again. "That's kind of wild," she said. "I guess when you're the owner you change your mind about being the elephant in the living room."

Mrs. Rain knew better. She knew exactly what had happened to change Laurel's mind. "Cherry, stop reading," she said.

"But there's more in this article, Mrs. Rain—"

"I've heard enough. I need a pen and my notepaper. It's upstairs in my bedroom. In my desk, I think. Or it might be in the nightstand. I can't remember, damn it!"

"I'll find it. Don't worry."

"Worry? Child, I'm so relieved I can't stand it!"

Her instincts hadn't been wrong. Laurel Selene McCready was being bullied, in the same way Myrtis and Peggy had been bullied. Laurel needed to know the truth so she could fight off the enemy.

Mrs. Rain picked up the pen Cherry had given her. Then she put it down again. She wanted to tell her tale from the beginning, but she didn't have time for that. She'd have to start with the hard part—the dangerous part. She'd be trusting a total stranger with secrets that had been kept for over seventy years. Her hand hesitated over the pen, then she picked it up.

"Dear Ms. McCready," she wrote. Her handwriting was shaky, but that couldn't be helped. "You don't know me, but I want to tell you a story. It begins in the summer of 1933 when two young girls got on a train for Georgia."

Chapter Fifty-two

IVA CLAIRE

1933

Small towns and farms passed by the train window, but Iva Claire didn't see them. It was the middle of the afternoon, they'd been traveling for two and a half days, and Beneville was the next stop. She hadn't been able to sleep, unlike Tassie, who was snoozing in the seat next to her.

She and Tassie hadn't talked about the future, not that there was much to talk about. The act was finished. When they went back to New York they wouldn't have work or a place to live. They didn't even know how they were going to get to New York. But all that would come later. Iva

Claire couldn't look farther ahead than the train's arrival in Beneville.

After she'd snuck off to Atlanta to meet her father years ago, her mother had finally filled in some of the blanks about his illustrious background. His family had founded Beneville to support the cotton mills they owned. They'd gotten rich off the mills, sold them, and gotten even richer in cotton brokering and banking. They were like royalty in Beneville, Mama said. Her father, whose name was Randall Benedict, was treated like a prince. And now his illegitimate daughter was going to show up and make the prince say he was sorry. She'd finally realized that was what she was traveling all this way to hear. It might not seem like much to anyone else, but she'd just buried her mother in a pauper's grave in a state she was never to see again. He couldn't change that, but, by God, she was going to hear him say he was sorry.

I'm as crazy as Mama after all. If Tassie's smart she'll get away from me and go off on her own.

If he hadn't known Mama was sick, it wouldn't have been so bad. But he'd read the two letters she'd sent from the Normandy Hotel, begging for his help. He'd read them and sent them back to her instead of the money she'd humiliated herself to ask for. He'd sent them back because he wanted to hurt her.

He'll say he's sorry for that. I'll make him say he's sorry.

The train was slowing down. Soon she'd see her father again, and this time it would be different. This time she wasn't a little girl he could throw out of his hotel room. This time she was going to make him admit what he'd done.

She leaned over to wake Tassie up.

The afternoon sun was starting to fade when they got off the train and stood on the Beneville platform. On either side of them, a pretty little town spread out in a neat grid of intersecting streets, with the train tracks running through the middle of it. A sign on the station house said the town had been founded in 1874 by the Benedict family. Her father's family. Not her family.

Beneville was a classic mill town. At its edge ran the river where the mills were located. Closer to the railroad on the right were the cotton warehouses, a hotel, and two long low buildings that looked like some kind of dormitory housing, probably for mill workers. All these structures were made of red brick.

The streets that ran perpendicular to the railroad tracks were narrow and tree lined. On her left, Iva Claire could see a small town square. In the distance, overlooking the center of the town, was a gently sloping hill. Iva Claire could make out a large white house perched on top of it, almost completely hidden by trees. She didn't have to check the address. That had to be her father's home.

"Iva Claire? What do you want to do?" Tassie asked quietly.

"I'm going up there."

"Do you want me to come?"

"I've got to do this alone."

Tassie seemed to understand—or was she a little relieved? "There's no train back to Atlanta until tomorrow morning," she said. "I'll get us a room in that hotel. Give me your suitcase."

Iva Claire handed it to her. "I'm not taking a bus or a taxi. I'll walk," she said. "It'll be easier to hide that way."

"Why do you have to hide?"

She had a brief memory of opening the door to the hotel room in Atlanta and seeing a face that was unmistakably like hers. She didn't want word getting out in this small town that a girl who looked like the prince was walking around.

"I don't want anyone to see me until I've seen him," she said. "I want to surprise him."

"If you don't want anyone to see you, I'll wait for you out on the porch of the hotel. That way you won't have to ask what room I'm in."

Iva Claire nodded, and Tassie started to pick up the suitcases. Then she stopped. "Iva Claire, you know your father's a son of a bitch, don't you? I mean, you're not expecting him to be nice to you."

"Don't worry, I'm not expecting a thing." *Except an apology.*

She began walking toward the big white house on the hill.

Because of all the trees, she hadn't realized how isolated the house was. By the time she finally reached 51 Mill Street, the address she'd memorized so many years before, she hadn't seen another building for at least half a mile. The winding drive leading from the street to the house was shaded by a canopy of oaks. The sun was setting by the time she reached it, and the trees made it even darker and harder to see her surroundings. She could make out flower beds laid out in formal patterns on either side of the canopy and, on her right, ahead of her, a garage with a car parked in front of it. To her left, almost behind the house, she could see some headstones and three mausoleums surrounded by an iron fence. Two statues of angels faced each other at the gates. Her father's family had a private cemetery. Her father would never end up in a pauper's field in a town where no one knew him.

The canopy of trees ended abruptly, and the house was in front of her. It was two stories high, built on a raised brick foundation with a square porch that wrapped around three sides. Two wide steps led to the porch and the front door. At first she thought the house was dark, but then she saw a light in one of the windows upstairs. He was home.

He'll be angry, warned a voice inside her head.

So am I. She walked up the steps and

knocked on the front door. Nothing happened. She knocked louder. She banged
with her fists. He was not going to get away
from her. Not now. She banged even louder.
The door swung open.

And in the half-light of the porch, Iva
Claire found herself staring at her own face
for the second time in her life. Her father
was a masculine version of her, but the
young woman in front of her was almost her
mirror image.

"Who . . . are . . . ?" she managed to get
out.

"I'm Myrtis Benedict."

Chapter Fifty-three

There were differences between them. But you had to look closely to see them. Myrtis's hair was a lighter brown than hers, and it had been cut fashionably short; Iva Claire and Tassie kept their hair long to look young for the act. Myrtis's eyes were a lighter blue than Iva Claire's and perhaps more deep-set. Myrtis's mouth was smaller than hers, the lips were thinner, and Myrtis was shorter by about an inch and fuller in the hips and bust. But the shape of their faces and their eyes was the same; they had the same nose and the same distinctive chin.

The resemblance was as stunning to the

other girl as it was to her. They stood on either side of the doorway staring at each other until Iva Claire finally pulled herself out of her trance.

"I'm Randall Benedict's daughter—" she started.

The sound of her voice roused the girl. "Get inside!" she commanded in a whisper.

"If you could tell him—"

"Get in here. Now!"

Iva Claire went in. A wide hallway ran from the front door through the center of the house to a back door at the other end, with rooms opening onto it on either side. In the front, a heavily carved staircase led to the second floor.

"This way!" Myrtis was still whispering as she opened a door on one side of the hall and pushed Iva Claire into what looked like a small parlor. "Don't move," she hissed. Then she left, closing the door quietly behind her. Iva Claire could hear the heels of her shoes clicking down the hall to the back of the house.

There were sounds of female voices talking, followed by noise of a door opening and closing—the back door, Iva Claire guessed—and a few minutes later she heard a car driving off. She listened for other signs of life, but there were none. Was she alone? Where was her father? Her mind was whirling, from lack of sleep and from the shock of finding her mirror image standing across from her. She could call out and see if her father was in the house, but the place seemed to be deserted and she didn't want to hear the sound of her voice echoing through that long hallway. Besides, if he wasn't there, she was damned if she was going to stay all alone in this strange house in the middle of nowhere. She'd come back in the morning, she told herself, when the sun was shining.

She started out, but her eye caught a small writing desk next to the parlor door. On the desk was a picture of her father. A black ribbon with a small black rosette was attached to the frame. Iva Claire remembered something she'd registered in the back of her mind when she first saw Myrtis Benedict standing in the doorway of the house. In the height of a Georgia summer, the girl was dressed in black. With the world spinning, Iva Claire hadn't had time to wonder why she was wearing what were probably mourning clothes—or whom she might be mourning—until now.

There was a large brick fireplace on one wall of the parlor. Next to it was a chair and a small table with the only lighted lamp in the room. Iva Claire moved to the stiff little chair, sat down, and waited.

She was still sitting there when she heard the car come up the drive and stop. A couple of minutes later, the back door of the house opened and there was more shoe clicking in the hallway. Then Myrtis was back, standing in front of her, and Iva Claire once again had the unreal sensation of staring at herself without a mirror.

"I had to get the maid out of the house," Myrtis said. "She always takes the late bus, and I don't even remember how I explained driving her home to Colored Town. Thank God I've already let the other servants go."

She had an unusual speech pattern. In spite of its weariness, Iva Claire's brain started analyzing it. *Her pitch is like mine, but the accent is fussy—almost theatrical. And there's a southern lilt.*

Myrtis was still talking. "How did you get here?" she demanded.

"Walked from the railroad station." *I wonder if this feels as nutty to her as it does to me.*

"You came by train? Well, you won't be leaving that way. There isn't another one out of here until tomorrow morning."

"I know that."

"Yes, I'm sure you checked. But you miscalculated. I'm not going to let you stay overnight." She had a way of biting off her words like she was cutting a thread with her teeth. And she arched her eyebrows at the end of her sentences. Watching her was like being in a strange dream where someone else was using your face.

"I didn't expect—" Iva Claire started to say, but the thread-biting teeth cut her off.

"I can't tell you how unimportant your expectations are to me. I'll drive you to the next town. You'll stay there tonight, and tomorrow you can go back to wherever you came from."

She was used to pushing people around and getting her way.

"I came here to see my father," Iva Claire said.

"Daddy died six months ago."

Of course. She'd known he was dead as

soon as she'd seen the picture frame, but hearing it made it official. She'd traveled hundreds of miles to make him say he was sorry, and he was gone. The son of a bitch had gotten away from her. She wished Tassie was here. Tassie would understand what a big stupid joke it was. But instead of Tassie, her father's idiot daughter was standing in front of her, talking and talking. Iva Claire tried to make her tired reeling brain comprehend the words.

"But you knew Daddy was gone," Myrtis said.

"No, I—"

"Of course you did. I'm not stupid. I know why you're here."

You couldn't. But she didn't say it.

"You're wasting your time," the daughter went on. "He didn't mention you in the will, and you have no claim on the estate."

"The estate? I never thought of that."

"And I'm selling the house, or it can rot for all I care. Either way, there won't be a dime for you."

"That's not why I came."

"Don't lie! You're after the money. You and your gold-digging mother have been milking him for years."

The scorn in her voice cut through the weariness and the shock. Iva Claire had had enough. She got up so they were facing each other. "If I were lying, believe me, I'd be doing a much better job than this," she said. "Now tell me how my father died."

Myrtis didn't want to. But she didn't know what to do when someone stood up to her. "It was an accident," she said sullenly. "It was late; Daddy had been to a party. They said he was drunk and lost control of the automobile. There was a woman with him." She covered quickly. "A family friend."

I bet.

"His car went into a ditch on the side of the road," Myrtis went on. "They didn't find him until the next day. I was in England, and he died before I got here. I didn't know until it was too late."

That makes two of us.

"After the funeral, I went back to London to be with friends. I never got to say good-bye."

I never got to hear him say he was sorry.

Then it hit her—there was nothing for him to be sorry for. He hadn't cut Mama off. He hadn't deserted them. He'd died.

Myrtis was tearing up at the thought of their father.

He was a cold man, but she loved him.

"This is hard for both of us," Iva Claire said. "A couple of hours ago, I didn't even know about you."

"I, on the other hand, have known about you for six months. When I was here for the funeral and went through Daddy's papers. All those canceled checks. What a lovely surprise that was."

"I guess we've both been surprised."

"Don't even suggest that there are any similarities between us." Myrtis brushed away her tears angrily. "All those years when he sent me to England to school, I thought he was getting rid of me. I thought he didn't want me around."

That's a similarity right there.

"But it was because of you and your mother. He didn't want me to find out."

"What are you talking about?"

"Now I don't belong anywhere. I can't live in this country; I've been here by myself for two weeks and I'm going mad. But I'll never belong in England—not quite the right class. When I'm in London, I'm just an

American mill owner's daughter." She spat. "I'll always be an outsider."

So will I.

"They tolerate me. I'm the rich Miss Benedict, after all. But it'll never be home. I don't have one, thanks to you."

"No. Thanks to *him*." Suddenly it was important to make this girl understand. "Your daddy—and mine—is the one who did it to you. He did it to both of us."

"I told you not to compare—"

"I don't give a damn what you told me. He was selfish and—"

"You shut up!"

"He didn't care about either of us."

"He did! He would have cared if he could have, if he hadn't been seduced—"

"You don't really believe that."

"My mother knew about it. She knew he had a child. That's the way I remember her, crying over another woman."

"I'm sorry about that, but—"

"She was dying, for God's sake! And your mother—that whore—"

Anger quick and hot started inside her. "Don't say that again." Oddly, her voice was calm.

"What do you call a woman who takes up with a man whose wife is dying?"

"What do you call a man who takes up with another woman when his wife is dying?"

"You can defend her all you want. The happiest day I had in months was when I—" she broke off. And Iva Claire knew.

"*You* read my letters." The anger was bubbling up now. She pushed it back. "You knew my mother was dying. I was begging for money for her, and you sent my letters back without even answering them."

"I wanted her to know the free lunch was over."

"Mama never got a free lunch. Your dear daddy was just taking the easy way out."

"And your mother took the money. I believe that's called a whore."

"Sounds as if he had his share of them."

Iva Claire never saw the hand that came at her, but she heard it hit her cheek and felt the sharp pain. She felt the anger rushing to the surface and, under it, the anguish. It was all going to come out, and her tired mind couldn't stop it.

Leave! said the voice in her head.

She pushed her way past the table and

chair and started for the door. But Myrtis grabbed her arm and whirled her around. She was yelling something, but Iva Claire couldn't hear it. She felt herself yank her arm away, and then she felt herself pull back her arm to hit.

Mama's temper! the voice warned. But it was too late. Everything inside exploded. She wanted to smash bones and make blood spurt. She felt her hand connect with flesh with a force driven by pure rage.

Myrtis stumbled backward. Then she fell. She went down hard, too fast to break her fall with her arm, although she tried. It was too fast for Iva Claire to reach out—too fast to understand what had happened. At first.

She must have been off balance. I couldn't have hit her that hard.

But I wanted to hurt her.

Just for a second. One little second. When she sits up, I'll tell her I'm sorry. I'll get out of her house and never bother her again.

But Myrtis didn't move. When she'd fallen, the side of her head struck the raised corner of the brick hearth that jutted out from the fireplace.

I wanted to hurt her.

Don't think about that!

There was blood on the hearth where Myrtis's head had hit it. Most of it had seeped into the porous brick, but a little pool was collecting on the hardwood floor. Myrtis's face was white—the same white Mama's had been after she died.

I wanted to hurt her.

Don't think.

Iva Claire moved closer. Yesterday she hadn't known Myrtis Benedict existed, and now . . .

I wanted her to die.

Don't think.

She knew there was no need to call for help. She knew by the white face and the stillness she'd seen just a few days before. But even though she knew it was hopeless, she had to try. She picked up Myrtis's hand and held the wrist, feeling for the little beat in the vein that would say everything was all right, that the unthinkable hadn't happened. There was no pulse. She tried the other hand. She held on for a long time, to make sure.

She walked out of the room. She crossed the hall, went through the front door, and carefully closed it behind her. Then she started to run. She ran under the canopy of trees to Mill Street. She ran past the houses and the dark little town square and the railroad station. She didn't stop until she found Tassie sitting on the porch of the hotel, waiting for her.

Chapter Fifty-four

Tassie was the one who said they shouldn't walk through town together, because they'd be too conspicuous. So they took separate routes from the hotel back to the big house on the hill. Tassie was the one who said they should hurry because maybe Iva Claire had made a mistake, maybe Myrtis was still alive. Only Tassie called her *your sister*, which was the first time Iva Claire had thought about her like that.

Iva Claire got to the house before Tassie, and as she stood on the porch waiting, she let herself hope she'd been mistaken. But when Tassie showed up and they went inside to the parlor, they both knew that Iva Claire had been right.

"You've got to get away from here," Tassie said. "I know it was an accident, but you're a stranger, and that girl lying on the floor was important in this place. Nobody will want to hear your side. Nobody will care. All they're gonna know is what you did to one of their own."

Hearing it called an accident made it easier. It stopped being something dark and evil. It was almost possible to forget the rage that had caused it. Now there were problems to be solved, decisions to be made. She had to think about saving herself. But she knew running wasn't the answer.

"There's a maid who works here," she told Tassie. "If she comes back in the morning and sees the—what happened, she'll call the police. We can't even get a train out of here until ten o'clock tomorrow."

"We'll leave right now. We'll walk."

"Without knowing where we're going? They'll catch us before we get to the next town. Besides, all anyone around here has to do is take one look at my face, and—" She stopped. The words she'd just said seemed to bounce around the walls of the little parlor. She turned to Tassie to see if she had heard them, but Tassie looked blank.

"If they look at my face, they'll think they see *her*," Iva Claire said softly. And this time Tassie understood.

If they had been civilians, maybe it would never have occurred to either of them. But they'd lived in a world of flimflam and illusion. The world's tallest man was really a guy on stilts. They had listened to dear kind Benny laugh about scamming marks as the Great Otto. They had pretended to be sisters. They both knew what you could get away with.

Tassie shivered. "Oh, my God, you want to pull a switch," she whispered.

Chapter Fifty-five

Now their roles were reversed. Iva Claire was the one who was in charge. Tassie was good at practical things, but the con Iva Claire was about to pull off—or try to—was beyond her.

"My God, Iva Claire, are you sure you look enough like her?" Tassie asked.

That was the question. They were standing in the parlor, as far away from the hearth as they could get. Now Iva Claire moved closer. Behind her, she heard Tassie whisper, "Sweet Jesus!" but she kept on moving to the body—the body that had been a person, breathing and full of life, but now was

just a thing on the floor. She fought an impulse to run and made herself look down.
She could feel the room starting to spin
around her, but she made it stay steady; she
had decisions to make. She circled the
body, mentally checking its size against her
own. Close enough, she decided. She
moved in to get a better look at the face,
and the room threatened to spin again.
Again, she stopped it. But she had to know
what she was getting into, and the face was
the key. She studied it carefully. The eyes
were closed, but she remembered they
were blue although the shade was a little
off. The bone structure was enough like
hers, and the crucial nose and chin were
perfect. She turned her attention to the now
bloodless lips. The mouth was the problem.
But was it an insurmountable one? Could
she work against it? She turned back to
Tassie.

"I can do it," she said, "but I need a distraction prop."

A magician they'd once worked with had
an act that involved shooting a guy on one
side of the stage and having him seem to
reappear on the other side. After the "shooting," the "victim" started "bleeding" through

his white jacket. The shocked crowd was so mesmerized by the fake blood they never saw a second man get into position across the stage. The magician called the blood a distraction prop. He had dozens of them, and it had fascinated Iva Claire to see the way they always worked.

"You need a distraction prop?" Tassie's voice, shrill with fear, dragged Iva Claire back to reality. "Like what? What could possibly distract people enough so they'll believe you're Myrtis Benedict?"

I don't know, but I'll come up with something. I'm smart. And she was every bit as ruthless as Mama had been. She'd known that when she stole the gold dog collar and then conned Big Hannah. "I can carry it off," she said.

"How? You don't know anything about her! It'll be like trying to play a part when you don't know the lines!"

"I'll have to wing it. I look enough like her. And you've always said what a good mimic I am."

"That was onstage. This is for *real!*"

"It won't be any different from doing the act."

"We did the act for twenty minutes,"

Tassie said desperately. "This won't end, Iva Claire. This will be the rest of your life!"

"I can do it." *I can do anything. I can steal, I can lie, I can even kill.*

Don't think about that.

It was Iva Claire who remembered the family cemetery. It was Iva Claire who found the keys to the cemetery hanging on a nail in the gardener's shed. With Tassie shuddering behind her, it was Iva Claire who found the sheets in the linen closet and wrapped the body Tassie couldn't touch. She did help Iva Claire carry it out of the house, but she was so shaky Iva Claire was afraid she wouldn't make it to the cemetery. Tassie watched while Iva Claire fitted the big ornate iron key into the door of the first of the three mausoleums. Together, they put the body inside and locked the door. On the way back to the house, Tassie stumbled into the undergrowth and threw up. Iva Claire practically had to carry her.

"How can you be so calm?" Tassie whispered, when they were back inside.

Because I am my mother's daughter. But then, with hard terrible clarity, she realized she was far worse than Mama had ever been. *Mama was weak. I'm strong. I will get what I want.* She felt something cold creep inside her bones, and she shuddered. *I'll make up for this*, she told herself. *I'll make up for what I've done.*

She got a bowl of water and some soap from the kitchen so they could scrub the blood from the hearth and the floor, but Tassie couldn't go near it. So Iva Claire worked alone for several minutes, until the water in the bowl was pink and the stains had faded. No amount of scrubbing would remove them from the hearth completely, but the brick was old and discolored, so they weren't noticeable unless someone was looking for them. And who would do that?

She rinsed the bowl in the kitchen sink and put it and the soap back where she'd found them. When she reentered the parlor, Tassie had stopped looking sick.

"Tassie, you have to pay attention. To-morrow—later this morning, it's after midnight now—you'll go back to Atlanta," she said.

"You want me to leave you alone?"

"Myrtis Benedict doesn't have a friend named Tassie.

Tassie shrank back in her chair. "I see."

"You'll take the first train . . . no, you can't do that. If something goes wrong—"

"What do you mean, if something goes wrong?"

"If there's something I've forgotten, if someone figures out what happened, you're a stranger in town and they'll suspect you too."

"Oh, God!"

"Someone at the hotel might remember you. You'll have to have a reason for being in Beneville."

"Iva Claire, let's just run!"

"No, listen to me. This is a mill town. You came here because you heard there were jobs. You've never done this kind of work before, but you're desperate. Ask them at the hotel where you should go to put your name in. If they actually try you out at the mill, do whatever they ask you to do so badly that they wouldn't dream of hiring you. But I don't think you'll get that far. Then take the train to Atlanta. Check into the Georgian Palace Hotel."

"That ritzy place you told me about?"

"It's the only hotel I know there. I don't want to take the chance that I won't be able to find you."

"But it'll cost—"

"I've got money. I found her purse in the kitchen."

"Oh." Tassie rubbed her arm nervously.

"You wait for me at the hotel. It shouldn't be long. I'll get out as soon as I can."

Tassie nodded. She was rubbing both arms now.

"I can't leave if there's some reason she should be here, someone she's supposed to see or something she has to do. And I need to find out whatever I can about her."

Tassie was clawing at her arms now, digging at them with her fingernails.

"For God's sake, stop that!" Iva Claire snapped.

To her amazement, Tassie started to laugh, a loud hysterical laugh that made her double over in her chair and gasp for breath.

"Tassie, you can't fall apart on me. I need—"

But Tassie thrust out her arm. Big red blotches were starting up where she'd been clawing herself. "It's poison ivy!" she managed to get out. "It probably happened out there, when we . . . when I fell. If I don't put some calamine on it quick, I'll blow up like a balloon."

They found some in the medicine chest in the bathroom upstairs. Tassie smeared the thick pink stuff over her arms until the rash was completely covered.

The hunt for the calamine had delayed the inevitable for a little while longer, but now they had to face it.

"It's after three," Iva Claire said to Tassie. "You should get back to the hotel. Can you still get in?"

Tassie nodded. "The man at the desk left at eleven, but he told me they always leave a key on the top of the door in case guests come in late."

They walked in silence to the front door. Iva Claire opened it. But Tassie didn't go.

"Iva Claire, it was an accident. Maybe you could try to explain . . . and you wouldn't have to do this."

"I'll see you in Atlanta, Tassie," she said.

For a moment she thought Tassie was going to argue. But sweet, loyal Tassie was one of the weak ones.

"Be careful," Tassie said. Then she ran across the porch and disappeared into the darkness.

Iva Claire went back inside, locked the door behind her, took a deep breath, and got ready to start her new life.

Chapter Fifty-six

She didn't know how much time she had. Did the maid come every morning? Was she there for breakfast? When was breakfast? Did the maid cook it? There had to be a certain way things were done in this place. Or did there? Myrtis had only been back home from England for two weeks, she'd said. It took time to establish a routine. Still, she'd seemed like the type who would be sure her likes and dislikes were well known to the servants.

I'll have to have some kind of cover story ready, Iva Claire thought, *in case I do something unusual.*

She'd been handed some incredible pieces of luck, both good and bad. Myrtis hadn't spent much time in Beneville since childhood, so there wouldn't be a lot of old friends wondering why she'd suddenly developed an uncharacteristic taste for coffee, or raspberries, or polka dots. More important, no boyfriend would pop up to notice she'd started kissing differently. That was good. Not so good was the fact that Myrtis had been planning to sell the house and return to England permanently, and now she'd be changing her mind, which would have to be explained. There must be someone in England who should be informed that Myrtis would be staying on this side of the Atlantic. And some steamship line should be told that her tickets were to be canceled. But who? And which steamship line?

Iva Claire knew she had to get out of Beneville. She had to go someplace where the Benedicts weren't as well known as they were in their hometown. Perhaps Atlanta. Myrtis Benedict was used to living in London, so a big city would be a logical place for her to pick. Since Randall Benedict had always stayed in a hotel in Atlanta, it was a safe bet that he didn't have a home there, and Iva Claire assumed he wouldn't have a lot of friends in the city who knew his daughter well. If he did, she'd move somewhere else until she'd fully established herself as Myrtis. Then, when certain details like Myrtis's height and weight and the fullness of her mouth had gotten blurred in people's minds, she might come back to Beneville every once in a while, just to keep up appearances.

But the real danger was now, while she was still in town trying to cover her tracks. This was the time when she could give herself away. She felt herself getting cold. What would happen to her if they found out what she'd done? What happened to you when you killed your own sister? Cold as she was, she was starting to sweat. She made herself move, pacing in a circle, anything to keep the blood flowing. *You are not going to give yourself away. You are going to pull this off. You've got to.*

Moving around helped. Her mind cleared and the panic stopped. She decided to do a fast sweep through the house, starting with the ground floor, looking for clues about

Myrtis and her life. In the kitchen she found a grocery list with *Sally* scrawled across the top. That had to be the maid's name. She hoped. She noticed the kitchen door leading to the outside was unlocked and locked it. The dining room was useless, as was the living room. In a little sitting room off the back porch she found a sewing basket with the initials *M.B.* worked into the straw. Did Myrtis repair her own hems and mend her stockings? Did she do embroidery? Did it matter? Iva Claire pocketed a pair of scissors she'd need later for cutting her hair and hurried on. The rooms on the first floor and the long hallway were full of old furniture—probably family heirlooms that were loaded with history she should know but didn't. She'd have to find a way to learn about them.

She got her first break in the library. On a pedestal near the window was a thick book, very old and bound in leather. A Bible, with a family tree.

A horrible thought occurred to her: What if her father had had other children? From the way Myrtis talked, Iva Claire had assumed she was an only child, but what if she wasn't? With a trembling hand, she quickly turned the pages, skipping generations of Benedicts, until she reached the last entry. She breathed a sigh of relief. Myrtis hadn't had any brothers or sisters.

Except for me.

Upstairs there were five bedrooms, and the bathroom she'd already seen. She went through the bedrooms quickly, making note of things she'd have to go back and look at later: a fan that had been framed, a little music box that looked like it was handpainted, some old photographs. There was a child's picture that looked eerily like one of Iva Claire's old publicity stills. It had to be Myrtis. There were four more of Myrtis as an adult. As soon as she could, without making the maid suspicious, Iva Claire told herself she'd have to get rid of those. In the largest bedroom there was a canopy bed with big swirling *B*s carved all over it.

Four of the bedrooms were not in use. She'd saved the front room—the one where she'd seen the light in the window—for last. The door was open. She paused for a second at the threshold and looked in. The lamp was still on, the way Myrtis had left it

when she went downstairs to answer Iva
Claire's knock at the front door.

Don't think about that.

Iva Claire drew a deep breath and went into
the room. It was a mess. Clothes were
stacked in piles; there was an open trunk on
the bench at the foot of the bed. Myrtis had
been packing. But what day was she leaving? What time? What was the name of her
ship?

There was a desk in one corner. Iva Claire
raced through the drawers looking for
something—a calendar, an address on a
scrap of paper, or please, please, a ticket
that might indicate a time, a date, and a
ship's name. She found stacks of old letters, postcards, and some stationery. But
nothing to shed light on Myrtis's return trip
to England.

She mustn't keep looking. A little china
clock on the desk said it was four-thirty. It
was time to make herself look like Myrtis
Benedict—as much as she could.

She'd told Tassie she could wing it. But
winging it meant risk, and she'd always
been the kid who checked out each theater
to make sure there were no surprises.

Just one nice safe distraction prop. That's all I need.

Nagging at the back of her mind was the thought that there was one, and it was right here in this house. But she couldn't slow down enough to think of it. The best she could come up with was dying her hair. She was going to have to change the color, because her shade of brown was noticeably darker than Myrtis's had been. Matching Myrtis's hair color would be impossible, so she'd do something totally different. Later in the day, as soon as she could get to the pharmacy to buy some peroxide, Myrtis Benedict was going to surprise everyone by becoming a platinum blonde. It would be a radical change from her ladylike light brown, and Iva Claire knew she'd have to find some way to explain it. A girl of Myrtis's class would probably think bottle blondes were cheap and brassy. Iva Claire was hoping the startling change would distract people from noticing that her eyes didn't look as deep-set as they had, or that her lips were a little too full. She would have preferred a better distraction prop but this was the best she could think of. Until she could get her hands on some peroxide, she'd wear a scarf or the big leghorn hat she'd seen hanging near the back door, or she'd wash her hair and wrap it in a towel.

The slight difference in height could be handled by wearing flat shoes. If there weren't any in Myrtis's closet, or if Myrtis's shoes didn't fit, she'd use the ones she had on until she could find better ones. But what she was really going to rely on to bridge the gap between herself and Myrtis was wardrobe and makeup.

She'd do it all with confidence; that was the first rule to any good performance, and she'd get away with it. Because she had to. *Still, it would be better with a distraction prop.*

Don't think about that.

There was a lipstick in Myrtis's purse and face powder on her vanity. It was a pity she hadn't worn more makeup, but at least the lipstick was dark. Iva Claire could make her mouth look thinner by putting on the lipstick inside the lip line. The dark color would show up nicely. But how far inside the lip line should she go?

She ran to get one of the photos of Myrtis so she could work from the original.

Still, I wish I had a distraction prop.

She went into the bathroom to cut her hair, the first step in her transformation. She took the scissors out of her pocket and looked into the mirror. And for the first time that night, she screamed.

She forced herself to look back in the mirror again. The side of her face where Myrtis had struck her had started to swell, and there was a large red bruise on her cheek. Sometime after Tassie left, she'd been aware that her cheek had started to throb, but she'd been so busy with other things she hadn't let herself focus on it.

I killed her and she left her mark on me. My face is blowing up and . . . Oh, my God! Suddenly the nagging at the back of her mind clicked in. Tassie had said she'd blow up like a balloon from poison ivy. And then they had covered her arms. . . .

Iva Claire found the calamine lotion and slathered it over her face. She cut her hair without worrying about matching Myrtis's fashionable shingle and bundled it up under a scarf so the difference in color wouldn't show. If anyone asked, she'd say she was keeping it out of the way so it wouldn't irritate the terrible case of poison ivy she had. She looked at herself in the mirror. It didn't matter how blue her eyes were now, or how deep-set. It didn't matter how full or thin her lips were. All she—or anyone else—could see was the thick pink mask that covered her face. It was a perfect distraction prop.

Chapter Fifty-seven

After she covered her face with the calamine, she washed it off her hands with Myrtis's soap and cleaned her teeth with Myrtis's tooth powder—but not her toothbrush; she couldn't make herself do that. She found a nightgown in Myrtis's closet and put it on.

Now she didn't have to worry about some unexpected meeting Myrtis was supposed to have. An attack of poison ivy that was so bad your face swelled up would certainly explain a lady's inability to keep a social engagement. No one would wonder why she was staying in the house. She'd bought herself the time and the privacy to figure out what she was going to do next.

The china clock said five-thirty. She'd had a long night, and she had an even longer day in front of her—a day when she had to be at her absolute best. She cleared the clothes off Myrtis's bed and made herself lie down. Making her racing mind slow down was harder. Images belonging to some nightmare newsreel flashed through it: Mama's grave in the pauper's field in Indiana, a little dog dancing with a gold collar, Mama's hand going limp as she died, Myrtis opening the door, Myrtis falling back onto the fireplace hearth. There was blood seeping into the hearth bricks and somewhere Tassie was banging on the door. Only it wasn't Tassie, it was someone who wanted to get into the house. Which was strange because Iva Claire didn't own a house. But then she remembered that she did, and she sat up fast in the bed that was now hers. Downstairs someone was calling out, "Miss Myrtis!" She looked over at the china clock; it said six-thirty. She'd been asleep for an hour.

*   *   *

She hurried downstairs to open the door to a Negro woman who was tall, slender, and probably in her late twenties. This had to be the maid, Sally. Thank heaven she was young. The last thing Iva Claire needed was a servant who had been with the family for years. Sally wouldn't be reminiscing about things her mistress should have known but didn't. Even so, it would be a good idea to keep her distance from the maid which was probably what Myrtis would have done anyway.

"Miss Myrtis, I'm sorry to wake you up, but you locked my kitchen door," Sally said.

Of course, the kitchen door was left unlocked in this small town! Her first mistake. Meanwhile Sally was staring at her face.

"I seem to have gotten myself a bad case of poison ivy," she said. It was her first attempt at Myrtis's Mayfair-tinged southern accent. Her voice sounded light and uncertain to her critical ear, but Sally was still mesmerized by the pink mask.

"Don't stand out there gaping at me," she said, biting off the words. The result was much better. "Come in."

"In the front door, miss?"

Second mistake: Maids used the back door.

"You don't expect me to go racing around to let you in the back when I'm standing right here, do you?" She remembered to arch her eyebrow at the end of the sentence. It seemed to work. Sally said, "No, Miss Myrtis," and came inside.

"I'm sorry about the door being locked," she said to the maid. "I'm all turned around because of this poison ivy. I have a terrible headache." Did you get a headache from poison ivy? "I'm going back to bed."

"Do you want your hot tea, miss?"

She would rather have had coffee.

"I'll get it in a minute."

"You don't want me to bring it to your room the way I always do?"

She'd been right, there were routines in this house—and every one of them was a potential for disaster. "Yes, I'll get the tea when you bring it to my room," she said. "That's what I meant." And then, before she trapped herself further, she ran up the stairs.

Inside Myrtis's bedroom she leaned against the door and tried to assess her performance. Clearly, it needed work, but for the first time in front of an audience it hadn't been half bad. If her luck would just hold. But hoping for good luck was like asking for a reward, and after what she'd done, how could she? What if, instead of a reward, she were to get what she deserved?

But suddenly, inexplicably, she was furious.

Exactly what do *I deserve?* She looked around the pretty bedroom in the house Myrtis had said could rot, for all she cared. *I never had my own room. I never even had my own bed. She went to a fancy school in England. He threw me out of his hotel room. She got everything. And I didn't mean to kill her. She was the one who hit me. It wasn't my fault, and I'll be damned if I'm going to go to jail or feel guilty. I'm the one who had a hard life, and—* She stopped herself.

"No!" she said out loud.

That was the way Mama thought. It was never her fault. She never did anything wrong.

She sat on the bed and took a deep breath. "I killed Myrtis Benedict," she said to the empty room. "I don't want to be caught and I'm going to do whatever I can not to pay for it. But I killed her. And I have to live with it for the rest of my life."

And someday I'll find a way to make up for it.

She climbed into bed and pulled up the sheets. That was when she saw it. And she knew her luck had held after all. Sitting on the bedside table was a little leather-covered book with *M B* embossed on the front. Myrtis Benedict had kept a diary. Iva Claire grabbed it and began to read.

Myrtis was scheduled to sail from New York to England the following week on a ship called the *Rex.* Her ticket and passport were tucked into the back of the journal. As for people who should be contacted about the change in plans, Myrtis didn't appear to have had many close friends. She seemed to have a pattern of meeting people, finding them delightful, and then discovering some terrible flaw and dropping them. There was one girl she seemed to like; her name was Allison Stanton-Jones. She and Myrtis had gone to school together, at a place called Gracewood, and Allison's family had a house in London where Myrtis seemed to spend a lot of her time. Myrtis had a small

apartment of her own—a flat, she called it—
but she was not happy with that arrangement. She wanted control of her money so
she could afford to buy her own house in
the city.

The only other person who appeared with
regularity in the diary was someone Myrtis
called *the hateful Mr. Jenkins.* How or why
he was hateful was never made clear. However, there were references to *frightful rows*
she'd had with him.

Iva Claire let herself relax against the pillows. She'd cancel the booking on *Rex* immediately, and as soon as she'd taught
herself how to imitate Myrtis's elegant
handwriting, she'd send a note to Miss
Stanton-Jones saying Myrtis would be staying in America after all. She still had to go
through the contents of Myrtis's desk
drawer, and she wanted to practice Myrtis's
strange accent some more. But for the first
time in hours she felt safe. Until she saw the
note Myrtis had made on margin of the last
page of her final entry: *Luncheon with Mr. J,*
it read. The note was underlined several
times, circled heavily, and there was a string
of exclamation points after it. Clearly, lunch-

eon was going to be a momentous occa-
sion. Added as an afterthought was a date.
Iva Claire read it and sat upright in horror.
She had three days in which to get ready for
this meeting with the enemy, Mr. Jenkins.
Whoever the hell he was.

Chapter Fifty-eight

She couldn't ask Sally outright about Mr. Jenkins. She racked her brain, but she couldn't come up with an indirect way to get the information out of the maid. She spent two days and nights reading every scrap of paper in Myrtis's room, looking for something that would shed some light on the man's identity, but she came up empty. She wanted to scream in frustration. She couldn't even figure out where she was supposed to meet him for the damn luncheon!

Finally, in desperation, she accepted the fact that she'd have to bluff her way through. And it had better be the bluff of a lifetime. On the morning of the luncheon, she put on one of Myrtis's oldest dresses, and applied her calamine thickly. She was now a white blonde—she'd sent Sally to the pharmacy for the peroxide and more calamine lotion—and the bleach had made her hair dry. If she didn't curl it, it looked awful. Which was what she wanted. Because she was going to miss her appointment with Mr. Jenkins—there was no way to avoid that—and she needed to look believable when she claimed that her physical discomfort had pushed the whole thing out of her head.

She'd gone through all this for Sally's benefit. Servants noticed everything, she was learning, and they could be a scary source of gossip. She was very careful to cover her tracks with Sally. She wasn't expecting to see Mr. Jenkins that day, although it never hurt to play it safe. He might come over to the house when she didn't show up at their meeting place. She was living in the sticks and it might be considered the neighborly thing to do. She was hoping he'd just telephone the house, and she could simper some apologies and try to get some idea of who he was.

She looked at herself in the mirror. She certainly looked like a girl with no social obligations for the day. What she needed now was a cup of coffee to steady her nerves. The only beverage Sally ever served was tea, hot and cold. She'd never drunk it before she came south; the stuff tasted like dishwater as far as she was concerned. But southerners liked iced tea and Myrtis had lived in England, where hot tea was the national drink. Iva Claire figured she'd be stuck drinking the swill for life. But not now. Now what she needed was a good strong cup of joe. There had to be some coffee somewhere in the kitchen.

Before this, Iva Claire had avoided the kitchen. It was Sally's domain, and she wasn't sure about the proper etiquette for invading your servant's turf. Or for dealing with a servant. But now she was desperate. To her dismay she found Sally sitting at a table, mixing up something in a large bowl. The maid was on her feet in a shot.

"Something I can get you, miss?" she asked.

Mr. Jenkins's life story and the name of the restaurant where I'm meeting him.

"Nothing, thank you." Sally was looking at

her quizzically. She had to think of something to say. "Please go on with what you
were doing. What are you cooking?"

"That's the chicken salad you wanted me
to fix for your lunch with Mr. Jenkins."

She couldn't believe it. He was coming to
the house! Her luncheon was happening at
home!

"Right. Well, do get on with it."

She raced upstairs. She grabbed one of
Myrtis's black mourning dresses out of the
closet and yanked it on with shaking hands.

I've got stay calm. I can do this.

She put a ribbon in her hair. She was
about to smear some more calamine on her
face when she stopped. The bruise was
gone, and the swelling had gone down. If
you really looked at her, you could see there
was no rash. *He won't look that closely.*

He might.

She ran back downstairs again.

I can do this. I can do this.

She went into the sitting room, got her
scissors out of the sewing kit, and sailed
through the kitchen, calling over her shoulder, "I'm going outside to pick some flowers
for the table, Sally," as she went out the
back door.

She found the patch of poison ivy Tassie had fallen into. The leaves were shiny and evil looking. The rash was going to drive her crazy. She hated it when she got a mosquito bite.

Don't think about it.

She reached out, picked several of the shiny leaves, and carefully, thoroughly, rubbed them over her face. For good measure she rubbed one over her neck as well. In for a penny, in for a pound. She checked her watch, hoping she'd react as quickly—and violently—to the nasty weed as Tassie did.

Thankfully, by the time she'd cut an armful of daisies, her face was already starting to itch. She couldn't wait to get into the house to smear more soothing calamine on it.

An hour and a half later, with a pounding heart and a face that was now covered with red blotches, she was greeting her mystery guest at the front door. Mr. Jenkins was well dressed. A preacher? A doctor? A lawyer? He looked like the kind of person who was very sure of himself and expected people to listen to him, but at the moment he was frowning. Which could be explained by the "frightful row." Or her calamine coverup. He was trying not to stare, but he couldn't help himself. He was fascinated by her distraction prop.

Or maybe he hadn't been distracted at all. Maybe—please God, no—he had noticed that Myrtis was suddenly slimmer and taller than she had been.

"Mr. Jenkins, do come in," she said, in her new accent. "I apologize for my appearance, but I'm afraid I have a dreadful case of poison ivy. I haven't been out of the house in three days."

She held her breath and waited.

"How unpleasant for you," he said.

There wasn't a trace of suspicion in the look he was giving her. She'd passed the first test! But the big one was still in front of her, because unless she could find out who he was and what he meant to Myrtis, she wasn't going to get past the chicken salad at lunch—or survive the rest of her stay in Beneville. She had to make him reveal himself.

Suddenly, she remembered the hours spent backstage with Benny Ritz and his stories about his days as the Great Otto the mind reader. "You gotta get the mark to tell you what you want to know without him knowing it," Benny had said. "There's two tricks that always work. Keep him off balance, and keep him talking. If one thing don't make him open up, try another. And watch him like a hawk. Not just the eyes, watch the hands, the feet, everything. Eventually something you say is gonna hit pay dirt, and you'll see it in his body. Then you got to take the leap and go with it."

Iva Claire eyed the stern middle-aged man who was standing in front of her and began to talk. "I'm sorry about the way we left each other the last time we spoke," she tried.

His eyes narrowed. "It was unfortunate," he said, through lips that were so tight they barely opened. He was really angry about something. Iva Claire thought back to her initial impression that he was a man who expected to be listened to. What kind of person felt like that? A preacher, she thought, and decided to take a leap. "I really enjoyed the sermon you gave last week," she said.

He looked at her blankly. "The sermon?" he repeated. He wasn't a preacher! She'd leaped too far. Now what?

Don't panic. You can do this.

She made herself smile. She could feel the calamine cracking and thought the effect had to be grotesque. Mr. Jenkins was looking away again. Good. He wouldn't see the terror in her eyes. "I'm sorry," she said. "That was a bad joke."

His mouth tightened even more. "If you feel my attempts to give you advice are humorous—"

"Oh, no!" she said quickly. "Please let me explain." But how? What would Myrtis say? "I've been under so much strain since Daddy passed. . . . But of course you were just trying to give me good advice." Yes, that was it.

"I assure you, I have only your best interests at heart." His mouth eased up. It wasn't a big improvement, but she'd take what she could get.

"I've been thinking about what you said," she ventured. There was a softening in his eyes. "Maybe we can talk about it over luncheon." He hardened up again. He didn't like talking, he wanted to be agreed with. She calculated his age and the fact that he had Myrtis's best interests at heart. An old family friend? Should she try another leap?

A smaller one this time? She had to do something. "Daddy trusted you so much."

"I take my position as your executor very seriously," he said. She'd hit pay dirt! Myrtis had an estate; of course, there would be an executor who was in charge of it! She'd read about that kind of thing in novels. Myrtis had wanted to have control of her money so she could buy a house in London. But if Mr. Jenkins was her executor and he was standing in her way, wouldn't that explain the frightful rows?

"You were just trying to help me, Mr. Jenkins," she said. "I realize that now." He was still wary. She wondered if she should try to cry a little.

"You were listening to your friends. On the other hand, as a professional I have to be firm with you."

A professional—what?

"I understand, you were just doing what you had to—as a professional," she vamped.

He didn't pick up the cue.

Keep talking. There had been something in the way he said the word *friends*. Time for another leap. "I know you don't like my friends," she said.

He sighed wearily; they'd had this discussion many times before. "I don't know your friends, Myrtis. Or anything about your life abroad. As you have pointed out to me, I am hopelessly provincial. But if the trustee of any bank in England would allow a young woman in your position to run through her money the way you seem to want to do, I'd call him damnably irresponsible."

He was a banker! That made perfect sense. And he didn't like it that Myrtis lived out of the country. Time to give him the good news.

"You don't approve of my living abroad . . ." she began.

"I merely suggested that you might want to try your own country before you abandon it," he huffed.

"I agree with you. That's why I won't be going back to England, Mr. Jenkins."

He looking at her in disbelief. She'd told him too fast. In another second he was going to notice her full mouth and the fact that she was too tall.

Keep talking.

"I know I said I wanted to go back. But this is where I was born, and my family has a history here. . . ." She wasn't getting through. He was still looking at her like he'd never seen her before. Which he hadn't.

Don't think about that.

She made herself smile. "It's all your fault, Mr. Jenkins," she said. "I've been thinking about all the things you've said to me. It must have seemed as though I wasn't listening because I've been so angry. But you know how sometimes even though you're fighting with someone, the words they're saying sink in? That's what's happened with me. And everything you said made so much sense, Mr. Jenkins. So I canceled my reservation on the *Rex*, and I won't be leaving," she added desperately. She'd run out of things to say. All she could do was wait. And pray. It seemed to take forever, but he finally smiled at her—a big beaming smile with lots of teeth.

"I'm glad to hear this, Myrtis," he said. "Very glad."

Not half as glad as I am.

"Shall we go into the dining room, Mr. Jenkins?" she asked, a little breathlessly.

He wasn't half bad once he stopped frowning, and he really did seem to have Myrtis's best interests at heart. But, unlike Sally, he had known the Benedict family for years. And while Myrtis hadn't lived in Beneville for a long time, there had been vacations and Christmases at home. Iva Claire got through the chicken salad by doing a lot of smiling and nodding while Mr. Jenkins reminisced, but there were traps everywhere. She had to get out of town quickly. She broke the news to Mr. Jenkins over dessert.

"But why would you want to live in Atlanta?" he demanded. "A young girl on her own in that big city? This is your home."

He had that disapproving look again, and she didn't want him getting angry.

Keep him off balance. Benny's voice came at her from the past.

It gave her an idea, a dangerous one. It could backfire on her so easily. And if it did . . . but she didn't want to leave Beneville without his approval. It would be so much easier if he was on her side. And besides, if she played her cards right, she'd find out what, if anything, Mr. Jenkins knew about Mama. And Mama's daughter.

Her hands were in her lap. She gripped them together so tightly she could feel the nails cutting into her palms, and said, "Mr. Jenkins, what do you know about the woman my father was supporting?" She lowered her eyes as if she was too embarrassed to face him, but she heard him draw in a sharp breath.

"I . . . don't. . . ." he stumbled.

"Daddy sent money twice a year to a woman. I found the canceled checks. What do you know about her?"

"Nothing," he said, and she believed him. "I was never sure there was one specific—" He stopped short, embarrassed. "I mean, I knew there were withdrawals, but I never . . . I had my suspicions."

"Well, there was a woman. I found out when I was going through Daddy's papers. All those years . . ." And suddenly she was crying—for real. It was partly relief, she knew that. But it was also grief. She was crying for Mama, and the years when the checks had kept them safe, and for Mama's sad little dreams. The sobs came up inside her, and for a moment she couldn't fight them back, until she felt the tears start to wash away the calamine mask. That stopped her. But the tears had had their effect. Mr. Jenkins looked like he'd rather be anywhere else in the world.

"I want a fresh beginning, Mr. Jenkins,"

she said, calmer now, but with total honesty. "I want to get out of this town. Daddy died in a car with a woman. There were others, too—Lord knows how many—and everyone in Benneville gossips about it. Can't you understand why I want to start over?"

The statement didn't make much sense in terms of Myrtis and her life, but a new start was what Iva Claire needed with all her heart, and her feelings were so real that Mr. Jenkins was swept away. Like Benny always said, if you gave your audience something real and fresh, you'd get them every time.

It only took her two days to tie up the loose ends and get out of town. She took the house off the market on Mr. Jenkins's advice; she knew he was hoping she'd get over her prejudice against Beneville and come back home where she belonged. Sally was hired to keep the place running in her absence. Mr. Jenkins opened an account for her in an Atlanta bank. Her money, it seemed, was in trust and she'd receive an allowance every quarter. Mr. Jenkins mentioned the amount in passing and she was so shocked she almost gave herself away. She couldn't imagine spending a fraction of it. And when she was twenty-one she'd get control of her entire inheritance. She was relieved when Mr. Jenkins didn't say how much that was.

She packed up Myrtis's wardrobe, and a boy hired by Mr. Jenkins took a small mountain of luggage to the railroad station; her days of lugging heavy objects were over. But she did carry the suitcase with the swirling *B* monogram herself as she boarded the train for Atlanta. Where Tassie was waiting for her at the Georgian Palace Hotel.

Chapter Fifty-nine

At first they tried to pretend that everything was going to be fine, even though Tassie was going to leave Atlanta and Iva Claire was going to stay there, and visiting was out of the question.

"We only played the South once," Iva Claire said, "but we were on the stage together for six years. If anyone who caught the act even saw us together now, it could ruin everything."

Tassie nodded. She was trying not to let the tears in her eyes spill over. Iva Claire was fighting tears too.

"It's just for now," Iva Claire went on. But

they both knew better. It was going to take a long time before they could see each other face-to-face without taking an unspeakable risk. "We'll write all the time and we can talk on the telephone. We can afford the long-distance calls now."

"That'll be as good as seeing you," Tassie said. But of course it wouldn't.

"What will you do, Tassie?" Iva Claire asked.

"The only thing I know. Work in the business."

"Honey, vaudeville's finished."

"I'm going to go legit. I'm going to be an actress."

"You want to go back to New York?" Iva Claire asked, trying not to sound worried. There were people in New York who knew them.

"I can't. The first time someone asked me about you and Lily and what happened to the act, it'd be over. I'm a rotten liar."

Unlike me.

"The Sunshine Sisters never booked out of California," Tassie said. "No one will know me there. I'll go to Hollywood and be a movie star." She was smiling bravely, but Iva Claire knew what it was costing her.

Tassie had loved New York from the second she got there. And she wasn't the movie-star type.

"There's a lot of work in moving pictures," Iva Claire said, trying to be cheerful. "If Shirley Temple can have her name up in lights, why not me?" They both tried to laugh, but the tears in Tassie's eyes threatened to spill over.

"I'm no beauty," Tassie went on, "but they always need second bananas."

"And it's supposed to be very pretty. The weather is perfect."

"Yeah, for growing produce. Can't you picture it? The second banana out there with all those oranges—a regular fruit salad." The tears that had been threatening to spill over finally did.

"Tassie, if you don't want to go . . ."

"I'll be fine!" It took her a second, but she pulled herself together. "One thing. I'm changing my name back to Tassie Ritz."

She didn't have to do it. They hadn't used the name *Rain* professionally in years, and it would have been safe for her to keep it. But she didn't want to. And after everything that had happened, who could blame her?

"Tassie, I'm so sorry. . . ."

"It's not your fault."

But it was.

"I'll send you money, as much as you need. You can have a house with a swimming pool. And a new car. No more subways. No more hot water and ketchup soup at the Automat."

Tassie frowned. "I don't want you carrying me."

"Just as long as it takes for you to get on your feet." Then, because Tassie still looked troubled, "Please. I know you don't want to live off the money we got . . . I got . . . this way. But please let me help you make a start. Mama would have wanted you to have a *real* chance."

Tassie looked at her again. This time she nodded.

Tassie was leaving on the night train. Iva Claire had insisted she get herself a sleeper, and a taxicab was going to take her to the train station. Iva Claire wouldn't be going with her. There was no use in taking any dumb chances, Tassie said.

Her small suitcase was packed and sitting by the door of the hotel room.

"Iva Claire?" Tassie's voice was achy. "Are you going to miss the old days?"

"I'll miss you and Mama."

"But not the Sunshine Sisters."

She had to be honest. "No, I won't miss the act."

Tassie nodded, but her eyes were full of pain. Iva Claire searched for the words that would explain—somehow—and make it easier. She wasn't sure if she was doing it for Tassie's sake or her own. "This is a terrible time, Tassie. Remember the hobo jungles alongside the railroad tracks when we were going to Indiana, and all the little kids begging every time the train stopped? And the bread lines back in New York? There are people who are trying to do something about all of that, and I've got money. Lots of it. I can't change the way I got it; I can never fix that. But maybe I can do something to make things better . . . and maybe if I do, it'll all be worth it. You, me, Mama, and—" She couldn't make herself say the rest, but she didn't have to, Tassie knew what she meant. "Maybe I can make up for it all, just a little. You understand?"

"Yes," Tassie said. But Iva Claire knew she didn't. Tassie didn't want to change the world or do good deeds. She hadn't done anything horrible that she had to make up for. She just wanted to go back to the days when the Sunshine Sisters were on the road, getting their laughs doing five shows a day in the vaud-and-pic houses.

It was time for Tassie to go. She picked up the suitcase and started out the door. They'd already said good-bye too many times. But suddenly she turned and hugged Iva Claire as hard as she could. "You're a good person, Iva Claire," she whispered. "What happened that night was an accident. Don't blame yourself." And Tassie left.

Iva Claire moved to a big new apartment in a fashionable building north of Ansley Park and settled in. On her first night in her new home, she unlocked the water-stained suitcase with the swirling *B* on the side. There, where she'd crammed them on top of her old clothes, were her Sunshine Sisters costume and the sheet music for "Beautiful Dreamer." She threw the clothes in the trash—she'd worn them when Mama was dying—put the costume and sheet music back in the suitcase, and hid it in the back of her closet.

*   *   *

Tassie settled in too, in her new home in California. She wrote long letters about her swimming pool and her new car, and the orange tree in her backyard. She didn't mention auditions, or acting, or the past. Then one day she called on the telephone. "I thought you should know. I decided when I get to be a great big star, Tassie Rain is gonna look better on a movie marquee than Tassie Ritz." she said.

Until that moment Iva Claire hadn't known how much it mattered, but now it hit her. For a moment she couldn't talk. The gesture meant Tassie had forgiven her. And it meant that somewhere in the world, someone would still be using the name she couldn't claim. There was still a Rain working in show business.

"Iva Claire?" Tassie's voice came over the phone. "Did you hear what I said? I decided to go back to my real name."

"Yes, I heard," Iva Claire said. "Mama would be so happy about that, Tassie."

"That's what I thought," said Tassie Rain.

Chapter Sixty

MRS. RAIN

2004

It was late, probably after midnight, and her hand had been clenched around the pen for so long she was afraid she wouldn't be able to move her fingers. She pried them open, slowly and painfully, and rubbed them until the feeling came back. She was a little light-headed too, and for a moment that scared her, but the dizziness passed and didn't come back. She was just tired, she told herself.

Her infant doctor would not approve of her nocturnal marathon, nor would her specialist, but a kind of euphoria was driving her. The relief of writing the story down, of seeing it on paper after all these years, was like the end of a low-level pain you weren't really aware you'd had until it suddenly went away.

She was going to need a large envelope. She'd used up all her personal stationery long ago and was now writing on the big yellow pad Essie used to make her grocery lists. Which was a good thing because the pages of Essie's pad were lined, and in the last few hours she'd had a tendency to run things together.

She picked up her pen again, then put it down. She'd written the dangerous part of the story; now came the part that was simply sad. And heartbreaking, really—as if her heart wasn't already dicey enough. Would Ms. McCready understand why she was doing this? Would this letter really give her the courage she needed? She picked up her pen again.

Laurel, I know you're afraid. That's why I want to tell you this story. You need to know that people are not always what they seem. You mustn't be scared of anyone. Don't let yourself be bullied. Do what you know is right. Myr-

tis couldn't, and neither could Peggy, but you can. I'm telling you this story so you can set things right for both of them.

She paused for a second and added, *and for me.*

She sat back and reread what she had just written. She wasn't sure it would get the message across, but it was the best she could do.

Chapter Sixty-one

LAUREL

2004

It was the middle of the night, but Laurel couldn't sleep. She got up, amid protests from the dogs, and went into the living room. The *Charles Valley Gazette* was on the couch where she'd left it after she read it. She picked it up and took it into the kitchen, but she didn't open it. There was no need to read it again. She'd memorized Gloria's editorial.

"The vehement Ms. McCready," Gloria had called her, and then made her sound like a mealy-mouthed phony. No, it was worse than that. Gloria had made her sound like every rich bitch who took the money and ran. All her life, Laurel had thumbed her nose at the gardens and the resort. Anyone who had ever heard one of her beer-fueled rants at the Sportsman's Grill knew how she felt about Charles Valley's leading family. In a few short sentences, Gloria had made her into the enemy—an ignorant white-trash Garrison. Accent on the ignorant.

> Ironically, the vehement Ms. McCready is now the owner of the resort, and she has the deciding vote on the board of trustees that makes policy for the gardens. And, according to yesterday's announcement, the gardens and the resort are now planning to raise the cost of health insurance premiums for those workers for whom Ms. McCready expressed such concern. When asked to comment, Ms. McCready replied, "I don't know anything about business. There are people who know what they're doing, and they say this is the way it has to be. My opinion doesn't matter."

Laurel cringed at the memory of her own words, immortalized in print. No one in town would say anything to her—but they'd all be thinking plenty. Going to the post office would be a nightmare. Everyone in Charles Valley read the *Gazette:* Sheralynn and her vast tribe, Maggie and Li'l Bit—and Perry. Laurel threw the paper on the floor.

The Lawrence family certainly knew how to deliver a gut punch. Stuart softened you up, and the ladies finished you off. If Myrtis Garrison had had the brains God gave a canary, none of the damn clan would have ever set foot in Charles Valley.

That, Laurel realized, was part of what was driving her crazy. Somewhere in all the conflicting stories she'd been hearing about Miss Myrtis, she'd started feeling a weird connection to the woman whose home, money, and life she now owned. She almost felt sorry for Miss Myrtis and, in a way she couldn't begin to explain, she'd come to think of her own battle with Stuart and his gang as a victory for the young woman who had been so nice to Li'l Bit and Maggie and then had had to back down on all her plans and dreams. Laurel Selene McCready, from the wrong side of just about everything in Charles Valley, felt like she needed to win one for the great Miss Myrtis. But she hadn't won. And she wasn't going to. Laurel threw the newspaper on the floor. The only thing she had in common with the great lady of Charles Valley was being as big a hypocrite as Miss Myrtis had been.

Chapter Sixty-two

MRS. RAIN

2004

Something strange was going on. She was sitting in . . . a thing . . . a piece of furniture. It had a name . . . a name she knew, but she couldn't bring it to her lips. Where was she? Backstage in the greenroom? But this wasn't a greenroom, it was a . . . some other kind of room. And there was something in her lap that had a name she couldn't remember. How had this happened? Sometimes when she first woke up, she didn't remember where she was or how she got there, but she hadn't been asleep. This was like the last time there had been an incident . . . a cardiovascular incident. . . .

"Myrtis?" she called out, panicked.

She came running into the room. Only it wasn't Myrtis, it was . . . someone else. Whose identity was lost in the same black hole that seemed to have swallowed her brain.

"Yes, Mrs. Rain," said the young girl, who wasn't a stranger but was, for the moment, nameless.

I know who you are, just help me a little with your name. Give me a hint.

"Mrs. Rain, why are you awake? It's three in the morning."

If I knew that I wouldn't have called you, whoever you are.

"You're still writing that letter, aren't you?"

She looked down at the pile of yellow papers on a tray in her lap. That was what it was, a letter! She was writing to Laurel Mc-Cready. Everything started clicking into place. Words were coming back. She was sitting in a chair in her sunroom, and she had a pen in her hand. The girl, whose name was not Myrtis but Cherry, was right. She had been writing through the night.

"Shall I get Essie? Or the doctor?" Cherry asked.

"No, dear, I'm fine." But the moment of

confusion had inflicted a little sting of fear. Like a bite from an insect or a rash from poison ivy.

"Have you been in that chair all night?"

"I couldn't sleep."

"The doctor is gonna be mad."

"Then don't tell him."

"Let me help you get into bed."

"As soon as I finish."

"Mrs. Rain, I'm responsible for you."

She wanted to shout that she was a grown woman, and if she chose to stay up all night, writing letters or dancing on tabletops, that was her decision. But the child looked so stricken. And there had been that scary little moment in no-man's-land.

"Please, Mrs. Rain."

So she let the girl put her to bed. And after young Cherry left she really did try to sleep. But the letter, which Cherry had put on the dresser, was calling to her. She waited for what seemed like hours; then she turned on the light and retrieved her yellow pages, the tray, and the pen. She got back into her bed with the tray on her knees, to finish the last sad chapter of her story.

Chapter Sixty-three

IVA CLAIRE

1936

Iva Claire hadn't counted on the loneliness. She was used to sharing everything, first with Mama and then with Mama and Tassie. It had been the three of them against the world, onstage and off. Now she was alone and she felt lost. She needed friends, but she'd found out fast that the old-time vaudevillians were right when they said civilians were a different breed. In Atlanta, thanks to the Benedict name and money, she'd been accepted into a circle that was young, rich, and well bred. The belles in this crowd could never have imagined rolling around on a stage in a silly costume or waiting in a dirty hotel room with a dying mother for a check that never came. The pain of Mama's last days, her horrid little funeral, and all the other memories that haunted Iva Claire would have sounded like a bad dream to them. But they were real for her.

That was the second thing she hadn't counted on. She could mimic Myrtis Benedict's speech, wear flat shoes to make herself look shorter, and play Myrtis to perfection, but she could never lose her memories of life as Iva Claire. The memories could trip her up. Theater slang she had used all her life could slip into her conversation if she relaxed her guard; so could references to Hell's Kitchen and Brooklyn.

So she was afraid to let anyone come too close for a variety of reasons—which made the loneliness worse.

It might have been easier if she'd had something to do. She'd worked since she was five, and she was accustomed to being useful. But now she was expected to spend her time going to parties and picnics. She read books, volunteered for socially acceptable charity work, and secretly gave large amounts of money to radical causes, but sometimes she thought her boring new life was worse than the old grind of doing split weeks on the Small Time.

The wealthy privileged people who had taken the wealthy privileged Miss Benedict into their homes and clubs whispered to one another that there was something a little off about her. They put it down to her foreign schooling, but that didn't stop them from wondering. All of this made friendship a gamble and romance a danger. Besides, she was finding she didn't like her new acquaintances very much.

The casual bigotry she encountered in the parlors of the spoiled never ceased to amaze her. She wasn't naïve. She'd played theaters where Negro customers had to sit in Coon Heaven, and she knew that in parts of the South they had their own circuit. Certainly, ethnic and racial stereotypes formed the basis of many successful comedy acts. But backstage, performers of every background were thrown together in the melting pot that was vaudeville, and prejudice simply couldn't last when you were trooping around the country on a five-a-day tour. But the sheltered girls and boys of Atlanta had been raised to look down on anyone who didn't look or sound exactly like they did.

Being with them often meant biting her
tongue until it was in danger of bleeding.
And she was discovering something else
about them and their parents; they were
amazingly ignorant about the world around
them. And they were mean.

Georgia had been hit hard by the Great
Depression, and Atlanta was a hotbed of
New Deal activity. People would have
starved without federal relief and the jobs
handed out by government agencies. As far
as Iva Claire was concerned, Roosevelt was
a great man.

But she was going to dinner parties
where the president was more likely to be
called a communist than a savior. And because she was afraid of attracting the
wrong kind of attention, she was afraid to
argue. In private, she read the *Women's De-
mocratic News* and Mrs. Roosevelt's column, "My Day," in the *Woman's Home
Companion*, but she couldn't talk about any
of it in public.

The worst part was, she couldn't even tell
Tassie how isolated she felt, because Tassie
seemed to be having problems of her own.
She still never mentioned acting jobs, and

she sounded discouraged. Iva Claire sent more money and tried not to think about it.

But sometimes all of it—the loneliness and the boredom and the worry—got the better of her. Then she would start remembering the night in the house in Beneville when her life changed. Those were the bad times.

She was in one of those moods when Bonnie Taylor Talbot invited her to spend a weekend in a small town a few hours outside Atlanta.

"One of Daddy's oldest and dearest friends has this garden," Bonnie burbled. "Well, it's not just a few rosebushes. This is acres and acres of trees and plants, it's all very scientific and horticultural, and for years he had this hunting lodge there for just his friends, but now he's made it into a resort. Mama says Uncle Grady—I call him that because I've known him since I was tiny—would make money in the outer rings of H E double toothpicks. But I don't think that's vulgar necessarily, not unless you wear too much jewelry. This weekend we're going to Charles Valley for the party Uncle Grady is going to open Garrison Gardens and Garrison resort to the public. You'll love it there, it's so rustic, with loads of tranquillity."

Normally, Iva Claire would have run from the idea of a weekend with Bonnie, her thimble-size brain, her overbearing daddy, and her hypochondriac mama. But she wanted to get out of Atlanta, and at least Uncle Grady's hunting lodge would be a change. So the next day she sat in the backseat of Daddy Talbot's Cadillac, heading for Charles Valley.

Chapter Sixty-four

The Garrison resort was rustic, as Bonnie had said, but in the most luxurious way possible. The lodge's façade featured weathered wood and rough stonework. Inside, the bedrooms were palatial, each with its own private bath, thick rugs, and hand-stitched linens. There was a reception area with heart-pine floors and a massive fireplace. Behind it were two small dining rooms to be used by guests for private entertaining. Next to the smaller rooms was a large dining room that seated one hundred and opened onto an outdoor terrace. This was where the party launching the resort would be held. But before the big shindig, the host had commandeered the smaller rooms for drinks and dinner for a few select friends. The exclusive little gathering included Iva Claire, the Taylor Talbots, the Garrisons and their son—there were two older sisters who were married and lived away from home, she learned—and three prominent families from Charles Valley.

One family in particular fascinated Iva Claire. The wife had been a beauty when she was younger and still would have been attractive if she hadn't tried to fight time with too much makeup and a dinner gown designed for a girl twenty years her junior. The husband, a lawyer, was the only man in the room not wearing a dinner jacket. He had a weary, slightly twisted smile that didn't show up very often. Their daughter didn't smile much either. She was a large gawky girl, and under the best of circumstances she would not have been considered pretty. Her nose was too large, her chin was practically nonexistent, and her pale blue eyes were hidden behind thick glasses. In the beginning of the evening her hair had been styled in tight waves, but it had rapidly become a bush of frizz in the heat. She should have dressed simply, in clean lines and neutral colors, but she was wearing a yellow dotted-Swiss frock with puffed sleeves, frills at the neck, and endless rows of ruffles that went the length of the dress from the shoulder to the hem. It would have been hard to find a garment that looked worse on her substantial frame, and the poor thing knew it. Iva Claire looked at her overdressed mother and thought she knew who was responsible for the choice. The girl's father was introduced as Harrison Banning; his wife was Beth.

"And this big old giantess is my daughter, Margaret Elizabeth," said Beth, with a smile totally lacking in warmth or affection. The daughter flushed bright red, which didn't help her looks, but she reached out calmly to shake hands.

"Call me Li'l Bit, Miss Benedict, everyone does." Her voice was high and fluty.

At her side, her mother tittered angrily. "Good gracious, Miss Myrtis is going to think you're a fool, asking her to call you that." She gave her daughter a quick look up and down to drive her point home. "Any-one who didn't know that's your daddy's silly pet name for you would think you're peculiar."

The girl flushed an even deeper red. Ignoring the mother, Iva Claire said warmly, "I think Li'l Bit is a charming nickname. And you must call me Myrtis." Mercifully, before Beth Banning could say anything more, they were called in to dinner.

Iva Claire had been placed at the end of the table. The scion of the Garrisons, whose name was Dalton, was seated at her right. At his right was Beth Banning, and across from her was Li'l Bit. Iva Claire immediately dismissed Dalton as another good-looking boy who had played football in college rather than study and now spent his time doing a token job for his family and showing up at appropriate times in a dinner jacket. Li'l Bit was far more interesting. But the girl seemed to have retreated into herself. Iva Claire was searching for something to say when Beth leaned over.

"Miss Myrtis, tell me about Atlanta. It's where I was raised, and I miss it so. And now I hear it's being destroyed by *that man*."

When people like Mrs. Banning said *that*

man, they meant the president. Iva Claire repressed a sigh. This was exactly the kind of dinner talk she'd been trying to escape.

Be careful, warned the voice in her head.

"I'm not sure I'd say Atlanta has been destroyed—" she began, but Beth leaped in.

"Oh, please, I beg you, don't say you're a supporter of the Roosevelts! My friends say I'd just cry my heart out at the way they've destroyed my old hometown."

"Things in Atlanta are different. . . ." Iva Claire paused and was helped out by an unexpected source.

"President Roosevelt had the runways at Candler Field graded, Mama," Li'l Bit said, as she carefully buttered a roll. "And I believe there's a new orchestra now. You know how you're always saying you're devoted to culture." Was she making fun of her mother? It was said innocently enough.

"I was addressing my remarks to Miss Myrtis," said Beth.

"The president also fixed the Cyclorama. Remember how you said it just broke your heart into little pieces to see it go to rack and ruin?" There was no mistaking it, she was practically imitating her mother. People around the table were looking uncomfortable. Obviously they were used to these clashes.

A mean little smile played across Beth's mouth as she eyed her daughter across the table. "What is that funny little poem about the Roosevelts?" she asked. "Oh, yes, I remember." She began to recite: " 'You kiss the niggers, and I'll kiss the Jews, and we'll stay in the White House as long as we choose.' "

The table became silent. Several faces were scarlet, Iva Claire noticed. But there were also a couple of grins. Beth giggled like a naughty schoolgirl. "Isn't that just awful?" she said.

From across the table, Li'l Bit said clearly, "Yes, Mama, it truly is." She stared at her mother for a moment, then deliberately turned away. Suddenly Beth seemed to become aware of the hush in the room and the spectacle she was making of herself.

"My daughter is devoted to FDR," she said shrilly into the silence. "And she is even more enamored of *Mrs*. Roosevelt. Personally, I can't understand why anyone would be, but perhaps it's comforting for some to see such a homely woman in the White House. Most plain girls aren't that lucky."

There was a sudden intense fascination with the cutlery on the part of everyone sitting around the table. Li'l Bit looked like she was going to cry.

"I agree with you, Li'l Bit," Iva Claire said, throwing away three years of discretion. "I think Mrs. Roosevelt is splendid. Did you hear her last speech on the radio?"

She was rewarded with a grateful smile and a nod from Li'l Bit.

"And I admire her work at Arthurdale so much, don't you?" That opened the floodgates. Li'l Bit Banning worshiped the president and his wife the way only a lonely, sad, smart youngster could. She shook off her mother's barbs and launched into a political discussion that soon left her listener far behind. Iva Clare's understanding of the New Deal was general, and she believed in broad issues like unionization, public health care, and the new Social Security program, but Li'l Bit knew in minute detail the history and purpose of every federal agency. She raced eagerly through an alphabet of abbreviations—NRA, TVA, NYA, WPA, CCC, FEPC, and NLRB—and documented the finer points of the anti-lynching bill and the argument for national participation in the World

Court. Her face was still flushed, but with an attractive glow now, and her eyes were sparkling. Although she was plain, as her mother had said, surely the right man would see the passion in her someday.

Beth broke in again. "I do hope Li'l Bit isn't boring you to death, Miss Myrtis. You're so sweet to let her go on."

"I can't remember the last time I've had such an interesting conversation," Iva Claire said honestly. "You must be proud to have such an intelligent daughter."

The woman really couldn't leave well enough alone. "You mustn't encourage her to show off," she simpered. "I keep warning her that boys don't like a girl who's too smart. They'll always prefer a pretty face."

"A boy might. But a *man* knows that a good mind will last long after a pretty face has" . . . Iva Claire paused to let it sink in . . . "faded," she finished coolly. Once again silence descended on the table. Beth Banning shot her a look of pure venom, but before she could attack, Dalton Garrison intervened.

"Now, Miss Beth," he said, "you must tell me what that scent is you're wearing. I've been enjoying it all evening." He hadn't really distracted the woman—she was still seething—but the difficulties of waging war at a dinner party with a gentleman sitting between her and her opponent, seemed to dawn on her. She opted to let the young man flirt with her.

Across the table, Li'l Bit was smiling as she polished off her dinner. And at the other end of the table, Bonnie Taylor Talbot was staring at Iva Claire with a mixture of curiosity and disbelief.

Iva Claire kept quiet for the rest of dinner and moved with everyone else to the big reception in the large dining room. The place was pleasantly crowded, but not jammed—clearly the Garrisons knew how to entertain—and the terrace was deserted. Knowing it was only a question of time before she was accosted by Bonnie, who would be panting for an explanation of her bizarre behavior, Iva Claire ducked outside.

Myrtis would never have interfered between mother and daughter. She never would have talked politics at a dinner party either.

I was careless. I forgot.

But the truth was, she hadn't forgotten

anything. For one glorious moment she'd been herself. But that was dangerous.

"I don't believe I've ever seen anyone draw out Li'l Bit Banning the way you did tonight," said a voice behind her. She whirled around to see Dalton Garrison. He was standing in the half-light coming from the party inside and holding two glasses of champagne.

She realized he was much more attractive than she'd thought at first. His sandy hair was thick and curled over his forehead. His eyes were a hazy golden brown, and not only did he wear his white dinner jacket well, he filled it out nicely too. But there was something else about him, something even more attractive than his good looks. She saw it as he stood there smiling at her. Dalton was one of those very rare men who are totally masculine but love being around women.

This is the last thing you need.

"Doesn't anyone ever stop that woman when she's picking on her daughter?" she asked.

He had the grace to blush—at least, that's what it looked like in the half-light. "Beth Banning can be . . . difficult. Most of the town is afraid to stand up to her. But you did a fine job. Won't you have a glass of champagne with me?" He had such a sweet smile.

She'd been planning to have a headache so she could leave the party before she got herself into any more trouble. But there was a rebel in her tonight. She took the champagne.

They sat on a stone wall to drink after he brushed It off for her. "Did you mean all those things you said to Li'l Bit?" he asked. "About unions and workers' rights and all of that?"

"Every word," she said recklessly. "Shocked?"

He shook his head. "I like it when a girl who's beautiful is also kind—like you were with Li'l Bit tonight. But when a girl is beautiful *and* kind *and* smart, she's a girl I have to know."

He was a dangerous young man.

"I think . . . I mean, shouldn't you go inside?" she said. "Everyone will be wondering where you are."

He stood up. "Dance with me first."

He was *very* dangerous. But he looked so good, standing there in front of her with his happy, sweet smile as he held out his hands to her, so she moved into his arms and danced with him to the music that was playing for his daddy's big party. And when the band stopped playing, they kept on moving without saying a word. Somewhere nearby, there were early roses blooming and sending out their scent into the dark, silent night.

She didn't sleep well, and the next morning she got up before everyone else. She left a note for Bonnie, saying she'd decided to go exploring and wouldn't be back until dinnertime. That way she only ran the risk of running into Dalton at one meal, which was a lot better than two, plus cocktails.

He was sitting in the reception area with a blanket and a picnic basket, waiting, as if he'd known she'd be there.

"I couldn't sleep either," he said, when she walked in. "Come on, I want to show you our gardens. I have some coffee and ham biscuits for us."

She could have said no. It would have been the smart, safe thing to do. But he made her want to forget about being smart and safe. He made her want to forget everything. Just for one day, she told herself. She was going back to Atlanta tomorrow, and she'd never see him again.

He took her to a trail that had been cut through a forest of pines, oaks, and maples, where dogwood bloomed in bursts of pink and white against the green and brown of the big trees, and he pointed out the pools of dappled sunlight under the trees where hostas, caladiums, and coleus grew around lacy ferns. He showed her the sweeps of purple, pink, red, and orange azaleas that had been planted at the edge of the woods.

They left the hiking trail and he took her to see the formal gardens, where beds of tulips, irises, hyacinths, poppies, snapdragons, pansies, and sweet william bloomed behind hedges of boxwood and holly, ringed by crepe myrtle, tea olive, and magnolias. They walked past the gardens through open fields where small orchards of pecan, pear, and peach trees were flowering. There were still the remnants of cotton fields and vegetable gardens with sunflower borders, and the occasional rosebush or gardenia growing next to an old shed or fence. They climbed to the top of a hill, where he spread the blanket and unpacked

their breakfast. Beneath her, patches of daffodils and crocuses dotted tall grass that
sloped down to a flat meadow.

"This has to be the most beautiful place in
the world," she said.

"Daddy wants to put in a golf course
down there," he said, indicating a place
where the land leveled off. "And he's going
to build a lake too. The engineers say it can
be done."

"What a pity," she said, and then realized
that sounded insulting. Being with him
wasn't doing much for her manners. But he
didn't take offense. Something was bothering him, she could tell. She sat still and
waited for him to say what was on his mind.
It wasn't easy for him. He liked things to be
light and happy. She wasn't sure how she
knew that about him, but she did.

Looking down at the ground, he said quietly, "My father wouldn't agree with you
about Roosevelt. Daddy thinks he's de-
stroying the wage hands. The federal government pays them seventy-five percent
more than we do. Who's going to work for
us?"

"Maybe you'll have to start paying better."

"And with all this talk about unions and

health care and now this Social Security, Daddy says it'll cut into our profit."

"Your family's wealthy. How much money do you need to make?"

"Daddy would say as much as we can."

"What do you say?"

He drew in a deep breath and looked out over the field. "All this used to be farm-land—*little* farms with one family working it usually. Times have been hard around here for a long time, even before the Depression." He looked at her and looked away quickly. He was embarrassed by what he was about to say. "Daddy started picking up the land for cheap way back. Whenever some farmer was going broke, we'd buy him out. We never paid what the land was worth. When cotton went down to five cents a pound, that was when we really closed in. Daddy didn't do the buying himself since the farmers would have held out for a higher price; he had agents working for him. I was in charge. We'd go in and scare the hell out of the man—" He stopped, but he still couldn't look at her. "Sorry about my language."

"Don't be."

"A couple of times it was a woman," he

went on. "A widow, sometimes with kids. I forced them out of their homes too. This hill where we're sitting? There used to be a house on it; it wasn't more than a shack really. An old man lived in it. His vegetable garden was right over there; that's his peach tree. When I came to give him his money, he cried. He had these big old hands, all knotty and scraped up—" He stopped again. His eyes were bright as he looked down at the ground. She wanted to put her arms around him. Instead, she reached out and took his hand.

"I think . . . I *believe* that if you've done something you wish you hadn't, you can always find a way to make up for it," she said.

He finally turned and looked at her. "Daddy wants to retire, and he's going to put me in charge of running the gardens and the resort. He says it's time for me to show what I'm made of." He was still looking at her; she had a feeling he was testing her in some way. "I'm sorry to be so serious on a pretty morning, but after the way you took up for Li'l Bit last night, and then when you were talking about the New Deal and all— well, I just wanted to tell you this."

He had been testing her, and even though

she'd never be seeing him again she wanted desperately to pass the test. She tried to think of some answer that would be wise and clever, but in the end she just told him what she felt. "I'm flattered that you told me," she said. "Thank you."

His smile seemed to burst over his whole face. "See there? No other girl I know would have said that."

She'd passed.

He had asked for her address in Atlanta, but she wouldn't give it to him. However, one week after she left Charles Valley, he showed up at her door with a big bunch of flowers he'd picked at Garrison Gardens.

"Drove them up to Atlanta in a bucket of water in the front seat of my roadster," he said, as he held them out to her.

When someone had gone to all that trouble to bring you the most beautiful bouquet you've ever seen, you couldn't tell him to take it back. And you couldn't accept flowers from a man and leave him standing on your doorstep. She let him come in. Just this once.

"How did you know where to find me?" she asked.

"Your friend Bonnie. She didn't want to tell me."

"Really. I wonder why?"

"I think you shocked her at the dinner table with your views on our president."

"Why would that keep her from telling you where I live?"

"She was protecting me, of course. Bonnie is a dear family friend. Fortunately, I'm very persuasive."

Iva Claire didn't like the way he said *dear*. She thought Bonnie was a jealous little cat who probably wanted him for herself.

"The thing is," he went on, "when you and Li'l Bit were talking about FDR, that's when I knew you were the right one for me."

She hadn't heard him properly. "What did you say?"

"I said, I know Myrtis Benedict is the girl for me."

"Dalton, I'm not good at flirting—"

"I am. Very good. But that's not what I'm doing now. I've finally met a girl I want to talk to for the rest of my life." Dalton's smile faded. "I don't want to be like my daddy, Myrtis. I don't want to take people's homes when they're down on their luck, bully my friends, and never even bother to hide my girlfriends because I know my wife won't stand up to me."

"If you don't want to, then you won't."

He didn't laugh, or even smile. "Don't be so sure. When I take over the business I'm going to need someone special with me. The moment you opened your mouth I knew you were different."

She had to stop him. "Dalton, I like you. And I'm sure we'll always be friends—"

"But, I want to kiss you too—more than I've wanted to kiss any other girl I've known."

"Oh."

"The only way out is for you to marry me."

"You . . . just met me," she stammered.

"But I'll never do better, so what's the use of waiting? I can court you for months or years if you want, but it won't change any-thing." He was smiling, but his brown eyes were anxious.

"Dalton—"

"If you don't think you could love me, maybe you could think of it as saving me?"

He was so serious. And so sweet. And so handsome. "Saving you from what?"

"Myself. I want to do right at the gardens and the resort. I want to make it a good place for people to work. But Daddy'll start going at me about keeping costs down, and"—he paused—"I'm not a strong person, Myrtis. I'm not like you."

"You don't know what I'm like. You don't know me."

That made him smile. "Yes, I do. I may not be good in business like Daddy, and the Lord knows I wasn't much for studying in school, but I know about people. I know what kind of person you are."

I hope not.

"There's nothing you and I couldn't do together, Myrtis," he said, his eyes shining. "We'll be a great team."

The sad part was, he was right. With his heart and her backbone they would be unbeatable.

"If you come with me, we can do so much good. And I'll make you love me one day, I promise."

But she couldn't say yes.

He came back the next week. This time he didn't have flowers, and he kissed her before she had a chance to protest. She'd never been kissed before, and she wanted it to go on and on. She wanted him to keep kissing her so she'd never think again. But he broke away.

"I should have done that ages ago," he said, his voice ragged.

It took her awhile to catch her breath. "There are things about me you don't know," she said, which was stupid, and risky, but she didn't care.

"That's okay," he said softly.

"I'm not going to tell you what they are. But I can't marry you. And you have to go now."

But instead of leaving he brushed a wisp of hair away from her cheek and said, "You lived away from home for a lot of years, without your parents or any family around. You were on your own, and things can happen. I understand. I wasn't exactly an angel when I was on my own at college."

He was so gentle. She had to make him leave, but he was still smoothing her hair.

"I don't care what you did before I met you," he said. "I know the girl I see in front of me right now, and that's all I need." He took her face in his hands and forced her to look up at him. "I promise you I'll never ask you anything you don't want to talk about." She believed him. Partly because he was kind and thoughtful, and partly because she knew he would never want to hear anything unpleasant or difficult.

"If you don't marry him, I'll never forgive you," Tassie said over the telephone. Her voice sounded weary and hard. "One of us should be happy, for Christ's sake."

"Tassie, are you okay?"

"I'll be fine as soon as I hear you're going to marry Dalton Garrison."

"It's not that simple."

"If you won't, what did we do it all for? What was the point, if you're going to be alone and miserable until you die?"

"Tassie, I can't."

"Why not? You love him. I can tell that all the way out here in California."

"You know why."

"Are you afraid you'll slip up? You've been Myrtis Benedict for three years. You know what you're doing."

"It's not that. I can't lie to him."

"It's not a lie anymore. You're the only Myrtis there is." She paused. Iva Claire could feel her gathering her thoughts. "When you told me you wanted to pull this switch, I didn't think you could do it. Well, you have. But you've been . . . trapped. You had all those ideas about making a difference, but you haven't done anything. Because you can't, on your own. You need him."

She did. In so many ways. "If I did marry him—and I'm saying if—do you have any idea of the kind of wedding I'd have to have? The Benedicts and the Garrisons are important down here. There'll be hundreds of people."

"You can get away with it for one day."

"There'll be relatives I'd have to invite. There are a couple of Benedict great-aunts, and an uncle who lives somewhere in the West, and cousins. And God only knows about Myrtis's mother's family."

"Have any of them ever come to see you or written to you?"

"Someone named Great-aunt Weedie invited me to tea in Charleston. I never went and she never asked again."

"So they don't care about you."

"My father didn't like his family or his wife's family, and none of them liked him."

"Then you're safe. If there's that much bad blood, they won't show up."

"But what if they do? This is going to be

the wedding of the year. What about my father's old friends? He had a lot of them, and they'll be sure to come. All it will take is one person who knows something I don't— something that happened years ago."

"You're going to be the bride at the wedding of the year. No one will expect you to remember your own name."

"You make it sound like nothing can go wrong."

"Something can always go wrong. But you can't play it safe, Myrtis. The time for that is over."

"Myrtis?" It sounded strange coming from Tassie, and she wasn't sure she liked it. "You don't call me Myrtis."

"I'm starting now."

"I need someone in my life who remembers Iva Claire."

"No, you don't. Not anymore. Because you're going to be Myrtis Garrison."

"I didn't say—"

"Good night, Myrtis."

It took her three more weeks to say yes. And when she told Dalton and saw the look on his face, she knew what it meant to be happy.

*   *   *

For a wedding present, Grady Garrison gave the engaged couple a piece of land at the tip of a pie-shaped wedge in the middle of Highway 22, and Dalton told her to build the home of her dreams there. She designed a mansion made of logs with four big beautiful skylights and called it Garrison Cottage, although she had much grander plans for it than the name implied. She saw it as a place where she and Dalton would invite the powerful and the thoughtful writers or professors—maybe even a senator or a governor. Maybe even the president. Important people would talk about important ideas in her new home. Great things would happen at Garrison Cottage.

She wanted to have modern furniture designed for the entire place, but she was afraid it would seem strange if she didn't take the Benedict antiques with her. So the treasures her father's people had been collecting and hoarding for generations were hauled out of the house in Beneville to furnish the bedrooms on the second floor. She even brought the big canopy bed to Charles Valley. And if she wished she could have left all the heavy furniture behind, with its heavier history . . .

Don't think about that. You have to play the part, and you need the props.

The truth was, she wasn't thinking about much of anything. She was so happy to be leaving Atlanta behind her. In a few months she'd be living in Charles Valley with Dalton, helping him do all the good things he'd dreamed of. They'd be a team, as he'd said, and maybe in time she could start to see herself the way he did. Charles Valley would be another step farther away from Beneville.

But first she had to survive her wedding, and the whirlwind that would precede it. Dalton wanted a big party. Miss Lucy, Dalton's mama, was delighted to help the bride plan one, and Mr. Jenkins not only gave her a blank check to pay for it but offered to give her away. If any of them thought it was strange that Myrtis Benedict wanted to be married in Atlanta instead of in Beneville they didn't say so. Her maid of honor was Bonnie Taylor Talbot, whose only real talent was shopping, and together they purchased a trousseau with enough dresses, suits, coats, hats, shoes, and lingerie to last any woman a lifetime.

Her future in-laws seemed to know hundreds of people, all of whom wanted to entertain young Dalton and his fiancée. Even her acquaintances from Atlanta wanted to celebrate the upcoming nuptials. She tried to avoid the showers and luncheons with girls she'd never liked, but there was no way to talk Dalton out of accepting all the invitations to dinners, cocktail parties, and dances thrown in their honor. There was a diamond ring that cost more than she wanted to know, sparkling on her finger. She managed to get through all the fuss and be happy because she knew Dalton loved her. And because Charles Valley was waiting for her.

Chapter Sixty-five

MRS. RAIN

2004

She looked at what she'd just written and thought back to that brief time when her friend was so happy. The joy had come through the pages of her letters and was in her voice on the phone hundreds of miles away. For a little while she'd had so much hope.

Mrs. Rain closed her eyes. It was hard to remember that good time because of what had followed. She'd been so sure she could write about it—the sad part—but maybe she couldn't. Maybe she should just rip up the damn letter. No one would know if she did. It wasn't like anyone had asked her to beat herself up reliving things she'd spent so long trying to forget. So what if it would help Laurel Selene McCready to know the truth?

"Mrs. Rain regrets that she is unable to fix Ms. McCready's life. Mrs. Rain is old and tired and doesn't feel like raking up old hurts. She has retired."

But of course she hadn't retired—not yet. And raking up old hurts could be good for the soul, if someone else could make use of them. Wasn't that the real reason she wanted to fix Ms. McCready's life? So she could fix her own?

She bent over her pad of yellow paper and continued with her story.

And while Iva Claire—only I called her Myrtis by then—was falling in love, what about me? What was I doing all that time? Making the rounds and getting nowhere, that's what. I could afford to take lessons in acting and speech— to this day I talk half cracker and half Lady Astor—but it never worked. I still don't know why. There was a time when I told myself it was because of what happened that night in Beneville. After that, I never felt young the way I had before. But the truth was, by the time it happened I'd already gotten too old to be cast as a kid. Maybe that was what was wrong. Maybe I was one of those child performers who can't pull it off when they get older. Or maybe it was just that I was a vaudevillian, and once vaudeville was finished so was I. All I know is, I hit my peak with Lily and Iva Claire doing the Small Time around the country and I never could top that.

What made it worse for me was I didn't have to face the truth. Because of the money I was getting, I was able to hang on long past the time when I should have quit. But maybe I would have hung on anyway—even without the money. Who knows?

All I can tell you is that while the wedding of the year was being planned in Atlanta, I was miserable out in California. I wanted to go back east. I wanted to see Iva Claire—Myrtis—get married. And when I said that, I caused a catastrophe.

Chapter Sixty-six

IVA CLAIRE

🌿

1936

They were talking on the telephone again. Tassie seemed to need to do that these days. "I wish I could be at your wedding," she said. "I'd love to see you walk down the aisle."

Iva Claire said, "Then come to Georgia."

"I didn't mean it for real."

But suddenly Iva Claire did. "I want you there, Tassie. I want to be like everybody else on my wedding day. I want my family there." There was silence on the other end of the phone. "It's just one day," Iva Claire urged. "I want to pretend I'm a normal person for just one day."

More silence. Then Tassie said, "It *has* been a long time since the Sunshine Sisters worked. And if I came to the wedding, we wouldn't have to talk to each other."

"*When* you come, we'll make sure we're never together. But I'll know you're there. That's what counts."

"And I'll get to see Dalton for myself," Tassie said.

When Tassie came to the wedding, she actually did speak to the bride, but only for a few seconds when she went through the receiving line. Other than that one moment, they were never together. By then it seemed silly to Iva Claire. Her wedding was so big she probably could have had Tassie as her maid of honor and no one would have noticed. But they were playing it safe.

It was hard to keep avoiding Tassie. She was dying to hear what her old friend thought of her wedding, her husband, his family, and hundreds of other things. But all that would have to wait for letters and long-distance phone calls. That's how they were playing it. Because they were so careful, they were sure they'd gotten away with it.

But the Garrison-Benedict wedding was

news, and a picture of Mrs. Dalton Garrison dressed to leave for her honeymoon appeared in the *Atlanta Constitution*. Behind her, in the distance but still close enough to be clearly visible, was Tassie. It was an accident, of course.

The new Mrs. Garrison saw the newspaper picture when she got home from her wedding trip.

Don't think about it, she told herself. *We've gotten away with it for this long. We'll get away with it again.*

And for almost a year she was right. She moved into her beautiful new house, and began her new life, and felt so safe that instead of getting rid of the old suitcase with the swirling *B* on the side, she hid it and its potentially damning contents in the back of the window seat in her bedroom. And everything was fine. Until the letter came.

It arrived on the day when she was hosting a luncheon. Harrison Banning, Li'l Bit's father, had introduced her to a woman doctor who was trying to set up a practice in Charles Valley. Dr. Maggie, as she was called, was a pretty doll-like little person with a husky voice. Iva Claire quickly realized there was a will of iron behind her delicate façade.

"The patients I see can't afford to pay me," Dr. Maggie said, "but they're the ones who need my help the most. I have children dying of diseases we've been curing for years. The other day I saw a case of smallpox—in this day and age! People like you, Miss Myrtis, have been vaccinated against smallpox for decades. This isn't just unfair, it's criminal, and I—" She stopped herself. "I'm sorry. I've come here to ask you for help and I'm being rude."

"Don't apologize," the lady of the house heard herself say. "You're frustrated. I understand." Then she asked—and, oh, the power and the sheer pleasure of saying the words—"What can I do to help?"

Over lunch, with Harrison Banning's assistance, they set up a plan for a clinic to be built on the grounds of Garrison Gardens. In exchange for her rent, Maggie would treat Garrison employees for free.

"When you talk this over with Dalton, do make sure he understands that I treat both Negro and white patients," Maggie said, as she was leaving.

It wouldn't make any difference to Dalton,

but his daddy was going to have a fit. Still, Dalton's wife nodded her head and said confidently, "My husband would expect that, Dr. Maggie." After all, this was just the kind of fight he'd married her for.

Two minutes after her guests left, the maid gave her the mail.

She was standing in the foyer under her beautiful skylights when she first saw the square white envelope; for some reason she always remembered that. She didn't recognize the handwriting, and no warning bells went off in her head. She was in her own home, with all the weight of the Garrison name behind her and the Benedict antiques respectably scattered through the bedrooms above. Nothing could hurt her. But as she opened the letter she had a quick vision of Mama ripping open the envelopes her father sent twice a year.

Don't think about that.

The letter began with the words *Dear Iva Claire.* The writer said he'd met her before, and they had things to discuss. His name was Stuart Lawrence.

*   *   *

He had chosen a little café on Ponce de Leon Avenue in Atlanta for their meeting.

"I'll know you the second you walk in the door," he'd drawled on the telephone. "So don't you worry none about recognizing me."

But she *had* recognized him as soon as she saw him waving at her from his table. His face was nice enough, but forgettable. It was the thick hair that had gone white that she remembered. And the big smile that stopped at his cold brown eyes. He was the lawyer Mama and Benny Ritz had hired to draw up the document making Mama Tassie's guardian. It had been ten years, but she still remembered his dingy little office and the sense she'd had, even as a kid, that the "guardianship" papers for which he'd charged them a week's pay wouldn't have stood up in court for five minutes. She'd had the feeling that Mama thought so too, because she'd lost them as soon as they got back to New York. And now Stuart Lawrence, who knew her real name, was smiling and beckoning her over.

She had debated about answering his letter. When something went wrong onstage, you ignored it. Either the audience wouldn't notice it or they'd forget it if you just went on as if nothing had happened. But she was too frightened to ignore Stuart Lawrence. Clearly, he knew something, and sooner or later he'd use it against her. So she'd agreed to meet him. Now, as she worked her way around the tables to the back of the empty café, she felt herself getting dizzy and breathless the way Mama used to. Perhaps she'd already made a terrible mistake.

"Iva Claire. It's been a long time, darlin'," he drawled, as she sat across from him.

"Please call me Myrtis," she said. She was surprised at how strong she sounded.

He sighed elaborately. "I thought you were going to be smart, Iva Claire. You can't con me. I spent a whole year making sure of my facts."

"I'm not trying to con you. I came to hear what you have to say."

"I know the truth, little girl. I knew it when I saw that picture of you and Tassie together at your wedding."

The one time we took a chance. Just once in all these years.

Don't think about it.

"And here's the part you'll love," he went on, in his fake friendly way. "I don't even

read the *Atlanta Constitution* normally. I still
live down in Mercier—remember that little
office I had, Iva Claire?"

She stared at him, keeping her face
blank.

He leaned back in his chair and smiled
the smile that never reached his eyes. "Life
is funny. I never would have seen that picture, except I happened to be in Atlanta on
business the very day it ran in the paper. I
was sitting in a little restaurant not too far
from here, and I saw your face, and right off
I had a feeling I knew you. In my kind of
work it helps to remember faces." He studied her for a second. "Although I think if
you'd had your hair like you're wearing it today, I might not have known. Changing
yourself to a blonde was real smart, darlin'.
But I couldn't see the color under the veil
you were wearing.

"Anyway, it bothered me that I couldn't
place you. Then I read that you were this
high and mighty society belle named Myrtis
Benedict, and I knew I'd never had anyone
like that in my office, so I told myself I'd
made a mistake. I was about to drop it, but
then I saw little Tassie's face in the background. There was no way I was ever going

to forget those big round eyes and the way they were staring at me when I wrote up those papers for your ma to 'adopt' her. You know?"

Iva Claire told herself not to blink or move a muscle.

Stuart Lawrence chuckled; he was enjoying himself a lot. "Once I recognized little Tassie I remembered where I knew you. At first I thought to myself, Well, I'll be! Iva Claire Rain snagged a rich boy for a husband! It wouldn't be the first time a little actress did that. But you were calling yourself Myrtis Benedict. And that didn't sit right at all. So I started digging." He leaned forward, obviously delighted with his story. "And all because I happened to be in Atlanta on the wrong day. Well, as the poet says, 'The best-laid plans of mice and men.' "

It had been a long time since she'd been this afraid. She kept on staring blankly at him.

"Don't you want to hear what I know?" he demanded.

Yes! But she gave him a careless little shrug. "I thought that was why you got in touch."

"You were born in New York City. Did you

know that? Too bad it wasn't a town in some little out-of-the-way place where they don't keep good records. I'm afraid the record-keeping in New York City is first rate." He paused. She waited. "Your mother checked herself in as Mrs. Lilianne Benedict and she listed her husband as Randall Benedict. That was your father's name, wasn't it?"

She realized with a little shock that she'd almost never said his name out loud. She always referred to him as Daddy, the way his daughter—his other daughter—had.

Don't think about that.

"I guess your mother just couldn't face giving birth to a bastard. Wonder what she told them when the loving papa never showed up at visiting time. Or maybe he did. Maybe he came up to New York City to be with her when she had her baby. Wouldn't you love to know?"

"No." *Yes.*

"Let's play a little game," he said. "Would you like to guess what Randall's mother's name was?"

She didn't have to.

"She was named Iva Claire," he said.

"Your Ma must have been very sentimental."

No, Iva Claire thought, *Mama believed in insurance policies.*

"Iva Claire is such a pretty name," he went on, "and it's so unusual. I thought that when you and your mother and Tassie came into my office all those years ago. It was the kind of name you don't forget." He settled back in his chair, watching her, trying to see past her blank stare.

"Is that all you have?"

"It's quite a lot. Because Randall Benedict had another daughter. And I may be just a l'il ol' country lawyer, but I think that raises a couple of questions. Don't you?"

If her heart didn't stop racing she was going to faint. She forced herself to breathe and said steadily, "I think you wasted a whole year on nothing."

"Then I guess we'll have to see what happens when I bring the police into it. You're smart, Iva Claire, but I'm sure you've messed up once or twice. And of course, there's your friend Tassie."

"What about her?" she blurted out, before she could stop herself. Because, of course, Tassie was the weak spot. She'd always known that. Tassie wasn't a natural liar the way she was.

She made herself look at him calmly, but it was too late. He'd seen her panic. And he knew where the vulnerable spot was.

"That time when you came to my office," he said gently, "when you were young'uns, I could tell you knew the papers I was drawing up were worthless. But sweet little Tassie, she believed every word I said. She's not tough like you are, is she? If they question her long enough, who knows what she'd say?"

She managed to keep her face a blank.

"Iva Claire, I'm not the enemy," he went on, in that same gentle voice. "I'm just a little guy trying to make my way, get some of the good things in life. And now you have more than enough to spare. All I want is for you to share some of what you've got with an old friend."

She looked at him, and she saw herself sending him checks in long white envelopes for the rest of her life.

Like father, like daughter, she thought grimly.

But Stuart Lawrence wouldn't be like her mother. He wouldn't take the money and stick to the rules. He'd want more and more. And he'd always be trying to play another angle. She needed to keep her eye on him. But how? Suddenly she had an inspiration. It would be a bad bargain, and it made her feel sick to think about it, but it might be the best she could do. She eyed the man across the table from her and shoved her fear aside. First she'd try one more time to get rid of him.

"I can't give you money," she said. "I can't do that without making my husband suspicious."

That threw him. For the first time he didn't look sure of himself. "I thought you had money of your own."

"I'm a married woman. You don't know much about my husband's family if you think I handle my own finances." The truth was, now that she was of age she could use her funds any way she wanted. Dalton would never have dreamed of interfering with her. But Stuart Lawrence didn't know that. "My hands are tied," she said.

"Then I guess you're out of luck."

"What good would it do you to ruin me?"

"Why shouldn't I?"

The cold eyes were staring at her across

the table, assessing and judging her as hard as she was assessing and judging him. She returned his stare and he didn't blink. He wasn't going to back down or go away either. She accepted defeat. It was time to make her bad bargain if she could.

"I can't give you money, but maybe there is something I can do for you," she said carefully.

A nasty little smile played around his mouth. "I thought there might be," he said.

"How would you like a job?"

She'd thrown him for the second time. "Working for you?"

"For my husband and me."

His eyes narrowed as he weighed it. Then he grinned. "Well, now, Miss Myrtis, I'd take it right kindly if you was to put in a good word for me with Mr. Dalton."

It was the only thing she could have done, she told herself. At least she could watch him and stay a step ahead of him. She couldn't have been more wrong.

She never dreamed sweet Dalton would find a kindred spirit in Stuart Lawrence. She'd known for a while that her husband was getting tired of wrangling with his daddy about "babying" their workers, but she hadn't realized how much it was bothering him. Dalton was an affectionate man who wanted everyone around him to be happy. The fights with his father were breaking his mama's heart, according to his two older sisters, who wrote him long plaintive letters. On the other hand, he loved his Myrtis and he still wanted to "do good." Dalton was in the kind of mess he hated most.

It didn't take Stuart Lawrence more than a couple of weeks to grasp Dalton's situation and turn it to his advantage. He asked Dalton's wife to come into his new office. As she walked in, he shut the door so his secretary wouldn't hear them.

"From now on, all this communist New Deal crap is gonna stop," he said. "You understand?"

"Who do you think you're talking to?"

"Darlin', I know exactly who I'm talking to. Remember? That's why you're gonna shut up and listen to me. I've been getting an earful from Mr. Grady. He's not happy about the way his son is doing business. And he's no fool. He knows where the trouble is coming from."

"It sounds as if you've been doing a lot more than talking to my father-in-law," she said.

"You better believe it. I aim to become his best friend."

"I would have said *boot licker*."

His cold eyes hardened. She'd gotten to him, but he wasn't going to give her the satisfaction of admitting it. "Is that the best you can do? I thought you were better with the snappy comebacks, Iva. . . ." He paused to let the threat sink in and then said, "I mean, Miss Myrtis."

That was when she realized just how bad a bargain she'd made. "What do you want?" she asked, fighting to keep her voice steady.

"Like I said, Mr. Grady isn't happy about the way things are going. And what with you suggesting me for this job and you and me being such old friends—well, he's asked me to use my influence with you. You better believe I'm not going to let him down."

He leaned back in his chair and smiled at her.

"This is the best tub of butter my behind has ever landed in, and no little nickel-and-dime vaudeville girl is gonna mess it up for me. You stick to your church, if you want to do good works, and leave the business to the men. Beats me why the hell you'd want to risk your own tub of butter by making your father-in-law mad, but that's not my business. Getting you to be quiet is, and you know what I can do to you . . . Myrtis."

And she did.

The first of her causes to go was Dr. Maggie's clinic. "Mr. Grady don't want it on Garrison grounds," Stuart said.

"We'll put it someplace else. I'll pay for it out of my own pocket."

"Not if the woman is going to have niggers in there, you won't."

"There are plenty of doctors who serve Negroes and whites."

"But those doctors aren't getting their money from Grady Garrison's daughter-in-law. He won't like it, and I aim to see that everything goes the way Mr. Grady likes."

There was nothing she could do. She had a second luncheon with Dr. Maggie in which she tried to apologize for withdrawing her support. Later on, when she got pregnant, she insisted on Dr. Maggie delivering her baby, which helped the little doctor get a foothold in the community. But that was the only help she could give.

Without Myrtis to back him, Dalton stopped fighting his daddy and began listening to his new adviser, Stuart. Thanks to Dalton's instinct for pleasing customers and Stuart's talent at cutting corners, they made money, even with the Depression going on. Dalton's father was proud of him, his mama and sisters were happy, and if his wife wasn't, she never said a word. She went back to writing checks for worthy causes, as she had before she was married, and closed her eyes when her husband took advantage of the employees he overworked and underpaid.

Her big log home never did become a place where great ideas were born, although famous people did come to visit. When her idols, the Roosevelts, came for a picnic, Charles Valley was thrilled. Even those who had hated *that man* were bursting with pride. It happened in the forties, during the height of the war, and by then young Mrs. Garrison understood that her role was restricted to accepting compliments for deviled eggs and pointing out the different varieties of azaleas.

Over the years she continued to be the perfect hostess. Her male guests went hunting and played golf with Dalton and Stuart while she took the women on tours of Garrison Gardens. Their visitors always said how much they enjoyed sleeping in the bedrooms she'd decorated with the Benedict family heirlooms.

Despite Stuart's presence in her life, she had been blissfully happy when she learned she was pregnant. But then she started dreaming about Mama. The dreams were always the same. She and Mama were back at Big Hannah's boardinghouse and Mama was in a rage, yelling and crying. Then the room changed and Mama was in the parlor in the house in Beneville. Myrtis grabbed Mama's arm, and Mama pulled her hand back to hit too hard.

And Mama's daughter would wake up panting and sweating in the big bed with the Benedict *B*s carved into the canopy. She'd get up carefully so she wouldn't wake Dalton and open the window for air so she could breathe. She'd look down at her swollen stomach and tell herself she'd have to be extra careful raising the child she was carrying because it had her blood. And she was a thief. And a liar. And a killer. She would have to be on guard every second.

She tried. Her son was named Grady after her father-in-law, and almost from the first moment the baby could talk she set the highest standards for him—too high, according to Dalton. She saw to it that little Grady was exposed to all the good things—books, museums, and fine music—as well as the sports his daddy loved. She enrolled her son in the best schools, and when he was old enough she filled his spare time with lessons and travel to broaden his horizons. She took him with her when she worked at her rescue missions, hoping it would make him compassionate.

By the time Grady was three he was throwing temper tantrums that terrified the other children who came to his house to play. By the time he was ten he was a full-fledged bully with a nasty temper who was, in the words of Charles Valley locals, meaner than a junkyard dog. Maybe she was too hard on him, as Dalton said. Maybe she pushed him away without meaning to, because she was afraid if she loved him too much he'd grow up to be like her. Or maybe her son was a small monster because of bad blood. Whatever the cause, she knew what Grady was. And she made sure she never had another child.

As the years passed, she missed Tassie desperately and she knew Tassie missed her. But with Stuart in such close proximity, they didn't dare get together—another reason to regret bringing the man to Charles Valley, as if she needed any more.

She was worried about Tassie. After Stuart dropped his bomb, Tassie had given up on her career because being an actress was too public. "Look what happened the last time I got my picture in the paper," she wrote. That could have been the reason, or maybe she'd just gotten tired of fighting for her dream. But she was lost without it. She moved around the country. She tried living in San Francisco, Boston, Chicago, and Philly before she finally went back to New York. She got married and divorced twice. Tassie was trying to make a connection with someone or something, and she wasn't able to do it. There didn't seem to be any way to help her.

Then Dalton started pressuring Iva Claire

to sell the house in Beneville. She never used the old place, he argued, and it was a crime to let it sit empty. She panicked. And she sent a letter to Tassie.

"I don't want anyone to live there," she wrote. She didn't have to explain to Tassie that she was afraid a new owner might decide to have a look at the historic old cemetery behind the house. It was a foolish fear after all the time that had passed, but Tassie understood it. She offered to move into the house.

At first it seemed wrong to let Tassie do it, but then Iva Claire realized the move would give Tassie a purpose again and the connection she needed so badly. So Mrs. Rain bought the house on the hill in Beneville. Tassie insisted on calling herself "Mrs." because someone once told her that was what actresses in the old days did.

She remodeled one room before she moved in—she had the parlor turned into a sunroom. It caused a bit of scandal in the town, because there had been a big fireplace in the parlor with a hearth that was said to have been built from some of the first bricks fired in the county, and many people felt it should have been preserved for posterity. She had it torn out anyway.

Iva Claire and Tassie—now safely established as Mrs. Garrison and Mrs. Rain—saw each other one more time. The meeting took place in a little barbecue joint halfway between Beneville and Charles Valley. It was the early fifties. Dalton's father had just died, and Iva Claire had news that was so exciting she had to celebrate with a face-to-face visit. It was worth the risk, she assured a worried Tassie. So Tassie met her and they managed not to cry so hard that they drew attention to themselves. Then Iva Claire told Tassie her news over glasses of the iced tea neither of them had ever learned to love.

"After my father-in-law died, Dalton and Stuart decided they wanted to expand the gardens and the resort," Iva Claire said. "And they needed cash to finish the work."

"So Stuart bullied you into giving them yours," Tassie said wearily.

"No! I told you, this time I have a happy ending."

"My favorite kind." Tassie gave her the old cocky smile. "Tell me."

"They did want me to help them. But I said if I put in my own money I should have shares in the resort, and a seat on the board at the gardens. Dalton agreed with me."

"So what does that mean?"

"I get to vote, Tassie! Whenever they make a big decision about anything to do with the resort or the gardens—wages, hours in a workweek, any of it—I have to be in that meeting! *They have to listen to me!*"

Tassie leaned across the table to hug her, tears in her eyes. "You can do what you want now! So it was all worth it!"

Of course nothing would ever be *worth* what had happened; they both knew that. It was just that they were so glad for something good to come out of it.

When she got home that night, she was told Stuart was coming to supper. She thought Dalton seemed less than happy during the cocktails, but she was flying so high she didn't care. After dessert, her husband got up from the table and, looking guilty as sin, left her alone with Stuart. And Stuart handed her a form to sign, a power of attorney so he could vote for her at the resort and the gardens.

"I told Dalton I knew I could persuade you," he said, smiling his cold smile. And, of course, he could.

She signed. She never sat in on a single meeting at the gardens or the resort. She watched her husband and Stuart institute polices she hated, and there was nothing she could do to stop it. And no matter how much money she gave away, she always knew in her heart she'd never make up for what she'd done so many years ago in the house in Beneville.

Chapter Sixty-seven

MRS. RAIN

2004

The letter was almost finished. She'd told everything. She just had one final request for Laurel.

Please don't judge my old friend harshly. Perhaps you don't know what it's like to grow up poor. When she was young, my friend wanted to go to college. It was her only dream, but it never came true. She never had a father. She watched her mother die, and she didn't have the money to make it easier. And no matter how much she loved her mother, Lily Rain wasn't cut out to be a parent. *These things leave their mark on a person, Laurel. I hope you'll remember that and try to understand. Lord knows, my friend paid for what she did. She built a beautiful house, but she was never happy living in it. She did some good in Charles Valley, but she wanted to do so much more.*

I've told you about her because I hope it will help you stand up to whoever is pushing you around. Take it from an old show-business trooper, no one can do that unless you let them. I hope you'll take over the gardens and the resort. I hope you'll live in Garrison Cottage and be happy—for my old friend's sake.

Then she signed her name: *Tassie Rain*.

She leaned back on her pillow, but she didn't close her eyes. Tired as she was, she couldn't rest yet. She eased herself out of bed but had to grab at its edge to keep from falling. A little wobbliness was perfectly normal after the night she'd put in, she told herself. She waited until the floor had settled under her feet, and then she made her way out of her sunroom and down the long hall.

She was still a little light-headed when she reached the living room, so she leaned against the piano as she opened the bench. The picture was on the top of the sheet music where she'd left it. She pulled it out of its envelope and looked at it. There she was, in the child's dress that was too big for her, with the large silk roses in her hair and on her skirt. Even in the faded old photograph, she still had a glint in her eye and a little grin to tell the audience that laughs were coming. God, what she'd give to make a crowd laugh again!

Her balance was still a little off, so the return trip down the hallway to the sunroom took awhile. She gathered up the pages of her letter and shoved them into the envelope with her picture. Then, even though she didn't have a full address, she wrote *Laurel Selene McCready* on the outside. She'd have to find out where the girl lived tomorrow . . . no, actually, today, because it was now morning and the sun was coming up. She'd find Laurel later, after she'd had some sleep.

When she was a kid, she always slept well after she'd done a successful show, and she knew she'd sleep well now. But first she wanted to put the letter on her dresser so she'd be sure to see it when she woke up. Otherwise, she'd never remember where she'd left it.

She started to walk to the dresser, but her right leg wouldn't move. Scared, she reached out for the bed to steady herself, but her arm wouldn't move either. She felt the letter drop to the floor and knew she was going to fall too. Then the pain came, hot and white and bright, like a crack of lightning inside her brain. And finally she knew what was happening. But it was all right. The letter was on the rug near her face. That was all right too. Someone else would find it and make sure it was sent to Laurel. She couldn't stay any longer. She had to run, because Lily and Iva Claire were waiting backstage and the house orchestra was playing the opening bars of "Beautiful Dreamer."

Chapter Sixty-eight

LAUREL

2004

Laurel hadn't left her house for two days. She'd slept on the sofa like she used to when she was a child. Only she wasn't a child anymore, so she'd awakened on the second morning with a crick in her neck, which provided the perfect excuse to loll around until afternoon.

When she finally dragged herself into the kitchen for some coffee, the *Gazette* was still on the floor where she'd thrown it. Not one of the dogs had thought to shred it or pee on it. They hadn't even accidentally ripped it up by walking on it. Clearly, it was protected by the forces of evil. She tossed it into the trash.

Her phone hadn't rung during her hibernation because she'd yanked the jack out of the wall. Stuart Junior must be having major withdrawal pains because he couldn't leave messages for her every two minutes. She was lucky he hadn't come over in person. Or, maybe, since he must have assumed he'd be getting his damn power of attorney, he'd decided to back off for a couple of days—being graceful in victory or some such classy crap.

She swallowed her coffee and went into her bedroom to get dressed. Until now she hadn't missed an afternoon on Li'l Bit's porch in two years, and she wasn't going to let it happen again. Gloria Lawrence and the *Charles Valley Gazette* be damned.

"We were worried about you," said Li'l Bit.

"Are you all right, Doodlebug?" Maggie asked.

"No. I'm pissed. Quoting me in the *Gazette* was a shitty thing to do!"

Maggie frowned. "Did Gloria get it wrong?"

"I sure as hell didn't expect her to print

what I said when I was talking to her on the phone. And she knew it."

Maggie and Li'l Bit looked at each other. Peggy used to say you could always tell when they were serious about something because that was when they did "the duet." Maggie's low cello tones would start and Li'l Bit's high flute would take over, until they were finishing each other's sentences. The two voices would flow back and forth, and there was no way you could interrupt. The duet was now beginning.

"Laurel, are you happy about what you're doing?" asked the cello.

"At peace with your decision?" piped the flute.

"Because, if you are, why shouldn't it be reported in the newspaper?" The alto was warm and earthy.

"If you were absolutely sure you were doing the right thing, you wouldn't mind reading about it." The soprano was firm and final.

"If you're upset, it's probably because you're conflicted, dear one."

Laurel felt herself snap. "Conflicted?" she shouted. "I hate this! But Peter Terranova's going to pull out his entire frigging team and leave if he doesn't get his way. I can't let that happen. I wish I could run the damn resort myself. I wish I could make the gardens such a big deal that everyone in the country would want to come." And as she said the words, she realized they were true. While she'd been fighting to be mature and realistic, the child inside her had been playing with dreams of running the place. Unrealistic, immature, stupid dreams. "I wish I could tell that son of a bitch Terranova to take his perks and his bonuses and stick them where the sun don't shine. I wish I could tell Stuart to hop up and kiss my rosy red ass. But I can't. Because I'm the wrong person."

Maggie and Li'l Bit were listening without saying a word. Peggy used to say there was something in the concentrated way that Li'l Bit and Maggie listened that would make you say all the things you hadn't even admitted to yourself you were thinking.

"I'm going to let them win, because I have to!" Laurel's eyes were starting to fill. "All my life, people like Stuart were the enemy. But if Peter Terranova and his team walk out, the resort and the gardens will go under. And I won't have three thousand people with no benefits on my hands, I'll have three thousand people with no jobs *at all*." And then before she demonstrated her mature acceptance of reality by breaking down and bawling all over Li'l Bit's porch, she ran to her car and got the hell out.

That night, she couldn't fall asleep. She believed what she'd said to Li'l Bit and Maggie, that she didn't have any choice. But as she lay awake in her bed, all she could think about were the changes she would have made at the gardens and the resort if she had been the right person for the job.

Chapter Sixty-nine

CHERRY

🌿

2004

Mrs. Rain's body was at the funeral home. The service would take place tomorrow.

"Not that it's going to matter much," Essie sobbed to Cherry. The housekeeper couldn't stop crying. "You and I will probably be the only ones there."

Essie knew where Mrs. Rain's will was and what was in it. "I'll be taken care of," she said. "And she left something for you, Cherry. The rest of it will go to some people she never even met." Essie shook her head, which made the tears in her eyes spill over. "It's all tangled up with an old theater she wanted to save. The place is called the Venable Opera House. I guess it's historic or something, I never did get the straight of it. I tried to talk her into giving everything to the Baptist Church. I mean, can you imagine leaving your money to someone you don't know? But she wouldn't listen to me." Essie dried her eyes, which immediately started streaming again. "Well, she was stubborn, that's for certain, and where she got some of her ideas, like leaving her money to total strangers just because of some trashy old theater, we'll never know."

"She was an actress," Cherry said.

"Mrs. Rain? Are you sure?"

"Well, it wasn't acting exactly. Singing and dancing was more like it. She told me about it."

"I don't know that I'd believe everything she said these last few months," Essie said. "She was old. She couldn't remember her own name without writing it down."

"Old people can remember things that happened a long time ago even when they don't know what day of the week it is," Cherry said. "She must have had some reason for giving her money to that theater place."

"She should have given it to the Baptists.

She put it in her will she wanted to be buried in their graveyard and they're going to do it, even though there's a perfectly good cemetery right here on the property."

"She said it was a family cemetery, and she wasn't a Benedict."

"Well, she wasn't much of a Baptist either. I doubt she went into that church more than three times in her life."

Cherry was the one who found the letter. They were cleaning up the house and Essie couldn't go into the sunroom without crying, so Cherry went in alone to clear it out. She didn't see the envelope at first, because it was partially hidden under the bed. After she found it she walked slowly to the kitchen and handed it to Essie.

"It's that letter Mrs. Rain was writing," Cherry said. "I guess it fell off her dresser. There's a name on the front."

Essie took the letter and looked at the name. "It's no one I ever heard of," she said slowly. "And there's no address." She sat down at the kitchen table and studied the envelope. Cherry could tell she was trying to make up her mind about something. "I just don't know," she murmured to herself.

She smoothed out a crease in the envelope with her finger. "She wasn't herself," she murmured again. "Ever since the stroke, she wasn't herself." She got up and said, "I can't let that happen to her." She walked over to the trash basket and threw the letter in.

"What are you doing?" Cherry protested. "She stayed up all night writing that thing."

Essie's eyes started to swim again. "She was dying, sugar," she said. "She didn't know what she was doing."

"But maybe we should look at it."

"Does it say *Cherry* on there? I know it doesn't say *Essie*."

"But—"

"Whatever is in there, she didn't mean for you or me to see it. Just let it stay where it is."

"But she put a name on the front."

"Cherry, I knew her much longer than you did. I know this is what she'd want me to do." Essie headed out into the hallway. "Come on, we'll make up that sunroom. I'm through being so dang stupid about it."

"Okay," Cherry said. But she waited until Essie was out of sight, and then she ran to the trash pail, grabbed the letter, and quickly stuck it in the knife drawer. She was pretty sure the scrawl on the envelope said Laurel Selene McCready. Reading about her in the *Charles Valley Gazette* had been what made Mrs. Rain start writing the letter. Maybe, Cherry thought as she hurried down the hall to join Essie, there was a way to find this Laurel Selene person.

Chapter Seventy

LAUREL

2004

When Laurel finally fell asleep, she slept hard. According to the clock by her bed, it was past nine when she woke up—which had to be a mistake. The dogs never let her stay in bed that late, they wanted to be fed. . . . She sat up fast. Everything was much too quiet, there was no barking or growling. She raced into the kitchen to find Patsy Cline lying on the rug in solitary splendor. Laurel ran to the window. The backyard was empty.

"Where the hell is everyone?"

Patsy's tail beat out a triumphant *good riddance* on the floor. Laurel dashed outside, picturing Peggy's beloved dogs wriggling through a hole in the new fence, tunneling under the chicken wire, getting lost in the woods or, worse, playing in traffic out on the highway.

Please let them be okay! Laurel prayed. *I can't screw this up too.*

Assuming the worst, she ran back into the house for her car keys. A note from Perry was on the key rack.

I figured Peggy's dogs would like to visit their old homestead. I used the key you gave Denny to get into your house. You were sleeping and you didn't hear me. I took the whole bunch over to Garrison Cottage in the van.

Then he'd added:

Don't bother looking for your Garrison ID card. I stole it so I could get past the security gate at the cottage. You really should find a safe place to keep your valuables.

She was going to rip his head off. Then she was going to stomp on his dead body.

Not only had he scared the shit out of her, he'd set her up. He knew she'd go to Garrison Cottage to make sure the dogs were all right. He also knew she'd been avoiding the damn place. Obviously, Perry had decided she needed some tough love. She was really going to kill him. Right after she checked on Peggy's babies.

The drive up to Miss Myrtis's castle was as magical as ever. Laurel had forgotten how the thing rose up out of its sea of wildflowers, and the way the sunshine soaked into the logs of the house and made them glow.

As she rounded the center island in the front drive, she heard exuberant barking from the pen at the side of the house. The dogs did sound happy to be home, damn their ungrateful little hearts. She parked and went inside.

As always, the soaring ceiling with Myrtis Garrison's skylights made her catch her breath.

"They are amazing, aren't they?" said a voice behind her.

She whirled around to see Maggie, staring up at the skylights. At her side was Li'l Bit.

"Look at the way that ceiling reaches for the sky," Maggie went on, still looking up. "She wanted wonderful things to happen in this home." There was no need for her to explain that the *she* in question was Miss Myrtis. Maggie tore her eyes away from the skylights and focused on Laurel.

"Li'l Bit and I come from a time when friends didn't give one another advice," she said.

"It may not have been the time, it may have been us," Li'l Bit added.

"Either way, it's hogwash," said Maggie. "We need to change. Come sit down, Laurel."

She didn't have to obey. She could say she didn't want to hear any advice, thank you. She could make some excuse and leave. But she let them lead her to one of the big couches in the living room.

"You've been floundering around for weeks and it's got to stop," said Li'l Bit.

"It's a hard—" Laurel began, but Maggie cut her off.

"Yes, it's a hard decision you've been asked to make. But you have to stop letting yourself off the hook."

"I'm not—"

"You know you don't want to give in to Stuart and Mr. Terranova," said Maggie.

"You weren't in that meeting," Laurel protested. "You don't know what they said."

"That the only way they can keep the gardens and the resort open is by laying off people and taking away all their benefits," said Li'l Bit, "because they have to give themselves outrageous salaries and bonuses—"

"And blah-blah-blah!" Maggie finished up.

"The gardens were in trouble and the resort was on the verge of bankruptcy," Laurel said wearily. "Stuart and Pete Terranova turned it around."

"Did they?" Li'l Bit asked. "Or would business have picked up anyway when people started traveling again?"

"I can't take that chance. This town would die without the gardens and the resort."

"Who knows?" Maggie asked. "We might prove to be very enterprising if we didn't have the gardens and the resort to depend on. Or maybe people would stop being afraid to leave and go make better lives for themselves somewhere else."

"Maybe they'd stop settling for crumbs," Li'l Bit added.

"But there's nothing that says we have to lose the gardens and the resort," Maggie said.

"Stuart—" Laurel started.

"Maybe you could do a better job than Stuart," Li'l Bit said. "Did you ever think of that?"

"What's to say you can't?" demanded Maggie.

"For one thing, I didn't—"

"Go to college or business school or blah-blah-blah," said Maggie, repeating a phrase that seemed to have pleased her.

"That's a big deal," Laurel said. "So is the fact that I've never run a business that takes in several million dollars a year."

"Katherine Graham never had a speck of experience publishing a newspaper when that husband of hers killed himself and left it all on her shoulders," Maggie said.

"And just look at Watergate," Li'l Bit added.

"To say nothing of the Pulitzer," said Maggie.

The duet was well under way.

"Mrs. Roosevelt was an appalling public speaker," said the cello.

"Until FDR had polio," said the flute. "Then she became the greatest woman of her day."

"People can do wonderful things when they have to."

"Especially women."

"You're extremely intelligent, Laurel."

"And you're not proud. You admit what you don't know, so you learn."

"You'll ask for help."

"That character trait is worth more than years of experience."

"Charles Valley is your home. No one has to bribe you to stay here. That's another plus."

"People will want to help you. You have to stop thinking you're alone."

"You do have friends."

"When you're doing the right thing, people are drawn to you, you'll see."

"And you'll always have Li'l Bit and me. And Perry, of course."

"Being angry and downplaying your abilities probably helped you get through some bad times when you were young. But for a while now it's been self-defeating."

"Self-indulgent."

"Unworthy of you."

"Stop making excuses for yourself, Dear One."

"It's time to grow up, Laurel."

A car honked outside. The duet was over. They both stood up, and Maggie looked at her watch. "I have to get to the clinic," she said.

"I nood to work in my garden," said Li'l Bit.

They started out.

"Wait!" Laurel called out. They turned, two sets of smart old eyes watching her. "Who's that outside?" she asked

"Gloria drove us over," Li'l Bit said.

"We felt it would be better if you didn't see a car outside," Maggie explained proudly. "The element of surprise, you know."

"Gloria would be another excellent friend for you," Li'l Bit added firmly.

"Yes, Doodlebug, she would." Maggie looked around the room. "I do hope you decide to make this your home. It's such a beautiful place."

"Neither of the two women who lived here before you were very happy," said Li'l Bit. "It would be nice if you could change that."

"I still don't know what I'm going to do," Laurel said. But they had both moved to her, and each bent over to kiss her on her cheek.

"You'll figure it out. Don't get up, dear one," Maggie said.

"We have faith in you. We'll see ourselves out," said Li'l Bit.

And they were gone.

The sun was directly overhead, pouring light in though Myrtis Garrison's skylights. The house was full of the history of the two women who had lived there. Laurel could feel it crowding in on her, with all its fears and hopes—and secrets.

Chapter Seventy-one

CHERRY

2004

It was late, and Cherry was exhausted. She and Essie had worked all day long without stopping, because Essie was determined that Mrs. Rain's house was going to be spotless before they left. Tomorrow, after the funeral, the FOR SALE sign would go up next to the mailbox in front, and in a week or two the real estate agent would hold an open house. The contents of the old place would be sold with it. Cherry's bags were already packed. She'd be spending the night with Essie, and in the morning she'd leave Beneville. The agency already had a new job for her.

Essie was walking through the house pulling down the shades; Cherry left her and sneaked into the kitchen. It was the first time she'd been able to get away from the older woman all day, and she wanted to retrieve the letter she'd hidden. When she got settled she was going to call the *Charles Valley Gazette* and ask for Laurel Mc-Cready's address. If they gave it to her, she'd send the letter on to its rightful owner. She opened the knife drawer. The letter wasn't there. Frantic, she searched through the other drawers, even though she knew where she'd put it.

"Sugar, if you're looking for that letter, I took it."

Cherry turned to see Essie standing in the doorway.

"Essie, where is it? I want to send it to that girl Mrs. Rain used to talk about."

"I ripped it up."

"Oh, no!"

"I have my reasons." Essie got a glass from the cabinet and filled it with water from the faucet. "When I came to work here, I thought Mrs. Rain was the strangest woman I'd ever seen. Well, for one thing there was that *Mrs. Rain* business, instead of calling

herself a good Christian name like Miss An-
nie or Miss Elizabeth. And she was all alone:
no family, no friends, no children. In all the
years I worked for her I don't think anyone
ever came to visit in this house. No woman
wants to live like that, Cherry." She took a
sip of water. "I couldn't figure out if she was
shy or so mean people didn't want to have
anything to do with her. Then I realized she
had secrets. I never asked what they were;
it was none of my business. But if she told
you she was an actress—well, there are all
kinds of actresses in this world. And maybe
when she was an actress she did some
things she wasn't proud of."

"She sounded very proud—" Cherry
started to say.

"She wasn't in her right mind, Cherry, not
at the end. And she didn't live that lonely life
all those years just to go spilling her secrets
in her last days because she'd gotten fee-
bleminded." Essie finished her water, rinsed
and dried the glass, and put it back in the
cabinet. "Mrs. Rain was a good person, she
always treated me right, and if she's not
here to protect herself I'll do it for her. Now
let's go. There's nothing more we can do

here, and I need to put my feet up. I swear I don't know when I've been so tired."

"Just let me get my bags," Cherry said.

"I'll wait for you in the car," Essie said, and she left.

Cherry walked down the long hallway to the sunroom and looked in. The big wing-back chair they'd brought in when Mrs. Rain got sick was still there. They hadn't carried it back upstairs. Cherry went in and sat in the chair.

I'm sorry, Mrs. Rain, she thought. *Essie's wrong. You knew what you were doing when you wrote that letter. You wrote it for Laurel McCready and I'm sorry I couldn't send it to her. I know you had a reason for telling her your story. And now she'll never know what it was.*

Chapter Seventy-two

LAUREL

🌿

2004

Laurel walked out to the dog pen, filled the water bowls, and patted Peggy's happy pack. She got into her car, drove back to her cabin, rounded up Patsy Cline, and picked up enough clothes for an overnight stay at her new home. In the morning she'd come back for anything else she wanted. Later on, she'd put the little house on the market. Or rent it out. She wasn't sure exactly what she'd do with it, she just knew she'd never spend another night there.

When Perry drove up to Garrison Cottage after work, she was waiting for him on the front steps. He was carrying a large round lump of something on a plate that was covered with tinfoil.

"You were expecting me," he said.

"You had to be curious. Cute stunt with the dogs, by the way."

"Maggie's idea. How are they doing?"

"They're happier in their own home. Patsy and I are joining them. Starting tonight."

"You're going to live here?"

"Looks that way."

She could feel how much he wanted to let go with one of his rebel yells, but he was being careful not to be pushy. "What about the gardens and the resort?" he asked, a little too casually.

"I'll be taking over. Any of the guys who want to stay on without the bells and whistles are welcome, but I don't think they will."

"Maggie and Li'l Bit did their number on you."

"Mostly, they said what I'd been wanting to hear. I was just too chicken to admit it."

He couldn't resist a triumphant grin. "I like this, girl!"

"One thing you won't like. I'm giving up the Viper."

"Why would you do a terrible thing like that?"

"It's a leadership thing. I just sent Pete Terranova a memo telling him the perks are history. I can't go around in an expensive car that guzzles gas when I've kicked his daughter's horse out of its stable."

"Couldn't you give up something else?"

"We leaders have to make the tough decisions."

"What are you going to trade it in on?"

"I thought something earth-friendly."

When he let it loose, he had the best laugh in the world. It was as good as his smile—maybe better.

"What's that?" She indicated the lump.

"Mayonnaise cake."

"You baked a cake for me?"

"Lord, no, you have enough problems without me cooking for you. This is from Maggie. And it isn't yours, it's mine. It's my birthday."

"I'm sorry, Perry, I didn't know. I'd have gotten you a present."

"I'm only seven years younger than you now."

"Oh."

"Now you don't have to be afraid people will say you're robbing the cradle."

"I was never afraid!"

"Good," he said, and he leaned over his cake to kiss her.

She'd been right about his potential in that department. He *could* make a woman's knees turn to jelly. Pulling away from him was almost impossible, but she had to. "You have to listen to me now," she said.

"It would be easier if you'd stop stroking my cheek."

She pulled her hand away. "When you were a kid, you had a crush on me because I was a lot older than you."

"Only seven years. And I thought you were the prettiest thing on two feet. Still do."

"But you don't know me. You're remembering a girl from twenty years ago. You were just a kid. That's ancient history."

"I saw you with Peggy when she was dying. I watch you with Miss Li'l Bit and Dr. Maggie every day. That's not history."

"You can do better than me. Don't interrupt. I'm not . . . you know what I am. And you should have the best. You're handsome and smart and funny. You can find someone who's not a mess."

"Someone boring."

"Someone who's educated—"

"And boring."

"Will you stop screwing around? This is serious."

"All right, seriously; about this boring woman of yours—"

"I never said boring!"

"Oh, yeah, you did. So, the boring woman: Will she read *The Great Gatsby*? Will she be rich? You're very rich, you know, and I've decided to become expensive."

"Dammit, Wiener—"

"Nothing but eighty-dollar blue jeans for this boy toy—or is eighty selling myself too cheap? I'll have to look into that."

"Don't make fun! I'm trying to do what's right."

So he kissed her again.

"I don't want to disappoint you," she said.

"I know what I'm doing," he said softly. "And I know what I want. Do you?"

Sometimes you had to stop fighting. "Yes," she said.

So they went inside her house and she gave him one hell of a birthday present, after all. And later on, when they cuddled up on one of the big couches in the living room, eating Maggie's mayonnaise cake, Laurel thought how easy life could be when you just let it. And how amazing.

The next morning, after Perry went to work, she drove to the cabin to get the books her father had left her and her ma's guitar. She'd been afraid that leaving the only home she'd ever known would be hard, but as she put her stuff in the Camaro she felt light and free. There were two more items she wanted; she ran back into the cabin and came out with a slim white jeweler's box and the battered old suitcase she'd found in the window seat in Myrtis Garrison's master bedroom. She added them to the pile on her front seat and drove back to Garrison Cottage.

Outside, the sun was shining, but Myrtis Garrison's master bedroom was dark because the shades were drawn. Laurel turned on a lamp and looked around. In the

half-light, the pink walls, swagged draperies, and thick carpets looked oddly unreal,
like a set for a movie or a play. But maybe
that was just because it wasn't her taste.

Before she'd come upstairs, she'd made
a brief stop in Peggy's little bedroom on the
first floor. The object she wanted had been
right where she'd thought it would be, on
Peggy's crowded makeup table. Now she
put it on Myrtis Garrison's bed along with
the old suitcase and the box from the jewelry store. She opened the suitcase and
looked at the contents. She'd never know
the story behind the dress and the sheet
music, but she couldn't make herself toss
them. She was going to put everything back
where she'd found it. Maybe in some future
generation, another woman living in this
house would open the window seat, see the
gleam of a rusty gold hinge in the darkness,
pull out the old suitcase, and wonder what
the hell she'd stumbled upon. But first, Laurel had a couple of gifts of her own for this
mythic person. She opened the white box
from the jewelry store and took out the
strand of pearls the nurses had taken off her
ma's wrist after she died. Laurel looked at

them for a moment and then dropped them into the suitcase next to the faded pink rose. Next, she picked up the artifact she'd snitched from Peggy's makeup table, the monogrammed thermos Peggy took everywhere because she never knew when she'd need an emergency swig of Gentleman Jack. In a way it was a shame to lock it away; it was one of the few things in this house that was unmistakably Peggy's. But this was for posterity. Laurel laid the thermos in the suitcase monogram-side up. Her Ma's pearls gleamed next to the rose. She closed the suitcase gently.

Outside the bedroom door, Patsy whined. The dog was not a happy girl, now that Peggy's dogs were back on their home turf and she was the interloper. She had reacted by sticking to Laurel like Velcro.

"Okay, I'm coming," Laurel said to the dog. "Hang on." She put the suitcase back in the window seat and started out. Before she turned off the light, she took one last look up at the canopy bed. She'd already called the antiques dealer to come and haul it off, along with the rest of the Benedict furniture and knickknacks. Somehow doing that had made her less angry at the great Miss Myrtis.

But I still wish I knew why Peggy was so afraid to get rid of all that stuff. Why the hell didn't she dump it forty-five years ago?

Chapter Seventy-three

MYRTIS AND PEGGY

1958

"Peggy, I want to talk to you," Miss Myrtis said.

Peggy put down the book she'd been getting ready to read. It had been almost three years since she had started working as a companion for Myrtis Garrison while the older woman recovered from her heart attack. Congenital heart failure, the doctor had called it. According to him, it ran in families.

Peggy's job was supposed to be temporary, lasting only for one summer. But congenital heart failure could be tricky, and Miss Myrtis's recovery dragged on. Without anyone really mentioning it, Peggy had become a fixture in the Garrison household.

After Miss Myrtis's first heart attack there was a second, and then a third. The doctor stopped talking about a recovery, and Miss Myrtis spent more and more of her days in the pink master bedroom, lying on the big canopy bed she'd had moved from the Benedict family house so many years before. Peggy stayed by her side, playing canasta or reading to her to distract her from the pain, until Miss Myrtis fell asleep and Peggy went downstairs to have supper with Dalton.

It was a routine that hadn't changed in three years. Until that night.

"I want to talk to you about Dalton," Miss Myrtis said. For no reason at all, Peggy felt a twinge of guilt about all the suppers she'd had downstairs.

"I try to keep him company, Miss Myrtis," she said. "He gets lonely without you."

"Yes, he does. That's why he has to get married again after I die."

"Miss Myrtis, we don't have to talk about that. You're going to get better—"

"I'm not, and we both know it." The sick

woman winced; the pain had been particularly bad that evening.

"You're hurting. Let me get you your pills."

"Just listen to me, that's all I need."

Peggy sat down at the side of the bed.

"Dalton will need a new wife. This time it should be someone gentle and sweet, who'll think he never does anything wrong. I wasn't like that." She was having trouble breathing now, but Peggy knew she was determined to finish her thoughts. "Dalton didn't marry me to be sweet. Back then he thought he needed something different. But that's all over now." She turned to look at Peggy. "The girl who marries Dalton now won't have an easy time of it. He'll be kind, but he's used to having his own way. I couldn't stop that."

"Miss Myrtis, you've been a wonderful wife; everyone says so."

"I couldn't keep my promises. That was the sad part. For Dalton and for me." She looked around the room, and her eyes came to rest on the window seat. She stared at it for a long time; then she turned away and looked up at the canopy bed. "When I brought all the Benedict antiques to this house, I hated them. I didn't want them here. But then I realized they were a part of me, after all. They belonged to my father's people. Now, I'm glad they're here. I hate to think of this house without them." Miss Myrtis was taking deep breaths now; her voice was hoarse and tired.

"You should lie back," Peggy said. "I'll stay here with you and you can tell me more when you're rested."

"No, I'm through talking. You can go."

"I'll come back to see you later."

"You don't have to; I'll sleep tonight. Turn out the light, please." Suddenly she reached out and took Peggy's hand. Miss Myrtis never touched people. "Peggy, one more thing," she said, in a voice that was so exhausted it was nothing more than a whisper. "Be careful of Stuart Lawrence. He knows all the secrets and he'll use them. If he's crossed, he could hurt everyone. Do you understand me?"

And even though she didn't at all, Peggy said, "Yes, Miss Myrtis."

"Now go have supper with Dalton," said the exhausted woman.

*　　*　　*

After she married Dalton and lived in the house Myrtis had built, Peggy signed over her power of attorney to Stuart Lawrence as Myrtis had. And she kept the house exactly as Myrtis had, with all the Benedict antiques.

But sometimes when Dalton was out hunting helpless animals or fishing, Peggy went into the foyer and looked up at the skylights and thought about the strange conversation she'd had with Myrtis so many years ago. She wished she could tell Myrtis that her secrets, whatever they were, were safe.

Maggie and Li'l Bit always said Myrtis was a woman who had failed herself.

"It's a pity, really," said Maggie, "because her heart was in the right place."

"She just never had enough courage," said Li'l Bit.

Peggy knew a little something about that. She'd look up at the beautiful skylights and think about the child she'd never had—the child she'd always dreamed would be a daughter. More than anything else she would have wanted her daughter to have courage.

Chapter Seventy-four

LAUREL

2004

Laurel stood in the foyer of her new home with a beer in her hand. She looked up at the skylights and held her beer up high in the time-honored toastmaster position. "Okay, Peggy," she said loudly, "here's to you. I'll do my best to make you proud." She started to drink and then stopped. "Here's to Miss Myrtis too." And she took a nice long swallow of the beer.

ABOUT THE AUTHOR

Louise Shaffer, the author of *The Three Miss Margarets*, Is a graduate of Yale Drama School, has written for television, and has appeared on Broadway, in TV movies, and in daytime dramas, earning an Emmy for her work on *Ryan's Hope*. Shaffer and her husband live in the Lower Hudson Valley.